Impulsive Connections

MARIE REYNARD

IMPULSIVE CONNECTIONS

ELEMENTAL BONDS
BOOK TWO

MARIE REYNARD

PEACE GARDEN
PUBLISHING

Cover by Moor Books Design

Illustrations by GetCovers

Beta read by Amy Pittel (LesCourt Author Services) and Megan Dischinger (Blue Beta Reading)

Edited by Kate Wood (Kate Wood Proofreading)

eBook ISBN: 978-1-958002-03-2

Standard Cover ISBN: 978-1-958002-04-9

Alternative Cover ISBN: 978-1-958002-05-6

First Edition

Published by Peace Garden Publishing, LLC

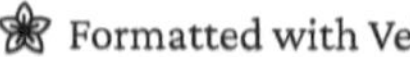 Formatted with Vellum

CONTENT WARNINGS

This book contains scenes with elements of dubious consent (including a twist on the sex pollen trope), mentions of rape in a historical context, and implied threats of rape. One main character also suffers from PTSD and has panic attacks.

IMPULSIVE CONNECTIONS

Ignited by accident, fueled by fate. Some bonds burn brighter than any flame.

Kade Mills has spent over a decade dreaming of his ideal meet-cute. Surely the universe wouldn't toss the perfect mage at him while he's a scarred shadow of his former flirtatious self, recovering from his last encounter with the malicious spirits haunting his pack's territory.

Liam Batiste is a man of simple pleasures; a quiet room and a stack of books are all he needs to be happy. He's only in Lost Creek to help his friend save the Mills pack from the unknown evil infesting their land, but everything changes when he and Kade are paired up to capture the supernatural threat.

After a run-in with a spirit leaves them entangled—physically and magically—they must learn to control the newfound power their unwanted connection grants them. As they struggle to resist the heady pull of their bond, they begin to realize it may hold the key to defeating the dark forces that are endangering far more than just Kade's pack... and perhaps it's not as unwelcome as they first thought.

Impulsive Connections is a steamy 149k M/M paranormal romance featuring a playboy wolf shifter, a nerdy mage, and friends who are trying their very best not to meddle. This simmering slow burn is perfect for readers who love reluctant mates, unintended bonds, forced proximity, unfortunate bed shortages, and knotting. While it guarantees a happy ending for its main couple, the overarching plot does contain cliffhangers, and the series should be read in order. (This series does not contain mpreg.)

PROLOGUE

Elijah held the map out in front of him so Victor could see. Smears of ash traveled across its surface, each different from the last—scores of unknown spirits haunting the forest. Some were nothing but pinpricks, motes of dust with no discernible features. Those, they'd have to ignore for now. The larger ones were more pressing.

The way they moved, the forms they took; no two were the same. A few skittered and scurried, spiders darting over the paper, making Elijah's skin crawl with their erratic movements and alarming speed. Others flowed, cascading in sinuous waves. This one hovered lazily, an ethereal, smoky specter; that one pulsated, expanding and contracting as if it were a living, breathing organism.

They slithered like serpents, spiraled like tornadoes, wheeled like birds in the air. Half a dozen left trails of *something* in their wake—jagged shards, ashen residue, smudged shadows.

Elijah's heart pounded as he traced the path of the

largest spirit, all crystalline cracks and creeping devastation. The magnitude of the task ahead staggered him. There were so many of them, and no one knew what they were doing to the land.

Victor leaned in, looping an arm around his waist, and Elijah found himself melting into his touch, leaning against his muscular body. He inhaled Victor's comforting scent, let the buzz of his energy wash over him, finding solace in the emotions and sensations that hummed through their bond.

They could do this. They'd defeated one of these things before, and they'd do it again. Whatever it took.

"You need to know what they are before you can capture them?" Victor asked.

Elijah nodded. "We have to identify them, or the sigils won't work. Last time, we knew the spirit was rot and corruption, so Liam could create a sigil that named it. They can't be bound without that."

"Okay. The little ones will be difficult to find, but any leaving trails should be easier to locate." Victor echoed Elijah's earlier thoughts. "Let's check out the largest, at least. This one first?" He pointed to the streak Elijah had been tracing—the shattered, cracked blotch.

"We have to start somewhere." Elijah frowned at the map. "I wonder why some leave trails and others don't."

It wasn't a matter of size. A few small spirits had ashy remnants marking their path, while most of the large ones did not.

"I guess we'll find out." Victor reluctantly let him go, his hand lingering on Elijah's hip.

They headed into the forest. The scent of pine perfumed the air, mingling with the earthy smell of natural decay, welcome after the putrid stench of the rot they'd faced during the battle just days before. Sunlight filtered through a canopy ablaze with autumn colors, creating dappled patterns of light on the blanket of fallen leaves. A soft breeze rustled through the branches.

The land was as alive as it always had been, but there were scars now, areas badly damaged by the spirit they'd defeated. They passed firs and hemlocks that had toppled to the ground, hollowed out by the rot, their needles brown and gray. Others stood withered and lifeless, evidence of the destruction that had taken place.

There wasn't much Elijah could do about that, but Aran would fix it when he arrived... ideally while staying as far from Kade as possible. The last thing Elijah needed was the inevitable, excessive dick jokes and fuckboy flirting that would arise if those two were in the same room.

But Aran had a way with plants like no one else. If anyone could salvage the trees, it was him. While he tended to the forest, Elijah, Liam, and Miles would trap the spirits. Then they'd figure out where the fuck they'd come from and how the hell to destroy them.

One might have been a fluke; dozens of them attacking Victor's territory was not.

"I know you don't want to talk about it..." Elijah said.

Victor sighed, following his train of thought. "I hoped banishing him would be enough. But if he's behind this, him and that fucking mage, maybe I should have—" He cut himself off, but Elijah knew how that sentence ended.

Should have killed his own father.

In Elijah's mind, Victor's presence was equal parts sorrow and anger, his dark eyes stormy with turmoil. Elijah reached out and squeezed his arm. "We'll keep that as a last resort."

Before he could say more, a crisp polar draft hit him, like he'd walked past an open door to a shop in the middle of summer, the blast of air-conditioning a stark contrast to the sweltering heat.

He looked at Victor and got a nod. Victor had felt it too.

Elijah checked the map. They were nearing the trail left by the spirit they were tracking.

Victor jerked his head toward where the frigid gust had come from, and they veered in that direction.

From one step to the next, the temperature plummeted, drawing a shiver from Elijah. His lightweight dress shirt was doing nothing against the sudden chill.

Whatever he'd been expecting, this wasn't it.

The forest appeared fine. Radiant autumn hues painted the trees, yet the temperature kept plunging. An icy pit formed in Elijah's stomach, and more shivers racked his body, but there was no other sign of the spirit, only this bone-deep cold.

They continued walking until Elijah was certain he'd never experience warmth again, and then they saw it.

The fiery reds and oranges on the ground ahead of them began to shimmer, almost imperceptibly at first, but spreading, growing. A glimmering veneer coated every blade of grass, every fallen leaf.

"Winter comes early here," Elijah said, his breath a billowing fog, "but there shouldn't be frost yet, right?"

"Not like this."

"They can affect the weather?" Elijah had never heard of a spirit with the ability to do that, but then, nothing about this situation could be explained by the knowledge he'd gained from his apprenticeship.

"Apparently." Victor's tone was terse. His presence through their bond was awash in apprehension and worry for his pack.

Autumn subsided to winter with each step they took.

The frost crept up the trees, crystallizing each branch, twig, and leaf.

It should have been beautiful—a picturesque scene fit for a holiday greeting card, the hoarfrost reflecting sunlight in a dazzling dance of colors. But its unnatural, twisted splendor made it horrifying. This wasn't the perfect stillness of a winter morning; it was a swath of frozen desolation consuming the lush forest, vibrant life suffocating under a film of glittering white. An eerie silence settled around them, the creatures in the area having long since fled.

And fuck, it was cold. Teeth-chattering, lung-burning, breath-stealing cold. Elijah trembled and quaked under its onslaught.

"Should we turn back?" Victor asked, but Elijah shook his head.

They needed to see the spirit itself, not just its aftermath.

The frost under his feet crunched. Leaves hung in suspended beauty, like delicately spun sugar that'd crumble with a touch.

Another glacial minute later, Elijah pulled up short. A thick fog floated through the trees ahead, a haze of bitter ice that sparkled with a mesmerizing, deadly allure. Disturbing energy emanated from the spirit, as malevolent as the rot before it, though this time cloaked in winter's icy crystals and frosty tendrils.

"Can you capture it?" Victor's words were whipped away by a piercing gust of arctic wind.

"No, I—" Elijah couldn't get more than that out. The tremors shuddering through him were too violent for speech.

Victor grabbed him, hauling him toward safety.

It wasn't until they were out of the spirit's wake that Elijah started to warm. The heat of Victor's body pressing into him eased his shaking.

"Well, that sucked," he said, and Victor chuckled as he ran his hands over Elijah's arms and back.

"At least I don't feel the urge to scrub my skin raw until I'm clean."

"Sure, frostbite and hypothermia are so much better than sludge and decay. I also don't want to find out what happens if it possesses someone."

If the rot spirit had corrupted Kade from the inside out, what would this do?

Victor grimaced, clearly thinking the same thing.

Elijah shivered again and used it as an opportunity to change the subject. "If my scent is wintry like you and Kade tell me, shouldn't I be better at handling cold than this?"

"Nah. That's from your naturally frigid bitchiness whenever you're pissed off."

"Thanks. Love you too, asshole." Elijah couldn't quite keep the fondness out of his voice.

"Wouldn't want you to smell any other way." Victor grinned at him. "Now, what were you saying before your fragile mage constitution stopped you from speaking?"

Elijah pinched him. "I was saying that even though we know it's a frost spirit, I have no clue how to create a sigil to embody that, but Liam will. When he arrives tomorrow, he'll be able to make whatever sigils we need, and then we can get rid of this shit once and for all."

Victor nodded. "So, ready for round two?"

"The last time you said that, it was significantly more fun than this is going to be."

"Tonight." The word was full of promise, their bond

warm with affection, and Victor nipped at his ear. "But until then, which one do we track down next?"

Elijah pointed to a twisting mass of ash on the map, not too far away. "Let's see what the fuck this is."

Victor gave him another squeeze, then they set off together.

ONE

Kade paced through the tiny airport. He made his way from the check-in counter, prowled past the car rental agencies, turned sharply at the lone baggage carousel, then retraced his steps and did it again.

Note to self, he thought. *Confirm the flight's on time* before *leaving.*

Not that it mattered. He wasn't going anywhere. There was no danger of him missing a flight. He'd be staying right there in Lost Creek.

Still, arriving at the airport to find he was ninety minutes early hadn't been the best of surprises. Especially when his phone battery was at seventeen percent. He'd read until it had dropped into the single digits, then attempted to occupy himself with other things. Nowhere nearby was worth the drive to help kill time.

A milk frother whirred and an espresso machine gurgled in the cramped coffee shop he'd passed at least ten times. Roasted beans and creamy froth beckoned him, but there was no point in getting a cup. It'd be bland and dull, as flavorless and muted as everything he'd eaten and drunk over the last few days.

The air should have been filled with the heavenly aroma of freshly brewed coffee. Instead, it was the olfactory equivalent of a blank slate, mocking his inability to register even the strongest of scents. He told himself that, on the plus side, it was also saving him from the stench of harsh disinfectants and people who'd been traveling too long. But sense of smell was an integral part of being a wolf shifter, and the sudden lack was unsettling, leaving him off-kilter ever since the spirit had—

He breathed in as he reached a tall bank of windows, each and every one sealed shut, then pivoted on his heel to stalk back to the ticket counter.

His body might have healed, but not all his senses had recalibrated yet. Thankfully his hearing had returned to normal, as had his sight and perception of touch. He focused on the hiss of the air-conditioning vents and the brush of that slight breeze against his skin. Tiny airport or not, it was still a large open room with plenty of clean air in it.

Clean air and not much else.

Sunlight streamed through the windows, giving the wooden floors a warm glow. The whole place was remarkably modern, despite its location in a remote corner of the Rocky Mountains. A lot of money had been spent on the minuscule number of people who used it—likely no more than a hundred or so passengers on any given day. At least the architecture and decor were interesting. Not an hour's worth of interesting, but better than the dated designs he'd been expecting from such a rural airport.

The sole rack of travel brochures had held his attention for a whole two minutes until he'd realized he'd been to every place they advertised—all local and nothing he cared to see twice. Places he'd dragged Victor to when they were younger, rarely more than a few hours' drive away.

Was it too much to ask for a tropical island or a world heritage site? Maybe glossy pictures of white sand beaches and azure water? Something different from the snow-covered mountains and windswept plains he'd grown up around? Probably. 'Welcome to the middle of nowhere! Wouldn't you rather be somewhere else?' wasn't exactly a winning tourism campaign in the making.

He really should have checked the arrival times.

Rolling his shoulders, he continued his circuit, each lap a ritual of frustration and impatience, but no amount of pacing seemed to alleviate the itch gnawing at him.

Usually, he only got this restless on a full moon, when his wolf's need to run shivered through him. But that wasn't the case now.

This simmering inside him, this too-tight feeling of his skin—it was entirely human. It had to be human; there was nothing more to him than that at the moment.

His wolf's absence cut deeper than losing his sense of taste and smell. It had taken the bulk of the damage when he'd been—

Kade inhaled, concentrating on the air entering his lungs, then slowly exhaled.

Without his wolf, everything was off. Everything was wrong. He'd never felt like this before. So incomplete. So broken.

God, how lame was he? How pathetic? Who'd ever heard of a wolf shifter with a defective wolf? One who couldn't smell.

It had to be temporary. His wolf must be in some kind of hibernation while it healed. Anything else was unimaginable. His mind shied away from the thought of losing such a huge part of himself, of never experiencing the pleasure-pain of transformation again. Of being stuck forever in his human form.

He scoffed. After what he'd done to Victor and Elijah, after trying to rip them apart when they'd just found each other, it wasn't like he didn't deserve it. He should have been stronger, should have stopped the spirit from—

Invisible bands tightened around his chest, and he forced himself to take a deep breath, casting about desperately for a distraction.

In the coffee shop, the barista leaned against the counter, his eyes tracking Kade's journey. He wasn't hiding how blatantly he was ogling Kade.

Well, that would have helped pass the time. If it weren't for the wedding ring on the guy's finger. Cheaters could go fuck themselves as far as Kade was concerned; he certainly wouldn't be doing it.

Though it wouldn't have made a difference if the barista had been single. Kade's sex drive had always been so tied to his wolf. Horny on full moons, marginally less so on new ones. He tried to imagine having sex when he couldn't smell, couldn't taste, couldn't feel the primal spark of his wolf, but it was impossible.

Apparently close brushes with death had adverse effects on a shifter's libido. Go figure.

He looked away before the man got the wrong impression.

With a sigh, he shuffled over to a bench in the arrivals lobby. Its fake leather creaked as he took a seat. He struggled to sit still, his leg bouncing.

In front of him, two enormous TV screens hung on the wall. One announced the day's arrivals and departures—all to or from Salt Lake City, all delayed. The other played cable news, subtitles rolling as the anchor talked about events in places Kade would never get to visit.

When the program broke to commercials, Kade snorted as an older couple strolled hand in hand along a white sand beach. But then the camera dipped into the clear water, and a crushing, suffocating panic twisted around him. He squeezed his eyes shut and refused to gasp. Instead, he drew in slow, deliberate breaths.

This was a large room filled with clean air, and he clung to that knowledge. He wasn't submerged in filthy water. No rot flooded his lungs. He could breathe just fine.

He shook his head, trying to rid himself of the memory. Karma, she was a bitch. He'd wanted something tropical. That the ad had been hawking erection pills was a nice little twist of the knife.

To distract himself, he pulled out his phone. Eight percent and one notification. Messages were good. They'd keep his mind off the shit show that had been the previous week.

ELIJAH

A quick reminder! I'm perfectly capable of throwing fireballs at your head. You're not allowed to hit on my BFF.

KADE

What if he hits on me?

The reply was immediate.

ELIJAH

He won't. You aren't his type.

KADE

I'm everyone's type.

Elijah sent an eye-roll emoji.

ELIJAH

To quote a different friend, Liam needs someone who can fuck him while he reads.

Kade blinked at his phone.

KADE

Huh. I've never done that. It sounds fun. What would he be reading?

ELIJAH

No! Bad Kade!

KADE

You're the one who brought up fucking.

ELIJAH

No. It means, like, anyone who wants to date Liam will have to share him with his books.

He needs as much mental stimulation as he does physical.

KADE

So what I'm hearing is I should be looking up Shakespeare quotes to use as pickup lines.

ELIJAH

Why did I think having you pick him up was a smart idea?

Pick him up in a platonic manner!

KADE

Because you're an excellent friend and know he'll enjoy the ride I'll give him?

ELIJAH

NO RIDES.

I mean, except in your car. Obviously.

KADE

It'll be a tight fit, hopefully in more ways
than one, but I can make it work.

ELIJAH

Ugh. No.

Please behave? In everything but blood,
he's my brother. I want him to like my pack.

KADE

Aww. New pack member card well played.

Fine. I'll behave.

ELIJAH

Thank you! I'm leaving for the shop now.
Will see you there.

But remember, FIREBALLS TO THE HEAD!

Kade sent him a thumbs-up, grinning.

Elijah had spent the morning warding the wooden boxes they'd use to trap the spirits infecting their pack territory. He and Victor were needed on the pack land; Kade was not. Picking up Elijah's friend was the only way he could help, the only way he wasn't completely useless.

He scrolled up and clicked on the picture Elijah had sent, clearly cropped from a group photo and complete with a caption.

ELIJAH

This is Liam. Don't even think about it.

Unheard laughter glittered in Liam's deep brown eyes,

crinkling them at the corners. His wide grin revealed a row of perfect teeth, while his light brown skin told of blended ancestry and contrasted with the dark shadow of his buzz cut.

Elijah was probably right. Kade doubted he was Liam's type any more than Liam seemed to be his. He couldn't imagine anyone with a smile that friendly and genuine wanting a dirty fuck in the back room of a club.

He put his phone away to save the remaining battery, leaned his head against the wall behind him, and stared at the ceiling.

Elijah's friends wouldn't be his type; he already knew that. It was too soon for him to find his mage. His thoughts drifted to his grandmother—she'd never been wrong when she had visions.

And honestly, given the screwed-up state of his life, that was preferable. How shitty would it be to meet his mage like this? He wouldn't be able to sweep them off their feet, to make them swoon over his charms. No, he wasn't ready for a proper meet-cute. It was not the time for his reformed rake redemption arc. He hadn't earned his happily ever after yet. If his mage walked through those automatic doors right now, they'd take one look at him and throw themselves onto the next plane out of there.

He prodded at his wolf, attempting to coax it awake but knowing it wouldn't react, just like every other time he'd tried over the last couple days.

Come on, dude. We aren't this pathetic. Wake your ass up.

His wolf stirred.

Kade's breath caught.

It was sluggish and groggy after days unconscious, but it stirred.

The lump in his throat prevented him from swallowing,

and his eyes burned, but he didn't pay that any mind. All he could do was sit there, frozen, as his wolf roused itself. He forgot to breathe, forgot to move, forgot anything else in the world existed.

His wolf was awake. Grumpy and unhappy about it, weak from the healing it had done, but awake.

It shook itself, its long slumber falling away like snow from its fur.

Relief didn't seem a powerful enough word, not after days of worrying, days of not telling Victor or their pack. Joy surged through him, so overwhelming it bordered on painful in its intensity. He let out a shuddering exhale and pressed his eyelids closed, savoring the connection to his instinctual side. The lack of that familiar presence had been haunting him like a phantom limb. When he inhaled again, no scents registered, but it didn't matter. His wolf was with him once more, a missing piece restored. He could wait for the rest.

The roar of jet engines and the skidding of landing gear on the tarmac interrupted his thoughts, and he blinked his eyes open, swiping at them with the heel of his hand as he looked at the TVs and saw one plane's status change to 'Arrived.'

Kade's wolf stretched, and it stunned him how comforted he was by something he'd taken for granted before this. His desire to get home, to shift and run, had his foot tapping against the floor, but he stopped the movement with effort, though he couldn't keep his fingers from drumming on his leg.

The minutes crawled by until the automatic door from the security-cleared area opened and passengers spilled out. The rattle of luggage wheels accompanied them into the lobby.

He scanned the travel-weary faces—barely three dozen of them, with Liam nearly the last out.

As he stepped through the doors, Kade did a double take and almost rechecked his phone. But no, this was the guy in the picture, though it didn't begin to do him justice.

He was a striking figure. His expression, so radiant and cheerful in that photo, was more serious now, accentuating his strong jawline and high cheekbones. The warm brown of his skin made him stand out in the crowd. The soft-looking sweater he wore pulled tight across a broad chest and hinted at the body beneath, while his backpack appeared to dig into his shoulders with its weight.

As Kade watched Liam, his wolf stilled. Far from its recent near lifelessness, this was a predatory quiet, a lurking silence, the moment of suspended anticipation before the strike. Kade shivered.

Ah. There was one of the feelings he'd been missing, and at the worst time too.

He shouldn't have been checking out Elijah's friend, but Liam was undeniably attractive, and if Kade had met him in a club, he would have tried to pick him up—in the decidedly spicier meaning of the phrase.

Elijah had to be insane if he thought Kade wouldn't flirt with a guy who looked like Liam.

But Kade had said he'd be good, and he would be... After he took another beat to appreciate the view while Liam surveyed the crowd. He had about three seconds before their gazes met and recognition flashed on Liam's face.

Kade stood. As Liam walked toward him, his eyes raked down Kade's body in an almost physical caress that made Kade's lips quirk.

He won't. You aren't his type.

Yeah, right.

And if Liam was giving him a thorough once-over, there was no harm in Kade doing the same as he moved to meet him halfway across the lobby.

He found himself inhaling deeply, the instinct impossible to deny. Like he'd somehow catch Liam's scent when he was incapable of detecting anything. He got nothing but frustrating blankness.

"Liam, I take it," Kade said as they reached each other. He received a nod in reply. "I'm Kade." He extended a hand and had to suppress a grin when Liam's eyebrows shot up.

Shifters didn't do this to mages often. The gesture spoke of familiarity and ease around magic. A willingness to smell like it. Not that the usual reek of magic presented an issue for him in his current state.

As their palms met, Liam's magic flared between them, alive and licking along Kade's skin, a new sensation. Something that made him want to slide his hands over Liam's body to get more of it.

He'd shaken Elijah's hand before. This wasn't like touching Elijah, not at all.

Liam felt it too, if the widening of his eyes was any indication. There were golden flecks in his irises—little sparks of light in the rich brown, fireflies in the dark. He was a few inches shorter than Kade, the perfect height to wrap in his arms and grind against as they danced together in a club.

None of Elijah's friends were his mage, but that didn't mean Kade couldn't *enjoy* their company while they were there.

He stroked his thumb along the back of Liam's hand and swore magic rippled under his touch.

Liam tugged his hand away, shaking it out, his eyes narrowing. "Elijah said I should be prepared for you to offer me a ride."

The ghost of a Southern accent clung to his words, but his tone was flat and left no doubt which kind of ride Elijah had warned him about Kade offering.

Right. He'd promised to behave and fully intended to honor that, no matter how the hum of electric magic lingered on his skin, making him seriously reconsider that vow.

A loud buzzer sounded, and the belt of the baggage carousel jerked into motion, saving Kade from having to come up with something that wasn't a pass at Liam. A salvation he was doubly thankful for because, for some reason, the only questions he could think to ask were if Liam was a bank loan or a parking ticket. On top of those being beyond lame as fuck, Elijah would not approve of him saying Liam held his interest and had fine written all over him.

The first suitcases started making their rounds as Kade and Liam approached the carousel. Given the size of the flight, it didn't take long before Liam hauled a sizable black suitcase off the belt. In the bright light of the lobby, Kade saw the faintest chalk markings on the fabric—runes, maybe. Liam muscled the bag to the floor.

Kade hoped Elijah was proud that he hadn't checked out Liam's ass when he bent over... much. It'd scarcely been a glance. Totally didn't count.

A matching suitcase followed, also marked with a hint of chalk. Kade lifted it, grunting as he belatedly noticed the orange overweight baggage tag on the handle. While it wasn't exceptionally heavy, he hadn't expected it to be quite so solid.

He opened his mouth to comment on it when Liam grabbed a third suitcase, and Kade realized there was a fourth behind it, also sporting those nearly invisible runes.

He snagged that one as well, its weight similar to the other.

"Okay, that's it," Liam said.

That was it? Was he helping Elijah out for a couple of weeks, or moving across the country?

Kade should have borrowed Victor's SUV. He wasn't sure these would fit in his car.

Liam started to arrange the bags so he could roll a pair in each hand, but Kade nabbed two. No guest should be lugging four suitcases on their own.

"What do you have in these?" he asked as he led Liam out into short-term parking.

Liam shrugged. "As much of the library as possible."

Books. He'd brought four massive suitcases full of books.

That called to mind Elijah's comment about Liam... How much fucking could a person get done while reading four suitcases' worth of books? Kade frowned as he tried to puzzle it out. He'd need to know shit like how many books were in each suitcase and how quickly Liam read to answer it.

He'd never paid attention in math class, but none of the word problems in his textbooks had been like this.

Not that Liam was there for fucking. And not that Kade wanted to risk Elijah's wrath to find out. He was being good.

He cleared his throat. "So. What's with the marks on the bags?"

"Protection runes. Most of these books are hundreds of years old and one of a kind. I wasn't taking any chances with them."

Kade nodded. How should he respond to that? Definitely not by asking about Liam's favorite kind of protection or what else he might be packing. Those were absolutely off-limits. And regardless of Liam's preference for large suitcases, Kade shouldn't ask if he also liked large sacks. That was a horrible idea. Innuendos about emptying said sacks were not tempting in the least.

The four sets of luggage wheels clattered over the pavement, and Kade watched Liam out of the corner of his eye.

Damn was he good-looking. Did he have to have this whole tall, dark, and nerdy thing going on? His neat, modest clothing seemed like a front, a failed attempt at hiding the effortlessly smoldering hotness beneath. The contrast was doing things to Kade. Did Liam ever wear glasses? He might be even hotter in glasses. In *only* glasses, as he read, and Kade—

No. Bad Kade, Elijah's voice said in his head.

Damn it. Behaving generally didn't involve imagining giving someone a blow job, did it? But it was fine. He could do this. Asking if Liam always needed over an hour to *arrive* was a terrible idea. As were any questions about the mile high club.

Elijah just had to go and play the new pack member card, didn't he? So unfair of him. Had he met Kade? Had he seen Liam? Was he trying to give Kade an aneurysm by making him repress a fundamental part of his nature?

For such a small parking lot, it took forever to reach his car, and then Kade needed to perform some serious tetrising to get Liam's suitcases inside.

He managed it. Barely.

As he shut the trunk, he heard a jet engine accelerating and looked up to see a private jet taking off. It banked up and around the airport as he watched it fly away.

When he turned back, Liam was studying him.

"Have you ever flown?" Liam asked.

Kade forced out a chuckle. "Wolves aren't known for flying."

Typically they preferred to stay close to their packs, and when they did travel, they'd rather drive, willing to sacrifice the extra days on the road to avoid hours trapped in stale air with too many smells and noises assaulting their senses, while not being in contact with the ground. They would fly, if they had to, but most avoided it. They didn't just leave to go jetting around the world.

Liam's gaze assessed him, but he didn't comment.

The first thing Kade did when they got into the car was crack the windows. Liam snorted, and Kade inhaled, about to say he wasn't doing it because of Liam. He could use magic the entire drive for all Kade would know. With as messed up as his senses were, not even the abrasive scent of non-pack magic would register.

Most wolf shifters found the scent repulsive enough that they'd do everything in their power to not be stuck in a car with a mage for any extended period. That wasn't Kade's problem, but he had no desire to discuss the real issue. He didn't want to explain why he couldn't smell Liam's magic, why he needed the windows open and fresh air constantly flowing through the car.

Liam could believe whatever he wanted about Kade. It was easier. And with three non-pack mages on their territory, it might be a blessing that his sense of smell wasn't working.

He pulled out of the spot and pointed the car toward the exit, racking his brain for something to say. No pickup lines allowed. Safe, unflirtatious topics only. Those had to exist.

His wolf wasn't doing him any favors; it thought

picking up Liam was precisely what they should be doing, but Kade was being good, goddamnit.

"So... do you come here often?"

Well, that was not it.

Liam glanced at him, expression impassive, and Kade held back a wince.

How the hell was he supposed to have a conversation with a hot guy without hitting on him? That was such an unreasonable restriction, particularly when they had nothing in common. At least with Elijah he had the option of teasing him about Victor.

"This is my second trip out here," Liam said after a few painfully slow seconds. "I helped Elijah move in, but I haven't been back since."

"Ah, I see." Kade drove to the nearby highway. Fields rolled by, brown and empty, waiting for the oncoming winter, and Liam seemed content to watch them pass.

Silence settled between them, the purr of the engine and the hum of the tires the only sounds.

Come on. You've got this, Kade thought. Surely there were tons of non-sex subjects to talk about. Like... the weather? People talked about the weather, didn't they? That wasn't flirty. Yeah, he'd do that.

"Hopefully we take care of this soon," he said. "Otherwise, by the beginning of next month, you'll need to be ready to handle a thick six or seven inches."

Liam raised an eyebrow at him.

Ah, shit. That came out wrong.

"Of snow," Kade clarified. "We can get a lot of snow."

Liam sighed, adjusted his seat belt, then returned to staring out the window. "It's a thirty-minute drive, right?"

"Yep. Though, just so you know, normally when I give

someone a ride, I make sure it lasts lon—" Kade clamped his mouth shut. *Fuck.* Why was this so hard?

He huffed. The fact that it couldn't be hard was the problem.

Liam shot him another flat look, unimpressed by his attempts at not flirting.

It really was going to be a long ride, and not in the fun way.

TWO

Liam's palm tingled with the buzz of energy he'd gotten from shaking Kade's hand, but he refused to rub it against his pants to alleviate the odd sensation. He hadn't used shifter energy since his apprenticeship, but it was as appealing as it always had been, maybe even more so.

While the mage council jealously guarded most contract work, they made exceptions for mages who taught, allowing apprentices to experience shifter energy in a controlled setting. The council never let them work with shifters as strong as Kade though. Few would be able to resist the lure.

Definitely second-in-command with that energy. Victor's pack had to be powerful for Kade to be so close to alpha level.

As the car sped past barren fields and scattered homesteads, Kade shifted his weight in his seat, and Liam tried to ignore the fidgety restlessness emanating from him.

Liam had no issue with silence—the same could apparently not be said for Kade.

He was gorgeous, though that wasn't a surprise; most shifters were. Liam would guess Kade to be half a dozen years older than him. His sun-kissed brown hair hung loose and was just long enough to tie back, the kind that might tempt a person to run their fingers through it—the complete opposite of Liam's. He was well-built, and his t-shirt and jeans did nothing to hide all the muscle beneath.

Multiple people in the arrivals lobby had been checking him out shamelessly, and Liam had been one of them. He shared Elijah's aversion to being tied to a shifter pack—or what *had been* Elijah's aversion—but he had eyes and had to admit Kade was easy on them.

Elijah's heads-up about Kade had been both vague and ominous.

ELIJAH

I'm sending Victor's second, Kade, to pick you up, and hopefully not in the way he usually picks up guys. I don't have a picture of him on my phone, but he's the shifter version of Aran. You'll know him when you see him. I apologize for him in advance!

Liam had reread the message a hundred times, trying to puzzle out what was waiting for him when he landed. As much as he would have loved to have Elijah meet him at the airport, Elijah had more important tasks to take care of. Liam could wait a little longer for their reunion.

Kade drew in a breath like he was about to speak, then snapped his mouth shut and shook his head almost imperceptibly, frowning at the road.

Despite himself, Liam was curious. What horrible pickup line had he just missed out on?

No. He didn't want to know.

Even without a picture, the moment Liam's eyes had

landed on Kade, he had indeed known who he was. There was something about shifters—their appearance, their bearing, the aura surrounding them. It was obvious once a person knew what to look for.

And on the off chance there'd been two shifters there... Well, Liam still wouldn't have needed a physical description. Kade looked nothing like Aran—he was muscular where Aran was lean, their coloring different, their ethnicities not the same—but Kade's fuckboy energy rivaled Aran's like few others'. It was as unmistakable as the smooth, predatory grace of his movements. His eyes had gleamed as they'd skittered down Liam's body, and the smirk on his lips had given him away. Liam had understood Elijah's apology without even talking to Kade. He'd seen hundreds of guys like him in the clubs Aran had dragged them to, each one offering a good time that night and little else of substance.

Now that they were sitting in the quiet car though, Liam wondered if his initial impression had been wrong. Sure, Kade had the look down, but he seemed to be trying so hard not to say anything inappropriate. It was kind of cute. And there had been something wistful in his expression as he'd watched that private jet take off.

Liam's money was on Kade's attempt at good behavior being Elijah's doing. It wasn't difficult to imagine Elijah putting the fear of god into him, making it more than clear that hitting on his friends was off-limits. There'd probably been a threat or two involved, most likely aimed at various parts of Kade's anatomy. Promises of pain in a supremely inventive fashion.

No wonder the poor guy was struggling. He didn't seem like he had many conversations that weren't flirtatious. But if that were the case, Kade wasn't remotely as bad as Aran.

When it came to dick jokes and pickup lines, Aran never would have been so readily deterred.

Liam caught himself rubbing his palm against his thigh and forced himself to stop. Man, did Kade have potent energy, and a lot of it.

In more ways than one, if the drumming of his fingers on the steering wheel counted. Kade noticed Liam glancing at the movement, and he squeezed the wheel tight before relaxing his grip. The memory of Kade's hand on his flashed through Liam's mind.

He'd been surprised by the offer to shake hands—less so by the lewd manner in which Kade had done it. Perhaps working with Elijah had desensitized him to being around magic. But then they'd gotten into the car, and that theory had quickly been disproven.

It was a shame. Liam had liked the scent inside before Kade had cracked the windows. It'd smelled warm. He wasn't sure how *warm* smelled, but it had to be something close to the scent that had permeated the air—a heat blanketing him, sinking into his bones.

Shifter scents fascinated him. Each shifter he'd met during his apprenticeship had possessed a distinct scent with notes he could never put his finger on. This one a hint woodsy, another sweet, though they didn't wear perfumes or colognes. It made him wonder what they smelled like to each other. He had a decent sense of smell, but nothing compared to enhanced shifter senses.

Although none of them had smelled bad, they also hadn't had the same effect on him as Kade's scent. It had wrapped around him for a few brief seconds, bringing with it a sudden ease, his muscles loose as tension seeped out of him. He needed to bottle that scent. It was the type he'd buy and wear. A subtle fragrance that would linger on his clothes and fill his lungs with every breath.

But it was gone now, stolen by the wind.

He suppressed a shiver. The weather was pleasant—warmer than he would have expected for mid-October—but it held the inevitable looming end of fall in each gust and breeze, and he was glad he'd worn a sweater.

"So..." Kade was clearly grasping for anything to break the silence. "You... like books?"

"I do," Liam said, then unable to stop himself, added, "*Big, thick* ones."

Kade jerked his head over to look at him.

Liam waved a hand in front of him. "Go for it. Do your worst. I won't tell Elijah."

There was no point in Kade being a jumble of nerves because he thought Elijah might castrate him if he used a double entendre or two. Liam had known Aran for far too long not to be able to handle that.

But Kade froze, his mouth hanging partially open. "You, uh, must prefer the hard ones over soft when you're craving a nice, lengthy... read?"

Liam refrained from snorting. Maybe Elijah hadn't scared him off; maybe he was terrible at this. "You're struggling to come up with something book-related, aren't you?"

Aran would be ashamed. How could Elijah think they were on the same level?

"Just 'books' is too hard. You've got to give me something more to go on here."

Liam could have quipped that Kade seemed the type to like hard things, or how he needed to rise to the occasion, or, 'Instead of something to go on, wouldn't you rather I give you something to come on?' But it wasn't a good idea to encourage that sort of behavior, so he tamped down the urge.

When Liam didn't answer, Kade tried again. "So, books. What did you bring?"

"Anything I could find about spirits. Trapping, destroying, banishing them. All the relevant books I haven't looked through yet. They might not contain the information we're searching for, but I wanted us to have as many of the books we haven't archived as possible."

Elijah had most everything covered as far as supplies went. That was the benefit of having the inventory of a magic shop at one's disposal. But when it came to books, nothing beat the library, and as hard as Liam had been working, only a tiny percentage of its collection had been archived. The handful of tech magic specialists aside, most mages were resistant to digitizing their knowledge base. Which meant Liam's four suitcases and backpack were almost entirely books, though the ones in his backpack were for his own research, not Elijah's. His clothes and personal items were afterthoughts, stuffed in the pockets of space remaining around the volumes and tomes. He swore he heard the curses of the luggage handlers who'd had the misfortune of lifting his bags.

"You archive books?" There was a note of genuine curiosity in Kade's voice.

"I work for the main mage library in the US. We're currently digitizing our collection, trying to get the books scanned and into a system so they can be accessed by any mage who needs them."

Under his breath, Kade muttered, "I can't use that either." He said it low enough that he must have thought Liam wouldn't hear it.

"I work at a library, and you can't even come up with a

'checking things out' line?" Liam asked, holding back a laugh.

Kade let out an amused huff. "In my defense, there's not much of a library in Lost Creek. It's a half-full bookshelf of farmer's almanacs, and that's it. But I suppose there should have been a joke somewhere in there about whether you'll shush me if I get loud."

"I'm not a librarian. I'm an archivist."

Kade faltered, a furrow forming between his brows.

"I don't just archive books. I handle priceless objects, including family jewels." Some unwise part of Liam's brain wanted to help Kade out, to throw him this lifeline. It was spurred on by the incredibly depressing mental image that had popped into his head of Aran suddenly incapable of making dick jokes. Not that he'd tell Aran that.

Kade's posture eased. "As an archivist, you must insist on wearing a glove?"

"Common misconception. Gloves are often unnecessary. As long as certain precautions are taken, it's preferable without. Bare skin means you can get a better feel of the object at hand."

Kade shot him a sly glance. "You'll have to give me a demonstration later."

Liam shook his head, but he was grinning. None of his friends were allowed to know he'd said something worthy of Aran. He wouldn't be making a habit of it. Better steer this conversation to safer topics.

"What kind of books do you read?" Liam asked.

"Do I look like a reader to you?"

That was a deflection if Liam had ever heard one. "There's an aphorism that might apply here. Something about books and covers?"

"I know that one. If you want a good time, you should get under the covers."

"Under? I would have assumed you'd prefer none at all." And it was official. His friendship with Aran had ruined him. That was the only reason he could be almost flirting with some shifter he'd met less than an hour ago.

"I could be persuaded." Kade's smirk was as warm as his scent had been. It was doing things to Liam he hadn't been prepared for.

The night before, Aran had sent a message in the group chat.

ARAN

> Just so you know, Elijah, after this is over, I might stick around for a few days to take advantage of the local amenities. Emphasis on the second syllable.

Liam had rolled his eyes, but Aran might have had the right idea. He'd been so busy getting the archiving project off the ground that he'd scarcely thought about anything else.

Not many people did it for Liam. He'd never felt the urge to pick someone up in a club. He didn't mind when Elijah or Aran did it—the latter far more often than the former—but it wasn't for him. The occasional need did crop up though, and Kade, for all his lame pickup lines, wasn't the worst option. Guys like him were never interested in relationships. He might be up for a night of fun.

Maybe Liam should take a page out of Aran's book and stay an extra day or two after this was over. Then he'd return to archiving the library.

Something to consider.

After they'd defeated the spirits.

The horrible lines seemed to have relaxed Kade further. "Alright. Tell me about this research you've been doing. What have you found out?"

"Truthfully? Not much." Liam launched into a summary of what little they knew and the massive amount they didn't. All the research they'd done and how it had come up empty.

To his credit, Kade didn't zone out the way most people did when Liam talked about his research. He asked questions and seemed interested, though from time to time, his grip on the steering wheel tightened. He'd take in a slow, measured breath before his attention was on Liam again, and Liam had to wonder if it was the stress of the situation, of knowing dozens of spirits were on his pack's territory.

The half hour flew by surprisingly fast and with shockingly few dick jokes.

Kade pulled off the highway and into a small town, though after the minuscule villages they'd passed, it was practically a city. The Welcome to Lost Creek sign proclaimed it home to nine thousand people, which boggled Liam's mind. He'd always lived in cities. He couldn't fathom daily life in such a rural location.

Vaguely familiar sights drifted by as Kade drove through the town until, finally, he was parking next to Elijah's car in front of a building with a brick storefront. The shops along the street were mostly shuttered—even the magic shop was glamoured to appear closed. The row of old-timey buildings made it look like the town was stuck in the Wild West, like there'd be a quick draw at high noon on the dusty main street between a steely-eyed sheriff and some notorious outlaw.

Before Liam could unbuckle his seat belt, the shop door opened, and Elijah stepped outside. Crisis or not, he looked more relaxed than Liam had ever seen him. Since they were preteens, Elijah had always been so buttoned up, so careful. Buttoned up both literally and figuratively. And while he was still in a tailored dress shirt, he had the top buttons undone and his cuffs rolled back, something he rarely did.

It was a good look on him. Happiness suited him. He deserved it... and needed some serious teasing about the reason for that happiness.

Liam's smile was so wide it hurt his cheeks. He threw himself out of the car and rushed toward Elijah. They collided, pulling each other into a tight hug. As nice as trading messages was, after years of friendship and then working together closely during their apprenticeship, being away from Elijah for over a year had been too long. When this was over, they needed to visit each other more, not let themselves get so tied up in their jobs that they couldn't spare a weekend.

"Thanks for coming," Elijah said as they pulled apart.

"Anytime. Though, I have to ask..." Liam's grin turned wicked. "Have you told Mom yet?"

The tension that ran through Elijah's body gave away his answer. "About that. I've been so busy. I haven't had a chance."

"Excellent. I was planning a quick call to let her know I arrived. It'll be the perfect time for you to tell her your news."

Elijah's pale skin blanched even paler. "Ah, I think that can wait. Like I said, we've got so much going on."

Liam slung an arm around his shoulders. "No, I don't think it can."

Elijah looked for anything that would save him. His eyes locked on Kade, standing next to his car, his expression bemused.

"First, we should get you unpacked." Elijah stepped away from Liam. "Did he bring the entire library?"

"He damn well tried."

Liam and Elijah grabbed a bag each while Kade took two, and they hauled them upstairs to Elijah's apartment, though Kade seemed to want to take all four up himself.

Once they were inside, Kade inhaled and started chuckling. "It seems you and Victor had fun moving you out yesterday."

Elijah's cheeks went red. "Fucking shifters," he muttered.

Kade snorted. "Exactly."

Liam's eyebrows rose. He glanced around the narrow efficiency, past the bookshelves to the neatly made single bed pushed against the far wall.

"No, the bed remains un-broken in," Elijah said. "Lady wouldn't allow that to happen in her apartment."

That didn't assuage Liam's concerns. If it hadn't been the bed... "Do I even want to know?" He eyed the kitchen table tucked in the corner near the door. Surely not. It didn't appear solid enough to support any amount of weight or vigorous activity.

Elijah winced. "The bathroom."

"How?" The bathroom in Elijah's apartment was the tiniest known to humankind. Liam's knees knocked against the door when he sat on the toilet.

"Wait a minute." Elijah spun on Kade and pointed at him. "I thought you couldn't smell right now."

An emotion Liam couldn't identify flashed on Kade's face, but it was swiftly replaced by a shit-eating grin. "Educated guess."

Elijah glared at him.

Kade couldn't smell? Liam frowned. But then why had he cracked the windows in the car?

"Who's Lady?" Kade asked, not-so-subtly changing the subject.

As if on cue, she strolled through the open door to the apartment and gave Liam a flat look. Her white-and-gray fur was even fluffier and more majestic than when he'd last seen her. Liam belatedly remembered he'd meant to bring treats to bribe her into not killing him in his sleep.

Elijah leaned toward Kade. "Meet Lady. The real owner of this shop. She hasn't forgiven Liam for trying to erect a ward on the building door so she couldn't get in while we were carrying my boxes up."

Kade's confused gaze bounced between Lady and Liam. "You put up a ward... to keep out a cat?"

Liam winced, but Elijah answered for him. "No, he *tried* to. She got past it and has held a grudge ever since."

Lady circled Kade, sizing him up. He crouched, and Liam braced himself as Kade gambled his life by extending a hand to her and cooing, "Aren't you a pretty girl?"

She looked so thoroughly taken aback and insulted, Liam had to stifle a snicker.

After giving Kade a final sniff, Lady sneezed, then jumped from the floor to the counter to the top of the refrigerator so she could peer down at them imperiously.

Still crouched, Kade glanced up at Elijah. "Should I be offended?"

"The fact that you have your fingers after that move means she doesn't hate you. You and Victor are the only wolf shifters she finds marginally tolerable," Elijah explained.

Kade's surprise was written on his face, not that Liam

blamed him. He'd never heard of a cat who liked canine shifters.

Kade stood, his eyes darting to Liam, then back to Elijah. "Well, see you later tonight."

"I'm staying here for the night. We're having a research party in the hopes we find some clue or lead before we start trapping the spirits tomorrow."

Kade paused, his head cocked, then he shrugged. "Okay. In that case, I guess I'll see you in the morning."

"We'll be there a little before noon."

As Kade walked out the door, Liam did his very best not to check out his ass, but Elijah's smirk told him he'd been neither successful nor subtle.

"Don't even think about it," Elijah said. "He doesn't do relationships."

"I wasn't, and I don't do relationships either."

"No, he does one-night stands. You do, as Aran says, 'academically stimulating arrangements.'"

"That's not... I mean, I can't go around picking up random guys in a club. What if they can't hold a decent conversation?" He didn't enjoy hooking up with people he didn't know, and the people he did know, he had no interest in hooking up with.

There was a very limited group of people he was attracted to and willing to sleep with, and despite the god-awful pickup lines, Kade seemed like he might squeeze right into it.

"It's cute you think there needs to be conversation." Elijah looked him over. "But seriously, I'm sorry about him. Was it nonstop innuendos?"

"Actually, he wasn't that bad. I was prepared for another Aran, but he couldn't even come up with 'Do I need a card to check you out?' when I told him where I work."

Elijah grimaced. "He should have been able to do that, but he hasn't recovered fully yet. He got the brunt of the previous spirit. It possessed him and started to rot him from the inside. He's lucky to be alive."

When Elijah had told them what had happened during the fight, he'd mentioned someone in the pack had been possessed, but Liam hadn't realized it had been Kade. His tightening grip and steadying breaths took on a whole new meaning, and Liam wanted to wince. He should have been more tactful about the information he'd discussed.

"Is that why he can't smell?"

"Yeah, Victor says he needs time before he's back to his old self. Sense of smell, perverted jokes, and all. I'm worried that'll happen while Aran's here."

No good could come from two Arans in the same room. "That's a recipe for dick jokes and disaster. And speaking of disasters..." Liam pulled out his phone.

"Fine." Elijah groaned. "Let's get this over with."

"Wait. Have you told your parents?"

Elijah pulled a face. "Yeah, no. Not excited to hear them say they told me so."

"Screw that. They weren't right. Just from looking at you, I can tell as much. You aren't in some loveless transactional bond for power. You never would have done that."

"They won't see the difference. They'll think I'm another pathetic mage who let himself get tied to a pack in exchange for alpha energy, and I don't want them thinking about Victor like that's the only reason a mage would want him. I'll tell them eventually, but you know what? I'm happy. They can go fuck themselves if they can't accept that."

Liam tossed an arm around Elijah's shoulders again. "Good. So have you told the council?"

Elijah laughed. "That can also wait until this shit is done. One crisis at a time. We don't need to deal with two sets of life-sucking evil beings at once."

"Please tell me I can watch when you do tell them?"

"You bringing popcorn?"

"Hell yes. And Aran will want to place bets on how many of them have a heart attack at the news that one of their precious shops is in the hands of a mage who has a true bond to an alpha shifter. My money is on two out of five. Now let's call Mom."

Elijah's body stiffened, but Liam steered him toward the bed, Elijah dragging his feet the entire way. They sat on the edge of the mattress, and Elijah felt like he wasn't breathing as Liam opened his video chat app and the call started to ring.

Liam's mother answered at a speed that indicated she'd been expecting the call, and she didn't wait for him to say hello. "Oh, good. You arrived safely."

He tilted his phone so Elijah was in the frame as well.

"Elijah, honey, how many times do I have to tell you that you need to call more often, or am I going to have to come out there myself?"

"You're welcome anytime, Mrs. Batiste."

"You move away for a year, and we're back to Mrs. Batiste? I really do need to get out there."

Elijah grinned. "That's not much of a threat, Mom."

Liam's mother beamed.

That was easy for Elijah to say. Now that he was bonded, she couldn't try to set him up with the 'nice young man' she'd met at the gas station anymore. Liam wouldn't be so lucky if she visited him.

Whether he looked it or not, Elijah was family. He was the closest sibling Liam had. As much as Liam loved his younger bio sisters and brother, the large age gap between them meant the relationship dynamics differed greatly from what he had with Elijah.

But these touching, sentimental moments were not why he'd made this call.

He gave in to his mischievous impulses. Elijah shook his head slightly, but that wasn't going to deter Liam.

"Actually, Mom, you should visit. Elijah's got someone he needs to introduce you to."

His mom, bless her, being who she was, scented blood in the water. "*Someone?*"

Elijah chuckled nervously. "Sooooo..." He dragged the word out like he could put this off if he made the O long enough.

"Wait! I'll get Dad." Then she was off, moving through the house.

Elijah slapped a hand to his face, and Liam didn't bother trying to stop his laughter. This alone was worth the cost of his last-minute airfare.

"Darling," his mother said, "Elijah's got news. About a *someone.*" And then there were two faces waiting expectantly.

Elijah pulled himself together. "So," he said again, then ripped off the band-aid. "I'm bonded to a local pack alpha."

Emotions flickered over his mother's face. Excitement at Elijah being in a relationship, then confusion, and yep, there it was. The concern and worry Liam had inherited from her.

His father was as laconic as ever, simply raising an eyebrow in question.

Next to him, Elijah cringed, waiting for their judgment.

Liam elbowed him in the ribs. "Don't leave out the important bits."

Elijah stared at him, eyes wide, and Liam took pity on him, telling his parents, "The bond is true, not transactional."

His mother's jaw dropped for a solid three seconds before she asked, "A true bond?"

Elijah nodded, the movement shy.

To Liam's horror, the next sound out of his mother's mouth was a borderline squeal, followed by a rush of words.

"That's wonderful, Elijah! I didn't realize you were seeing someone. You need to tell us these things. Tell us about him. How did you meet him? What's he like? What's his pack like? This is amazing. I always knew you were meant for great things, but that kind of bond just doesn't happen. Who'd have thought? A true bond with an alpha shifter."

Before Elijah could respond to the barrage of questions, there was another sound, this one most definitely a squeal, and the older of Liam's two younger sisters came crashing into view, squeezing between their parents.

"Elijah is true-bonded to an alpha shifter? Oh my god. For real?" Bridget stared into the phone with a rabid glint in her eyes. "That's *so romantic*! Did you know right away? Like, when you first saw him? Is he hot? I bet he's hot. Shifters are super hot. Is he big and muscly? *Oh.* But he's an alpha? Doesn't that mean he's old? Aren't all alphas old? Is he, like, thirty? Eww." She wrinkled her nose.

"Ah... he's two years older than me." Elijah glanced at Liam, overwhelmed by the onslaught.

Bridget frowned, mentally calculating that. "So he's kinda old." At fourteen, she was nearly a decade younger than Liam and Elijah.

"Tell us how you met him, dear," Liam's mom said, but Bridget didn't let Elijah get a word in.

"*Oh my god.* Did he scent you? Like the day after you moved to town, were you running errands, and he caught a whiff of your scent and hunted you down because he knew he'd found his fated mate? And then when he found you, did he pull you into his arms or push you against a wall and—"

Liam's mom hastily covered Bridget's mouth with a hand, cutting off wherever that sentence was going. "You've been reading my books again, haven't you?" she hissed, and Liam's sister blushed, her light brown skin flaming to a dark red.

Liam and Elijah exchanged side-eyed looks.

"You were saying, Elijah," Liam's mother prompted, hand still firmly over Bridget's mouth.

Elijah answered her questions, haltingly at first, then more smoothly as his nerves eased and he realized she was genuinely excited for him—though they were getting a highly edited version of events. He didn't mention evil spirits or metaphorical shifter dicks once.

He'd honestly expected Liam's parents to care about anything other than whether or not he was happy. Liam knew where that came from. Elijah wouldn't get such an outpouring of joy when he told his own parents.

Liam's father even had a slight smile on his face and nodded his approval when Elijah admitted he loved it there, with the pack, and he was figuring out how to make things work with his shop since his bond with Victor meant he was no longer a neutral party.

"Well, that decides it," Liam's mother said. "We're making a trip out there. You tell us the dates, and we'll make it happen. I'd invite you both here for the holidays, but I have a feeling your wolf won't want to leave his pack. We could come for a visit next year though."

Elijah's grin was pure delight. "I'd love that."

"And while Liam's there, if there are any other nice young shifters—"

"*Mom*," Liam groaned. He should have seen this coming. His mother couldn't learn of Elijah being happily bonded without her thoughts straying to Liam's relationship status. Or lack thereof.

"Don't 'Mom' me. You both have been so against the idea of any sort of relationship because of your careers. I'm merely saying you need to give people a fair chance."

"I'm not getting bonded to a shifter, Mother."

"Elijah said that too, and yet, look at him. Don't limit your options. What matters is that they're good people. And make sure he enjoys a good book. You'll never be happy with a man who doesn't understand the value of a good book."

Liam groaned again.

Outside the apartment, a car door slammed, and Liam leaned over to glance out the window. "Gotta go, Mom. Aran's here."

She perked up. "While you're at it, get that boy a nice man too. He needs to settle down and put down some roots."

Liam refused to make a joke about how many nice men Aran had already had. "Aran is not in the market to get bonded either, Mom."

She shook her head. "Deep down, that boy wants someone to love and cherish him."

Aran wanted a number of things deep down, but Liam didn't think that was one of them. "We'll see what we can do."

They exchanged farewells, then ended the call.

"I take it you didn't tell her about the spirits before you left," Elijah said.

"Hell no. There's no way we'd be able to check in every ten minutes to reassure her we're alive. That's why you didn't tell her either." He nudged Elijah with his elbow. "And why she's never going to hear the true story of how you got bonded."

A sheepish look crossed Elijah's face. "Busted."

There were things his mom didn't need to know, at least not until well after they happened.

They stood and headed for the door, opening it to find Aran climbing the stairs, a duffel bag over one shoulder and a box of potted plants in his arms. His smile was easy, his black hair falling loose and soft around his face.

"Why do you have a box of plants?" Elijah asked, skipping the greeting and holding the door open for him.

Aran set the box on the table. "I've been trying a thing. And considering I've already put months of effort into these guys, I wasn't leaving them to wither and die while we handled this."

Liam squinted at the plants in the shadows of Elijah's kitchen. Was there a faint bioluminescence to them? Yeah, that was not a normal green.

"What's going on with those plants?"

"It's a secret." Aran walked to the refrigerator to pluck Lady off of it. She looked disgruntled at being disturbed, but immediately snuggled into his arms, purring and making the tiniest biscuits in the air as Aran grinned at her. "There's my girl, my Queen of Cats, my Lady of Dread and Slaughter. I missed you."

Aran was on the short list of people who could snuggle Lady without dying in the process.

"We missed you too, jackass," Elijah said. "Now what the hell is up with your plants?"

Aran's expression was beyond pleased with himself. "I have this theory. My teacher thinks I'm nuts, but I'm trying it anyway. We're constantly searching for ways to draw out the magical properties of plants, but we do it after the fact. We expect the plant itself to do the heavy lifting. So I thought, why not help it along?"

"How?" Liam asked.

"That's proprietary."

"We're going to be living together for a week or longer. Are you deluded enough to think I won't discover whatever special technique you're using on your plants?"

"Fine. Ruin my fun." Aran pulled a tumbler out of the box and spun the lid open one-handed. A green glimmer emanated from inside, and the presence of his magic flowed over Liam, cool and refreshing.

"Is that water infused with your magic?"

"Yep. Basically, I'm using magic as a fertilizer to enhance the natural properties of the plants. I've been experimenting with these for three months, and last week, they picked up that glow. I can't wait to try spells with them."

It was an interesting theory, but potentially too time-consuming. The amount of magic that would require had to be insane. Though, if Aran made it work, there'd be a market for it. He'd have to ensure his magic wouldn't inter-fere with anything another mage might use the plants for, but it had potential.

Cradling Lady in his left arm, Aran set down the tumbler, then took the couple steps necessary to close the distance between them. He clasped Elijah's shoulder, making his knees nearly buckle before Elijah swatted him away.

"Don't fucking do that." Elijah cupped a hand protectively over his bite mark, and his cheeks splotched red.

Aran laughed. "I'd heard those things were sensitive and wanted to see if it was true."

"You could have asked." Elijah's glare promised retribution.

"Where would the fun be in that?" Aran glanced around the apartment, then at Liam. "So. Tonight. Little spoon, big spoon, or lucky middle spoon?"

As narrow as Elijah's bed was, those were the only options if they were fitting three people on it, but Liam had planned ahead. "I packed a sleeping bag."

"That's too bad. Fingers crossed Miles won't be as prepared." He eyed Liam's suitcases. "I'm shocked there was room for a sleeping bag in there."

"I vacuum-packed it."

Neither Elijah nor Aran seemed surprised by the confession.

Aran took out his phone, snapped a picture of them and Lady, then pulled up the group chat. Liam's phone buzzed with notifications for the picture and a message.

ARAN

Get here quick, or we're starting the orgy without you.

Miles, who was absolutely driving and should not have been looking at his phone, responded with disturbing quickness.

MILES

Oh no. I think I just got a flat tire. It'll be hours, possibly days, before I get there.

By which point, you'll be dead. Because Elijah's shifter will have killed you. But enjoy!

LIAM

Are you driving?

While on your phone?

MILES

Don't worry about it. This stretch of I-90 is so straight, I haven't had to use my hands for the last twenty minutes.

Liam stared at the screen in dismay.

MILES

Liam's freaking out, isn't he?

ARAN

Yep. Full Li-mom mode activation achieved.

MILES

Relax, Liam. I'm using speech-to-text.

LIAM

Put your phone away and focus on the road.

MILES

I'm a little over an hour out. Please clean up any bodily fluids before I arrive.

He sent a heart emoji, and the chat went silent.

"He used to be so sweet." Elijah shot Aran a look. "I blame you for this."

Aran winked at him. "I am more than willing to take the credit for any debauchery I inspire."

Elijah couldn't suppress his grin, and Liam wasn't successful either.

"Alright," Aran said. "Let's get this party started."

Liam grabbed a suitcase, and they got to work.

They paused their research when Miles arrived, his bright smile bringing life to the drab apartment.

"I'm so relieved you're clothed," Miles said.

"You and me both," Liam agreed.

"Hey now," Aran said. "Anyone should be so lucky as to see me naked."

Elijah scoffed. "If I had a dollar for every time I've seen your dick, I'd have paid off the shop loan already."

"That makes you extra lucky." Aran leered at him.

"Sure, keep telling yourself that."

Elijah's apartment was cozy with the four of them in there, and it made Liam realize it shouldn't take mysterious spirits wreaking havoc for them to meet up. When this was over, they needed to fix that. None of this once-a-year or less bullshit.

In the early evening, Elijah ran out to get dinner, though there wasn't much to choose from.

They sat on the floor of the cramped living area, containers of food strewn around them, after Liam had carefully piled the books to the side, safe from damage.

As they ate, he let their conversation flow over him. He'd missed this. Even with Aran's unnecessarily horny commentary, he'd missed it. He wouldn't be telling Aran, but he truly had.

Nights like this had been a regular occurrence when they were apprentices—talking about everything they'd been studying, everything they wanted to do with that knowledge, and the latest guys Aran had picked up.

The group chat was great, but it wasn't the same.

Besides, it was more fun to tease Elijah in person. The chat never captured how easily his pale skin tinted red when he was flustered, and Aran seemed determined to embarrass the absolute hell out of him.

"Alright, strip," Aran said as they finished their dinner.

"What?" Elijah asked.

Miles glanced at Liam. "I thought he was kidding about the orgy."

"That's not why I want him to strip, and you can't tell me you aren't curious."

"I've seen him naked multiple times," Liam said. "I don't need to see it again."

"No, not that. We're checking out how stretched he is."

"I'm definitely good without seeing that, thanks." Miles's expression was aghast.

"Not like that. Get your mind out of the gutter. I keep telling you not everything is about sex. Take your shirt off, Elijah, and channel your magic."

It hit Liam what Aran was doing, and he couldn't claim to be entirely disinterested.

Elijah rolled his eyes, but stood and unbuttoned his shirt, looking ready to throw something when Aran wolf-whistled at him.

"I do enjoy how you always wear dress shirts. It draws out the show."

Elijah flipped Aran off, but then he was standing shirtless, the bite mark at the juncture of his neck fresh and tender-looking.

"Well, get on with it." Aran made an impatient gesture, earning him a huff from Elijah.

The air in the room became electric, and Liam sensed Elijah gathering his magic, pulling deeply on it.

Slowly, working their way up from his wrists, Elijah's tattoos unfurled, glittering a soft purple as they snaked over his arms.

Liam had seen Elijah's tattoos on many occasions; he knew their pattern and how much skin they covered. Elijah had always been strong, and his tattoos had shown that. They'd twisted around his arms, ending near his shoulders, beginning to creep onto his chest. But this time, they didn't stop there.

While the tattoos on his arms hadn't changed, new ones now swirled out from the bite mark, crawling over his shoulders and across his chest, a few tendrils climbing up his neck.

Aran made a twirling motion with his finger, and Elijah obliged with a glare, turning to show the spiraling lines decorating his shoulder blades as well. A gasp caught in Liam's throat.

How much of a mage's body was covered by their tattoos was generally not discussed, though most apprentices had a phase that might be labeled the 'I'll show you mine if you show me yours' stage. The ones on their arms stabilized by the time they were adults, but for the most powerful mages, they kept growing well beyond that.

Someone more crass might equate it to comparing dick sizes; Liam couldn't agree. It didn't account for how the tattoos changed and grew over a mage's life. Though, he supposed certain people would point out that made the comparison even more appropriate.

Aran whistled again softly, and for once, he wasn't being lewd.

Liam stared in awe. If the increase in Elijah's tattoos corresponded with a similar increase in his magic, Aran had been right. Being bonded to a shifter had stretched Elijah's channels wider than they'd ever been before.

There were diagrams in books that compared the tattoos a mage had with the strength of their magic. Elijah was now up there with the strongest, and he was just getting used to the new level of power available to him. He'd only get stronger.

Liam couldn't think of anything to say, but he didn't have to. Elijah's phone vibrated where it was sitting on the floor, and Elijah snatched it up, his tattoos fading from view as he answered.

He'd barely gotten the phone to his ear when a gruff voice on the other end spoke. "Are you okay? Why did you have to use your magic?"

Elijah's face softened, his tone soothing as he replied. "I'm fine. I had to show my friends something. That's it."

"Are you sure? Do you need me to come there?"

Liam had never seen Elijah look as content as he did in that moment. He normally held himself so taut, so reserved. It had only been with them that he'd let his guard down, and even then, it was often like he was trying to project an image, forcing himself into a mold he hoped would make his parents accept his chosen path. But now he was standing there, radiating happiness, and Liam was thrilled for him. He spared a glance at Aran and Miles and found them both grinning, though from the unholy glint in Aran's eyes, Elijah was in for a world of teasing—something Liam would absolutely be helping with.

Elijah reassured Victor that there were no problems and he didn't need to storm into town to save him.

It was a quick call, but Liam swore Elijah had completely forgotten they were there in those few seconds. His theory was confirmed when Elijah hung up, smiling at his phone, then jumped when he looked up and saw them watching him. His gaze darted between the three of them, and he cleared his throat.

Aran was about to go in for the kill, but Miles was the first to speak.

"Aw, you go all soft when you talk to him."

Aran snorted. "That's no good. His shifter won't be happy if that happens. But I'm pretty sure him going soft isn't an issue when his shifter is around."

"I didn't mean it like that." Miles scowled.

"Ignore Aran," Liam said. "He's just jealous, thinking about how many more tattoos he could get if he were bonded."

"Full chest plate." Aran's voice was filled with hushed reverence, his eyes distant.

Aran's tattoos were impressive to anyone, mage or not. He'd found a tattoo artist in the supernatural community and had channeled his magic so the artist could create an ink design around his magical tattoos. What resulted was a negative space of twisting vines that curled up his arms, surrounded by leaves and flowers in black and gray. When he channeled his magic, the negative space filled with a shimmering green. The average person unaware of the supernatural would think the design was interesting, but for anyone aware, those tattoos showed precisely how powerful Aran was, whether he was using his magic or not.

It showcased the gap that defined everything that was Aran. Deadly serious when it mattered, though that side of him was hidden behind his fuckboy ways. His flippant behavior was a mask for someone who cared intensely.

Most mages were reluctant to show their tattoos; Aran's were visible for the whole world to see. An ostentatious reminder of his not-insubstantial power. The ink went up to his shoulders, since those tattoos were set. He'd have to wait years for them to grow much beyond that. If there was one thing that might tempt Aran to get bonded to a shifter —besides the dick—it was the prospect of getting more tattoos.

But then Aran shook himself. "Nope. Not worth it. I'll get there by myself, thank you very much. I'll leave the channel-stretching to Elijah and his shifter."

Elijah rolled his eyes again and put on his shirt. They cleaned up before returning to their research under the watchful eye of Lady from where she'd perched on Liam's backpack.

As they researched, Elijah became progressively more restless, his leg bouncing where he sat, the movement a distraction out of the corner of Liam's eye. Elijah's agitation grew as the night wore on. He was unable to sit still, frequently looking toward the north. It was extremely unlike him.

Finally, Miles said, "We've got this, Elijah. If you're needed back home."

Elijah froze like he'd been caught red-handed, and the pieces clicked together for Liam as Aran asked, "Are you already so addicted to that shifter dick you can't go twelve hours without it?"

"No." Elijah glared, then pointed to his head. "He's restless. This little ball of anxiety in my mind."

"Do you need to go to him?" Miles's brown eyes were big and soft.

"We talked about it. He told me he'd be okay for the night. Besides, this way, I can drive you out to the territory tomorrow."

Miles didn't seem convinced, and neither was Liam. He couldn't decide whether it was horrifying or adorable that they were so connected, so in sync with each other.

For the rest of their research session, Elijah tried not to fidget but didn't quite manage it.

They got through a suitcase worth of books. Not that it mattered. There wasn't anything of use. Liam enjoyed learning for learning's sake, but even he'd reached his limit on various aspects of spirits. He now knew more than he'd ever wished to know about possessions and exorcisms and hauntings. None of that helped them. Nothing was similar to what they were facing.

Shortly after midnight, they sorted out sleeping arrangements.

"I've got a sleeping bag." Miles looked at Aran. "It only sleeps one."

"Same," Liam said.

"Y'all aren't fun," Aran complained. "But I brought one too."

"You guys are welcome at the pack house. There are spare bedrooms. You could each have your own."

Liam declined Elijah's offer, and Miles and Aran did the same.

Mistrust of shifters was deeply ingrained in the majority of mages, as it had been for centuries, ever since the abductions—that dark era of their shared history when shifters had taken mages and forcibly bonded them to control their magic. For so long, mages had been raised to be careful around shifters, to be suspicious of their motives. Relationships between their kinds had begun to thaw over the last few decades, but hundreds of years of bad blood weren't easy to get over.

Liam trusted Elijah's pack; he'd be safe with them. They wouldn't try to bond him against his will. But staying the night on pack land still felt dangerous in ways he couldn't logically justify.

Elijah shrugged. "I figured that'd be your response."

"Let's get some sleep so we can start capturing these things in the morning," Liam said.

"Whatever the fuck they are," Aran added.

They crashed for the night, but before he fell asleep, Liam stared up at the ceiling and grinned, the banter and teasing of the evening replaying in his mind.

Moonlight shone through the window, casting a silvery illumination over the room and the sleeping forms of his friends. They were together again, as they should be.

Contentment draped itself over him, and he closed his eyes.

After this was over, he'd make damn sure they saw each other more often.

CHAPTER

THREE

Victor was pacing. Kade sat on the couch and watched him try to wear a hole in their flooring.

Most of their pack had discovered they had pressing business elsewhere, not wanting to deal with Victor when he was this wound up. He circled the coffee table, then headed toward the kitchen. His brow was furrowed deeply, his jaw clenched. He exuded a half-feral energy.

A few moments later, he was in the living room again, each step sharp, his movements those of a caged predator seeking an escape.

"You should have told him it was too soon for you to be apart," Kade said as Victor made his lap.

With obvious effort, Victor sat. Tension was written in the lines of his body, his shoulders stiff, like it took every ounce of his willpower not to rip open the front door, shift, and sprint until he reached Elijah.

"No." Victor's hands gripped the arms of the chair hard enough that his knuckles went white. "He needed to be with his friends. That was more important."

Kade scoffed. "I doubt he was having much fun while he had a giant ball of anxiety in his head from your self-restraining ass."

"Speaking of his friends," Victor said in an attempt to change the subject, "I didn't see you yesterday after you picked up Liam. What's he like?"

Kade shrugged. "He's a mage."

The glint in Victor's eyes was entirely too perceptive. "I feel like I know him already."

Kade had a flashback to sitting beside Victor when he'd said the same thing about Elijah, but how was he supposed to answer that? Should he admit he'd been utterly unprepared for Liam to look like a model? All high cheekbones, warm brown skin, and piercing eyes. Or that he seemed impervious to Kade's feeble attempts at his usual flirty innuendos? The spirit must have screwed up any amount of game Kade had, along with his senses.

After dropping Liam off, Kade had been even more off-kilter. To try to lessen the feeling, he'd driven around Lost Creek and up into the mountains in a large loop that had doubled the forty-minute journey. It had taken that long until he hadn't felt quite so unsettled, until he'd convinced his wolf they didn't need to return to the shop to prove they were much better at flirting than their disastrous first impression had shown.

But what he'd truly longed to do was shift and run. With his wolf awake again, he wanted to be in his other form. The dozens of unknown spirits on their territory made that impossible. It was too unsafe. Victor had expressly forbidden going into the forest alone. He couldn't afford anyone else being stupid enough to make the same mistake Kade had, and shifting somewhere off pack land by himself didn't feel right.

Speeding through the winding mountain roads had been Kade's only option to ease his restlessness. He'd been almost as bad as Victor was now, his grip on the chair tightening to the point he was likely putting permanent dents into it.

They had nearly an hour before Elijah arrived. Maybe doing something active would offer a distraction that'd keep Victor sane until then.

"Do you want to see if we can identify another spirit?" Kade asked.

Victor groaned. "Yes, please." He retrieved Elijah's map, showing it to Kade when he returned.

"These are the three we've already tracked down and identified." He pointed them out—a shimmering mirage of ash, glimmering crystal, and twisting growth. "Heatwave, frost, and this is causing a bunch of vine-like weeds to grow and choke out the native plants. Elijah said Liam will design sigils for them once he arrives so we can capture them." He motioned to the fourth largest on the map. "This is next on our list to identify."

It was a cracked thing, spidering slowly across the paper, leaving behind jagged lines of ash. It wasn't moving fast, just creeping along the southern line of the territory in an unstoppable trail. They'd have no problem finding it; the bigger issue was figuring out what it was.

They headed out the front door, and Kade paused, staring into the forest. The reality of what he'd suggested they do hit him like a punch to the stomach.

He hadn't been in the forest since the night they'd fought the decay spirit. Since the night they'd fought *him*.

His breathing grew shallow, his chest tight.

He was being pathetic and weak. This forest had been his home his entire life; the wind twisting through the trees had whispered secrets to him since his childhood. The idea of entering it shouldn't cause his heart to pound and sweat to prickle on his skin. He loved running through those trees. But now they loomed so tall, the shadows underneath them so dark.

Who knew what was out there, what those spirits could do?

What if another spirit—

Victor's hand came up to the back of Kade's neck and gave him a reassuring squeeze. Kade sucked air into his lungs.

Victor cocked an eyebrow. He didn't say anything; he didn't have to. The question was clear. *Are you okay?*

If Kade said the word, Victor would let him sit this out, and he wouldn't judge him for it either. But Kade didn't want that. What he wanted was to help defeat these fucking spirits.

He pulled himself together. There was no way in hell he was letting his pack down again. Memories would not keep him from doing his duty.

Victor nodded in acknowledgment. He then stripped out of his clothes, hung them on the railing, and shifted into his wolf form. Kade did the same.

He surrendered himself to the shift, letting himself be consumed by it. Pleasure and pain washed over him as he was reborn, as he became more than human. The familiar rush of adrenaline and energy coursed through him, and he welcomed it, welcomed the feeling of returning to himself more fully than he'd realized was possible. The relief of that transformation left him shivering in its aftermath, his fur ruffled by the breeze, the earth solid beneath his paws, power thrumming through his muscles. He exhaled, finally home after a long journey.

When he opened his eyes, Victor was watching him. Kade dipped his head. He was good, better than he'd been for days.

Victor led the way, his large frame loping gracefully through the undergrowth. They'd be faster on four legs, and unlike some of the other spirits, this one didn't seem to be moving quickly or erratically; they wouldn't need a map to find it.

For all Kade's determination to do this, his breath still hitched as he stepped past the first trees into the forest, but it was easier to push that aside in this form. Being in this body helped, like these weren't the lungs that had filled with decay.

They padded through the trees at a good clip, and Kade took in the forest surrounding them—the vibrant canvas of colors and sounds, the autumn leaves and scattered destruction. How long would it be until it recovered? Would it ever be the same, or would the scars of the rot spirit always be there, no matter how well new growth tried to cover them?

It wasn't far to the area on the map that had been smeared with ash in the spirit's wake.

Something in the air felt wrong, though Kade couldn't place it. It wasn't the skin-crawling filth of the decay from before. This was different. He scanned their surroundings, but didn't notice any immediate signs that made it apparent what they were facing.

They continued along the trail. With each step Kade took, the grass grew more brittle until it was breaking under his weight. The trees began to change too. They weren't simply colored by fall here; their leaves were shriveled and withered. The earth was parched.

He exchanged a glance with Victor, and they shifted to human.

"Drought?" Kade asked.

"Seems like it."

They walked farther, the cracked dirt harsh under their bare feet.

It was like the forest hadn't seen rain in weeks, in *years*. Kade's skin felt parched as well, and he wanted nothing more than a drink. He went to wet his lips, but his mouth was as dry as the land around him.

While none of these spirits were good, he preferred this over the rot. It didn't reek or make him feel unclean.

He was about to say as much when Victor stood up straighter, turning toward the road that led into their territory. He closed his eyes and exhaled, tension falling away from his shoulders.

Kade grinned. "I take it Elijah's here?"

Victor didn't bother answering. He was back in his wolf form, sprinting home.

Kade shook his head, then shifted and hurried to catch up, his paws rapidly covering the distance between him and the house.

He caught glimpses of Victor's fur through the trees and rounded the corner to see Elijah getting out of his car, a second vehicle parking behind him.

Elijah jumped when he noticed the large wolf barreling toward him, then relaxed when he recognized Victor. He didn't even have time to shut his door before Victor was there, shifting mid-run, crowding into his personal space. Victor pushed him up against the car and inhaled his scent like he'd been oxygen-starved, his hands roaming over Elijah's body.

Elijah's expression flickered from surprise to amusement, and then he melted into Victor, giving himself up to the kisses Victor dragged along his neck before finding his mouth and devouring him thoroughly.

Kade shifted at a more leisurely pace as Elijah's friends got out of the cars—Liam from the passenger side of Elijah's and two others from the second vehicle.

Grabbing his clothes from the railing, Kade studied the new arrivals and was tempted to take his time dressing when he noticed Liam and one of the other mage's eyes darting over to him.

Liam was as attractive as he had been the day before— the sunlight warm on his skin, his soft-looking sweater fitting him snugly. Kade tore his gaze away to check out the other two.

The driver of the second car was gorgeous, with Asian heritage, black hair, dark eyes, and a wicked grin, the type Kade would pick up in a club. His frame was slender but strong, his sleeves pushed up to reveal inky patterns twisting around his forearms. Kade had never seen a mage with real tattoos before, and he blinked when he realized the negative space in the design must align with the pattern of his magical tattoos.

The third was a cute blond who was carefully looking everywhere but at Kade slipping into his underwear and the very naked shifter currently mauling his friend. The only word Kade had for him was angelic. Where he would have picked up the tattooed mage in a club, the blond was an immediate no. Kade couldn't fathom dragging someone that pure into a bathroom stall for a dirty fuck.

He pulled on his shirt and hoped he wasn't imagining the disappointment in Liam's eyes.

It was a miracle Victor hadn't tossed Elijah over his shoulder and headed straight to their room. It really was too early for them to be apart, and Victor would need to reaffirm their bond until his wolf was satisfied.

Liam and the tattooed mage cast amused glances at Elijah, not that he noticed, and Kade had the distinct feeling Elijah would be getting his fair share of shit as soon as Victor let anyone near him.

Kade finished dressing and grabbed Victor's clothes.

"Victor," he said sharply, tossing them on the roof of Elijah's car.

Victor seemed to regain some semblance of control, though he lingered as he pulled away from Elijah and kept their hips pressed together, like that was hiding the situation that was happening down there. Elijah's eyes were glazed over, nearly as lost as Victor.

"Don't stop or get dressed on our account. I'm enjoying the show," the tattooed mage said, smirking as he leaned against his car, his gaze trailing down the bare line of Victor's back and over his ass.

Elijah flipped him off, but didn't push Victor away.

On the other side of the car, the blond surveyed the scene. He was grinning at Elijah and Victor too, but not in the 'I'm going to tease you relentlessly about this' kind of way. No, this was a genuinely warm smile, like he was thrilled for Elijah, for them both.

Liam leaned on the top of Elijah's car, mirth glittering in his eyes. He snapped a picture with his phone, the shutter noise drawing Elijah's attention.

"I'm sending this to Mom."

"You wouldn't," Elijah hissed, attempting to lunge for him, though Victor held him firmly in place.

Liam grinned and slipped his phone into his pocket. "We'll see."

Elijah looked ready to race around the car and make

him delete the picture, but Victor was boxing him in and didn't seem inclined to let him go.

Kade chuckled. "How about I take your friends to the back of the house and show them the maps?"

A low rumble of approval came from Victor, his stare not leaving Elijah, and Elijah swallowed hard. "Great idea. You do that."

"Aww," the tattooed mage said. "For a second there, I thought we might be treated to some live-action porn."

"Not everyone wants to watch Elijah get bent over the hood of his car and railed by his big-dicked alpha shifter, Aran." The blond seemed to realize what he'd just said, then clamped his mouth shut, his cheeks coloring.

Aran snorted. "Nice, Miles. I see you're already ahead of me on imagining positions."

Kade suppressed a laugh. With as worked up as Victor was, he doubted they'd get that far. He gestured for the mages to follow him. They did, each tossing a bag over their shoulder, and if there wasn't a book or two in Liam's, Kade would never shift again.

He'd heard people say there was something about shifters that marked them as supernatural, especially on full moons. Something a little wilder, a little more dangerous. He supposed that was true, but he felt the same about mages. Even from across the yard, he would have known Elijah's friends had magic. Whether he could smell it on them or not, he sensed it in the atmosphere around them— it was almost electric. The power was undeniable, and it made him wonder how humans could look at a mage and not realize they were something *more.*

The pack had smelled of magic until his late teens when his grandmother had passed, but having four mages in one place was a lot. There'd be more magic in the territory over the next few days than there had been in decades, and most of it wasn't pack magic. Once again he thought it might be a blessing that his sense of smell wasn't working.

The same wasn't true for his hearing though. He had to purposefully block out the choked-off cries and bitten-back moans that were coming from the front of the house.

They made their way around to where a pile of boxes had been stacked next to the porch. The boxes were rough things, assembled by Rick, one of the pack's betas. The cedar wood was raw and unvarnished, with simple hinges and a single clasp to keep them closed. Most would fit nicely onto the palm of a hand, but there were a few closer to chest-size and a couple in between.

He gestured to the pile. "Those, Elijah will have to show you. If he has the mental capacity to do so after Victor makes him come his brains out. But I can explain these."

The mages gathered around him as he grabbed three maps that were tucked under a box and handed them out. They weren't overly detailed, but they'd be sufficient to navigate the land. The major paths were marked, as were rivers and terrain. A few of the larger clearings were also noted.

As the mages unfolded the maps and saw the ashy blobs slithering and flowing over the paper, they each sucked in a breath. It was daunting how many spirits there were, how littered the forest was with them. Some had gotten bigger over the last few days; others were still small smudges. None were remotely close to the size of the decay spirit.

"Elijah explained what's happening, right? That they're all different, but we've only tracked down a few so far?" He got three nods in return, so he continued, stepping into Liam's space for the sole purpose of seeing the map he was holding better. The instinct to breathe in deep hit Kade, but he repressed it and pointed to the four spirits they'd already identified. "Drought, frost, heatwave, and vine-like weeds. The spirits grow bigger as they get stronger."

"You haven't checked out any without a trail yet?" Liam asked.

Kade leaned closer. It was impossible not to wonder how he smelled. How abrasive was the scent of his magic? Kade had never been with a mage before. Non-pack magic often made him feel like he was about to sneeze. Not the sexiest of sensations. But he wasn't having that issue with Liam right now.

He shook his head, half to clear those thoughts and half to answer Liam's question, but then the back door opened and Rick and Will walked out.

"We heard Elijah's car and figured it was time to get started," Rick said as they descended the stairs to join them.

"Made the mistake of glancing out front first," Will added wryly.

Kade snorted. They must have gotten an eyeful.

When he turned back to the mages to make introductions, he found Liam crouched at his feet with a massive book in his lap and a notebook open beside him. Liam muttered to himself as he flipped through the tome.

The book was like nothing Kade had seen before. It was full of intricate symbols, each with a block of text next to it, though Liam didn't stay on any page long enough for Kade to read them. The speed at which he jumped through the pages suggested he had the book mostly memorized. He flipped with his left hand and sketched with his right in the notebook, first rough chunks of designs, but they soon coalesced, twisting into sigils that he labeled, each embodying the spirit they represented. This one cracked like parched earth, that one twining around itself like over-grown vines.

Kade stared, impressed.

On his other side, Aran leaned in and said under his breath. "He's kinda hot when he does the super-focused genius book-nerd thing, isn't he?"

Kade jerked his gaze away from Liam and saw Aran's smirk.

He was saved from trying to deny that when Elijah and Victor appeared. Elijah looked weak-kneed and rumpled, his cheeks stained red, though there was a fond smile on his lips. Victor radiated smug satisfaction. He was also significantly more relaxed, and Kade found an additional reason to appreciate his senses being messed up, because otherwise, he'd be smelling how much they had to reek of sex.

"Well," he said, "I guess we can get started now that everyone's had a nutritious lunch."

Elijah blushed darker, Victor's smugness increased, and from where he was crouched, Liam huffed out an almost-laugh.

Aran and Miles's heads whipped toward him, and he looked guilty for a fraction of a second before he raised an eyebrow to ask, *What?*

Elijah cleared his throat and gently pushed Victor away. Victor grudgingly took a step back, giving Elijah room to walk over to his friends. Aran greeted him with another smirk.

"Don't even," Elijah replied.

Aran held up his hands. "I didn't say a word."

"Literally no one believes the innocent act, Aran," Liam said as he gathered his books and stood.

Kade had to agree with him. He knew next to nothing

about Aran, but even he could tell innocent was the last word anyone would use to describe him.

"Please. Would I make a comment about Elijah receiving such a warm, enthusiastic welcome? Or about how he just came home?"

"Yes," Elijah, Liam, and Miles said in unison.

Kade would have remarked that it was lovely Elijah had gotten his happy ending, but those worked too.

"*Anyway.*" Elijah made quick introductions between the mages and the pack members, telling them that Rick and Will were Victor's betas while Kade was his second-in-command, then picked up a box to show them.

Kade hung back with Rick and Will. They were there largely as guides and energy sources; the difficult parts would be up to the mages.

Elijah explained how he'd put a binding spell inside each box that would snare the spirits and reel them in, a contract that the mages could activate.

"The four base sigils are inscribed and ready to go." Elijah grabbed a map. "We just need to identify the spirits and inscribe the correct fifth sigil that will name the spirit we're capturing. This one is—"

"Frost," Liam said. "Got it. I've already made sigils for the first four."

"I should have known." Elijah's tone was amused. He shut the lid and flipped the clasp. A dazzling glow sprang up around the box before fading. "These wards should hold the spirits we capture."

The mages launched into a dozen questions Kade didn't completely understand. From what he could follow, the wards were impressive. He'd always gotten the sense that Elijah was strong, that he was a good mage, but their reactions to Elijah's wards told Kade all he needed to know.

What would his grandmother have thought of Elijah? Other than being thrilled Victor had found his mate, of course. She had been good with wards too, so that would have made her extra fond of him.

Victor was watching the scene with contented, possessive pride in his expression, perfectly willing to let Elijah take charge of the situation. There was no one else in the world Victor would so easily take a back seat to, and Kade found it adorable how smitten he was.

Elijah must have felt it through their bond, because he glanced up and smiled at Victor with such warmth that Kade couldn't help but grin. He hoped to have that one day, that perfect connection between two people.

But he'd have to wait a little longer, and he was okay with that.

"What do we do with the boxes after we've trapped a spirit?" Liam asked. "They need to be kept somewhere safe."

"We've got a room to store them in. I've warded the absolute hell out of it, so if the spirits somehow escape their boxes, they shouldn't be able to get out of the room."

Liam nodded, but he was frowning at the box in Elijah's hand. "The sigils are on the inside. That's ideal for trapping the spirits, but once we've got dozens captured, we won't have a clue which is which."

"Will we need to?" Aran asked.

"I'd rather play it safe and have us mark the outside of the box than have to open them up to figure out what's inside later."

That seemed reasonable to Kade.

"Okay, we'll do that," Elijah said. "After you've trapped a spirit, label the box. Now, I want to show you what you're dealing with before we break up to identify these things. This is the closest." He pointed to the drought spirit.

Liam hesitated, considering the map. "Actually, we should check out one that isn't leaving a trail. It's clear they're different somehow, and there are more of that kind. They might be harder to track, but we need to know what they are."

"This would be so much easier if we could trap them all at once," Aran said.

The mages looked at Liam expectantly, and Kade had a few seconds to picture that—a spell that would suck the spirits out of the forest in one go—before Liam shook his head.

"I've only seen binding spells that capture specifically named spirits, and I have no idea how to modify a spell to capture more, not without knowing exactly what they are. But I'll keep researching."

Of course that'd be too easy. Kade should have known.

"And we still have to find out where they came from and how to destroy them," Liam added. "So identifying them is only half the work."

He was right. They were on cleanup duty here. There must be something underlying it, and they'd have to deal with that eventually. Kade wanted to discover who was behind this so they could ensure it would never happen again, but making the forest safe for their pack came first. Their territory was too dangerous with the spirits on it. None of them had come near the pack house, but that might not last.

Elijah shrugged. "We'll take care of that when we have to. Until then, let's get as many of these things identified as we can. Today, we'll track them down, then tonight, Liam can make sigils, and we'll capture them tomorrow."

Liam cocked his head. "Why not message me when you find one? I can send a picture of the sigil."

Kade scoffed at the idea, drawing Liam's attention.

"There's shit reception in the forest," he explained.

"Oh." Liam frowned.

"Welcome to the middle of nowhere," Elijah said. "But some areas are better than others. We could try with the understanding that it's unlikely we'll get an immediate reply. If we do manage to send a message that you receive, and you can send the sigil while we're still in the area, it would save us from having to find every spirit twice. So just in case..."

He handed a few boxes to each of them, which they tucked in their bags, then he singled out a medium-sized smudge about fifteen minutes from the pack house. "Okay. Let's see what this is."

The spirit traveled in sharp bursts through the forest, leaving no trail behind, and Kade's chest tightened, each lungful of air harder to take than the last, but he forced himself to inhale.

Glancing up, he caught Victor watching him again and nodded. He was fine. He wasn't chickening out of this.

When he looked away from Victor's assessing gaze, he found Liam studying him too, a furrow between his brows.

"Alright." Elijah clapped his hands, saving Kade from having to respond to the concern in Liam's eyes. "Let's do this."

"And be careful," Liam added. "We don't know what these things are capable of."

It wasn't directed at Kade, but it still reminded him of how he hadn't been careful last time.

Keeping his breathing regular, he followed Victor and Elijah into the forest to face whatever awaited them.

They hiked for ten minutes, Victor and Elijah in the lead. Victor's hand found the small of Elijah's back before pulling away—a brief touch, a confirmation. Elijah leaned into it, then returned his attention to the land and the map.

Even if they had been idiots who'd taken forever to figure out how perfect they were for each other, Kade was glad Victor had finally gotten his head out of his ass. Elijah balanced Victor, made him stronger, made him happy. If only they were all so lucky.

The rest of their party trailed behind him—Liam and Will directly after him, followed by Aran and Miles, with Rick bringing up the rear.

They were nearing the area where the smudge was marked on their maps.

Kade looked around, expecting to see some sign of disturbance—leaves dripping with sludge, the cracked dryness of drought.

There was nothing.

Two squirrels yelled at each other in the trees, chattering aggressively before one chased the other away, and a crow screeched at them as they passed beneath its tree. Its warning call rang through the forest, picked up and echoed by other birds.

Kade almost ducked his head at the ruckus, and that irritated him. He wasn't afraid of a few crows.

From behind him, Aran called ahead. "Elijah, you aren't leading us into a scene from *The Birds*, are you?"

Elijah waved him off and kept walking.

Well, that was fucking rude. The least he could do was answer his friend's goddamn question.

Confused by his own thoughts, Kade's eyes narrowed. He didn't get irritated often, yet tension coiled under his skin. Anger was not a common emotion for him, but it was building in his chest.

He tried to push it down, tried to calm himself. It didn't work the way it should have, and that annoyed him even more.

Where was this fucking spirit? He wanted this over with so he could get the hell away from these people. Each and every one of them was annoying the shit out of him.

He frowned and cracked his neck. That thought wasn't like him.

When he glanced around at the others, their shoulders were bunched. Dark glowers marred their faces.

"Is anyone else feeling... irrationally angry?" he asked.

"Shut up," Will snapped, then paused. He exhaled shakily. "Sorry. Apparently yes."

They gathered in a cluster. Now that Kade was aware of it, he felt the anger inside him, the urge to lash out, to say something that would hurt.

This had to be the spirit, but how? It hadn't touched him, it hadn't...

He breathed in. No, that wasn't what was happening. It was affecting him, affecting *them*, and the animals too, but he wasn't in danger of being taken over by it.

"They affect emotions?" There was an edge to Aran's tone that glinted like steel.

"I guess so," Elijah said. "Which means they do leave trails, just not ones that show up on the map. And since the spirits that cause physical effects seem to feed off those effects, I'm going to assume the ones that affect emotions feed off the feelings they elicit. So the angrier we get, the more we're feeding it."

"Lovely." Aran spat out the word like a curse.

"How concerned should we be about that?" Liam asked. "Can they also possess people?"

Elijah frowned. "As far as we can tell, the spirits can only do that if they touch you. And it might only be the bigger ones that are capable of it, though we shouldn't assume. If these emotion spirits work similarly to the physical ones, they'll taint our emotions while we're in their wake, but shouldn't affect the areas outside that. So, as long as we monitor ourselves, I think we should be okay. But whatever you do, don't let them touch you."

The hot flush of shame raced through Kade, followed by annoyance at the emotion, but before he had time to process it, Liam shoved the thick tome of weird squiggles at him.

"Hold this."

Kade did as he was told, blinking at the book, holding it open so Liam could flip through it as he sketched out a spiky sigil.

When Liam was finished, he held up the notebook for Elijah to see. Elijah studied it before pulling a box out of his bag, opening its lid, and pressing his fingers to the bottom inside. A light flared briefly before dying out.

He exhaled forcefully, lowering his shoulders with deliberate effort. "Let's give this a try."

"Can you do it from here?" Kade immediately wanted to growl, frustrated at how weak that sounded, and he couldn't blame it on the spirit.

Liam stopped repacking his bag, and the mages exchanged contemplative looks. He tilted his head in thought. "If we only have to get close enough to identify the effects and not see the spirit itself, it would be a lot safer."

"Worth a try." Elijah held the box out, open on his palm. A brilliant light shone out of it as he activated the seal, and a purple glow sparked in his eyes.

Kade watched, holding his breath.

A few drawn-out seconds later, Elijah shook his head. "I can sense it out there, but the binding can't latch on. I need to be closer."

"Figures," Aran sighed.

They started to hike through the forest again, though this time, they stayed clustered together. Kade had to remind himself he didn't hate how fucking close Will was to him. That was ridiculous and not something he would have been annoyed by under normal circumstances, but it got harder to remember with every step he took.

Even so, this felt nothing like the spirit of decay. If Kade focused, he could separate his own emotions from the irritation it was amplifying inside him. It didn't have control of him.

"There," Elijah announced, pointing ahead of them.

A moment later, Kade saw it—sharp flashes, white-hot light exploding in bursts as it moved.

"Why isn't it trying to evade us?" he asked. When the decay spirit had been smaller, it had fled when they'd gotten close. It pissed him off that this spirit wasn't doing the same.

"They might all work differently," Elijah said. "Or they get smarter as they get more powerful. The rot hid until it was too late to do anything about it, but some of the others might not act the same."

"If each spirit embodies an emotion, they may also

mirror that emotion with their actions. It'd explain why no two look the same on the map," Liam said.

"So each might require a different tactic to—" Before Kade could finish his sentence, the spirit changed course, charging at them, its explosions getting brighter, leaving afterimages dotting his vision.

Kade froze, unable to breathe. Elijah held out the box and activated the binding contract, his eyes kindling to purple again. The power of his magic surged into it, causing a sudden change in the air around them as it pulled the spirit toward them. The closer it got, the more irritated Kade felt, and the tighter his chest became.

Anger swept through him, and he gritted his teeth against it, refusing to let a spirit control him again.

Elijah kept working, the tattoos on his arms glowing bright enough to show through his sleeves, a few tendrils peeking out over his collar. Victor's hand settled on the back of his neck, giving Elijah's magic an extra kick.

As the spirit was sucked into the box, it condensed, forming a volatile pool so blinding it was difficult to look at. Kade's breathing came easier, and the anger churning inside him lessened, then abated entirely. He exhaled. Next to him, Will did the same, tension leaving his body.

When the remnants of the spirit were trapped in the box, Elijah snapped the lid shut and latched it. The ward flashed around it as brightly as the explosions of anger. He pressed his hand to the top of the box, and when he lifted it, the sigil for anger was transcribed on the wood.

Nodding to himself, he turned toward his friends.

"Elijah," Aran said, "you just invited us to the shittiest bootlegged version of Pokémon GO ever, didn't you?"

Elijah's laughter was shaky but genuine. "Yep, sorry. You don't want to see what they evolve into. This won't be pleasant for any of us, but I think the best plan is for Victor and me to tackle the largest spirits, while you guys search for the medium and small ones to identify and catch if the reception plays nice and Liam can send a sigil."

"Will we be able to do that?" Liam asked. "You used a fairly sizable amount of energy, and we aren't bonded to shifters."

"This took less energy to trap than the decay spirit, so I think you'll be fine provided you connect to a shifter and stick to spirits smaller than this. That's why Kade, Rick, and Will are here. But if you have any doubts, leave them for us. If you can identify them at least, that'll help when we capture them."

Liam considered that, then spoke. "We now know they affect emotions, so we should make a list of potential spirits. That way, if we come across one of those, we can try to capture it immediately."

"Good idea. If this was anger, what else could there be?"

"Hatred? Sadness?" Miles suggested.

They started to brainstorm, and Kade found himself holding Liam's book again as Liam scribbled sigils in his notebook. He was so laser-focused on the task at hand, Kade wasn't sure he realized they were standing in the middle of the forest.

Kade absolutely was not distracted by the sweep of his dark eyelashes. They were standing so close, he should have been able to smell Liam, though everything was still frustratingly blank.

When Liam had a dozen sigils created, his friends took pictures of his notebook with their phones.

"Okay," Elijah said. "If you find a spirit that matches these and think you can handle it, give it a try. But err on the side of caution, alright?" They nodded. "Pair up so we can trap these damn things."

"Gotta catch 'em all," Aran muttered.

Kade snorted, their gazes locking. They looked each other over, and for one moment, Kade could imagine meeting Aran in a club. He saw the recognition on Aran's face, the knowledge that they might dance for a few minutes, a pretense to feel each other up, to grind against each other as foreplay before finding the nearest bathroom or back alley for a quick hot fuck. They wouldn't even remember the other's name by the end of the night.

Aran grinned at him, wide and wicked.

"Oh fuck no." Elijah jabbed a finger at them. "You two are *not* allowed to pair up. Even if no one is around to hear the resulting chaos, you'll use up the entire universe's quota of dick jokes. You'd probably just end up fucking while you're out in the forest."

Aran looked offended. "Hey now, I do not fuck while I'm working." He paused, then added, "Unless, you know, the work involves fucking."

Fair enough, Kade thought. That seemed like a sensible position to take.

"Also," Aran added, "you're one to talk." He gave Elijah a thorough once-over. "Pretty sure only one of us has gotten off in nature recently."

Elijah's cheeks heated. "Regardless. Nothing good can come from you two being paired together. It's not happening."

Kade glanced over to where Miles was standing, but Elijah cut in again.

"Nope. Nuh-uh. I'm not subjecting Miles to you either. He gets enough from Aran as it is. Liam?" he asked, apology clear in his tone.

"Got it." Liam didn't seem particularly surprised by the arrangement.

Okay. Liam it was. Kade could work with that. This might be his chance to prove he wasn't as pathetic as Liam had likely thought yesterday.

That settled, Elijah continued. "Miles, you go with Will. He's semi-decently well-behaved and mated with a baby on the way, so he should be practicing how to be a good role model." Elijah's expression held a clear warning, and Will beamed at him as innocently as possible. "And Aran, I'm pairing you up with Rick because I don't think anything you can say will faze him."

Aran assessed Rick with a leer. "Challenge accepted."

He was barking up the wrong tree with that one. In Kade's entire life, he'd never seen Rick show an ounce of interest in another person sexually, and he was unflappable when it came to double entendres and dirty jokes. Kade knew that well; he'd lost count of the times he'd tried to flap him, to get some kind of reaction out of him.

"Actually, Aran," Elijah said, "Today, I want you to concentrate on repairing the damage from the previous spirit. The forest is pretty beaten up in some areas. A few are almost dead zones. Whatever you can do to revive it would be great. If there are nearby spirits while you're doing that, definitely identify them and capture them if you can, but I'd rather have you focus on the forest itself. Make sure everything is recovering properly."

"I can do that. After all, I'm the best here at making wood grow nice and ha—"

Victor cut him off. "Rick, take him to the western border where the damage is the worst."

Rick sent Victor a flat look, but led Aran in that direction.

"Be careful!" Liam yelled after them.

Aran gave him a little salute. "Always, Li-mom. You know I'm a big fan of keeping things safe."

Li-mom? That was adorable.

Elijah tapped the frost spirit on the map. "We'll do this one, then take care of the others we've already identified, if you want to go in opposite directions and see what's out there."

Liam and Miles nodded.

"You guys be careful too," Liam said, getting promises from Elijah and Miles before they left.

Liam pointed to a dark ashy blob that was skittering across the map. "Should we try this spirit? It doesn't seem that far from here and isn't too big."

"Might as well."

Kade turned toward the spirit, and they headed deeper into the forest.

FOUR

Liam should have known he'd get paired with Kade. While Kade wasn't nearly as bad as Elijah seemed to think, Liam had to agree that they should keep him as far from Miles as possible. And the combination of Aran and Kade would indeed be nonstop dick jokes. No one needed that in their life.

The look Kade and Aran had exchanged—their acknowledgment of each other's fuckboy credentials—had spoken volumes. Liam would never be that compatible with Kade, but they could work together. He just had to check one thing before they got too close to another spirit.

"I want to channel your energy," Liam said as he came to a stop and held out his hand. If he had trouble using Kade's energy, it'd be an issue, but from their handshake at the airport, he suspected that wouldn't be the case.

Kade eyed him. "When Elijah used my energy, bodily fluids were involved. Am I going to get covered in yours as well?"

The corner of Liam's lips tried to twitch, but he

suppressed it. That was not funny. "I don't think that'll be necessary."

"That's no fun." Kade slid his hand into Liam's. The moment their skin touched, energy buzzed against Liam's fingertips. He opened himself up to it, let it flow into him, surge through him.

He inhaled, a little shaky at how easy it was, and Kade did the same, his wolf flashing in his eyes.

Using shifter energy always required conscious effort to channel. It never rushed into him like it was eager to fill him, eager to do his bidding.

A shiver ran through him. No fluids needed. He'd barely begun, but this could easily become addictive.

He dropped his hand and released Kade's energy, though a ghost of it remained in his system. That hadn't been as intense as how Elijah described Victor's energy, certainly not as overwhelming, but if this was a fraction of what he felt while tethered to Victor, Liam couldn't fault Elijah for getting lost in it.

"Huh." Kade tilted his head. "That was different from Elijah channeling my energy."

"How so?"

Kade paused before answering. "With Elijah, it didn't feel direct. If that makes sense? This was direct. I felt *you* pulling on my energy and it flowing into you. I didn't feel that with him."

"If it was before the last full moon, he might have channeled your energy through Victor. Whatever weird pseudo-bond they had likely made it difficult for him to connect to anyone else. Victor's metaphorical dick was too far up his channels for anyone else's to get in there."

The words were out of Liam's mouth before he could

stop them. He resisted the urge to slap a hand against his face.

Kade's eyebrows rose. "What?"

Liam was glad it was harder for people to tell when he blushed than when Elijah did, but he couldn't conceal his wince.

"Blame Aran. It was his theory. So... let's go trap this thing."

He started to walk in the direction of the spirit, hoping Kade would let it drop, but from his smirk, Liam doubted he'd be that lucky.

This spirit was smaller than the spirit of anger. On the map, it appeared darker than the other smudges of ash—almost as if it were absorbing light. Liam had no idea what that meant, but with as easy as it was to use Kade's energy, he was decently confident he'd be able to trap it. He didn't want to leave all the bigger ones for Elijah. That would be exhausting, no matter how strong Elijah had become.

As they hiked, Liam surveyed the forest. He'd never liked the outdoors, much preferring his books, but in small doses, he could admit nature held its own appeal. Even if a place like this would make him go stir-crazy, he understood why Elijah might love it. The bright colors of fall were welcoming in ways he hadn't taken time to consider.

But then they entered an area of unseasonably bare trees, the section stark and desolate.

"It's not usually like this. It still hasn't recovered," Kade explained.

Liam pressed his palm against a tree that looked dead, but when he concentrated, he sensed a spark of life inside it, hibernating deep.

"Give Aran a few days, and it'll be as good as new."

There was no question in Liam's mind that Aran would nurture those sparks and ensure the trees would be strong and healthy again once spring came. Aran was probably enjoying himself. Nurturing plants was in his blood.

From Liam's left, a large raven burst through the branches, its caw raucous and wings loud as it flew up into the canopy.

Liam jumped, then laughed. After spending most of his waking hours in the silent peace of the library, he needed to recalibrate to being outdoors. It was just a bird, not something sinister.

As he watched it fly away, the air took on a chill, making him shiver. It had been pleasantly warm when they'd arrived, but now goose bumps sprang up on his arms. Wind creaked in the skeletal branches, all rusty hinges and slamming doors, and Liam wanted to shiver for a different reason. It was like they'd stumbled onto the set of a horror movie.

He glanced over at Kade and saw the concern on his face. Any trace of joking or flirting had vanished, replaced by a pinched expression.

They continued on, getting closer to the smudge on the map. A small animal dashed past them, its eyes wide and terrified even through the streaking blur of its hectic movement. Liam's pulse accelerated; his breathing shallowed.

What would jump out next? What waited for them behind those trees? Was something about to attack?

He shook his head to clear it. There was nothing subtle about this spirit; it wasn't the slow-building boil of anger.

"Terror?" he asked, and Kade nodded. Elijah had been right; this wouldn't be pleasant.

"Do you have a sigil for that?"

"Close."

Liam got out his notes. He'd made one for fear during their brainstorming session, but this felt stronger than that. It didn't take much to alter the design and make it more extreme, changing fear into terror. He transferred the sigil into a box, then tucked his notebook away. The fear sigil might have worked, but it was best to be precise.

"Ready?" Kade's smile was cocky, bravado in his tone. Neither covered the strain around his eyes.

Liam held the box in his right hand, open for when the spirit came into view.

Now that he had identified the feeling, it was easier to separate the looming dread from his own emotions, but that didn't stop the branches from reaching out and clawing at him.

The sunlight spilling through the bare canopy started to fade, despite the early hour.

"Can these things make it night?" Kade asked.

Liam shrugged. "Maybe? Or it might be affecting our perception?" Either way, the results were the same.

In a few more steps, they were plunged into pitch blackness. Liam called fire into his free hand, its warmth radiating but scarcely piercing the deepest midnight that surrounded them, a darkness hiding the monsters that lurked under children's beds.

It hissed in his ears and rattled like death. Every step took effort; he faced his fears with each bit of ground they gained. All he wanted to do was turn, run, get to safety... If anywhere was safe.

Kade's hand wrapped around his arm above his elbow. He wasn't touching skin, but a jolt of energy shot through Liam. The fire flared, driving back the night, revealing nothing hidden in those inky depths.

They passed more trees, and the spirit appeared, a shadow among shadows, deeper black than the night. It skittered across the ground, iridescent, a teeming swarm of insects crawling over each other.

The spirit shrank away from the fire but still prowled just outside the light, twisting and terrible.

"What do you need?" The faintest tremor of nerves quivered in Kade's voice.

"Wrap your hand around my wrist," Liam said, and Kade did as directed, then his other hand found the back of Liam's neck the same way Victor had done to Elijah.

Immediately, his energy was there, ready for Liam. He had to force his eyes to stay open, force himself not to sink into that tempting flow. He should ask Elijah if this was how it felt to use Victor's energy before they were bonded, because he'd never experienced anything like this.

But he couldn't dwell on that. They had a spirit to trap.

He activated the contract and channeled Kade's energy into the sigils. His tattoos lit up, casting an orange glow over his skin.

The binding latched on to the spirit, and slowly, it was drawn toward them.

Liam gritted his teeth and stood steadfast, but that was easy to do with Kade's hands on him. The spirit crept closer as it was sucked into the box.

It was both harder and easier than he'd expected. Harder to control, harder to know exactly what he was doing. This wasn't the type of spell he was used to. It required more magic than anything he'd done in ages. But also, it was so easy with Kade's energy willing to help. It was a rush, but he didn't let it sweep him away.

Over a minute passed before the spirit was pulled

completely into the box. It pooled inside, a crawling iridescence.

The forest lightened, and daylight returned as the terror was contained.

He exhaled a sigh of relief, let his fire flicker out, and closed the lid before latching it shut. He marveled as Elijah's ward snapped into place. It was stunning work.

Liam was an abject failure at wards. He was much better at blowing things up. Having a fire affinity with a decent grasp of air lent itself well to spectacular explosions and not much else, but he could appreciate the beauty of this. It was the most delicate and intricate spellwork he'd seen Elijah create. This was a masterpiece, and it made him smile because he knew it could only come from the bond that Elijah shared with Victor. It wasn't something he wanted for himself, but looking at it now, it was impossible not to recognize its perfection. More of this kind of magic should exist in the world.

With a quick press of his fingers, he marked the box with the sigil for terror.

Kade let his hands drop, taking his energy with him, and Liam almost regretted the loss.

To distract himself from that thought, he put the box into his bag and pulled out the map again. One down, dozens more to go.

He glanced up, and for the briefest moment, Kade looked shaken, but then he grinned—bright and charming and entirely too appealing.

"Wanna see if we can capture more of these things than Victor and Elijah?"

Despite himself, Liam did.

While he excelled at theory and designing new spells or

modifying old ones, Elijah had always been better at doing those spells. It made them a great team, but that didn't mean the idea of one-upping Elijah on the practical side of magic held no appeal.

He nodded. "Let's do it."

FIVE

Kade stood next to Liam and looked at the map. There were three medium-sized spirits within a thirty-minute hike from their current location. One was doing lazy circles while another zigzagged, and the third was a hazy cloud that floated over the paper.

"I picked the last one," Liam said. "Your turn to choose."

"Wanna try something bigger?" Kade asked, putting some innuendo in his tone. He jabbed at the hazy smudge. It was slightly larger than the spirit they'd just captured, but they'd managed that without much problem.

Liam side-eyed him. "Should we get this on the way?" He pointed to a smaller spirit that swirled in on itself, a tiny vortex.

The detour would take them off the most direct path to the ashy haze, adding ten minutes to their trek, but it sounded like a plan.

Before Liam could refold the map, the cracked spirit of drought began shrinking. Kade grinned when he realized what was happening. "We better get going if we want to beat them."

"Then let's go." Liam was smiling too, a competitive spark in his eyes.

There was no way Kade was letting Victor and Elijah capture more of these things than he and Liam did. Turning this into a competition, even if Victor and Elijah weren't aware they were playing, was perfect. If he concentrated on showing Victor up, he didn't have to think about what the spirits were capable of.

He led Liam toward the smaller spirit. It'd be a good fifteen minutes before they'd get to it, and then the same again to the medium-sized one.

"Soooo." Kade drew out the O, as he often liked to do. "What were you saying about metaphorical dicks?"

Liam groaned. "You really are like Aran, aren't you? Fine. After the first ritual Elijah did for your pack, his magic was acting up, and Aran came up with this theory that Victor's energy was working like—" He paused, then rushed forward. "Like a knot. Keeping Elijah... Well, you get the idea."

He didn't finish the sentence, but Kade was more than willing to. "Stretched and filled?"

There was the tiniest trace of heat in Liam's cheeks, and Kade wanted to know if he could get more of that color.

"Yeah, that." Liam wasn't quite meeting his eyes.

That theory was too much fun to pass up.

"So in this metaphor of yours, when you channeled my energy to capture the spirit, you were taking my dick?"

"Just the metaphorical tip." Liam winced with instant regret.

Kade laughed. "I take it mages getting knotted by shifter energy isn't normal?"

"No. As far as I can tell, it happened because Elijah and Victor are freakishly compatible. Normally, actual sex is required, but the pair also have to want that connection. I'd never heard of a mage accidentally tethering themselves to a shifter before. I think they both subconsciously wanted it —or were interested, at least—though I doubt they'd ever admit as much."

If that didn't open up an entirely new line of teasing to use on Victor, Kade didn't know what would.

"Sex alone isn't enough?"

"No, otherwise mages and shifters could never do sex rituals without a connection forming. A sex ritual by itself wouldn't create the kind of tether Elijah and Victor have. Sex magic is merely that—sex and magic, not permanent. It's the same for bonds, isn't it? You have sex when you're bonding someone, but the sex isn't the important part, right?"

"Yeah, you don't accidentally give someone a mating bite; it has to be done with intention. There needs to be desire behind it, even if that desire is transactional."

"Actually, Elijah and Victor reminded me. Once, years ago, I was... reading this book about sex rituals—"

"Reading, huh?"

"Purely for educational purposes."

"Uh-huh. And I watch MateHub for the stellar acting and riveting plots."

"Right. Richard Knotz is a legend, a god among shifters." Before Kade could ask how Liam knew the name of his favorite porn star, Liam plowed ahead. "*Anyway*, as I was saying, there was this line about how sex rituals were best suited for incompatible shifters and mages, but there was no explanation why. Maybe it's unnecessary for compatible pairs to do those rituals, but it seemed like a warning to me. Like 'don't do these if there's a chance you're compatible.' But if that's the case, why?"

Liam's face was lit up, his hands gesturing wildly as he spoke and that faint trace of a Southern accent coloring his words. Kade couldn't tear his eyes away. There was something both charming and cute about it, something that made it impossible for him not to wonder if Liam got this passionate and focused about other things he did.

"Sex rituals aren't supposed to have any lingering effects, but this book warned about compatibility and sex magic. So what if you do a sex ritual with someone you're compatible with? And how should we define compatibility? I hadn't truly thought about it before Elijah and Victor, but if they ended up with a pseudo-tether from the ritual they did, what would have happened if they'd reset your wards with a full-on sex ritual instead?"

"You think any compatible pair would form a connection during a sex ritual, whether intended or not?" Kade mentally ran through their family history and the mages who had bonded into their pack, the ways they'd found their mates. He hadn't heard of anything of the sort, but he also didn't know the whole story of the ones further back in their pack's history, hundreds of years in the past.

Liam rubbed a hand over his buzzed hair and made a frustrated noise. "That's what I'm trying to figure out. Why include that warning otherwise?"

"If that's something you have to worry about, wouldn't there be more warnings?"

"I'm not so sure. Think about it. We've segregated ourselves into our own communities, and not just mages and shifters. Almost all supernatural beings stick to their own kind. Even different types of shifters don't mix much. Obviously there's no chance for real relationships to develop. Transactionally bonded pack mages aside, the only mages that regularly interact with shifters are the ones who run shops and, to a lesser extent, teachers and apprentices, but it's very controlled. And when our interactions are limited to brief periods, nothing's going to occur while we're so wary of each other. I mean, how often are shifters around mages enough to get past the scent of our magic? That alone has to have a distancing effect. I can't imagine we smell good to many shifters, if what I understand is correct."

"Fair point. Most shifters never get desensitized to its scent, and even then, there's a sharpness to it that can be unpleasant."

The sole exception was pack magic. When mages were bonded into a pack, the edges got shaved off, leaving their magic softer and more welcoming. For mages and shifters to enter transactional bonds, the shifter had to ignore what their nose was telling them for the sake of bonding a mage to their pack. Those pairs frequently couldn't stand each other; their relationships were nothing but a mutually beneficial business arrangement.

"There has to be something there, and if I could get my hands on better records from before the abductions, I might be able to prove it."

"The library doesn't have records from that time?"

"A few. It was long enough ago that books from that period are rare to begin with. The oldest books in our collection are over a thousand years old. There are a handful of grimoires from the Early Middle Ages, but most are damaged, which is to be expected with books that old. Even with protection spells, these are spellbooks that were meant to be used, not kept in pristine condition."

"None of them mention bonds or tethers?"

"See, that's the thing. We have grimoires from that time

with detailed information on what was known about the magical properties of stones and herbs, charms and spells, and basically everything else. However, when it comes to relationships with shifters, it's impossible to find anything concrete. Only the vaguest mentions remain. But some of those books are missing entire sections."

Kade frowned. "You think it was covered up?"

"Maybe? It's too suspicious. I've seen multiple books that have missing or unreadable sections. Yes, they're old, but the rest of the book will be in semi-decent condition with only that chunk of pages gone. What if those pages were about bonds? Maybe it was the council, but it might not have been a concerted effort to hide it. We were at war for generations; the worst of the fighting lasted over a hundred years. Even if there were mage families that previously had amicable relationships with packs, they might have destroyed those records during that time."

"Would it change anything? If tomorrow someone gave you a book that proves things were different back then, would that affect anything now?"

"It probably wouldn't. I realize that. But either way, it's something we need to figure out. Look at Elijah and Victor. I don't know if you're able to sense how perfect the magic Elijah can do with Victor's energy is, but you must feel how much stronger they are together."

There was no denying that. Kade felt Victor's strength in the pack connections. Their bond had caused Victor's energy to skyrocket, infusing the pack with power, and this was only the beginning of their relationship. As it grew and developed, as their bond solidified, it would strengthen the pack further, and from what he understood, Elijah's magic would increase with it.

Liam continued, his brown eyes intense and sparkling in the light filtering through the trees. "You can't tell me magic like that wouldn't have been written about in more detail outside folktales and legends. If what inspired the original abductions was jealousy over the power those bonds hold, it seems logical that there were more than just a few of them. If we're talking one or two true-bonded mage-shifter pairs, if they were a fluke, why would anyone think they were entitled to that level of power?"

"Versus them being commonplace, and some asshole alpha feeling they deserved a mage of their own because the neighboring packs all had one?"

"Exactly. If I can prove that, if I can show it was a thing, that it happened—that it was more accepted and that exquisitely beautiful magic can come from it—maybe it'll become more common again. Maybe transactional bonds won't be the only way we do things. More mages and shifters might find something like what Elijah and Victor have. The magic Elijah creates with Victor's energy is stunning. The wards he put around these boxes? They're priceless. Even I can tell that. It's *right*. Balanced. It transcends everything I've ever seen. What could a mage with that amount of magic at their disposal accomplish? What could they learn and discover? What advancements could they make? Elijah could double or triple the prices he charges for the spells he does at his shop, and people would pay for it. At least, anyone who can properly sense the quality. This kind of magic lasts centuries, if not longer."

Kade remembered Victor's father grumbling about how little their grandmother charged for her spells. If it had been up to him, she would have been charging more, but she'd been firmly against it. According to her, they were making more than enough money to support the pack; they didn't need to fleece the people who came to her for help.

"I might be imagining things," Liam said, "but I swear there's something there. Especially now that I've seen Elijah and Victor together, seen how his magic has changed. I can't shake the feeling. There's that saying—history doesn't repeat, but it often rhymes. If true bonds were common, if there was more trust between us before everything fell apart, wouldn't it be amazing if Elijah and Victor were the start of a new cycle?"

Kade would have been lying if he claimed Liam hadn't sparked his interest, that he wasn't curious about the answer. He'd never been particularly invested in any of the research papers he'd done during school, but this? This was more fascinating than any of the topics he'd been assigned.

"We've had a lot of mages in our pack over the generations. All true bonds," Kade said, and Liam looked over in surprise. "Elijah didn't tell you?"

Liam cocked an eyebrow in question.

"Our grandmother—Victor's and mine—she was a mage. But before her, we always had one, sometimes more. She told stories that mentioned the time before the abductions. How different things were then. She never gave specific details, but it sounded better. I thought it was just our pack, but you might be right. Maybe there used to be more packs like ours. Maybe it used to be more common."

The conversation faded as they walked on.

"Would you want that?" Kade asked after a few minutes.

Liam squinted at him for a beat before realizing what Kade meant.

"Oh, no. I have zero desire to be bound to a pack." Liam waved the thought away—an automatic no that he didn't need to consider. "Even if it gave me access to extra energy, if it made me stronger, it's not what I want in life." He groaned. "I sound like Elijah, but seriously, getting involved with shifters is not on my to-do—"

He pulled to a sharp stop. "Didn't we already pass that?" he asked as he gestured to a fallen tree.

Kade blinked at it. "We... did. Huh." He'd thought they'd been traveling in a straight line, but they'd made a giant loop.

Liam opened his map, frowning at it. "We're heading in the right direction. It should be just up ahead, if I'm reading this correctly." He looked at Kade for confirmation, and Kade nodded.

But when Liam started to walk, he pitched to the right, away from the spirit.

"Liam," Kade called after him, and Liam glanced back. "The spirit is this way."

"No, it's not. It's..." He checked the map, trailing off. "Huh."

Kade took a few steps forward. He wanted to go right too. He knew the spirit was in front of them, but that felt wrong.

The spirit was to the north of them. They just needed to keep going north.

Which direction was north?

He gazed at the sky, squinting. "Is the sun in the... south?"

"That can't be..." Liam looked up as well. "What the hell?" He spun in a circle, searching for anything to indicate direction. "Which way did we come from? Where's the pack house?"

Those were good questions. Kade had no fucking idea.

He was lost in the forest where he'd grown up. In the forest that was mapped on his soul.

He forced himself to focus. "Disorientation? Can that be a spirit?"

"I didn't think anger and terror could be spirits either, so why not?"

"Can you make a sigil for it?"

"You bet your ass I can."

"If we're making wagers, sure. But does that mean I get yours if you can't?"

Liam's head jerked up from where he was pulling his massive book out of his bag. There was color in his cheeks again. "Here, hold this."

Evil spirits aside, this wasn't a bad way to spend a day.

The sigil Liam sketched would have made M. C. Escher proud. Kade tried to follow its lines but kept getting lost.

"Okay," Liam said after transferring the sigil into a box. "Is the map any help?"

Kade doubted it. He had no clue which way was which.

Liam's brow furrowed. "Maybe if we go in the direction we don't want to go? It seems to be misdirecting us, possibly as a protective measure? So if we use that as a guide?"

That made sense. Kade stepped forward. He immediately wanted to veer to his left. When he took another step, he drifted off track, but Liam was there, straightening his path.

It was a slog, but they pushed ahead.

"Elijah owes me so much for this," Liam gritted out as Kade hauled him back in line, only to have Liam do the same to him a moment later.

"It's appreciated," Kade said, then stopped at the sight in front of him.

A twisting green mass whirled before them. When he attempted to look at it, his eyes slid off it and an inexplicable urge to wander away tried to take over.

For one heartbeat, he was in polluted water, unable to breathe as corruption filled his lungs.

Liam gripped his arm tight, his fingers digging into Kade's bicep, dragging him back to reality. Without being asked, Kade placed his hands on Liam's wrist and neck. His skin was warm under Kade's palms, and the buzz of magic kept the memory at bay.

He inhaled shakily as Liam activated the seal on the box and drew on his energy. Something in him opened for Liam, and his energy rushed out, eager to fill Liam again. The heady thrill of magic surged through him in exchange, giving him an anchor to latch on to in the churning disorientation of his mind.

It was so different from what he'd felt with Elijah. Their energy and magic mixed, making everything around him jump into sudden sharp clarity. The world grounded itself. He knew where he was.

The seal sucked the spirit into the box, and they stared as it churned in the most disconcerting manner. Liam shut the lid, Elijah's wards trapping it inside.

Liam labeled the box with a press of his fingers, exhaling a sigh of relief. Kade glanced up. The sun was where it was supposed to be. He could point to the pack house with his eyes closed.

"We need to be more careful," Liam said. "That could have been bad. We have to stay vigilant for anything that seems remotely out of place."

"Absolutely. But I think we've got this."

"On to the next one?"

As they headed toward the spirit, Liam continued.

"So, what I was saying before. I really do believe true bonds and tethers might have developed more naturally in the past, or at least have been more common. There are hints there, but it doesn't add up. I need to do more research."

"What kind of research?" Kade asked with a leer.

There was that slight blush on Liam's cheeks. A human wouldn't have even noticed it, but it was there, and he liked it more than he should have.

"Not that kind." Liam wasn't able to hide his amusement.

Kade didn't ask if Liam had done anything like that, some sex ritual with a shifter or anyone else. It wasn't his business, but that didn't mean he had to be completely well-behaved.

"If you do decide you want to get in a bit of *research* while you're here..." He left the invitation hanging in the air.

Liam shook his head, but it wasn't a no.

"Though..." Kade paused like he was thinking. "I've heard once you've had sex with a shifter, you'll be ruined for anyone else."

Liam snorted. "I doubt that."

"Only one way to find out."

"I'll have to survive with my curiosity unslaked."

"What sort of life would that be?"

"Sex with you is life-changing?"

"Like I said, only one way to find out."

Liam scoffed, but his gaze traveled down Kade's body, stroking over him.

Elijah had given Kade a clear warning to leave his friends alone, but now that Kade thought about it, how often did he listen when *Victor* told him what to do? If he didn't follow his alpha's orders, no one in their right mind would expect him to follow Elijah's.

Besides, Liam seemed to be showing signs of interest. Why not take full advantage of that?

Liam would never want someone like Kade. Not long-term. But then, Liam wouldn't be there long-term.

"You know," Kade said, this time with more than a hint of flirtation in his tone. "The shop's quite a drive, and you'll be here for a few days while we get these spirits trapped. Seems like a waste for you to commute back and forth every day."

Liam wasn't his mate; it was too soon, and given how quickly he'd dismissed the idea of bonding into a pack, he didn't want to be. But they could still have a little fun.

Kade was hit by a visceral image of Liam under him, tight heat wrapped around his dick. His wolf pushed toward the surface, sitting up with interest.

A drop of sweat slid down his neck. It was too hot in this forest for fall.

Could the next spirit be similar to the one causing a heatwave?

He held up a tree branch for Liam to pass under. The path was narrow, and Liam had to press against Kade as he went by. He didn't shy away from the contact. "Are you offering a bed here?"

"We could find you one, if you're interested."

Liam studied him, the quirk of his lips saying he had a good idea which bed he'd end up in if he accepted the offer.

Instead of responding, he glanced at the map. Kade looked at it over his shoulder, standing closer than was necessary or polite.

Even though he knew he wouldn't get anything from it, he inhaled, trying to get some of Liam's scent. The instinct was too ingrained not to. When he exhaled, his breath ghosted over the bare skin of Liam's neck.

Liam shivered, but steeled himself. "Considering the size of the spirit and the range they seem to contaminate, we have about five minutes before we start to feel its effects. We have to be careful."

Kade nodded and turned down another trail. "It's this way."

CHAPTER

SIX

The heat of the day was out in full force as they hiked toward the third spirit, the sun shining through the branches. Liam pushed up the sleeves of his sweater and wished he'd worn something lighter. He'd assumed mid-October would be cooler, but apparently, he'd been wrong. He envied the simple t-shirt Kade was wearing.

Wearing very well, Liam had to admit. He followed a few steps behind Kade, giving him the perfect view of his back. His gaze lingered on Kade's broad shoulders, then trailed down to his firm ass. From his tousled hair and warm brown eyes to his sensuous lips and strong jaw, there was no denying the guy was attractive. Even his attempts at flirting were growing on Liam.

Kade had the kind of back he could rake his fingers down, digging them into those shoulders as Kade pinned him to a mattress and railed him.

Liam blinked. That was... an extremely explicit thought. Not that he didn't have thoughts like those, but... He had been thinking about Kade in a less than platonic manner since the airport, so he couldn't say it was foreign...

Inhaling deeply, he tried to assess himself.

Fuck, Kade smelled divine. That scent from the car, warm and wholesome, teased Liam's senses, demanding he get closer and confirm it came from Kade.

He was so keyed to that scent. He'd never smelled anything like it. It reminded him of fields in late summer, ready to be harvested, cooling in the moonlight. The mental image it gave him was vivid. He took another deep breath, and even with the myriad scents of nature surrounding them, the only one that mattered was Kade's. It was intoxicating. What would it be like to have that scent all over him?

Kade would make it worth his time. Given how much of a flirt he was and Elijah's comments, Liam had no doubt Kade knew what he was doing in bed. Shifters were so physical, so instinctual; it'd be an enjoyable ride.

He frowned. His mind wouldn't let this go. He needed to concentrate, and not on the way Kade filled out those jeans.

Wait... was that weird? He had checked out Kade's ass before, Elijah could attest to that, and it had been a while since he'd had sex. He wouldn't say he had a high sex drive, not compared to shifters—or Aran—but it had been too long. Maybe that was why he was getting hot under the collar from looking at a set of muscular shoulders and an ass he wanted to sink his teeth into. How could he not fixate on that?

From a purely logical standpoint, whenever he did have sex or gave himself a good orgasm, he was more focused on his work afterward. And if he could concentrate on these spirits, he might figure out what they were.

So, really, he'd be doing it for the team. A selfless act.

And Kade was the perfect guy to lend a helping... hand. He wasn't in the market for a relationship. They'd have a fun round or two, and then Liam would return to his life. No feelings, no attachments, just a few mind-blowing orgasms and nothing more.

It was unquestionably the logical thing to do. He'd never hear the end of it from his friends, but he could deal with some teasing if he got to scratch the itch building between his shoulder blades, the raw need to get thoroughly fucked.

No. That wasn't logical at all.

"Are you feeling a bit—?" Liam cut himself off as Kade glanced at him.

God, he was gorgeous. Liam had never understood it when people said someone's eyes could smolder, but Kade's were doing precisely that.

Yes, his plan was flawless, absolutely genius. No one back home had to know. What happened in Lost Creek could stay in Lost Creek. Desire ran through him at the idea.

Kade had offered him a bed. Now to arrange it. He would mention to Elijah that the apartment was too cramped for three people and that he'd be willing to take a room in the pack house so Miles and Aran could have more space. Kade could slip in for the night. Into the room, into other things. Liam had never slept with a shifter before, but from what he'd heard, it promised to be an energetic night.

"Am I feeling a bit...?" Kade prompted.

What had Liam been saying? He shook himself. Right. The spirit.

"Are you... well, to put it bluntly, feeling excessively horny?" Liam wet his lips, and Kade's eyes tracked the motion.

"Always." He leered at Liam.

"I mean more so than usual?"

Kade tilted his head and froze. "My mind's not family-friendly on the best of days, but... yeah, I guess. I'm more horned up than the situation justifies. Though, feel free to justify it."

Liam exhaled. The thought of Kade being worked up should not have sent arousal quivering through him. It shouldn't have had him picturing Kade pounding him into a bed, fucking him until magic sparked at his fingertips, a hair away from uncontrolled. Until he was so sated, he wasn't sure he had muscles anymore, or if they'd been liquefied by the intensity of his orgasm. It really had been too long; he needed that. And he'd return the favor if Kade was so inclined.

No. Focus, Liam thought.

"Lust?" he asked, his voice rough.

Kade's gaze roamed over his body, taking a leisurely journey before landing on his crotch. "Yeah."

Liam took out his book. Lust. He could do this.

He didn't have to ask. Kade was there, holding the book for him while he sketched the sigil—its soft curves and hard lines, a sensuously entwined thing.

Liam pulled out a box and transferred the sigil into it.

Kade locked eyes with him and reached over, easing the sigil codex into Liam's bag, and fuck, why did that feel so dirty? Why did it make him picture Kade slowly slipping other things into other places?

No, no, no. He needed to focus. No matter how hot Kade was, they had a job to do.

With shaky hands, Liam checked the map. The hazy smudge was five minutes away, but it appeared larger than it had been.

Kade stepped behind him, looking at the map over his

shoulder. One hand settled on Liam's hip, and even through his sweater, Liam swore energy tingled against his skin.

"After we catch this spirit," Kade said, too close to Liam's ear for his sanity, "we should take a break."

"That's the spirit talking." Liam leaned back, his shoulder brushing Kade's chest.

"Is it?" Kade brought his hand up to trail over Liam's forearm. "We'll have to be careful then."

Energy buzzed against Liam's skin, and he saw his tattoos flickering, orange and bright wherever Kade skated his fingers, like flames licking up his arm. Kade's touch alone shouldn't do that, but Liam watched in fascination as Kade traced over the swoops and whirls.

"I've always been curious about these. It's true they're different depending on the mage?"

Liam nodded. "Different color, different shape. Depends on the mage and their magic."

"They grow as you get stronger?"

Liam couldn't tell whether Kade was asking out of genuine curiosity or as an excuse to keep touching him. He didn't care either way. "Starting at the wrists and working up our arms, covering more skin, getting more detailed and intricate."

"For your whole life?"

Liam shook his head. "The tattoos on our arms stabilize around eighteen or twenty. Only the strongest mages get more after that, on their chest and shoulders."

Kade pushed his sleeve up farther, revealing more of Liam's skin, following the curve of a tattoo on the inside of his elbow. "How far do yours go?"

That wasn't a polite question in magical circles, but Liam couldn't be offended. Not when he was imagining

Kade dragging his tongue along the few lines that had begun to creep over his shoulders.

Kade inhaled right behind his ear. "Show me?"

Fuck, Liam wanted that. But first... "Let's capture this thing so we can take that break."

They could do this. It was fine. They'd identified the spirit and how it was affecting them. They had this.

Kade's hands landed on Liam's hips, tugging him back, his half-hard cock pressing against Liam's ass. "Looking forward to it."

Liam needed to thank Elijah for pairing him with Kade. His plan was definitely happening.

After they took care of this damn spirit.

"Let's earn that break." Kade rolled his hips against Liam once more, then released him, but he didn't go far. He stayed in Liam's space, not touching him, but so close that it might have been less of a distraction if he had been.

Liam tried to stay vigilant for any signs of the spirit. The forest was beautiful, its fall colors in full bloom. The scars from the decay spirit weren't as noticeable in this area.

The humid air washed over him. Sunlight warmed his skin. It seeped into his muscles, into his bones, making his body loose and relaxed. Sweat trickled down his neck. He should have worn lighter clothes for this.

"You should take off that sweater," Kade said, still distractingly close.

"I'm not wearing an undershirt."

"Don't let that stop you."

Liam laughed. Maybe he should. Given the temperature, going shirtless would be a relief.

Before he could answer, they entered a clearing—gorgeous, idyllic, straight out of a painting. On the far side, a haze shimmered. White wisps of fog floated between the trees, their edges tinted red.

That had to be the spirit, the manifestation of lust. Now they needed… They needed to…

Kade's hands were on him, one curling around his wrist, the other sneaking under his sweater to rest low on his stomach. "Need me to touch you?"

"*Yes.*" The word was breathy. He leaned into Kade, his ass fitting into the cradle of Kade's hips, grinding back on his hard cock.

There was something he should be doing. Something important.

Kade rocked his hips, his dick nudging against Liam, offering to fulfill his every need, his every desire.

It couldn't be that important if he couldn't remember it, right? They deserved this break, and then they could… do whatever it was.

Wood clattered as he dropped the box. Why had he been holding a box? That was strange. His bag hit the ground a moment later, but he couldn't focus on that. Couldn't concentrate on anything but the patterns Kade's fingers were drawing.

"Lower," he said, and Kade dipped his fingers under Liam's waistband.

"Here?"

"*Lower,*" Liam demanded.

Kade's hands trailed downward, but not to where Liam wanted them. "Do I get to see how much of your skin your tattoos cover now?"

That sounded like an excellent idea. Everywhere Kade touched, energy caressed Liam's skin, thrilling and addictive as their magic and energy mixed. Liam needed that sensation all over his body.

Across the clearing, the fog grew thicker, dark red streaking through it. Should they be worried about that?

Kade popped open the button on Liam's pants, smirking against his neck. "And here I thought you wouldn't be any fun."

Liam grinned and turned in his arms. "I can be persuaded," he said, quoting Kade.

Kade slid his hands into Liam's underwear, cupping his ass, pulling him close.

This wasn't what they were supposed to be doing; it wasn't how this should have gone. But Liam couldn't hold on to those thoughts when Kade's hips fit against his so perfectly, when his dick was as hard as Liam's, when Kade's mouth was hovering over his, daring Liam to kiss him, challenging him to break first.

Before Liam could, Kade ran his nose along Liam's neck, inhaling. "Please tell me you bottom?"

"Only if you can make me see stars." Liam's skin was tight with how badly he needed that.

Kade nipped at his ear. "When I'm through with you, you'll have seen the entire fucking universe."

"Big words. Can you live up to them?"

"I'll show you something big."

Liam huffed. "Already felt it."

"It's going to feel even bigger when I'm sliding it into this cute little ass of yours."

Arousal shot like wildfire through Liam. "You have lube?"

Kade faltered. "Can't you just... magic us up something?"

"No, I can't summon lube out of nowhere. There's no spell for that."

"Why not? You and Elijah produce fire out of nowhere."

"Fire is elemental, lube is not. I don't think your dick would appreciate the fire."

"Lube would be so much more useful."

Maybe there was a vial of oil in his bag... Wait. His bag. Liam's eyes latched on to it and the box. He needed that box. They needed to...

"I guess I'll have to make you come twice then."

Fuck, yes. That was exactly what they needed to do.

"You think you can?"

Kade's gaze took on a wicked gleam, and he walked Liam backward until he bumped into a tree. "You're going to want something to hold on to."

He dropped to his knees, stripping Liam of his pants. Liam shucked off his sweater, tossing it aside. Bark scraped his skin as he leaned against the trunk.

Kade stared up at him, ravenous, his eyes flashing with his wolf and promising that Liam was about to be devoured.

And then he was.

Kade sucked him into his mouth, not bothering to tease, his sole purpose to make Liam come as fast as he could. His lips stretched around Liam's cock, his mouth hot and wet and with zero gag reflex in sight. Liam was torn between watching Kade and wanting to throw his head back and *feel.*

The visuals won out, but he barely had time to enjoy it, barely had time to thread his fingers through Kade's soft hair. He would have been embarrassed, but coming quickly was the point.

Kade pulled off so just the tip of Liam's dick was in his mouth as Liam came, ecstasy sweeping him away. Liam's knees threatened to buckle, but then Kade was manhandling him, dragging him down, flipping him over, arranging him so his ass was in the air. Kade spread his cheeks, spitting Liam's release onto his hole.

"I wish I could taste you. Next time we do this, we do it somewhere I get to swallow," he grumbled, then his tongue speared into Liam, and Liam's fingers clawed into the dirt.

It didn't take long until Kade had his tongue and two fingers in him and Liam was cursing him out for not fucking him already. He was so turned on, so ready for Kade, so relaxed from his orgasm.

"Another thing for the future," Kade said in a low rumble. "Someday, I'm going to rim you until you come from my tongue alone."

Liam clenched around his fingers, but Kade pulled away to undress with supernatural speed. He had less than a second to savor the sight of Kade's cock before Kade was on him, pressing into him, and damn, Liam wished they had lube. He'd feel this in the morning, and for days after, but the burn was too good, having Kade touch him, fuck him, stretch him open. While he didn't have shifter healing, his magic gave him an edge, and Kade's energy was filling him too, mingling with his magic, helping things along. The discomfort was worth the fucking he was about to get.

"You ready?" Kade asked, his breathing labored.

"Yeah, come on."

Kade pulled him up so they were both on their knees, back to chest as Kade thrust up into him, holding him close.

Even though Liam had just come, he craved more. His dick was hardening again, and Kade's hand was on him, stroking him as he moved in him, his teeth sharp as they grazed over Liam's skin. He mouthed at his neck.

"*Fuck.* You feel so good. So tight. I want you wrapped around my knot. Want to see how full I can fill you. Need to make you feel better than you've ever felt before. Fuck you so deep, no one will ever make you come as hard as I can."

Liam moaned. *That* was what he needed. If this felt amazing, how much better would being stretched open on Kade's knot feel? "Yes. Give it to me. Bite me. Knot me."

"You want that? Want my knot?"

"God, yes."

Kade scraped his teeth over the juncture of Liam's neck. "You want to be mine?"

More than anything he'd ever wanted or needed in his life. "Please, Kade," he said in a desperate whine.

Kade bit down, his teeth breaking skin, and Liam gasped in pleasure and pain. He clamped a hand around Kade's wrist, his magic surging out of him and into Kade, spiraling up his arm, then ricocheting between them. Heat seared into his back as tattoos unfurled over Kade's chest, Liam's magic marking him, claiming him as thoroughly as Kade's teeth had marked and claimed Liam.

The connections between them opened, flooding him with Kade's lust, bringing a completely new world of ecstasy—his and Kade's mixed, letting him sense how he was making Kade feel. Liam clenching around his cock was driving Kade wild, his wolf taking control. The need to knot his mate was overwhelming.

"Do it," Liam demanded.

Kade's knot pulsed and expanded, tying them together. In his mind, Kade was undone by the sensation of him—how tight, how hot, how perfect. *His.*

Sex had never been this good, could never be this good. Not without Kade.

Kade bit his shoulder again, and that single action engulfed Liam in pleasure.

He came with a choked cry, spilling over Kade's hand.

Kade's knot locked inside him, his world exploding in white-hot euphoria, echoing through their bond as Kade's orgasm hit. Liam gasped, riding out their bliss.

Kade rocked shallowly in him as much as his knot would allow, his come easing their grind. He sucked at Liam's shoulder, tongue tracing over the mark. He felt smug and satisfied, but also ready for another round as soon as Liam recovered.

"I knew you were mine from the moment I saw you," Kade said, a feral, animalistic growl behind his words. Claws pricked Liam's skin where Kade clung to him. "I wanted to claim you right there, fuck you in that arrivals lobby, let everyone watch me make you mine."

That should not have been so hot, but Liam was imagining himself bent over the fake leather chairs, a dozen eyes on him as Kade fucked his knot in and out of him. He was already getting hard a third time. It shouldn't have been possible, but with that vision in his head, there was no way he couldn't.

He ground on Kade's dick. Kade needed to keep fucking him. He never wanted this to end.

Liam rode Kade's knot, loving the stretch of it. Sweat poured off them and the clearing swam with that red-tinted fog, but he kept moving, driving them both toward the precipice of another orgasm, unable to think of anything except Kade's hands on him, his cock in him, how well they fit together. He reached behind him, burying a hand in Kade's hair and tugging his mouth to the bite mark.

There was a shout, and a sluggish corner of Liam's consciousness pushed forward, forcing him to register it as his name.

Kade growled, but Liam couldn't stop grinding on him. His orgasm was so damn close.

This was the best idea he'd ever had. Why had he been against fucking shifters? Kade's dick filled him like nothing had before, like Kade was meant to fill him.

He moaned, his movements growing frantic. A little more, and he'd come again.

Another shout of his name rang out, and it took all his effort to turn his head, to see where it came from.

He stared at Elijah and Victor, at the shock written on their faces. Elijah dove for a box on the ground. His hands shook as he opened it, the purple tattoos on his arms kindling.

Why was Elijah using magic? And why wasn't Kade moving? Didn't he know Liam needed him to move? But Kade was still snarling at Elijah and Victor, the warning clear.

He was being foolish. Elijah and Victor were bonded. They wouldn't want to join them, and Elijah was like a brother to Liam. But there was room enough in this clearing for them. It would be hot to watch them. Live-action porn, Aran had called it. They didn't have to touch to enjoy each other's pleasure.

Voyeurism had never been one of his kinks, his mind tried to tell him, but that was ridiculous. Elijah and Victor's cocks were straining their pants. Their faces were flushed, their breathing heavy. Obviously they needed to get off as much as he did. Why didn't they give in to their desires? Why fight it?

His eyelids drifted shut, and he rolled back onto Kade's dick, trying to get him to move. Kade made short, aborted thrusts, like he couldn't help himself even as he rumbled out another warning.

Liam heard a string of curses from Elijah, followed by muttering about it being too strong, feeding off them, and he didn't understand what Elijah was talking about. He didn't need to, didn't want to.

When he opened his eyes again, he looked over, waiting for them to give in. Elijah's left hand clasped Victor's, their fingers entwined, and Victor's other hand rested on the nape of Elijah's neck. In Elijah's right hand, he held that box.

There was something about it. Something Liam was supposed to remember. Something he had to do.

A hazy white tinted with red pooled in the box.

Sweat dripped down Elijah's brow. He seemed stressed, and that was so unnecessary. Victor should help him relax.

Liam watched them in a detached daze.

What were they doing? Didn't they realize how good it felt to be touching someone?

He frowned. Touching someone... it did feel good, didn't it?

He shifted his weight, then winced. That certainly didn't. Kade's knot pulled on his rim in an unpleasant way. The edge he'd been riding, his next orgasm, slipped out of his grasp.

There were twigs and rocks under his knees, digging into his skin. That was *not* pleasurable.

He went to stroke himself, attempting to reclaim that feeling, but he hissed at how oversensitive he was. He stared at a tree in front of him, his brain not processing the situation.

Why was he on his knees in a forest, naked, on Kade's dick, on his knot? Wait. His knot? Kade had knotted him... But that meant...

Kade's growling had cut off. He pressed against Liam's back, so motionless and rigid that it felt like he wasn't breathing.

Liam shifted his weight and winced again. Kade let out a choked-off whimper and gripped his hips, preventing him from moving.

His shoulder throbbed, and when Liam shrugged it, he inhaled sharply at how the skin there pulled, itching and burning as it healed.

Kade's presence in Liam's mind was chaotic, pervaded by a sense of discomfort and the impression that if they weren't tied together, he'd be putting distance between them.

Hold on. He could feel Kade's emotions? What the hell?

Liam was soft; the arousal he'd been experiencing had drained away. He was so open and exposed, his legs spread over Kade's thighs, Kade's knot stretching him wide. He wanted to grab his clothes, but they were out of reach. How had this seemed like a bright idea? He'd never done anything like this before. He wasn't this type of person. Even when he did hook up with someone, it was always very controlled.

He shivered, cold and uncomfortable, and Kade wrapped around him tighter, the warmth of his body bleeding into him. Liam took comfort in that, though he was unsure what was going on. When this had started, it had been so hot outside.

When this had started...

Liam sucked in a lungful of air, his heart rate skyrocketing. Shit. The spirit. They'd let it get to them. It had—

The lid of a box slammed shut, and a spike of magic flared, drawing Liam's attention.

"Got it," Elijah said, panting.

Oh god. Elijah and Victor were there. While he and Kade were...

Liam jumped. The movement made both him and Kade hiss. Fuck, that didn't feel good. Not even remotely.

He tried to cover himself, but they'd already gotten an eyeful.

Elijah cleared his throat, his cheeks a dark red, his gaze trained well above their heads. Victor's face was unreadable.

"Ah," Elijah said, "we'll just... We'll give you guys a minute?"

Kade swallowed, the sound loud in Liam's ear. "It, uh, might be more like five or ten." He was a whirlwind of emotions that disoriented Liam as much as the previous spirit had. His heart pounded so fast, it thudded against Liam's skin.

Elijah's eyes widened. He looked at Victor, then back. "Um. Okay." Victor helped him to his feet. "We'll... uh, we'll wait on the other side of these trees."

They left Liam and Kade alone in the clearing. It was unnaturally silent, with no haze or fog floating in the air.

Liam had no clue what to say. He stared out into the forest, trying to make sense of everything.

The spirit had possessed them. That had to be it. He'd found Kade attractive since they'd met, but he never would have done this. Kade wouldn't have either. And while they might have been willing to do some of it under different circumstances, neither of them would have wanted to bond.

He'd thought the spirits were all negative—fear, sadness, corruption. He hadn't been prepared for one to make him feel good, for it to merely amplify what he was already feeling, for it to weaponize his attraction to Kade until he hadn't noticed it taking over.

But he should have known, and he still couldn't decide

what to say. How did you start a conversation after something like this? He needed to soothe the jumbled ball of emotions that was Kade in his mind, and if that wasn't a headfuck and a half—sensing someone else's feelings, even just the impressions of them—he didn't know what was.

"I'm so sorry," Kade said, scarcely above a whisper. Guilt roiled through him, strong enough that Liam could pick it out.

"No, it was the spirit. We were both possessed by it."

Kade's grip on him tightened to the point of pain, his breath harsh and uneven, his body shaking, and Liam's chest constricted. Panic inundated his brain.

Oh, fuck.

"Kade." He squeezed Kade's wrist. "*Kade.* Breathe. The spirit is gone. Elijah captured it. We're okay."

He tried to project a sense of calm through their bond, focusing on his own breathing, keeping it steady.

Kade inhaled, filling his lungs to their full extent before letting out a shuddering exhale. His churning presence eased marginally.

"There you go. Just breathe. We're fine. Everything's okay."

He felt Kade shake his head. "No, we aren't. You don't understand. I bit you. I knotted you."

Liam was quite aware of that. The throbbing in his ass wasn't particularly easy to ignore, but he didn't think saying that would help Kade. So instead, he said, "I may not have understood what was happening, but I clearly remember asking you to bite me, asking you to knot me. Neither of us was in our right mind."

"I should have been able to stop this. It wasn't the same as... But I should have recognized the signs, should have known this wasn't..." His breathing was going shallow again.

Liam tried to look at him, but they both winced when the motion jostled where they were tied together, so he gave up. "Listen to me carefully. What happened between us, it was the spirit's fault. Not yours. Not mine. The *spirit's*."

"I *bonded* you." Nauseous self-loathing twisted through Kade, settling sick and heavy in Liam's gut as he realized what Kade thought he'd done.

"No. It wasn't like that. And in case you didn't notice, I tethered myself to you in return."

"What?"

Liam channeled Kade's energy, marveling at how easily it rushed into him, even easier than before. As messed up as this was, it felt so good, that power flooding him, tingling in his veins. "Any new tattoos around your heart?"

Even without seeing them, he knew the answer, knew Kade felt their warmth, just as Liam felt the patterns spiraling out from the bite mark.

Kade pulled away slightly and gasped.

The lack of body heat had Liam's skin prickling with goose bumps, and Kade tucked him back against his chest before he could shiver. It was so tempting to melt into him.

"You have control of your magic?" Kade asked.

"Complete and total control." And even if he hadn't, Liam was certain Kade would never take advantage of that.

"Oh, thank god." Kade's relieved exhale gusted past Liam's ear.

"We'll figure this out," Liam assured him. "From what I've read, shifter bonds can be severed on new moons."

Another wave of nausea rolled through Kade, standing

out from the swirling mass with its intensity, but he nodded.

"This situation is screwed up," Liam said, "Literally, physically, magically. But it's not irreversible. We'll deal with it for the next few weeks, then sever the bond."

"Okay." Kade's voice was gruff, and Liam wished he could see his face. The emotions coming from him were too confusing to parse.

"I guess I get to find out if there are magical knots after all."

The joke hung awkwardly between them. Kade didn't seem to want to pick up their banter, so Liam dropped it. Whatever flirting Kade had been doing before must have been because of the spirit.

The next few minutes were spent in silence as they waited for Kade's knot to deflate.

When it did, Kade withdrew gingerly, his release leaking out, and Liam cringed. He'd never let anyone come inside him before, and this wasn't a small amount. His cheeks burned.

"Sorry," Kade murmured, gliding a soothing hand down Liam's side. When it made him shiver, Kade stopped.

Regret poured off him, but when Kade stood, when they were no longer touching, it became removed and indecipherable. Liam turned to look at Kade. "It was the spirit, not us."

Kade hauled him up. His touch brought more guilt and a hundred other emotions that were too fast and violent to name. His face was drained of color, his eyes pinched. Even his movements were jerky, lacking their usual shifter grace.

Something inside Liam ached to comfort Kade, but just standing was difficult enough. His legs weren't cooperating with him. He'd never been this shaky after sex. But then, he'd never come twice in such a short period, and he'd never been knotted.

He leaned against a tree as Kade grabbed their clothes and Liam's bag. Normally, he'd feel self-conscious being naked outside in the daylight, but he was too exhausted to care.

Kade helped him dress, his expression shell-shocked. Each brush of their skin was accompanied by the buzz of Kade's energy and the stab of shame. Liam would have to make sure Kade believed him when he said this wasn't their fault.

When they were presentable, or at least as presentable as possible while covered with come and sweat, Kade called out to Victor and Elijah. He sounded absolutely wrecked.

Elijah's face was concerned as he peeked around a tree. Liam wasn't used to being on this end of things. He did the worrying, not the other way around.

"Are you okay?" Elijah asked.

Liam sighed. "Yeah. I'll be fine."

"Did you... bond?"

A sharp burst of guilt tore through their connection.

"We did," Liam said, his tone as reassuring as he could manage. "But we've discussed it and will sever it on the new moon. It isn't a big deal."

Both Elijah and Victor looked skeptical.

"Alright. Well, we should return to the pack house and regroup." Elijah stepped toward Liam, but Kade growled, freezing him in place.

Victor tugged on Elijah's arm, pulling him back. "Kade's not going to want anybody near Liam right now."

Elijah glanced at Victor, his surprise evident.

"Like I said, ideally, after bonding, you spend at least a week alone in a room, reaffirming the bond. Two weeks is better. When it's this new, it's difficult being around other people, especially having them close to your mate."

"I thought that was just the first day or two. I've been around your entire pack these last few days. You've felt twitchy, but I didn't think it was that bad."

Victor looked sheepish. "It's been a struggle to not kill anyone who gets too close to you. To let you out of my sight. But it's what we have to do, so I've been tamping down those instincts."

Elijah's eyes softened, and he squeezed Victor's arm. "When this is over, we'll do things properly."

That seemed to please the hell out of Victor, and Elijah appeared equally happy. Liam loved seeing Elijah at peace with himself, not trying to live someone else's life or impress people who would never accept him for who he was in his entirety.

Kade was a distant tangle of turbulent emotions that Liam couldn't begin to read until Kade wrapped an arm around him to help him back, but even then, it was impossible to sort through all those wretched feelings.

As they walked, Liam's legs started to cooperate, but Kade seemed reluctant to let him go, so Liam didn't pull away.

SEVEN

As they walked through the forest, Elijah kept up a steady stream of conversation, like he could ward off the awkwardness of the situation if he held the silence at bay.

"We checked the map while tracking the frost spirit and noticed this hazy smudge was growing at an alarming rate. We knew there had to be a problem and ran here. But man, that thing was potent. I think the only reason we managed not to get caught in it was our bond. It's only been a few days, but I've gotten used to sensing lust from an external source. When it's from Victor, it feels right, but from that spirit, it felt so wrong."

He babbled about how they'd captured two spirits, but Kade couldn't concentrate on what Elijah was saying. His thoughts were a tangled mess.

God, he'd fucked up. Again. And he'd dragged Liam down with him.

Liam might not think it was Kade's fault; Kade knew the truth. This had happened to him before. He should have recognized it, should have known there was no way Liam would respond to him like that.

But this had played out so differently. Last time, he'd been caught off-guard. The decay spirit had come at him from out of nowhere. One moment he'd been searching for the spirit, and the next—

Panic clawed at his chest; water closed over his head, filling his lungs. The world tilted and blurred.

A hand clamped around his wrist, and the ball of foreign emotions in the back of Kade's mind seemed to pulse with a calming warmth. It eased through Kade, seeping into his muscles, loosening the vice grip that constricted his lungs.

He breathed—shaky at first, but gradually steadying as he brought Liam's face into focus.

His expression concerned, Liam stared at him with an intensity that made Kade want to shield himself from the scrutiny.

"Everything alright?" Elijah asked, and both Kade and Liam jumped.

"We're fine." Liam's hand fell away from Kade's wrist. "All good here."

That wasn't remotely true, but Kade followed Victor and Elijah as they hiked. Elijah shot them another skeptical look over his shoulder.

Kade had no clue how Liam did it, but he continued to project calm through their bond. It was faint but soothing, something Kade could cling to in the chaos. And somehow, that made him feel worse.

Liam shouldn't have had to reassure him. He'd identified the spirit; he'd known how it was affecting them. Everything after that had been Kade's doing. Kade had been the one pushing things, escalating things. He should have been setting Liam at ease, not the other way around.

His only offering was physical support, though Liam no longer seemed to need that. And to make it worse, his wolf radiated smug satisfaction at having Liam pressed against their side. It kept reminding Kade of how Liam's body had felt—hot and tight and perfect—and how much it wanted Liam under them again. It didn't care if they'd been possessed. They had a mate now; that was all that mattered. Everything else would fall into place.

But his wolf was wrong. Other things mattered. How it happened. Who it was. It mattered.

Victor hadn't trusted his wolf around magic, and Kade had thought he was being ridiculous. Their wolves never misled them. Apparently, he'd been naive.

He'd lost count of the number of times he'd fantasized about getting bonded, the scenarios that had played out in his head. Candlelit dinners, kissing under the stars, edging his soon-to-be mate until the need to be tied together was their entire universe.

Not once had he imagined this. Fucking someone who only wanted it because of a lust spirit, pushing them down in the dirt, taking them when they weren't properly prepared.

Whatever his wolf's opinion, the more logical, human parts of Kade's brain were horrified. Nausea pooled in his gut.

Liam glanced at him, frowning, and Kade wrenched his mind away from that line of thought before another panic attack threatened to take over. The last thing Liam needed was to have to deal with Kade's shit on top of everything else.

Kade was pathetic, and his wolf was confused. The lack

of scent must have thrown it off. If they could smell Liam, his wolf would understand how they weren't compatible. Liam was too smart to be stuck out here. He'd said it himself; he didn't want to be tied to a pack. This situation didn't warrant his wolf's smugness.

He didn't need his sense of smell to know this wasn't when he was supposed to find his mate. The day his grandmother had foreseen him getting bonded to a mage was etched into his memory. This was not what she'd predicted.

She'd known Victor would bond a mage since before he was in elementary school. It had been an accepted fact for decades, and Victor had gotten his fair share of teasing over it. Their pack had been waiting for Victor's mage to arrive, but they didn't know that Victor wasn't the only one she'd predicted ending up with a mage.

Kade had been thirteen and alone with his grandmother when the foresight had hit her. Her gaze had gone distant, seeing something Kade couldn't.

"You'll bond a mage too," she'd said, her eyelids sliding shut, a soft smile on her lips. "After Victor."

But then she'd paused, and Kade had waited, breath held.

She'd shaken her head and opened her eyes.

"It won't be right after Victor finds his mage. It'll take a while." She'd reached over to pat his hand. "You'll need to be patient and give it some time, but you'll have a true bond too."

A handful of days was not a while. Not even close.

Their pack had always had mages, but with Victor predicted to get mated to one, Kade had figured he wouldn't. Her vision had thrilled him though. Most of their history was about pack members with true bonds to mages. They were the strongest, the best leaders, the ones who protected their pack from anything that was thrown at them. He'd wanted that. Not to be a pack alpha—that was Victor's destiny, not his, and Kade didn't envy him for it—but strengthening his pack through his love for his mate spoke to something deep in his soul.

Sure, he might sleep around to kill time while he waited, but having that kind of connection with someone, the same thing Victor and Elijah shared, what his grandparents had shared... He longed for that more than he'd admitted to anyone, even Victor.

But this? This wasn't how it was supposed to happen. No true bond started like this.

His grandmother had never brought it up again. She hadn't told the pack. Maybe there was a reason for that. Maybe that pause had been her realizing something was wrong with his bond. What if she'd seen him getting bonded and assumed it would be a true bond? She never would have conceived of a wolf in their pack fucking up to this extent.

It'd be fitting after everything Kade had done to Victor and Elijah. This was karma. He'd been given the thing he'd always hoped for, but would never be able to keep it, and he only had himself to blame.

Ahead of them, Elijah stopped and spun around, startling Kade out of his spiraling thoughts.

"I'm so sorry," Elijah said, and a flash of surprise filtered into Kade before Liam took a step toward Elijah.

Kade let him go.

The calming wash of Liam's emotions went with him, leaving Kade cold and bereft at the sudden loss. Now that they weren't touching, Liam was a distant, fuzzy impression, and if Kade needed any more proof that this wasn't meant to be, that was it. If they'd had a true bond, he would've felt Liam regardless of how far apart they were. They'd be completely open to each other, too connected for anything else. Whatever they had, it was closer to something transactional than what Victor and Elijah had.

"*You're* sorry?" Liam asked.

Elijah winced. "If I hadn't rearranged the groups to keep Kade and Aran apart, things would have been different. Kade would have been helping Aran heal the forest. You might have gone after another spirit."

"It's fine." Liam sighed. "Can you imagine if you hadn't? Maybe I would have had sex with a mated man. Or Kade and Aran would have gotten trapped by that spirit instead. Even I'm glad that didn't happen. Let's just say I took one for the team. Literally."

A strange look crossed Elijah's face. "You do realize that sounded more like an Aran joke than a Liam joke, right? Has Kade already been that much of a bad influence on you?"

He was kidding, trying to make the best of the situation, but it caused Kade to spiral deeper.

Some of his feelings must have bled through, because Liam narrowed his eyes at Kade like he was a puzzle to solve.

A twig snapped to Kade's left. Leaves crunched underfoot, and branches rustled. People were drawing closer.

Unable to repress the instinct, Kade pulled Liam against him, his grip tight enough that Liam squeaked in surprise.

A few seconds later, Will and Miles appeared. As they approached, Will scented the air, his gaze zeroing in on Kade and Liam. He glanced at Victor for confirmation, and Victor nodded. Will's eyebrows rose, but he didn't comment.

Miles seemed oblivious to that wordless exchange. "What's going on? We saw a spirit getting bigger on the map and headed this wa—" His eyes took in how Kade was holding Liam.

"Are you okay?" He stepped forward, but Will grabbed him, holding him in place.

Miles slapped at his hands. "If you don't let me go this minute, I will punch you in the face."

Will looked startled and let Miles go.

Miles's gaze jumped around the group. "Someone needs to tell me what happened. *Now.*"

There was silence for a beat, an increasingly murderous aura building around Miles, until Liam spoke.

"Kade and I had... a run-in with a spirit, and long story short, we're bonded. Temporarily."

His explanation didn't appease Miles. "That was entirely too short. I need more details. But before that, would you like me to heal you?"

Kade growled, the reaction instinctual and uncontrolled. From what he knew of healing, it required touching, and true bond or not, anyone else getting that close to Liam was not something he could handle.

Liam's hand found his wrist and squeezed. That simple touch was enough to reassure Kade. As long as Liam was there, everything would work out. Another foolish belief coming from his wolf.

Liam forced out a laugh, but hints of his embarrassment floated through their bond. "I'm not sure how I feel about you healing my ass, and honestly, it's better than I expected. The spirit... uh, relaxed me? That was... nice of it? And I'm healing surprisingly fast."

"That extra shifter energy really helps things along." Elijah's pale cheeks flushed pink when his brain caught up with his mouth.

Miles's eyes widened.

"Oh god, can we not tell Aran about that?" Elijah asked.

"That'd be my first choice," Liam said wryly.

There was more movement through the forest, and Rick and Aran joined their group.

"First choice about what?" Aran asked.

Elijah groaned. "Figures you'd show up now."

Aran's gaze landed on Liam, and any trace of humor in his expression vanished. He marched over and tugged aside the collar of Liam's sweater, ignoring Kade's warning growls.

"Oh, shut up. If you're a decent guy, you won't attack me."

Kade blinked at him. He couldn't guarantee that. His wolf hated that someone else's hands were on Liam; it prowled below the surface, rumbling its discontent. But Aran wasn't looking at him. He stared Liam dead in the eye.

"Do I need to kill him?" His voice was low, a dangerous edge to each word. Shimmering green twisted through the negative space of the ink on his arms.

Liam batted Aran's hands away. "No. I'm fine."

"Are you sure?" Aran's dark eyes bored into Liam's, searching for any indication otherwise. Tension coiled around him, thick and heavy as a brewing storm, a feral predator restrained, a heartbeat away from springing on his prey.

He'd seemed so similar to Kade before, always ready with a dirty joke, but this version of him left no room for questions. He *would* kill Kade if he thought Kade had done this against Liam's will, and Kade would deserve it.

"I'm good," Liam said, equally serious. "We got caught up in a spirit and things happened. And you'll be happy to know you and Miles will probably have the apartment to yourself."

Aran studied Liam's face for another drawn-out beat. Whatever he saw, he must have believed Liam. The looming threat that hung around him dissipated, and he smirked. "I bet you're good."

Kade shifted his weight on his feet, only to almost trip. He looked down. Roots were tangled around his shoes. It took effort to break free of their grasp. When he glanced up, Aran gave him a cool smile that was nothing but a warning.

But then Aran turned to Elijah.

"Just so you know, Elijah, I fucking love you. Thank you for not letting me go out into the forest with him. Dodged a bullet there. You saved my skin. Or—" He paused, considering. "—my ass, I guess."

Liam glared, but a soft feeling hummed inside him that Kade had to assume was affection.

Aran paid him no heed. "And thank god you didn't let Miles go either."

"We must protect Miles at all costs." Elijah nodded solemnly.

Miles beamed at them.

"That's not it. I mean, Miles Mills? All that alliteration. It'd be a fate worse than death."

"Hey. I'm not taking anyone's name." Liam's tone was annoyed, but his body was more relaxed than before.

Kade couldn't believe how quickly Liam seemed to have adjusted. How was he not blaming Kade for this? How was he not freaking out?

"Let's get to the house," Elijah said.

The trek back was quiet. Kade was lost in his thoughts, none of them pleasant.

They stopped outside the house and gathered in a circle, Kade still offering unnecessary support until Liam stepped away and stood on his own.

"Do we need to move Liam into the pack house?" Elijah asked.

Victor nodded. "Ideally in Kade's room."

"Are you alright with that, Liam?"

"I'd assumed as much. It's fine. Better than sharing a bed with Aran."

"You should be so lucky," Aran said.

"Besides," Liam continued like he hadn't heard him, "Lady will be thrilled to get me out of her apartment. If there's one thing she knows how to do, it's hold a grudge."

Something threaded between them, and while Kade couldn't fully read it, it hinted that Liam was not as comfortable with the situation as he made it sound.

Miles's brow furrowed. "It was a lust spirit?"

"Yeah," Liam said.

"So they aren't all bad? Or at least, not until they're in excess." Miles tilted his head. "We came across one that was... amusement? Hysteria? Suddenly, everything was funny. Will was practicing his dad jokes on me, and I actually thought they were amusing, which was weird, but then a leaf fell on the path in front of us. We were laughing so hard we couldn't breathe. It was beyond creepy and difficult to focus long enough to get away from its influence."

"You know when you were a kid and someone was tickling you, and it was funny until it started feeling like you were about to die?" Will asked. "That's what it was. It was that severely uncomfortable, want-to-crawl-out-of-your-skin level of laughter. Do not recommend."

"Okay," Elijah said. "When we go out tomorrow, we have to keep that in mind. Be on guard for anything out of place, not just negative emotions."

That wouldn't have helped Kade. He'd been attracted to Liam since he first saw him. The spirit had amped that up, but none of what he'd felt had been foreign. Except bonding Liam, which had been his wolf's doing.

The wind shifted slightly, and Rick inhaled, his nostrils flaring before his eyes darted to Victor. Victor gave him an almost imperceptible shake of the head, and Kade wanted to snarl at them. At Rick for smelling Liam when he couldn't. At Victor for thinking he knew what the hell was going on. At himself for being so stupid about this.

It wasn't real.

But no matter how many times he told himself that, he couldn't rein in his instincts, not right then. Not with the bond so new. Standing out there, exposed, Liam out of his room, was making him twitchy. He needed to get them somewhere quiet and safe. Somewhere it was just them. He needed to touch Liam, to do so much more than that.

He had to suppress that though, because, for whatever reason, they had to stand there and keep talking, attempting to figure everything out. It made him want to sprout claws.

Liam's hand circled his wrist, squeezing once, and Kade was instantly calmer. Liam squeezed again, then dropped his hand. Kade fought back the desire to chase after his touch.

"Listen, guys." Liam cracked his neck like he was restless too. "Let's hash this out later? I need a shower."

"I bet you do. I can't get over how much shifters co—" Elijah cut himself off, his cheeks red.

Aran cocked an eyebrow at him, and Elijah scowled.

Kade would rather not dwell on how thoroughly Elijah was acquainted with the amount shifters came when they knotted.

"Let's call it a day," Victor said, clearly trying to move

the conversation along. "Maybe Miles and Aran could run to the shop and pick up Liam's things before dinner?"

"Liam can borrow some of my—" Elijah started to offer, but Kade growled before he could stop himself. "Or not."

"Kade won't want your scent on Liam. Especially with how tied to my scent yours is. Even if he can't—" It was Victor's turn to cut himself off abruptly.

Even if he couldn't smell. That was what Victor had been about to say. Kade knew it was ridiculous, but the idea of someone else's scent covering Liam had his hackles rising.

"No problem," Miles said. "Aran and I can pick up his stuff. Anyone up for placing wagers on how many dick jokes he can tell me during the hour-and-a-half round trip?"

In the betting chaos that followed, Liam tugged on Kade's wrist, and they slipped into the house through the back door.

Inside the kitchen, they ran into Katrina.

"Will the mages be joi—" She froze and sniffed the air, her expression shocked. "Yes. I'm guessing yes."

She sent Kade a look, but didn't say anything else as they passed.

Kade herded Liam up the stairs, hoping to avoid meeting other pack members.

The moment he had Liam in his room, his wolf exhaled. Some of his tension drained away now that they were alone.

He crowded into Liam's space, trying to breathe him in, running his hands over him, the instinct too strong to deny. There was still no scent, though his wolf urged him to try again.

Liam seemed surprised, but didn't push Kade off. "I

thought you couldn't smell. Why are you inhaling like that?"

That brought Kade up short. He forced himself to stop touching Liam and back off. "Sorry. It's... it's a shifter thing. My wolf is convinced I'll be able to smell you if I breathe deep enough."

"I suppose I need to get used to the smelling and scenting for the next three weeks?"

Three weeks. This was so messed up.

"I'll keep it to a minimum."

"Okay."

Silence settled between them, and Liam took in Kade's room.

Their bond was too weak for Kade to sense Liam's emotions as he surveyed his surroundings—the open window, the armchair, the door to the connected bathroom. He purposefully ignored the bed. Instead, his eyes latched on to the lone bookshelf.

He walked over as if drawn to it, and Kade was painfully aware of how empty it was. There were books on it, sure, but Liam had more in one suitcase than Kade had on that shelf. He doubted Liam would be interested in any of the books he owned.

As if confirming his theory, Liam turned away from the shelf, a small frown on his lips as he finally looked at the bed.

Kade wanted to cringe.

Only one bed. His life was such a cliché. He just hoped they didn't wake up cuddling.

It was a big bed. They'd both fit, but Kade wasn't going to presume.

"We can share, or I'll sleep on the floor. Either way, I promise I won't touch you more than necessary."

Liam raised an eyebrow. "How much is necessary?"

Kade rolled his shoulders, uncomfortable. "From what I've heard, bonds are demanding at the beginning. My wolf will want us to be close, to reaffirm the bond." Liam's other eyebrow joined the first, so Kade rushed on. "We don't have to have sex."

Even people with new transactional bonds tended to have a lot of sex though, regardless of the lack of emotions between them.

But that didn't matter. He hadn't controlled himself in the forest, but he sure as hell would now. It might be torture—his wolf would want to touch Liam, scent him, mark him, knot him—but Kade would do his damn best to keep those instincts tamped down. It'd be better for them both.

"I'm fine with sharing." Liam shrugged, then glanced down at himself. His clothes appeared mostly clean, but even without his sense of smell, Kade knew a considerable amount of his come had leaked out of Liam's ass into his underwear. "Can I use your shower?"

Kade bit back the urge to apologize. He'd screwed the absolute hell out of this.

Liam tilted his head, listening to something. "Would you stop that?"

"Stop what?"

"That..." He waved his hands haphazardly around his head. "This. You. Whatever you're feeling. Guilt? Is that what this is? It's something not good."

Kade stared at him incredulously. "Why wouldn't I feel guilty? I forced myself on—"

"*NO.*" Liam got into Kade's personal space, and Kade thought he was about to strangle him. Instead, his hands settled gently along the sides of Kade's neck, magic licking against his skin.

Kade wasn't certain what was happening.

"This helps, right? When there's skin contact, you can feel me better? Sense my emotions?"

"Yes?" While Liam's presence wasn't clear or easy to read, with his hands on Kade, he was more at the forefront. Determination radiated from him.

"Good. So sense my emotions, or whatever, while I'm saying this. *I don't blame you.* I feel pretty damn violated, but *not by you.* I'm pissed that I got possessed by some bizarre lust spirit, but that's *not your fault.* And it's not my fault either. It's *the spirit's fault.* And I will tell you that as many times as you need to hear it to get it through your thick skull. But believe me when I say *I don't blame you.* All this shit just makes me want to defeat these spirits more. I want to destroy them and whoever's behind them."

He let out a frustrated huff, his eyes not meeting Kade's. Warmth curled between them as Liam sped through the next part so fast Kade almost couldn't comprehend his words. "And I might not have noticed the spirit affecting me immediately because I thought you were hot from the moment I saw you in the airport and I wouldn't have wanted to bond but I might have slept with you if it didn't interfere with helping Elijah and even if it was fucked up I enjoyed some of it though that doesn't make it okay or make me any less pissed at the spirit but basically what I'm saying is that I absolutely probably would have had sex with you if you'd been willing and no spirits were involved."

He snatched his hands away, blushing a shade of red that would have given Elijah a run for his money.

Shell-shocked didn't begin to describe Kade's state of mind.

"Right. I should shower," Liam said. He turned, but Kade grabbed his arm and spun him back.

Liam looked at him questioningly, and Kade copied his gesture, placing his hands along Liam's neck, though he carefully avoided the bite mark, as tempting as it was to touch it.

"I also absolutely probably would have had sex with you without the spirit. And I want to kick these things' asses too. I'm really, *really* done with getting possessed by them."

He was sick of having panic attacks, sick of letting the decay spirit have power over him. Sick of not having agency over his own body. It needed to stop.

Liam let out a breath. "So we're on the same page? Fucked-up situation, but we aren't to blame?"

Kade felt lighter than he had since he'd returned to his senses in the clearing. He let his hands fall from Liam's neck. "Yes. No more guilt. We'll get through this, and we'll find a way to kick incorporeal spirit ass."

Liam nodded decisively, then winced. "I really need a shower."

"Do you want fresh clothes? Underwear?"

"Yes, please."

He wasn't that much smaller than Kade. A little thinner and shorter, but they were close enough. Kade picked out underwear, sweatpants, and a sweatshirt and handed them over.

They'd make it through this. It'd work out.

Except Kade had to physically restrain himself from following Liam into the bathroom.

He and Liam might have been on the same page; his wolf was not.

The bathroom door shutting felt too final, like Kade would never see Liam again. But that was his wolf talking. How had Victor survived an entire night as far from Elijah as he had when Kade could barely stand being in a separate room, with one door between him and Liam?

Kade paced and waited for the shower to shut off, managing to sit in the chair and pretend he was gazing outside before Liam came out.

He had to grip the arms of the chair not to go to Liam when he saw him in his clothes. They were baggy, but so fucking perfect. It made contentment want to rumble in his chest.

Kade ignored it, grabbed clothes for himself, and went to shower.

As the water streamed over him, he looked at his chest. There were no marks, but he couldn't shake the memory of what he'd seen in the clearing. The orange glow on his skin, sinuous swirls like the patterns he'd traced on Liam's arm. Graceful swooping curves that were thicker and more intricate than the elegant spiraling lines of Elijah's tattoos.

They were invisible now, but he swore he felt them—a pleasant heat under his skin. The magical tether that connected him to Liam.

Better not get used to it, he reminded himself, then finished showering. It wasn't his to keep, not this time.

When he stepped out of the bathroom, Liam was sitting in the chair, reading on his phone.

And like too often when he was around Liam, Kade had no idea what to say, but it was almost dinnertime, so they should head downstairs.

Kade tried to leash his instincts. It felt unnatural to

smother that part of himself, but that was what he had to do.

He led Liam away from their private sanctuary. His hands twitched with the need to drag Liam back inside the bedroom and not let him leave until Kade's wolf was satisfied that Liam knew they were meant to be together.

Victor eyed him as they entered the dining room. Kade read his concern, but he shook his head. He'd handle dinner. Liam wasn't his. Screw what his wolf thought.

The pack would judge him, but it couldn't be any more awkward than having food brought to his room so he could sit in silence with Liam while they struggled to find things to talk about for the rest of the evening.

Victor slid into the seat Kade had come to think of as Elijah's, and Elijah sat to his right without comment.

Kade blinked, then exhaled, his shoulders lowering. With the chair at the head of the table empty, he could put himself between Liam and the pack, no one on Liam's other side. It was as big of a buffer as he'd get, but he was grateful for that concession.

Aran and Miles, freshly arrived with a suitcase for Liam, sat in the two seats to Elijah's right. Kade gestured for Liam to take the chair opposite Victor.

After Kade sat, he realized the seating arrangement was as far as his pack's courtesy stretched. He'd figured Victor had explained the situation, but when they began to pass around dishes, an older pack member *tsked* at him.

"You of all people should know it's too early for you to be out of bed," Marcia said.

The pack didn't stifle their chuckles. Victor opened his mouth, but Kade could handle his own mess.

"It's not like that. It's temporary."

Frowns appeared around the table, and glances were exchanged. Their pack didn't do transactional bonds.

Liam's presence lingered in his mind, a buzz of emotions, nothing distinguishable, nothing like he'd be feeling if this were a true bond.

Marcia and a few other members started to speak, but Victor cut in.

"This is a lovely meal, Katrina." A hint of power colored his tone, the warning subtle but clear.

The pack played along, complimenting the food and letting the subject drop. For now. Kade wasn't lucky enough for that to be the end of it.

Elijah looked at Victor, some unspoken question in his gaze, and Kade knew they'd be discussing it later. Discussing him, *them,* later. Victor would tell Elijah how their incompatibility was written in their scents, how Kade was the first member of their pack to bond a mage when it wasn't true.

Maybe that was another good thing about his faulty sense of smell. He wouldn't get a constant olfactory reminder of his mistake.

After he'd confirmed that Liam was tucking into a full plate, he took a bite from his own, then suppressed a grimace at the bland, tasteless food. He concentrated on the textures instead, but it wasn't the same.

Across the table, Katrina's son, Oliver, was sitting next to Miles, more focused on the mage than the food he was shoveling into his mouth with a gusto Kade envied.

"You smell funnier than Elijah does," Oliver declared, and Katrina sighed.

"Oliver, we've talked about this."

"But he does, Momma! Elijah smells like Alpha and only makes my nose itch a little."

"No worries." Miles's eyes sparkled with laughter. "We know how we smell to shifters."

"See, Momma. He knows he smells weird." That settled, Oliver squinted up at Miles. "Elijah built a wall *in my head.* Can you build a wall in my head?"

Miles shot a look at Elijah.

"It was a spell to try to protect them from the spirit."

"Ah." Miles turned back to Oliver. "No, Elijah is much better at that than I am."

"Then can you make dirt move under my feet? Elijah can make dirt move under my feet."

"Nope, not that either."

"Elijah can do a lot more than you can."

"He can, actually." Miles laughed. "But there are things I can do that he can't."

Oliver looked skeptical. "Like what?"

Miles pointed to the steam floating up from a serving dish of beef stew. "See that? Watch."

His brown eyes took on a faint blue glow as he stared at the steam. It coalesced, twisting around itself until it formed a hummingbird that fluttered over the table, then flew off, fading as it went.

"*Oooh.*" Oliver leaned forward to look at Elijah. "Can you do that?"

"Not with air," Elijah said.

Oliver considered this, but as he sat back, his gaze caught on Aran. "What can *you* do?"

Aran eyed Oliver's plate. "You going to eat those lima beans?"

"Momma will make me." Oliver wrinkled his nose.

"Can I have one?"

"You can have them all." He pushed his plate toward Aran. Miles obliged by passing it over.

Aran plucked a bean off the plate before Miles set it back in front of Oliver.

"He can take more," Oliver hissed.

"I only need one," Aran said. "I don't want your mom angry at me."

He enclosed the bean in his fist. Green filled his tattoos, and then he opened his hand to reveal a tiny, sprouted plant.

"You make *more* vegetables?" Oliver asked. Words would never do justice to the pure horror on his face, and Kade grinned. He would have agreed as a kid.

Aran laughed. "Yep. That's my main talent. I'm particularly good with eggp—"

With zero subtlety, Elijah punched him in the side.

"Certain species of the nightshade family." Aran gave Elijah a flat look.

Kade snorted. He took another bite without thinking and grimaced.

"Still not tasting anything?" Victor asked, catching Kade's slip-up.

Kade shook his head, and Elijah sat up straighter.

"Oh, right. With everything going on, I forgot. Miles, could you check Kade over? His senses are a bit messed up."

Miles's attention immediately snapped to Kade. "May I?"

Kade shrugged.

Miles stood and took a step to his left, then paused before taking the long way around. It was a little thing, but Kade appreciated it.

He pushed out his chair, but Miles motioned for him to remain seated.

"Is it okay if I touch you?"

"Go for it."

Miles cupped Kade's face. Kade's heartbeat ratcheted up with nerves almost everyone at the table could hear.

Miles's eyes glowed blue again as they stayed trained on Kade, though he wasn't looking *at* Kade; he was looking *into* him.

He inhaled. "*Oh*. That's... Huh. I've never seen that before. Here. Let me..."

A tingling swept over Kade, making his nose twitch as it washed through his sinuses and into his brain. It was the oddest feeling—not painful, but nothing Kade cared to experience again. He took a deep breath through his nose, getting a whiff of non-pack magic that nearly made him sneeze, and then the world was scentless again.

"That spirit did a number on your senses," Miles said. "The pathways are already regrowing though. I'm not positive how your shifter healing will affect the timeline, but I'd give it two or three more days before your senses of smell and taste return. I gave it a boost, but it's better if things grow naturally, even if it does take some time to develop properly."

"Thank you."

As Miles walked back to his chair, Kade felt overly self-conscious as he took his next bite, like everyone was watching how he'd react. For a moment, he thought he might be tasting something, but then it was gone.

An instant cure had been too much to hope for. At least Miles seemed certain he'd recover.

The remainder of the meal consisted of small talk and pleasantries, with Kade growing progressively more restless. The pack went out of their way to include the mages in their conversation, and Kade learned more about Liam in that single dinner than he had during the car ride or in the forest.

It was nonsensical how much he was bothered by people talking to Liam and asking him about his family— his mom, dad, and three younger siblings. But Liam seemed genuinely happy telling them how they'd moved from Louisiana to the suburbs of Seattle, where he'd met Elijah as a preteen. They'd gone to the same elementary school and studied magic together in the afternoons.

Liam and Elijah traded conspiratorial looks, and Kade wondered what kind of trouble they'd gotten into as kids.

They'd met Aran and Miles while they were apprentices in Seattle, with Liam and Elijah learning under the same mage, and Aran and Miles working with nearby teachers.

Kade would have enjoyed the flowing discussion and banter if it had been any other time, but as it was, he had to consciously keep himself from bouncing his leg with the urge to get Liam out of there.

For as excruciating as the dinner was, he also wasn't ready to go to bed with Liam. In the least fun way imaginable.

After dinner, they saw Aran and Miles to the door.

"We packed your things, but left the books at the shop," Miles said as they passed the suitcase they'd brought.

Liam frowned.

"Should we have brought them? We figured if they were at the shop, we could do research in the evenings."

"Oh, yeah, that's fine." Liam waved them off.

It was fine? Really? It seemed inconsiderate to Kade. Why wouldn't they have brought Liam's books? He shouldn't be without them; even Kade knew that much.

But if Liam said it was fine, who was he to argue?

They exchanged goodbyes, and Kade carried the bag upstairs despite Liam's protests that he could do it. But Liam was a guest. He should be taken care of.

Once they were in the room, Liam rubbed a hand across his five o'clock shadow, and Kade's wolf wanted Kade to copy the movement, to slide his hand along Liam's sharp jaw.

"So..." Liam said. "Right or left?"

"Left." It was closer to the door.

Liam glanced at the window, a cool breeze blowing inside. "Do you always have that open?"

"I prefer it that way." That wasn't answering the question, but that was all Kade was willing to divulge.

Liam scrutinized him before saying, "Okay. We'll leave it open."

They got ready and into bed, then turned off the lights.

And lay there, staring into the darkness, the silence falling over them with suffocating thickness.

His wolf unhelpfully suggested they pull Liam close, but Kade would not be doing that.

After half of forever had passed, Liam's breathing changed, a deliberate slowing, a measured count, and then he was asleep.

Kade wished he could do the same. It was much longer before he fell asleep as well.

Fuck, this scent was perfect. Kade pressed his nose against skin, his arms wrapping tighter around the body he was spooning. That body snuggled back, melting into him, and he rolled his hips, his morning semi waking faster than his mind. He ground against that warmth, loving the sleepy little moan it caused.

A flood of emotions rushed into him—arousal, followed by groggy disorientation and confusion—and it stopped Kade cold, his brain coming back online.

He was wrapped around Liam, his erection pressed into Liam's ass. It felt so fucking good. Without looking, he knew Liam was as hard as he was; he sensed it. Sensed the aching need.

Kade inhaled. Everything was blank. Hadn't he been—

No, that must have been a dream. He tried to recall what he'd been dreaming about, what scent he'd been smelling, but that was gone too.

Mustering all his willpower, he peeled himself off Liam and flopped onto his back, putting distance between them. He groaned, his dick protesting his decision to be gentlemanly.

In a million years, he never would have imagined himself thinking fondly of the days his libido had been nonexistent, but he shouldn't have been surprised it had returned to top form in time for him to wake up with his cock digging into Liam's ass like it was aiming to live there permanently.

Liam rolled onto his back as well and cleared his throat, glancing over. "So. Want some help with that?"

Kade really did. Images ran through his mind of all the dirty things he could do to Liam, all the dirty things Liam could do to him.

But he couldn't with this sham of a bond.

"Not gonna lie, that's a tempting offer, but it isn't a good idea."

He swore a thread of disappointment wormed through their bond.

"Anytime we have sex," he explained before Liam could ask, "it risks deepening the bond. It's part of why newly bonded pairs often spend the first few weeks in bed. Usually, the more sex a couple has, the deeper the bond becomes, assuming there are emotions involved. Which makes the sex feel better, so then they have even more sex. It's a truly vicious cycle. But that makes the bond more difficult to sever."

"Difficult how?"

"I've never done this before, obviously, but I've heard the worst thing you can do to a bonded pair is force them to sever their bond. The deeper the bond, the more painful it is to remove. But if we keep it shallow and not reaffirmed, it shouldn't be horrible."

Liam squinted at him, clearly confused. "When Elijah was having trouble with his magic because of his pseudo-bond with Victor, I researched how bonds were severed, but there was nothing about it being exceptionally painful."

"It might not be for mages, but for shifters, it can be like losing a limb. Like half of you has been ripped away. There are stories of shifters going insane from it, but it's not something we talk about outside of shifter circles, and like I said, it doesn't sound as bad for transactional bonds. Honestly, true or transactional, bonds are rarely severed. I'd just rather not risk strengthening the bond with three weeks of what would doubtlessly be very enjoyable sex."

"That makes sense. So no sex, huh?" Liam actually did sound disappointed. "When you said sex with a shifter is life-changing, I didn't think you meant like this."

Kade chuckled and rolled out of bed. "Neither did I. I'm going to take the coldest shower in history unless you need in there."

"I'm good."

Kade headed into the bathroom, thankful for the distance it put between them this time.

Waking up pressed against Liam with the remnants of his dream floating around him was messing with his head, and staying in bed wasn't doing his cock any favors. For all his talk about the reasons they shouldn't have sex, it hadn't flagged in the slightest.

He stripped and jumped into the shower, cranking the water to frigid, but it didn't do anything to kill his arousal.

"Seriously?" He glared at his dick. "I can't believe I'm saying this, but could you go back to being down for the count?"

Groaning, he adjusted the water to a more comfortable temperature and wrapped a hand around himself.

His wolf whispered that he was being an idiot. Liam was right outside. They didn't need to be doing this alone. Liam had offered, and fuck, it had felt amazing to grind against his ass.

Kade focused on that, focused on how it had felt to be inside him, how perfect and tight he'd been, how he'd wanted to hold Liam against him as they rocked together until they both got off. The thought of it had his stomach clenching and his toes curling.

It didn't take much to come, but it left him decidedly unsatisfied, like he hadn't begun to scratch the itch.

Grumbling to himself, he got out of the shower and toweled himself dry, pulling on jeans and a t-shirt before exiting the bathroom.

The room was quiet. Liam was sitting against the headboard, his legs drawn up, his cheeks flushed, his hands gripping his knees.

It hit Kade how stupid he'd just been.

Of course Liam had felt that. They might not have a true bond, but arousal was strong enough to register through even a transactional one.

The need in his mind became clearer. It wasn't Kade's dissatisfaction; it was *Liam's*. Liam needing to get off because he'd had a front-row seat to Kade's orgasm.

"Oh *fuck*." Kade winced. "I didn't think that through. I'm so s—"

"It's fine. And apologies in advance for this too!" Liam sprinted past him, shutting the door behind him. The water was on a moment later, and that need blazed like a bonfire. It was all Kade could do not to bust down the bathroom door, to invade the shower. To fall to his knees and get his mate off, because Liam needed to come, and Kade wanted to get him there, to make sure he was satisfied and his desires were fulfilled in every way possible.

But he didn't. No matter how easily he could picture it, or how this was a whole new kind of torment.

Could he fuck this up any more? Even with as distracted as he was, even with this faint bond, Liam was there, hot and throbbing with pent-up need.

Kade gripped his dresser, the wood creaking under his fingertips. He was already hardening in his pants again, his body buzzing with the pleasure coursing through Liam, with how close Liam was to coming, but he wasn't going to touch himself.

When Liam did come, Kade almost fell over the edge with him.

This was his punishment. He'd made Liam sit through his orgasm, so it was only fair he sat through Liam's. After everything that had happened recently, he deserved a few weeks' worth of blue balls. Probably more.

Liam spent longer in the shower than could be expected for a guy with a buzz cut. He was avoiding Kade. Not that Kade could blame him. But that extra time allowed him to cool off.

How he would survive three weeks without jerking off, he didn't know. He was used to regular orgasms; he hadn't gone that long without one in his entire adult life.

And *fuck*, the full moon was coming up. Wonderful.

But he'd manage; he'd deal with it. He wouldn't make this more awkward for Liam than it had to be.

When Liam came out, they stood there, not meeting each other's eyes.

"Well," Kade said, forcing himself to look at Liam, "this'll be a fun couple of weeks."

Liam huffed. He was scrubbed clean; the scent of soap had to be heavy on his skin.

There was no reason for that to bother Kade. He couldn't smell Liam, so why did he care? Why would Liam being fresh and clean nettle him?

Whether Liam smelled like soap or like Kade, it shouldn't cause Kade's wolf to prowl unhappily under his skin. He didn't need to do anything about that. To fix it. To ensure Liam was covered in his scent before they left the room.

Kade turned toward the door. As Liam seemed so fond of saying, it was fine—no problem at all.

The real issue he had to worry about was the amount of shit his pack was likely to give him once they got downstairs.

It was *fine*, and to prove that, he just had to walk out this door.

Kade paused, his hand on the doorknob, and Liam stared at his back. He couldn't read Kade's emotions beyond that he felt conflicted.

After a moment, Kade turned, looking sheepish. "I'm sorry, but before we go downstairs, can I... uh..."

He held his hands out, and Liam eyed them. "Can you...?"

"So. You just showered."

"Yes." Obviously. It'd been a whole thing.

"But now you don't... And I kind of... I mean, my wolf sort of needs..."

The realization of what he was asking to do hit Liam. "Oh! The scenting thing? Sure? I guess that's fine."

"Sorry," Kade said again, brushing his hands against the sides of Liam's neck. His presence leapt forward in Liam's mind as he stroked downward, avoiding the bite mark. His palms slid firmly over Liam's shoulders and along his arms.

Liam's eyelids fluttered closed, and he melted under the caress. God, that felt amazing. Wherever Kade touched, whether bare skin or over clothing, his energy buzzed. The pleasure of the sensation was equaled by Kade's satisfaction at doing it, at covering Liam with his scent. Even if he couldn't smell it, everyone else would.

Kade repeated the gesture. He kept his hands to the safest areas possible, but all Liam could imagine was Kade doing this to his entire body. When he tried to push the thought aside, it stayed lodged in his mind, like a—

Nope, he wasn't going there.

Kade's hands fell away, and Liam blinked his eyes open, feeling almost drunk. When he'd agreed to this, he hadn't expected it to have quite this effect on him, for it to make his blood rush and his breath catch.

"Right." Kade stepped back, the effort it took apparent. "We should..."

"Right. We should."

There were many things they had to do, and Kade stroking his hands over every inch of Liam's body was not on that list.

Unfortunately.

Liam exhaled as they left Kade's room. When he took another breath, Kade's scent invaded his senses.

It figured. He'd wanted that scent all over him, and now he was getting it in the most torturous way possible. It lingered on him like a cologne, so warm and wholesome.

Wholesome was not a word Liam would have associated with Kade, but somehow, it fit.

Though Kade could stand to be a good deal less wholesome. These next three weeks would have been a lot more enjoyable if he'd been willing to make this a 'reluctantly bonded with benefits' situation. Liam could have knocked getting laid off his to-do list. What had happened in the forest didn't count. And now he wasn't just dealing with his own sexual frustration; he had Kade's to contend with as well.

While sharing a bed. Lovely.

Feeling Kade get off through their bond had been strange... and insanely hot. But he'd respect Kade's wishes and not push for more.

As much fun as 'more' would have been.

But instead of having regular and thorough... fun, he had to resign himself to being stuck without sex in a room with entirely too few books. The lone bookshelf had looked more ornamental than anything, with a collection of photobooks and multiple shelves empty except for a few pictures and knickknacks. It was a sad thing begging to be filled with books.

That made Liam think of other things begging to be filled, and he sighed. He'd turn into Aran at this rate.

Kade's head swiveled toward him, but Liam waved away his concern.

He didn't like people tiptoeing around him. Being concerned about him. Fussing over him. He was supposed to be the worrier of their group, goddamnit.

Was he in the weirdest situation he'd ever been in? Yes. Yes, he was. Could they do anything about it before the new moon? No. No, they couldn't. There was no point in people worrying about him. They needed to accept it and move on, as he had. But that didn't seem to be the case.

Elijah's expression was anxious as they descended the stairs, and Liam had seen more than enough of that. He grabbed Elijah by the arm and marched him outside.

Elijah glanced at Kade, but for once, he wasn't growling, too caught off-guard by Liam's actions.

"Would you stop worrying about me?" Liam asked as the front door closed behind them, and Elijah scoffed.

"You do realize how ridiculous it is for *you* to say that, right?"

"Oh, shut up." There was no heat to Liam's words.

Elijah gestured away from the house, and Liam realized almost everyone inside could hear them.

He followed Elijah down the driveway, and they kept their voices quiet as they walked.

"Are you sure you're okay?"

Liam checked in with himself before answering. He'd screwed up yesterday; the least he could do was give Elijah an honest answer. "Physically, I'm healed. Mentally? I don't know. I can't say I enjoyed the lack of control over my own body, and I'll probably need some therapy after this is finished. Are there therapists who deal with spirit possessions?"

Elijah opened his mouth, then closed it, expression torn.

"What?"

Elijah hesitated.

"Tell me."

"I... I don't think you were possessed?"

That hit Liam like a backfired spell. It took him a moment to respond, and even then, all he got out was a strangled, "What?"

Of course they'd been possessed. They wouldn't have done that otherwise.

Elijah grimaced. "I could be wrong. Every spirit acts differently. But the last time? The rot spirit had hooks in Kade. In his brain. I had to remove it from him. But when we found you guys, when I was trapping the lust spirit, it wasn't in you. Not directly. Not the same way the other spirit had infected Kade. It was feeding off you, yes, but it didn't have hooks in you. I think it was affecting you, not *controlling* you."

Liam stared blankly at the forest, his mind refusing to wrap around that idea. The spirit hadn't possessed them? They'd only been under its influence?

Elijah continued, his voice soft. "Kade said the rot spirit surrounded him, that it filled his lungs, and when it possessed him, he had zero control. He was along for the ride as the spirit used him to do what it wanted. Is that what happened? Did it touch you?"

Liam shook his head, realizing there was truth to Elijah's words. He hadn't felt like he was being controlled. Sure, he'd been abnormally fixated on how horny he was. That one emotion had been amplified to an impossible extent. Nothing else had mattered. But his actions had felt so natural, like he'd been meant to do it, not like he was being compelled to do it by an outside force.

The spirits of terror and disorientation had affected them, but they'd fought through those effects and over-come them.

The lust spirit might have removed his self-control and inhibitions about acting on his desires, but it hadn't put novel thoughts in his head... the bonding and knotting aside.

He swallowed down the lump in his throat. "It didn't touch us."

"To be clear, whether it was possessing or affecting you, it's not your fault. Yours or Kade's. That shit was powerful. We barely kept it together enough to trap it. Like I said, if I didn't have the bond with Victor, I don't think I would have been able to. This was *not* your fault."

Liam snorted. "I told Kade the same thing last night. Whether we were possessed or not, I wouldn't have had sex in the forest under normal circumstances. And for all his dick jokes and bad pickup lines, I doubt Kade would have either. Or, well, he definitely would, but not when he was doing something to protect his pack."

He scrubbed a hand over his face, and Elijah waited for him to continue, concern in his eyes.

"Stop looking at me like that. I'm fine."

"Don't pull that 'I'm fine' bullshit with me."

"Seriously. I'm *fine*. I wouldn't have chosen any of this, and I do not want a repeat with another spirit affecting me that much. But..." Liam exhaled forcefully, then sped through the next part. "The reason I didn't realize what was going on sooner was because I'd already thought about him in that way."

Elijah cocked an eyebrow at him.

"Please don't judge me. Or tell Aran."

"Yeah. I'm going to judge you for thinking a shifter is hot. What absolute lunatic would want to fuck a shifter?" Elijah said, voice deadpan.

"I think Elijah from a few months ago would have had some thoughts on the matter."

"Lies. All lies. There was no priority-rearranging metaphorical shifter dick or anything."

"Uh-huh."

"But are you—"

"*I'm fine*. The situation is fucked up. I never would have done it of my own volition. I wouldn't have even hooked up with him if we'd met in a club. And I absolutely never would have gotten bonded to him." Liam rubbed a hand over the back of his neck, glancing away from Elijah. "But this morning, I wasn't affected by the spirit, and when we woke up..." He wasn't willing to admit he'd wanted to grind against Kade's dick until they both came. Some of that had to have been the bond, but not all of it.

Elijah's eyebrows rose again.

"Nothing happened, but I also wasn't opposed to it happening. I mean, if we have to be bonded, we might as well, right? But he's against the idea. The situation is messed up, and we'll have to get through it, but I'm..." Liam trailed off. He couldn't say *fine* because Elijah wouldn't believe him and he wasn't, not completely. So instead of his default, he said, "Better than I would have thought."

"That's as good as can be expected."

"Plus, can you imagine if it had been Aran?"

"Let's pray to any and every power listening that we get through this without him ending up in bed with one of the pack."

They both cringed.

"But you'll be able to sever this, right?"

Elijah hesitated. "You really want me to do that?"

"Who else would I trust to do it?"

"No, I didn't mean—" Elijah huffed. "I'll do it if you want me to. But how are you adjusting to it? It's intense, isn't it?"

Liam cocked his head, studying Elijah. "How so?"

"You can't sense him in your mind?"

"Kind of? He's there."

"But you aren't constantly aware of how he's feeling? It can be overwhelming how exposed the bond leaves you. There's no hiding from it. I doubt I could keep a secret from Victor if I wanted to."

"That's not what I'm experiencing. I get hints of his emotions when they're strong. Like right now he's... restless? Maybe. It's pretty nebulous. More of a vague impression? Definitely not overwhelming."

"Oh, no. It's so much deeper than that. Especially when we touch, I can sense *everything* Victor's feeling."

"Thankfully, it's not like that." Liam was more than a little relieved. Sharing himself with someone the way Elijah was describing sounded too intimate. "When we're touching, I do get more of his emotions, but it's still a guessing game. The only clear emotion I've felt when we aren't touching is... arousal."

"Oh." Elijah looked distressed.

"*I'm fine,*" Liam insisted. "It's not the first time I've been a mistake."

"*Liam.* Don't start with that shit. You know that's not true. And it'd break your mother's heart if she heard you say that."

Liam grimaced. "I know, I know."

His parents hadn't been married when they'd had him. They hadn't even been of legal drinking age. They'd talked about getting married someday, having kids *someday*. Liam had happened significantly before that someday had rolled around, before they'd been prepared for it, before they'd created anything remotely close to a stable life. His three younger siblings had been much closer to that someday than he had.

"You happened when you needed to. Don't ever think anything different. If you'd been closer in age to your siblings, maybe you wouldn't have been so willing to let me glom onto you."

"Screw that. I don't care how many blood siblings I have or what their ages are, you still would have been my brother from the day we met."

Elijah grinned. "Exactly."

"Fine. But that doesn't change the fact that this was a mistake."

"You honestly don't feel anything through your bond?"

"Not really. Other than the... you know." Elijah didn't need specifics about the shower incident. "But that's a relief. I don't want some stranger in my head, feeling everything I do."

"I wonder why though. When our connection was unbalanced, I didn't sense Victor's emotions as much. Maybe that's the reason? Did you tether yourself to him?"

"Yeah. This is as balanced as it's getting. It must be the difference between a true and a transactional bond. From what I've read about transactional bonds, they sound more like what I'm experiencing than what you are. None of it suggests transactionally bonded pairs have a connection like you and Victor do, and we aren't freakishly compatible, unlike some people I could name."

Elijah frowned. "You aren't interested in him? If you can ignore all the dick jokes, he's sort of sweet."

Liam waved his hand dismissively. "I've been ignoring dick jokes on a regular basis since the first year of our apprenticeship. But no, I'm not interested."

Elijah's frown deepened. He was about to speak, but then he paused before saying, "If you tethered yourself to him, how's your magic?"

"Oh." Liam gave a start. He hadn't tested it. It didn't feel uncontrolled like Elijah had described his magic when he'd had the pseudo-bond with Victor, but Liam also hadn't used it for a spell yet.

He gathered his magic and inhaled sharply at how different it felt. Not foreign, but transformed, and beneath it, a pool of energy—deep and powerful—called to him. He ran phantom fingers through that untamed energy. It wanted to pull him in, to sweep through him, leaving him tingling from his fingertips to his toes from how potent and heady it was.

But when he went to channel it, it didn't flood into him to the extent he'd expected. It was still there, still available to him, but throttled somehow. Limited. Those depths weren't his to use as he willed.

That didn't mean he couldn't use any of it though. He pulled on a thread of that energy and called forth a spark of fire above his palm. It made the tattoos on his arms light up, and the fire that sprang to life wasn't the tiny flickering flame he'd intended. It was a fireball that had even him jumping back.

He looked at Elijah, surprised.

Elijah laughed. "You should see how bright your eyes are glowing."

Behind them, the front door slammed open. Kade hurried out onto the porch, his expression panicked. Victor followed at a more sedate pace.

Kade strode down the stairs toward them, and Elijah stepped away from Liam. "I should have known he'd feel that."

Oh, yeah. Obviously, he would notice Liam pulling on his energy.

"We're testing his magic," Elijah explained, not bothering to raise his voice. "There's no threat."

Kade was so fixated on Liam, he either didn't hear or didn't believe Elijah.

"But while you're here," Elijah said, "we should have him test it further. We should make sure he can use your energy without blowing anything up. Otherwise, there could be issues."

Liam winced, but if he couldn't channel Kade's energy

without losing control, if his magic was unstable, he'd be a hindrance to the team.

So when Kade neared him, Liam reached out, and Kade's hand found his.

When they touched, energy rubbed against him, wild but ready to be used. He opened himself up to it, and it filled him so full he gasped. With it came a total awareness of Kade—his body, his mind, their skin pressing together. How that wasn't enough. How he needed more. Was that his thought or Kade's? Did it matter? Either way, he was consumed by it, by all that energy, all those sensations. Was this what Elijah was talking about? What he experienced with Victor?

Kade shifted closer to him, his hand coming up to Liam's neck, his body crowding into him, and Liam shivered, liking the possessive curl of Kade's fingers, that warm scent coming off him.

"Ah, Liam?" Elijah's voice broke through the fog that had overtaken him. "You might want to use some of that magic before it explodes."

Liam peeled his eyes open. The trees surrounding them were moving in a breeze caused by the sheer amount of magic he'd channeled. It swirled around him, waiting for his command.

He shook himself. Right. He needed to make something. With so much power available to him, he didn't want to use fire. That seemed unwise in the middle of a forest when he couldn't predict how big the spell would be. But there was another thing he wanted to try.

As his friends often reminded him, he was terrible at wards. Would he be better with this level of power?

Kade moved with him as he knelt, and Liam pressed a palm against the ground like he'd seen Elijah do a dozen times or more. Then he called up a ward, the best he could manage, pouring magic and energy into it. It was tempting to use every last drop, but he restrained himself.

The ward snapped into place between him and Elijah.

Liam stood, swaying from the magic he'd used. Kade's hand fell from his neck to his waist, steadying him, and Liam leaned into his touch. Arousal sparked inside him, but he tried to calm himself, tried to regulate his breathing.

Elijah placed a hand against the barrier and studied the ward, amusement and curiosity written on his face. "This isn't bad. It's fairly strong." He focused on it, his gaze getting distant as he sensed the threads, his mouth opening in a small gasp, but then he pulled his hand away, his expression shuttering. He shot a look at Victor before turning to Liam. "I wouldn't have guessed you were capable of making this."

"Thanks," Liam said dryly, though he had to agree. Terrible at wards or not, this one was decent.

Regretfully, he dropped the barrier. Releasing Kade's energy was even harder.

After he did, he caught Elijah sending Victor another look and Victor's near imperceptible head tilt in return—the perfect communication of two people so closely linked that they knew each other's every thought. But Liam was unable to follow.

Elijah's next question was hesitant. "So... can you control it?"

Liam had almost lost himself in it. If Elijah hadn't been there to jar him out of it, what would have happened? All he'd wanted to do was crawl into Kade, to get closer to him, to feel more of that energy.

"It's intoxicating," Elijah admitted, reading Liam's uncertainty. "As shitty as it was to have my magic acting up for a month, it helped me get used to Victor's energy. Once I was tethered to him properly, everything fell into place. I didn't have to fight to control it; I could just welcome and accept it. I don't know how I would have handled having immediate control over that level of power, and I'd rather not have you out in the forest until you're certain you won't get overwhelmed by it."

Elijah wasn't outright saying it, but Liam could read between the lines. He and Kade were a liability they couldn't afford. None of them wanted a repeat of yesterday.

"My strong suit has always been research."

"That's probably for the best. Miles, Aran, and I can wrangle the worst of the spirits, and you can find out what they are."

Liam nodded. It was what it was. He refused to drag down his team.

"Good thing I packed so many books," he said with a humorless laugh. "Hopefully I can finally figure out how to destroy them too."

It was too bad Miles and Aran hadn't brought his books yesterday, but the plan had been to capture the spirits during the day, then do research in the evenings at the apartment. It made sense to leave most of the books at the shop, and considering how twitchy Kade became when people got close to him, being alone might ease his nerves. Or his wolf's nerves? Liam wasn't sure which.

They decided to grab breakfast before heading to the shop and had finished eating when Victor looked in the direction of the main road and said, "Miles and Aran just passed through the wards."

A few minutes later, they met them in front of the house. On the way out, Liam hoisted his bag onto his shoulder. He'd packed the codex so he could make sigils as needed.

Aran pulled up, and he and Miles got out of his car. He went to tuck his keys into his pocket, and a jolt of surprise flashed in Liam's head.

Liam glanced over at Kade, who was staring at Aran.

"Is that a DickHunt keychain?"

What was DickHunt? And what did that have to do with the weird little eggplant Aran had on his keychain?

"You know DickHunt?" An unholy light glittered in Aran's eyes.

"Dude, who doesn't? They're legends!"

"Fuck yeah, they are."

Liam exchanged a look with an equally confused Elijah.

"Are you on the forums?" Aran asked.

"Of fucking course. You?"

"Damn right I am. I'm MagicalHWood."

"*Dude*. No way. I'm KnottyWolf69!"

They proceeded to bro-hug each other, complete with back slaps.

Liam couldn't get past 'KnottyWolf69.' That was Kade's screen name on some forum? Jesus fucking Christ.

Kade looped an arm around Aran's shoulders and turned toward them. "This bastard and I have been friends for years! I can't tell you the number of times we've gotten off together."

The number of *what*? That didn't sound friendly. Liam frowned. "You know each other... online?"

"Yeah. We met on the MateHub forums."

Aran nodded solemnly. "Richard Knotz. The love of my life. Making people come together around the world."

Elijah slapped a hand to his face. "I tried to keep them apart, but it was too late. All my efforts were for nothing!"

Kade grinned, his arm still slung around Aran. Which was not bothering Liam. Not in the slightest. Kade could touch whoever he wanted.

"I've always wondered. What does the H stand for?"

"Ecchi. It's slang. Comes from hentai."

"*Nice.*"

Liam didn't see how that was nice.

"Have you watched their latest scene? The one announcing Hunter's merch?" Kade was all but bouncing with excitement.

"Do you even need to ask? Watched and preordered. That's how I spent my night in the hotel on my way up here. It was so fucking hot."

Liam's mouth was hanging open, but he couldn't bring himself to shut it. What the hell? Were they talking about videos on a porn site like they were a popular TV show?

"Right? Richard was about ready to kno—"

"OKAY," Elijah said, cutting through their conversation. "We've got a lot to do today. So. We should do that."

Liam agreed wholeheartedly. Anything would be better than standing around, listening to Kade and Aran discuss porn.

They executed some overly complicated handshake like they'd done it a thousand times before.

Kade pointed at Aran. "We're talking later."

It was one hundred percent bro energy, not even slightly flirty, but Liam didn't want to think about them getting off together. Or talking about it.

"Please, no," Elijah muttered under his breath.

Still confused, Liam followed Kade to his car. "Be careful," he called to his friends.

Aran gave him a dramatic thumbs-up. "Will do, Li-mom! As fun as it sounds, I promise to avoid getting knotted in the forest."

Liam sighed and got in Kade's car. What did he expect?

As Kade pulled out onto the road, he glanced over. "So... Li-mom?"

Liam let out another sigh. "I've been told I worry too much. Apparently that makes me the group mom. But Elijah will work so hard he forgets to eat, and Aran will go home with any guy with an above-average dick, and Miles? Like Elijah said, Miles needs to be protected at all costs. He's too sweet for this world."

Kade chuckled. "And here I thought I had it bad taking care of an alpha who's too repressed and self-sacrificing for his own good."

"Elijah will keep him from getting too sacrificial."

"And Victor will make sure Elijah has plenty to eat. I can't guarantee it'll always be a balanced meal though."

Liam shot him a flat look.

"Ass," Kade said, as if that required clarification. "I'm talking about Elijah eating—"

"YEP. Got it. Thanks." That was not an image Liam cared to have in his head.

They settled into silence. Liam hadn't realized how long the drive was when he and his friends had made it the previous morning, but a day later, it seemed to stretch on forever.

He gazed out the window and tried to think of it the way Elijah would. He was their best researcher; there was no question about that. If anyone was going to find out what was happening, it would be him. As much as he didn't like it, maybe this was where he needed to be. This was what he needed to do.

And Elijah was right. He had to get comfortable using

Kade's energy before they could safely work in a potentially volatile situation.

He took out his phone and wrote an email to the head librarian, explaining that his family emergency would take longer to handle than he'd expected. Initially, he'd taken a week and a half off, so he requested an extension. Since he worked on his own most days, doing a project that wasn't a high priority, it wouldn't be an issue. While the librarians thought archiving the library was a decent idea, they didn't think it was critical. Most of them were in their late sixties or older, so it wasn't too surprising. It had irritated him before, but it might play to his benefit. At worst, he'd run out of vacation time and have to go unpaid for a few weeks.

Well, no. At worst, someone would decide his tiny office would make a wonderful storage room, and he'd have to excavate it from mountains of boxes to reach his desk and scanner. But he'd deal with that.

Plus, he hadn't taken a day off in the year he'd been working there. He had some time saved up.

While he waited for the reply, he studied Kade. Wind whipped through the open windows, stirring his loose hair. His jaw was clenched, and his knuckles were white on the wheel. There was a murmur in Liam he couldn't identify, but looking at Kade, it was obvious. He was frustrated about getting benched. Liam enjoyed research; he doubted Kade was the type to spend hours of his free time combing through books on some obscure topic for fun.

"There's a workspace on the second floor above the shop," Liam said. "We can take occasional breaks from researching so I can practice using your energy, if you're okay with that."

Some of the tension bled out of Kade's shoulders. "If that'll get us out there helping again, whatever you need."

Once they were in Elijah's apartment, Liam headed over to the books Aran and Miles had piled up while emptying his suitcases to gather his things. All it took was a glance to make him wince. He loved his friends, but they needed to learn how to organize books.

"What's wrong?" Kade asked.

"No, it's nothing. They just mixed the books from my suitcases and backpack together."

"And that's... bad?"

"The ones in the suitcases were sorted by overarching topics—summoning, exorcism, and the like—and then subtopics. They're still mostly by topic, but the subtopics got disorganized. And the ones in my backpack are for my personal research on mage history, in case there's downtime, so those should be separate. But it's okay. It'll only take a minute to sort out."

"You brought... research? For downtime... during your research?"

"Of course. What else would I read?"

Kade's brow furrowed like he'd spoken a foreign language, and Liam suppressed the urge to justify himself. Instead, he selected a few books that dealt with the types and classifications of spirits, avoiding the ones about possession, and passed them over to Kade.

With a resigned expression, Kade took them, then glanced around the apartment. He gestured to the closed windows. "It's stuffy in here. Do you mind if I open those?"

It wasn't stuffy at all, but Liam doubted that was the real issue. "Yeah, that's fine."

Kade opened the windows, then walked to the small kitchen table, sat down, and dove in.

Liam had the books organized in no time, though he did wish he had shelves for them, but that wasn't happening.

With that finished, he had one more thing to take care of before he got down to business figuring out what these damn spirits were.

On his laptop, he pulled up the notes he'd taken while researching bonds when Elijah's magic was acting up. He knew what was written there, but wanted to confirm he hadn't missed anything. He skimmed the document until he hit the relevant section.

<u>Severing Shifter Bonds</u>

- ***RARELY DONE***
- ***Requires a mage to sever the bond.***
  - *A bonded mage cannot sever their own bond like they could sever a tether.*
  - *Most recorded instances performed by pack mages.*
  - *Familiarity with using shifter energy and working with pack bonds is highly advisable.*
  - *Also advisable the mage is strong, particularly in the case of long-established bonds, or bonds involving pack alphas or betas.*
- ***MUST happen on a new moon.***
  - *Diminished lunar energy makes the bond more susceptible to mage intervention.*
  - *Traces of the bond may remain if attempted outside the conjunction phase.*
- ***Ritual graded adept level with high intensity and basic complexity.***
  - *While it has straightforward instructions and minimal variations, it does require*

> *significant amounts of energy manipulation and concentration.*
>   - *Ritual should never be interrupted. One book warns of "profound consequences," though the exact nature is unclear. (Incomplete bond severing? Lingering effects? Death or injury? Making the bond impossible to sever?)*
> - *Ritual requires minimal preparation and supplies.*
>   - *The bonded pair must be in close proximity to each other and the mage. Touching skin is required.*
>   - *A diluted tincture of wolfsbane can be taken by the bonded pair to further dampen the energy that sustains the bond. Ratio of 1:20 or weaker suggested by most sources to ensure it only temporarily sickens the shifters. (Not required.)*
>   - *See following page for full ritual details.*
> - *Major side effects seem limited.*
>   - *Temporary disorientation and confusion appear most common.*
> - *Dissolving the bond is irreversible.*
>   - *Cannot be reestablished once severed.*
>   - *However, bonds with others are possible. This does appear to be rare though.*

So, regardless of their desires, they were stuck with this bond for three weeks.

He reread the ritual. Elijah could do it. It wouldn't even require that much magic.

Liam had left his plane ticket open-ended because he

hadn't known how long it would take to clean up the mess with the spirits, but hopefully that would be over by then and he could head home the day after the new moon.

His gaze caught on one of the bullet points. *"Major side effects seem limited."* Kade had made it sound like there could be a great deal of pain involved. None of Liam's research had indicated anything of the sort.

"Hey," he said. Kade's relief was palpable as he looked up from the book. "You mentioned that severing shifter bonds can be painful?"

Kade appeared less thrilled about the topic. "I think it depends on the bond itself, like how deep it is. There are MateHub stars who do transactional bonds so they can film knotting scenes, but most never do those contracts more than once. I'm assuming that's because breaking the bond after a few dozen scenes is too painful for it to be worth the money. It's part of the reason Richard Knotz is such a legend. He did it over a dozen times. But he's the exception, not the rule."

"That seems like a logical theory. Are there other side effects?"

"It's not a topic we commonly discuss, so everything I've heard is rumor at best. There are stories that float around. They say severing a well-established, wanted bond is painful to the point of death, and after a bond is severed, there can be residual pain from a phantom bond. There's a period of adjustment too. You need to relearn how to be yourself as an individual. It's like a mourning period similar to what you'd have if your mate died."

That tracked with what Elijah had explained that morning. It wasn't what Liam was feeling, but then, Kade had said their bond was shallow.

Liam started typing.

"What are you writing?"

"I'm updating my notes on severing bonds."

Kade's panic stabbed at him, intense enough that he whipped his head up in surprise.

"Maybe I shouldn't have told you that."

"Oh." Liam blinked at his half-finished bullet point.

- ***Can cause pain, even de***

He swallowed. "You think a mage would use that against you?"

Kade shrugged, his discomfort apparent.

"They'd need to be close to a bonded pair, on a new moon, with the intention of harming them. No mage would do that."

Kade looked away, then back. "Entire packs were wiped out by mages."

"But that was retaliation for the abductions."

"*Entire packs*. Including children. I'm not claiming the abductions weren't fucked up and wrong, or that most of the pack wasn't complicit, but *children*?"

That was valid. Almost no one's hands had been clean during that period of their history, but Liam could never condone slaughtering children in the name of revenge.

He hit backspace until the bullet point was deleted. The notes were his, and he had no intention of sharing them outside his closest friends, but he could understand Kade's concern. "I won't write it down, but I do appreciate you giving me a heads-up about it."

Something eased in Kade's presence. The stiff line of his shoulders relaxed.

Liam's phone chimed, and he opened the notification.

MILES

First spirit of the day: Nausea. Sigil, please?

There appears to be reception here, and
we're out of the spirit's area of influence, so
we're resting for a bit.

If you need me, I'll be vomiting up
everything I've ever eaten.

Liam winced and grabbed his sigil codex.

"What'd they find?"

"Nausea, apparently."

Kade pulled a face. "Kinda glad we avoided that one."

"Same. Not upset I only have to make the sigil for it."

LIAM

Here you go.

Get some electrolytes if you did throw up.

And remember to be careful!

He sent Miles the sigil and got a thumbs-up in reply.

Now that he thought about it, this could work out well. If he were in the forest, there might not be enough reception for him to make sigils for everyone as they went. But this way, they could identify one or two, get to a place with reception, and he could make the sigils straight away.

Maybe he wasn't benched after all.

With that settled, he picked out half a dozen books, then dropped into the second chair at the table.

He cracked open *An Exorcist's Guide to Evil Entities & Emanations* and skimmed through it. Over-alliteration of the title aside, it was an interesting read, but not what he was searching for. He put it on the discard pile and picked up *A Comprehensive Study of Possessions*, though he soon discovered it was less comprehensive than advertised. Everything in it was run-of-the-mill, but he diligently flipped through until the end, just in case.

As he read, it became harder and harder to pore over the tomes. This wasn't like him. When he was hunting down an answer, he locked in and could read any book, no matter how boring. If he had a stack of books in front of him, he could tune out the world.

It took him another book to register the constant impulse to fidget for what it was, but it should have been obvious.

Kade. He was restless. The need to move, to do something other than sit there, was causing him to twitch.

Liam couldn't work like this. He set down his book and pushed back from the table. The motion made Kade look up, a desperate hope in his eyes.

"Should we go practice?"

Kade sagged with relief. "Thank fucking god. Yes, please. Is it too much to ask for an occasional sex ritual to be thrown in with this dry educational stuff?"

"You only want to read books with sex rituals in them?"

"Is that an option?"

"No."

"Worth a try. I guess it's foolish to hope for an ancient grimoire to have high heat."

"High heat?"

Kade clamped his mouth shut, his eyes darting around before he said, "So, where's this workroom?"

Okay, then. That wasn't suspicious at all.

Liam grabbed his bag and led Kade to the workroom. It was the same size as Elijah's apartment, with a respectable amount of floor space to draw circles and two large storerooms at the far end full of supplies for any spell or ritual they might do.

But they wouldn't be needing that. No, they'd be starting much smaller.

He grabbed an armful of pillar candles, then lined them up on the floor as Kade watched him from the side.

When Liam was finished, he sat halfway across the room from the candles.

"Come sit by me," he said, and Kade did as told.

"Your affinity is fire?"

"Yes, with air as secondary, which makes me fantastic at blowing things up."

"So Elijah wasn't joking about you using the magic before it exploded?"

"Yeah, he meant that very literally."

"Remind me not to get on your bad side."

Liam huffed. "I don't make exploding things a habit."

"What do you specialize in?"

"Honestly? Nothing. Mages who have fire affinities are frequently battle mage types. Many work in magical law enforcement, but I'm not interested in that. Elijah's earth and fire, so he's amazing with barriers and wards, protections and things that are grounded and binding. Aran's water and earth, so that makes him ideal for Druidic magic, especially anything with plants. Miles is air and water and the best healer you'll ever find. But my particular flavor of magic doesn't lend itself to those skills. I'm excellent if you need to stay warm. Lighting fires, lighting candles. Bit ironic, considering how much I love books. But that's all I've got."

He'd never been fond of his affinities. There wasn't anything wrong with them, and there weren't others he'd rather have instead; he just didn't see much use in blowing things up.

"And creating spells," Kade said.

"What?"

"Exploding things *and* making spells. Or sigils, or whatever."

"Yes, but only creating and modifying them. I'm not great at doing them. When we were apprentices, Elijah and I would brainstorm together. I'd create the spells, but he was the one who could do them. We made a good team. I'd figure out the theory, and he'd handle the practical stuff. He has the impressive repertoire of spells he can use."

Ever since Liam had begun using magic, the spark of inspiration to create something new had been intuitive to him. It required knowing how pieces needed to fit together and balance each other out, but he couldn't always do the spells he created.

"And research," Kade added.

"Anyone can do research."

Kade leveled a disbelieving look at him. "I was five seconds away from smothering myself with a two-hundred-year-old book."

"I didn't say everyone would enjoy it."

Kade snorted. "And reading in multiple languages."

"Of course. That's a given. How else would I research properly?"

"Sure. You're only good at explosions. We'll ignore the creating spells, researching, and speaking, what? A dozen languages?"

"Ten," Liam grumbled. "And most of them are magical or dead, so I can't actually *speak* them."

"I guess if it's only ten..."

"All the other guys know at least two."

"Two, ten. Very similar numbers, what with them starting with T and having three letters."

"How did you know I spoke another language?"

"The third book you were reading. It was written in... runes?"

He hadn't realized Kade had been paying attention. "Ancient Germanic."

"Ah, yeah. Who isn't fluent in that by the end of grade school?"

"Fine. I don't just blow things up. Happy?"

"Extremely. Now I want to see you blow some shit up. Also, I should get bonus points for not making the obvious joke when you said you're excellent at warming people up."

Liam grinned and shook his head, then focused on the candles.

"I'm going to try to use my magic without drawing on your energy. That way, I can get a feel for the new baseline level of power at my disposal."

Taking a breath, Liam accessed his magic, attempting to keep the amount he channeled to a minimum.

He zeroed in on the center candle and snapped his fingers... then flinched back, cursing, as a massive fireball billowed over the candles. The entire row was alight, though the middle few had been half-melted from the heat.

"I... I was kidding about you exploding things," Kade said, staring at the candles.

"I wasn't, but I didn't think it'd be that big."

"That's what he said."

Liam did not laugh at that. Not even a little. That wasn't his brand of humor. "Once I've had some practice, I'll be able to handle it better."

Kade leered at him, and Liam rolled his eyes. Yeah, he'd heard it.

"Is this the whole metaphorical shifter dick thing you were talking about yesterday?"

Liam groaned. "I knew I'd regret telling you that. But essentially, yes. Your big metaphorical shifter dick has stretched my channels wide open, and I have to adjust to its girth before we use it for anything fun. And if you tell any of the guys I said that, your metaphorical dick will be the only one you have."

"Understood." Kade failed spectacularly at the somber tone he was attempting.

It took three more tries until Liam could light a single candle without producing a fireball.

Kade clapped.

"Okay," Liam said. "Now the difficult part. Let's see what happens when I—"

"Take my massive meta—"

"*Energy.*"

Kade snickered, and Liam's lips twitched with something that was not a smile.

"One of the first exercises mages learn to do is meditate with our magic. We hold it and get the feel of it, try to notice everything we can about it, be as aware of it as we can be. So I'll attempt to channel a thread of your energy and meditate with it."

"Did Victor and Elijah need to do that?"

"No. Like Elijah mentioned this morning, he had a month's worth of problems with his magic because of Victor's energy. After all that, it's easy for him, but I've been thrown into the deep end, haven't used shifter energy for over a year, and have never been great at the practical use of magic. Don't get me wrong, I will outperform Elijah on any theoretical test you give us, and I'll run circles around him when it comes to creating spells. But it's going to be harder for me to get used to your energy. That said, it won't take me a month as long as we're practicing."

"Fair enough. Whatever you need."

Liam held out his hand, and Kade took it. The connections between them opened wider, and Liam sucked in a breath, his eyes sliding shut.

Fuck, that was good.

Kade's energy flooded into him, a rush of endorphins like nothing he'd experienced before. The few occasions he'd used shifter energy as an apprentice, it had been with older shifters—low in the pack hierarchy, low in energy. It'd taken work to connect to them. But this? This was *easy*.

This was being filled impossibly full as energy coursed through his body. He wasn't actively using it yet, just letting the intoxicating rush sweep through him. He shifted his weight where he sat, his clothes rubbing against his skin—too harsh and restrictive, his pants too tight.

When was the last time he'd been this turned on by magic? It wasn't uncommon for mages to get aroused when channeling, especially when they first experimented with large amounts of magic and powerful spells. They eventually got used to it.

He wasn't used to this. He let out a shaky exhale, more of a sigh than anything.

Kade's presence was a bright fire, blazing lust in an endless feedback loop, want and need spiraling deeper and deeper inside Liam.

He felt pulled toward Kade, their bond demanding he get closer.

A low rumble built in Kade's chest, and it tempted Liam to crawl into his lap, to press against him, to feel that sound vibrate into his body.

Liam's eyes drifted open, and he found Kade staring at

him, his wolf making itself known in an amber flash. He looked ready to spring forward and pin Liam down, like Liam was his prey. If the energy and magic zinging through his system hadn't gotten Liam hard, that gaze would have.

Kade growled, leaning closer. He inhaled deeply, his eyelids hooded, his teeth showing in a predatory approximation of a smile.

Their lust entwined, and Liam shivered, fixating on Kade's mouth. They hadn't kissed in the forest. There'd been nothing intimate about what they'd done. It figured he'd somehow gotten bonded without kissing the guy first. That was not the proper order of operations. They should rectify that.

Liam wet his lips, and Kade's eyes tracked the motion. His expression was ravenous enough that it made Liam want to lay himself out like a feast to be devoured.

Kade moved closer still. Greedy hands pulled Liam in. Kade's breath was hot against his skin as he brought his nose to his neck, another pleased rumble thrumming through him.

In Liam's pocket, his phone buzzed multiple times in rapid succession.

He jerked away from Kade. The sudden loss of all that energy hit him like a punch. Winded, he dug for his phone, refusing to look at Kade.

There were four messages from Aran.

ARAN

RASHES.

UGH.

EVEN MY DAMN BALLS ITCH.

I take it back. Getting knotted would be so much better than this.

Liam's cheeks burned, and he angled the phone so Kade couldn't see the screen.

He got up and adjusted himself. Out of the corner of his eye, he saw Kade do the same.

"What is it this time?" Kade's voice was rough, stroking along Liam's spine.

Liam cleared his throat as he walked over to his bag. "Rashes."

"That lust spirit keeps getting more appealing."

"Aran said the same thing." Liam got to work making the sigil. The prickly lines and pieces fell into place as he flipped through the codex. He then took a picture of the sketch and sent it.

LIAM

Has the rash gone away?

Should I pick up some ointment for you?

Let me know!

He took longer than necessary to close his book and notebook, but he needed to collect himself.

"Okay." He sat next to Kade again. "Touching is a bad idea. At least for the time being."

"It doesn't feel like a bad idea, but yeah. I regret that we can't take advantage of this. Does magic always affect you like that? How do you ever get any work done?"

"To a much lesser extent, yes. Your first advanced spells can be *really* embarrassing, but you get used to it, and we'll get used to this. Also, concentration is required for magic. When doing spells and rituals, we have to focus on the task at hand. That keeps us from thinking about—"

"Other things that could be at hand?"

"Yeah. That."

Liam channeled a tiny thread of his magic and summoned a ball of fire. He held it, staring into the flame, trying to sense his magic and decide what to do next.

"Isn't that hot? When Elijah does it, it's more like a ball of light, but you're holding fire. Actual fire. How are you not getting burned?"

"Oh, no. I can't get burned by my own fire. Unless something goes seriously sideways. And my fire affinity helps protect me from fire in general. It redirects the heat around me."

"That explains your resistance to my hotness."

Liam scoffed, then paused. "Wait. Technically, you have some of my magic in you. There's an exchange, even if you can't use it like a mage would. I wonder..."

He held out the flame to Kade.

Kade stared at him, incredulous, but Liam kept his hand there, waiting for him.

After another suspicious look, Kade tentatively reached out until his fingers brushed the flame. His eyes widened, and he ran his hand through it.

"It's... it's warm, but it's not painful."

Liam had to smile at Kade's shell-shocked reaction. He tilted his hand, dumping the flame into Kade's. Kade blinked at it, stunned. It dimmed, but stayed alight.

Now that surprised Liam. He'd assumed it'd extinguish after a second or two, that Kade wouldn't have enough magic in his system to sustain it, but traces of Liam's magic plus Kade's energy seemed to be sufficient.

An idea popped into his head, and he was too curious

not to give it a try. He centered himself, then pushed his magic into Kade through their connection, reversing the tether. The flame flared before it stabilized.

Kade looked up at him, a hint of orange coloring his irises. "Did you just feed me some of your metaphorical mage dick?"

Liam couldn't stop himself from snickering. "Maybe just the tip."

"Fuck, if that's how the tip feels..." Kade bounced the flame in his hand, testing the weight of it, though it had no true mass. "Here. Catch."

He lobbed the ball of fire at Liam.

"Jesus fucking Christ. DON'T THROW FIRE." Liam scrambled, but managed to catch it, the tiniest wisp of a flame clinging to his fingertips. It latched on to his magic and grew until it returned to its original size.

A grin spread across Liam's face. "I have an idea."

He didn't need to say anything else; Kade was already scooting a few arms' lengths away.

Liam considered how to do this. "Okay, I think if I keep feeding you my magic, this will work."

"Bring it on. Give me more of that mage dick of yours."

This was what he got for bringing up Aran's ridiculous theory.

He carefully fed magic through the tether. Kade pressed his eyes shut, his head tilting from side to side, a hum escaping his lips. "That's... that's such a strange sensation. Like your magic is filling me up. I want..." He swallowed. "Can you give me more?"

It would have been impossible not to. Liam pushed more magic into him and got a breathy groan as a reward.

"Damn." Kade shifted his weight like he couldn't help himself. "That's... that's so good. Kind of tingling from the inside out. Is this how you feel when you're using my energy? Fuck me. I've taken massive dicks that haven't filled me this full."

And that was not a mental image Liam needed when he wasn't allowed to get himself off for three weeks.

Kade shook himself. "As much as I regret saying this, if we want to accomplish anything other than me coming in my pants, let's stick to just the tip."

Liam eased back the magic he was transferring, and Kade cracked his neck. He could not have been comfortable with the way he was straining his jeans. Liam's dick gave a throb of sympathy.

"Okay, that's definitely something I'll have to remember for the future," Kade said, giving Liam a rueful look. "So, any and all practicing with magic is going to be a constant state of blue balls, isn't it?"

"Seems like it."

"Fun times. Let's go. Throw that fire at me."

Liam had practically forgotten the ball of fire he was holding. To do this, he'd need to keep channeling a stream of magic into Kade while maintaining the fireball until Kade caught it. Then his magic in Kade's system should sustain it. It'd take concentration, but he could do that—theoretically.

He tossed the fireball gently toward Kade. It fizzled out halfway there.

Liam readjusted his magic, then tried again. The ball got farther, but still didn't make it.

"Shouldn't you be using more of my energy? I can't sense you pulling on it."

Kade was right; Liam was avoiding it.

Relaxing, he let Kade's energy fill him. It was so

distracting that it made it challenging to continue feeding magic to Kade, to balance the flow.

There was a give and take. A little of his magic in exchange for a little of Kade's energy. It took some tweaking, but then it clicked. Their connections balanced out— energy flowing into him, magic flowing into Kade. The same way it did when they were touching, but not as overwhelming.

He stared at Kade, seeing his own wonder reflected back.

"Are we... did we achieve simultaneous metaphorical dick penetration? A metaphysical sixty-nine?" Kade asked.

"I... I think we did?"

And fuck, did it feel good. But he could handle this. He got too much energy when they touched, but this small, tempered exchange was more controlled. Larger spells were still out of the question, but this gave him something to practice with, and it might help him learn how to control the connection between them better. He could build up a tolerance to using Kade's energy.

He lobbed a fireball at Kade. It dimmed halfway between them, and Liam's breath hitched. The seconds stretched out, but when Kade caught the ball, it rekindled to a steady flame.

Kade grinned at it, then looked at Liam, raising one eyebrow in question. Liam nodded, and Kade threw the fireball back.

It wasn't always smooth; sometimes it almost went out as they passed it, but with each throw, it became easier, the fire feeding off Liam's magic, then Kade's energy in turns.

Liam's phone chimed, and the balanced connection between them teetered, the flame guttering out. But they'd kept it up for a full ten minutes without either of them trying to screw each other or Liam losing control of his magic. That was one hell of an improvement.

Liam opened the group chat.

ELIJAH

Allergies. The hay fever, sneezing kind, not the throat closing up food allergy kind, if that matters.

Liam flipped through the codex, debating whether it mattered. Were all allergies allergies, or were there different kinds? While he pondered that, he sent a message of his own.

LIAM

Have you ever given some of your magic to Victor?

ELIJAH

There's a natural transfer anytime I use Victor's energy.

The bond and tether seem to balance out, and he ends up with some of my magic.

LIAM

How about intentionally?

ELIJAH

Oh, yeah. If you want a real wild time, transfer magic into him with your fingers as you're stretching him open.

LIAM

What?

No.

There is no stretching happening.

There will be no stretching happening.

ARAN

Excuse me? I came to ask for a sigil for headaches, but instead, what's this? I'd like more information. What exactly are you stretching?

LIAM

THERE IS NO STRETCHING HAPPENING!

He should have sent that message privately, not in the group chat.

ARAN

It sounds like there should be.

LIAM

I meant through the tether, Elijah.

Reversing the connection and feeding him your magic.

ELIJAH

Ooh. I'd never thought of that. We'll give it a try.

LIAM

Uh.

Wait until tonight.

In your bedroom.

ARAN

I definitely need more details now. Why am I just hearing about this?

MILES

I did NOT need to know any of that.

Sigil for air pollution, please.

And one that will make me forget what I just read.

Liam made the three sigils and sent them over.

LIAM

Here you go.

Be careful when you're catching them!

I don't want any of you hurt.

ARAN

Always, Li-mom. You enjoy that stretching!
And tell us the details later!

MILES

Or don't.

LIAM

Yeah, don't is good.

He turned to find Kade watching him.

"Allergies, headaches, and air pollution."

"And which of those three was making you blush?"

"Uh. Shall we try again?"

Kade shot him a knowing look but dropped the subject, scooting another arm's length away. "Let's do this."

They practiced for the better part of an hour, working their way farther apart, occasionally stopping so Liam could make a sigil.

Liam found Kade remarkably easy to talk to, even with the dick jokes and offhanded flirting.

"You and Elijah are close?" Kade asked, tossing the fireball.

Liam caught it, then threw it back. "He's basically my brother. I've got a younger brother and two younger sisters, too, but they're much younger. Elijah and I have been pretty inseparable since we met."

"Must have been weird moving so far from him then."

"Yeah. During our apprenticeship, we lived together. I

still have moments when I want to tell him something and then remember I have to do it via message instead of yelling at him from the other room. So as shitty as these circumstances are, I'm glad I get to see him.

"I'd assumed someday Elijah would move out to the East Coast too. To a bigger city there, since that's where the highest concentration of magic shops are located. Clearly that's not happening now, but I'm glad he's so content out here, even if it does mean he won't be moving near me."

"You could move out here."

"That's never happening."

Kade nearly missed the fireball, but snagged it on his fingertips. "Why not?"

"I've got the archive to get up and running, and then there's my research on magical history. Neither of those are things I can do out here. But what about you? Elijah told me you and Victor are close? I believe he said you're four years older than Victor?"

"Five," Kade corrected quickly. "And yes. He's also like a brother to me. Though a younger, 'pain in my ass because he's so stupid sometimes' brother."

"So... a brother? Aren't they supposed to be pains in the ass, whether they're blood or otherwise?"

"Fair point. It is in the job description."

"That it is." Liam caught the fireball and let it extinguish, then reluctantly released Kade's energy, trembling as it left his body.

He took a second to assess himself. He was mildly turned on, but not in danger of ripping Kade's clothes off. His magic felt stable. Kade's presence in his mind was still distant and unreadable. Not bad for their first practice session.

"Okay. It's been over an hour. We should get back to researching."

Kade groaned. "I was afraid you'd say that." But he dutifully trailed after Liam up the stairs to the apartment.

Lady was already there, perched on the books, waiting for them. She hadn't been inside when they'd left. It was creepy how she did that.

Liam had to assume she'd chosen the pile of books for his personal research as her throne out of spite, plotting to shed as much fur on them as possible.

She glared at them as they took their seats at the kitchen table, but before they could start reading, Liam's phone rang. He pulled it out and cursed when he read the name on the screen.

"You alright there?" Kade asked.

"It's my mom."

"Oh, you should get that. Guess we'll have to take a break."

Liam shook his head, but he was grinning. "Fine. Just don't make any noise."

He went over to sit on the bed, his back against the wall so there was zero chance of Kade wandering into the frame, then answered the video call.

"Hey, Mom."

"Hello." She peered around.

"They aren't here," Liam said before she could ask.

"Aw, I was hoping to catch all four of my adult boys at once. Where is everyone?"

"They're out, but I wanted to get some reading done, so I'm staying here."

Across the room, Kade cocked an eyebrow, but Liam ignored him. He'd explain later. There was no way in hell he was telling his mom what was actually happening. She'd fly out there and try to defeat the spirits single-handedly for daring to mess with her boys.

"And have you met Elijah's shifter yet?"

"We have. Victor seems very nice."

Bridget poked her head into view. "Hey, Liam!" She waved as she walked past. But then she froze. Slowly, she turned to squint at the screen. She leaned in, getting closer, her eyes wide. "What's that on your neck?"

Liam's hand flew up, his stomach sinking as he realized the bite mark was peeking out over the collar of his sweater.

His gaze locked with Kade's, panic echoing in equal measures through their bond.

Oh fuck. He hadn't checked if it was showing before he answered.

"Wait. It's not what it looks like. I can explain."

She shrieked. "OH MY GOD. ARE YOU BONDED TO A HOT ALPHA SHIFTER TOO? DO YOU HAVE A TRUE BOND LIKE ELIJAH?"

His mom pulled the phone out of Bridget's grasp. He had no idea how her expression managed to be shocked, hopeful, worried, and demanding answers all at once.

"Liam?" The threat of his middle name loomed in the air.

Liam winced. "I can explain. It's temporary for a project we're doing. Nothing to worry about. It's just until the new moon."

His mom frowned. "Was that really necessary?"

"OH MY GOD! Do you have an arranged bond? No, no! Those are the BEST BONDS. Listen! He secretly loves you and yearns for you because YOU ARE HIS FATED MATE, but he doesn't know how to—"

His mom covered Bridget's mouth with her hand.

He risked a glance at Kade, only to find him frozen in place, eyebrows at his hairline.

"Who is this shifter?" his mom demanded. "I want to meet him."

"It's temporary, Mom. You don't need to do that."

"I will be the judge of who I do and don't need to meet. And if you're bonded to a shifter, temporarily or not, I need to meet him."

"Aaahh..." Liam looked at Kade, who shrugged. "Okay. Hold on."

He muted the video call. "If you say anything inappropriate, so help me, I will make a fur hat out of you."

Kade walked over and sat next to him. "Your sister, or whoever that was, might be more of a threat as far as saying inappropriate things."

Liam couldn't argue with him on that. He unmuted the call and held the phone to include Kade in the shot. "This is—"

"OH MY GOD, HE IS SO HO—" His mom's hand cut off the rest of Bridget's sentence, but she still managed to mumble, "He's kinda old though."

"Kade," Liam finished. "He's Victor's second."

"Nice to meet you, ma'am," Kade said.

His mom was having none of it. "And what are your intentions with my son?"

"Ah..." Kade's gaze darted to Liam. "Liam is helping our pack, and he, uh, needed access to my energy. So we're bonded, but just for a few weeks."

Well, that wasn't a lie. Liam had to give him credit for that. He didn't like lying to his mother. Not telling her everything, sure, but he always tried to avoid flat-out lying.

"Wait." Bridget knocked away their mom's hand. "That

means you and my brother had... EW. GROSS. I don't wanna think about my brother doing *that.*"

Liam was too distracted by the supremely unhappy expression on his mother's face to respond.

"So. Kade." Oh god. She didn't even know Kade's middle name, and it still hung like a threat over them. "You're the type to do a transactional bond for the sake of power? Do bonds mean nothing to you?"

Liam opened his mouth to defend Kade somehow. Before he could get a word out, Kade was speaking.

"A true bond is a fate one such as myself can only dare to aspire to. For as the moon casts its silvery glow upon tranquil waters, so does a true bond cast its luminous radiance upon the lives of those blessed enough to bathe in its glorious effulgence."

...What?

Both his mother and sister sat up straighter. They traded a look, a truly disturbing amount of agreement passing between them, then leaned in, staring at Kade with a rabid glint in their eyes.

"I have heard it told a true bond is the music of the soul," his mom intoned.

Kade nodded gravely. "It is a symphony resonating in harmonious accord, where the strings of affection are plucked by the masterful hands of fate itself, a delicate melody of emotions, the ethereal cadence of two souls perfectly entwined."

Liam looked between the phone and Kade. His mother and sister were almost clinging to each other, their expressions growing more manic.

"Such a wondrous joining of the souls shall surely spring forth effortlessly," his mother said.

What the hell were they talking about?

Kade shook his head. "A rose does not bloom overnight. Its roots must delve deep into the soil of trust, drawing sustenance from the wellspring of understanding. Like the petals of a rare and exquisite flower unfurling to the kiss of the sun, a true bond blossoms under the nurturing light of genuine affection."

"A rose may hold fast to its thorns, guarding its fragrant heart."

"But a careful hand may navigate those defenses, discovering the tenderness within, embracing both barriers and blossoms." Kade responded without hesitation, the words a long-winded shibboleth that had his mother and sister nodding approvingly, though they left Liam even more confused.

His mother let out a relieved sigh. "I'm so glad Liam is bonded to someone with such good taste."

"Temporarily," Liam said. "*Temporarily* bonded to."

No one was listening to him.

"I'm looking forward to meeting you when we visit, Kade. We were planning sometime after the holidays, but I think we're going to have to make it sooner. Or, could you make it out here? I know it'll be difficult for Elijah to get his Victor away from your pack, but we'd love to have you for the weekend. We'll pay for your travel, dear."

What was happening? Why was his mother talking to Kade as if he were family?

"DAD," Bridget yelled, "ANDREA, FINLEY. LIAM GOT MATED TO A SHIFTER TOO. COME MEET HIM. HE'S TOTALLY HOT BUT KINDA OLD. LIKE, THIRTY OR SOME-THING GROSS."

Liam pinched the bridge of his nose.

That caused as much chaos as he'd been afraid it would.

His other two siblings spilled into the room, followed by his father.

Liam introduced them to Kade. "It's temporary," he stressed.

"That's what you said when you rescued Alexandria. It was 'temporary' until we found her owner, but somehow that 'temporary' lasted ten years. And now you've got yourself a wolf."

Kade leaned in and, under his breath, asked, "Did she just compare me to a stray dog or something?"

"Yep." Why was this his life? Why was his family like this? Was this his punishment for teasing Elijah?

At least the rest of his family weren't as bad as his mom and Bridget. His brother seemed unimpressed, but that was the age he was at. His father was as calm as ever, and his youngest sister mainly seemed bewildered. She cocked her head.

"Does this mean you're a wolf shifter now? That's how werewolves happen in movies. They bite people."

"No," Bridget said. "This isn't that kind of biting. When they bond, they have to—"

His mother's hand was over her mouth again, and not a moment too soon. Bridget glared, disgruntled, and Liam knew Andrea would be getting an earful the next time they were alone. He just hoped he didn't end up with *three* people in his family obsessed with romance novels.

"Ah," Kade said, a hint of nerves in his tone. "That's a different bite. Alphas have to do it while intending to turn the person into a shifter. It requires a lot of the alpha's energy and is not a pleasant experience for anyone involved, so it's rarely done anymore. And it doesn't work on mages because of your magic. Only humans."

Liam's phone flashed with a message from Elijah.

"Sorry, guys. Elijah's trying to get a hold of me. We need to go."

He wasn't remotely sorry.

"Okay," his mother said. "But next time, I expect to see all of you. Elijah's Victor, too. And, Kade, I hope to meet you in person soon."

"You too, Mrs. Batiste."

"Mom," she corrected.

"OKAY, MOM, GOTTA GO BYE." Liam ended the call and slumped back, covering his face with a hand. "I'm so sorry."

Kade laughed. "They seem sweet. Should I call my parents so we can see how that goes?"

"Oh god. Was that not enough for you? Are you trying to kill me?" Liam paused. "Hold on. Your parents? Aren't they in the pack?"

He felt like an ass for not asking sooner, but he supposed if they had been in the pack, he would have met them last night.

"Ah. No. My mother's originally from the East Coast. They rejoined her pack a few years ago. Victor's father and mine are brothers, but they never got along. So when Victor's father started getting power hungry, my parents decided it'd be better to be elsewhere. But I couldn't leave Victor to face that shit alone, so I stayed behind."

"Where on the East Coast?"

"Near Boston."

"That's close to the library."

Kade stood. "If I'm ever out there visiting them, you'll have to show me around."

"Sure," Liam said offhandedly, but there was a more pressing issue to discuss. "Why did you suddenly sound like some overwritten romance novel?"

Kade froze, then gave him a cheeky grin. "You caught me. I'm the shifter version of Fabio. You can see my hair blowing in the wind, my ripped shirt displaying my rippling abs, on dozens of manchest covers."

"Man... chest... covers?"

Kade glanced around, his eyes landing on the piles of books on the table. He groaned. "You know, the thing none of your books have. Thank your family for me. They momentarily made me forget the mind-numbing research that's in my future."

"Would it help if the grimoires had... manchests on them?"

"It'd give me something pretty to look at."

Liam wasn't sure how to respond, so he said, "Let's get back to it."

He checked Elijah's message and sent him a sigil for jealousy, then settled in at the table.

They got through a few more books before Kade cheerfully volunteered to grab lunch.

As soon as he was gone, Liam pulled out his phone.

LIAM

Aran, I need your help.

He then outlined what he wanted Aran to do that evening, and if he snickered while he was typing it up, well, no one was there to hear him.

Except Lady, who would judge him either way.

Five minutes later, Aran replied with a string of laughing emojis.

ARAN

ON IT. Oh, man. Bonded Liam is FUN Liam.
You never would have thought of this
before.

MILES

We're stopping for lunch, and Aran is rubbing his hands together with glee.

Liam, you've unleashed a monster.

LIAM

I refuse to admit I'm excited to see the chaos he's about to cause.

He was still chuckling to himself when Kade returned with their food. Kade narrowed his eyes in suspicion, but he'd have to wait until tomorrow to find out.

"Let's eat so we can do more research."

Kade groaned. "Oh, *awesome*."

They made it through a little less than a suitcase of books before it was time to head back to the pack house for dinner. That was two suitcases down with no answers. Liam tucked a few books into his bag but left the rest. Kade did seem more relaxed with them alone, and the workroom was perfect for practicing.

Hopefully they'd have better luck tomorrow, but even if it didn't pan out, he still had something to look forward to.

CHAPTER
NINE

Liam wasn't in bed when Kade woke. Probably a good thing. Kade would rather not have a repeat of yesterday. He didn't have the self-control necessary to routinely deny himself. Too many mornings like that, and he'd do something he wouldn't regret nearly as much as he should.

The quiet noises of a morning routine drifted from the bathroom. In Kade's head, Liam was a fuzzy presence, a shimmering lightness that floated like a feather on the breeze. Kade lay in bed, feeling almost weightless from the sensation, and realized Liam was amused. Something had him downright giddy.

Being able to identify a new emotion signaled their bond was deepening. That should have worried him, but he couldn't bring himself to care, not when mirth threaded between them, tickling his mind.

This had to be the end of it though. They couldn't let it get deeper than this.

Kade rolled out of bed and stretched. That had been the

best night's sleep he'd had in ages. He grabbed clothes for the day as he waited for Liam.

When Liam emerged, there was a devilish gleam in his eyes, though he tried to hide it with a bright smile.

Yeah, right. Kade wasn't buying it, but Liam could keep his secrets, even if he was terrible at feigning innocence.

Kade slipped into the bathroom and got ready for what promised to be another long day of research, then stared at himself in the mirror.

"You don't need to scent him. He isn't yours to scent."

His wolf huffed. It didn't care what the human side of Kade thought, but that was the bond talking. It was natural for his wolf to feel possessive over whoever they were bonded to. Liam was theirs as far as it was concerned, and they should act accordingly.

But his intentions to behave shattered when he stepped back into the room and Liam turned toward him, holding his arms out away from his sides.

"Do you need to do the scent thing?"

Before Kade could process his actions, he'd closed the distance between them, crowding into Liam's personal space. His hands stroked over Liam's neck and his arms. Magic moved under his touch, drawn like a tide to the moon, tingling against Kade's palms.

Liam's eyelids slid shut, his lower lip caught between his teeth. He inhaled, his chest swelling with the extent of his breath, looking for all the world like he was enjoying this as much as Kade's wolf was.

Damn, he was gorgeous. His strong jaw and those high cheekbones, the dark sweep of his eyelashes and the warm brown of his skin.

Kade's hands had stopped moving, resting on Liam's

shoulders, but he didn't notice until Liam opened his eyes, his gaze hooded.

"Finished?" he asked, his voice rough with arousal that blazed in Kade's mind.

Kade hadn't even begun. There were so many ways he could cover Liam with his scent, and this was far from the most enjoyable. But he took a step back, the movement knocking Liam out of the daze he'd fallen into.

Emotions played across his face and through their bond, though Kade never could have read the latter without the former—sheepish embarrassment, a sudden realization, and then the return of that curious amusement.

"We should grab breakfast so we can get going!" Liam spun on his heel and bounded out the door, a spring in his step as he descended the stairs.

Kade trailed after him, bemused.

It wasn't much past six, and most of the pack was asleep, with the two notable exceptions of Victor and Elijah. Victor had always been a late riser, but Elijah's early-bird tendencies had rubbed off on him. That didn't mean they were normally out of their room quite yet, though. They had other things to rub off on each other first.

When Elijah saw them, mischief lit up his expression too. The mages had to be up to something, but Kade had no idea what. He shot Victor a glance, but if Victor knew, he was keeping a straight face.

How did Elijah feel in Victor's head? Was he shimmering like Liam was? How much stronger could Victor sense it?

Liam ate so fast that Kade wasn't sure he breathed between bites. He should slow down. Using magic took a lot out of a mage. If they practiced, he would need to keep up his strength. But it was hard to insist he eat properly when Liam was practically bundling him up and carrying him out of the house. Elijah's laughter sounded as Liam herded Kade to his car.

The drive to the shop went quicker than the day before, like Liam's anticipation had a magic of its own, making the road fly by under the tires.

They passed Aran and Miles driving in the opposite direction out to the pack land. Kade honked in greeting and caught a glimpse of Aran cackling as they sped past. Liam's presence grew brighter.

The moment they were inside the apartment, Kade discovered why. His eyes landed on the books, and he laughed. Liam's amusement echoed back, dazzling and effervescent as Kade approached the table. Liam's entire body was shaking with barely contained snickers.

In the last fifteen hours, someone had turned a dozen of Richard Knotz's most famous porn posters into makeshift book covers, printing them out and folding them around the tomes. They'd included a few of his bonding series: *Bonding the Incubus, Bonding the Fox Shifter,* and *Bonding the Coyote Shifter. Bonding the Human*—the first of many scenes Richard had filmed with his mate, Hunter Savage—had been given a place of honor in front of Kade's chair. The rest were more of their scenes, including *Hunting Down Hunter,* the brand new *My Naughty Roommate Switched Places with My Sex Toy and I Didn't Notice until I Was Knot Deep!,* and the classic *A Mage Summoned My Knot and then Fell on It!*

It was *glorious.* Liam had arranged this for him?

"Is *this* what you were giggling over yesterday afternoon?"

"After you mentioned the manchest covers, I had to. Aran agreed to help. I have no clue where he got these though. I told him romance novels, but apparently this is his idea of romance."

"Hey, there's romance here. Have you seen this?" Kade held up *Bonding the Human*. "These two ended up staying together after their initial contract. It's actually really sweet, and their videos are scorchingly hot. They even have one where Hunter pretends to be a mage." Kade pointed to the knot-summoning scene.

Liam squinted at the cover. On it, Richard Knotz was laid out on his back, his mate riding him. "Are his tattoos magical sperm?"

"Yep."

"Well, if that's not romance right there, I don't know what is."

"You've never performed a ritual to summon a shifter's knot?" He should get bonus points for not adding, 'Would you care to dance around almost naked, then slip and fall and land ass-first on mine?'

Liam side-eyed Kade like he'd heard that unspoken question. "Let's get to work."

"Any chance there's a spell to make the contents of these books as interesting as their new covers?"

When Liam didn't bother answering, Kade sat and opened *A Mage Summoned My Knot*, then blinked. This was not one of Liam's books.

Liam looked up and raised an eyebrow, registering Kade's surprise and reacting to it like it was the most natural thing in the world.

Kade pulled off the paper cover and held it up for Liam to see, its actual title proclaiming it to be *Sex Magic and Rituals*.

Liam groaned. "That was all Aran."

"Does that mean I don't get to read it? Because it seems

more fun than everything else I've read so far."

"Sorry. We absolutely will not be needing that."

That was a shame. With a sigh, Kade placed it on the discard pile and grabbed another book, but in his mind, an idea took root. Other people could set up surprises too, and researching wasn't nearly as boring when Kade got to reward himself by brainstorming his plans between books.

When it came time for him to grab lunch, he might have stopped to put in an order that had nothing to do with food. He wasn't even bothered by paying the extra forty dollars for overnight shipping.

It provided a distraction from his wolf's smugness over bringing Liam food, providing for their mate. Kade blamed the upcoming full moon, but knowing that didn't make his instincts easier to ignore.

Being alone with Liam in the apartment helped soothe his wolf. This wasn't what it wanted; this wasn't how they were supposed to spend their first few days with their mate. But if this was all it'd get, it'd take it. If they couldn't fuck their mate until he was so boneless he couldn't walk— for whatever stupid reason Kade was claiming—they could have him to themselves. There was no one around who might get too close to him, who might touch him.

With his plans already in motion, Kade grew restless again after lunch. Every book was another dead end. They should have been tracking and trapping spirits, not sitting there, wasting time. At least Liam was in contact with his friends, pausing occasionally to make a sigil or two. He had something useful to do; Kade could only methodically flip through books that needed goddamn indexes.

Liam took mercy on him an hour later, closing his book and asking, "Practice?"

"Yes, please." Kade didn't add, 'for the rest of the day.'

Liam would never go for that. He followed Liam to the workroom.

Liam's magic pushing into him was such a strange sensation, but fuck, it felt amazing. Even if it was a gigantic tease—an hour of making out with no prospect of a climax in sight, leaving him aching for release.

Liam might not be his mate, but Kade hoped whoever he bonded would be willing to do this to him. This and so much more. He needed to get fucked while he was full of magic. It had to be beyond pleasurable.

That wasn't all he wanted, and he wasn't the only one who wanted it. He sensed Liam's desires. Magic sparked in his veins, rushing through him, exhilarating and provocative. His imagination ran wild with the idea of pinning Liam down and fucking him in the workroom.

But he was being good. It was a new thing he was trying. He couldn't say he recommended it though.

They settled into a rhythm tossing the fireball back and forth, but concentrating on that was difficult with the buzz of arousal in his system. He tried to distract himself by thinking of the least sexy things possible, and one in particular kept popping into his head.

"So, you're planning to do research in between your research?"

Liam nodded.

That sounded like pure torture to Kade, but everyone had their kinks, so he shouldn't judge. "About mage history?"

"Yeah. Even before this started, I wanted to create a comprehensive record of mage knowledge. The library itself isn't truly comprehensive. It's mainly books that have been donated, often from family lines that have died out, but it's the largest collection we have. However, you have to physically go there to read the books. Not everyone can do that, but they should still have access to that information."

"The archiving project you mentioned?"

"Yes. Our knowledge is compartmentalized, with each mage family or apprentice line specializing in something and keeping their own records."

"Wards. Our pack mages frequently excelled at wards."

That made Liam grin. "As if we needed another sign pointing to how Elijah was meant to be here."

Kade agreed. Elijah was perfect for their pack. Perfect for Victor. There was no denying that.

"Just so you know," he said, unable to help himself. "Shifters prefer oral."

Whenever Liam gave him that flat look, all it did was make Kade want to poke at him more.

"Lengthy, deep, thorough oral."

Liam stared at him blankly as he plucked the fireball out of the air and tossed it back, but there was a soft brush of amusement against Kade's mind.

"Seriously, though. Shifter history tends to be passed from one generation to another through oral storytelling, but our pack has quite a bit written down. I'm guessing thanks to our mages, because we're a total outlier."

Interest glittered in Liam's eyes. "I bet your pack mages had knowledge about wards that no one else did. That they had grimoires and books that were one of a kind, just like any other family of mages has spells only they know. That's why I wanted to archive the library. When knowledge is fragmented, when it's not shared, it's easily lost. Yes, the library has a massive amount of books, but what if something happens to it? All that information, all that learning, might be gone forever."

A thought hit Kade. "Alexandria. You named your dog after the Library of Alexandria?"

The way Liam beamed at him for making that connection felt like a victory, like a reward. "I found her right after I'd heard the horror story of the Great Library being burned to the ground. I know that's not what happened now, but at the time, my seven-year-old self was very traumatized by it, and it's stuck with me over the years. My parents are big on family trips, and around that time, they took me to the mage library. It was the coolest place I'd ever been, but I kept thinking, 'What would happen if there was a fire?' A librarian assured me they had safeguards in place, but still."

"That's the inspiration for your project?"

"More or less. Long story short, we visited there again when I was older, and I started corresponding with the head librarian. I think he was happy someone younger was interested in the minutia of how the library runs and how they preserve the books. He offered me a job after I completed my apprenticeship. I pitched archiving the library so more mages could access its information, and he helped me secure funding from the mage council for the project."

"It'll go online?"

"Yes, but it's just a start. I've always hoped to get the other mage libraries around the world to join the project after it's established. What's happening here has reaffirmed how important that is. Take finding information on these damn spirits, for example. It has to be out there. Some mage somewhere has to know what they are, but we've been so insular and fragmented for so long, finding those answers seems almost impossible. That was excusable before modern technology made the world so interconnected, but now? The current state of things is untenable."

"And that led you to research mage and shifter history?"

"No, that rabbit hole started with Elijah and Victor's situation. Like I was saying in the forest, I believe true bonds were more common than our records show, so I've been searching for references, and I'm hoping I can fill in the blanks in our shared history and make it available via the archive."

"But you said the books from that time are missing pages."

"They are, so I've had to get creative. Even if the direct references to true bonds were removed, there must be some remaining traces, right? Like that warning about compatible couples and sex rituals. I've found a few other hints too. Nothing direct, but inferences can be made."

"You think there's more in older texts?"

"Older texts or things derived from older sources."

Kade frowned. "What do you mean?"

"Specifically? I'm looking into mythology."

"*Oh.*"

Liam pointed to his head. "I *felt* that. You lit up in my mind. Light-bulb moment?"

Kade nodded.

"Tell me. What did you come up with?"

"Shifters and myths. There are a bunch of legends that likely came from humans stumbling across something they shouldn't, or hearing about it and not understanding it, and then incorporating it into their belief system. Like Romulus and Remus might have been inspired by some human seeing pre-shifting age kids playing with their pack. Or some horny swan shifter got caught boning someone's wife, and suddenly he's a god because, obviously, what else would explain it?"

"Exactly! It's the same for us. I'm under the impression

that mages, shifters, and other supernatural creatures weren't as careful in those days. They didn't have to be. So many things weren't explained, and there were no photographs or videos."

"We've definitely had to become more careful as technology has progressed. It's harder to keep our existence secret when everyone has a camera and the internet in their pocket. You can't escape a pissed-off husband by shifting into a large bird and flying off the way you used to."

Liam snorted. "Speaking from personal experience?"

"Nah, man. My dick isn't getting anywhere near a cheater. They can fuck right off."

People had called him a fuckboy, but he did have standards.

"So," Kade continued, "there are stories about true bonds in myths?"

"Maybe? They're some of our oldest records. Plus there are a ton of powerful magic users in mythology, and quite a few of them have familiars or an association with animals of some sort. Hecate had her pack of dogs, for example."

"True bonds between shifters and mages are literally the things myths and legends are made of?"

"The one fact we know for absolute certain is that mages who are true-bonded to shifters are the strongest, and what I've seen of Elijah and Victor confirms it. I don't know the full extent of what Elijah can do with his magic now; I honestly doubt he knows, and it's just starting. To some human unaware of magic, even to the average mage, he has godlike power."

That made a hell of a lot of sense. Increased power and access to shifter energy were part of the reason transactional bonds appealed to some mages, and that new level of magic didn't begin to compare to what came from a true bond.

Kade caught the fireball and blinked. He'd completely forgotten they'd been tossing it between them.

"I... was not paying attention to throwing this the entire time we were talking. Were you?" He tossed the ball.

Liam looked surprised, then grinned as he snagged it. "I was not. Okay. I think that's a good sign. Enough messing around."

"I feel obligated to point out that we haven't messed around at all."

"*Anyway*, I should try to use your energy directly again."

"I will do my best to keep my hands to myself. Or, well, as much to myself as I can while touching you."

Shaking his head, Liam scooted forward, and Kade met him halfway.

Liam held out his hand. "At least we know what to expect, so we should be able to control ourselves."

That was easier said than done.

Once Kade's palm pressed against Liam's, once Liam channeled his energy, their bond blazed to life, hotter than the fire they'd been throwing, more alive, burning brighter. A delicious heat spiraled out from his heart, along the lines of the magical tattoos on his chest, matching the patterns lighting up on Liam's arms and the ember glow of his eyes. Awareness of Liam filled him—his racing pulse, his shuddering breaths.

No, if they wanted to talk about easy, denying this wasn't it. But covering Liam with his body, rocking against him, fucking him senseless? Now that would be easy. Effortless. What Kade was made to do.

Even without the ability to smell, Kade sensed how turned on Liam was, how arousing he found the rush of

Kade's energy, how he wanted to open himself up to it and let Kade fill him, stretch him.

Kade shivered at the thought. It had only been two days. How was he going to survive another three weeks of this?

The instinctual need to breathe in Liam's scent was too strong to deny. He inhaled. Nothing registered to him, but his wolf rumbled its pleasure.

He had to focus and get himself under control. He should also consider constantly wearing sweats around Liam, because his jeans were too tight too often when they were together.

Liam channeled the faintest trickle of energy from Kade to light the candles. There was still a fireball larger than he'd meant to create, but it wasn't massive. It lit three in the middle and didn't leave them in a puddle of wax.

That was progress.

Liam let out a shaky exhale and dropped Kade's hand, swaying slightly as the orange glow faded from his tattoos.

"As long as that's the worst of it," he said, "I'm getting the hang of it."

Kade chuckled darkly. "The full moon is coming." He already felt her call, and his energy would swell with her.

Liam froze, his eyes widening. "Well, fuck."

"Unfortunately not."

"Okay," Liam said, trying to regroup. "After that. If the guys haven't trapped all the spirits, we'll get back out there."

Kade refrained from sighing. Four days of research as his wolf grew more restless, more in need of fucking their mate.

Yeah. This was going to be fun.

They stood, adjusting themselves, and headed upstairs.

Kade stared at the table of books. "Any chance we could keep tossing the ball around as we research?"

The sheer horror that washed through him was staggering. He glanced at Liam and found his mouth hanging open, his expression one of complete betrayal.

"Ah. Never mind. No throwing fire around the priceless magical books."

Liam nodded solemnly.

Kade did sigh as they got back to their research.

They worked for several more hours, supervised by Lady's judgmental glare and chaperoning presence, before heading home with no answers to show for it and another awkward dinner to face. The previous night, the pack had been holding themselves back from commenting so hard they'd seemed ready to choke on their own tongues. When anyone neared a breaking point, Victor would clear his throat and give them a stern look, and they'd snap their mouths shut, but that didn't stop their unspoken opinions from hovering over the table, palpable and oppressive. But what did he expect? Subtlety was not a trait their pack had ever embraced. It was a miracle no one had told him how badly he'd fucked up yet, but the chances of that lasting until the new moon were nonexistent.

As they walked into the pack house, he braced himself for the sideways glances that would be served during the meal. This was not how he'd pictured spending his third night bonded, not even close.

TEN

"Okay, hear me out," Kade said as they climbed the stairs to the apartment for the third day. "Strip research."

Liam suppressed a laugh but couldn't stop himself from asking, "How would that even work?"

"Whenever we finish a book, the other person loses a piece of clothing."

"Have you not noticed how quickly I read?"

"Have you not noticed how hot I am? I look fucking fabulous naked."

"And that's supposed to help us not have sex, how?"

"Fine. You're no fun. I was hoping for *something* to get me through today." Kade collapsed into his chair and eyed the books. "Are there more than yesterday? It seems like there are more than yesterday."

Liam shook his head. There were significantly fewer, and that was worrying him. They had two days of research left at this pace, and he had no idea what he'd do when he ran out of books. If these didn't hold the answer, where did they go from here?

Kade sighed and opened a book from his pile, then froze. A warm wave of arousal washed through Liam, and Kade slammed the book shut.

"What?" Liam asked.

Kade stared at him, his eyes wide. "When I said I wanted steamier content, I didn't expect that."

Liam cocked an eyebrow. "Expect what?"

"Didn't you tell your friends to do this?"

"Do *what*?"

Kade laughed. "Joke's on both of us then. Anything interesting in that top book on your pile?"

"All books are interesting."

"Anything *I'd* find interesting?"

Liam leafed through the pages, then paused, his cheeks heating.

Tucked into the book was a screencap that had been printed out. A very, *very* explicit screencap.

He recognized the men from yesterday's covers. The shifter porn star Aran always raved about was fucking the guy from *Bonding the Human* and that weird knot-summoning scene. The human's back was arched off the bed, only his shoulders touching, his legs locked around the shifter's waist. That one frame showed how hard Richard Knotz was railing his mate, how into it they both were.

Liam's mind unhelpfully supplied him with a mental image of Kade doing the same thing to him.

Kade leaned over to look. "Oh, I love that one. Such a hot scene. I seriously thought they were about to break the bed." He opened his book again. "I got *Hunter and the Hunted Hunter*."

Before Liam could comment on that mess of a title, Kade showed him the screenshot he'd found: one of Richard

Knotz strapped to a table, his legs spread open as the human fucked him.

"They switch mid-scene in this. I came so hard I nearly blacked out the first time I watched it." He flipped through the book, finding yet another screencap, the loose white sheet standing out against pages yellowed by the passing of centuries. Cackling gleefully, he held it up for Liam. "*Cooking with DickHunt: Tossing the Salad.*"

Richard Knotz was bent over a kitchen counter, the human's face pressed into his ass.

Liam swallowed, trying to get moisture back into his mouth. "I can't believe I'm asking this, but what's DickHunt?"

"Oh, man. Meet your new favorite porn stars."

Liam didn't bother pointing out that he didn't have a favorite porn star to begin with.

"DickHunt," Kade explained. "That's the fan name for Richard Knotz and Hunter Savage. They're MateHub's first true-bonded couple. Their scenes are the hottest things you'll ever see."

Liam was confident he could think of hotter things, all involving Kade. He slapped a hand to his face. "I'm going to kill Aran."

He took out his phone and typed exactly that into the group chat.

> **ARAN**
>
> I take it you found my surprise!
>
> **MILES**
>
> I tried to stop him!

Liam glowered at the screen.

"Are you sending a message to Aran?" Kade asked,

thumbing through multiple books enough to show there were screencaps hidden in them as well, though not revealing what they were. "Thank him for me. I'm actually looking forward to researching now. This is gonna be awesome! I hope they're all DickHunt. Ooh. Or MaxHard. MaxHard would be good too."

Liam huffed. He didn't want to know.

LIAM

Kade says thank you.

ARAN

Damn right he does, and you will too.

As Liam settled into research mode, he highly doubted that. His books had become minefields, no warning for when a... Richard might spring out at him from nowhere.

But he liked the amused, contented hum he was getting from Kade through their bond. Whenever Kade discovered another screencap, he lit up in Liam's mind, his desire and delight mixing in the most addictive manner.

That didn't mean Liam was required to admit he was glad Aran had done this though. Nope. Not at all.

He turned the page and blinked at the picture nestled there.

It wasn't particularly explicit; it wasn't even full body, no dicks in sight. Just a waist-up shot of the two porn stars clinging to each other, Hunter sitting in Richard's lap, sweat glistening on their skin as they traded the most passionate kiss Liam had seen in his life.

Kade peeked around a pile of books to get a look. "Right?"

Liam nodded numbly. He wasn't entirely sure what he

was agreeing with, but the answer was yes. Unquestionably, yes.

"*Celebrating the Exclusive Contract,*" Kade said. "It's the first scene they released after announcing they had a true bond. Check it out."

Staring at the image, his words failing him, Liam nodded again. He would be doing that. After the new moon. When he could... He shivered at the idea, his cock starting to fill.

"*Fuck,*" Kade groaned. "I retract my previous statement. Tell Aran he's an evil bastard and no longer my favorite DickHunter."

Liam snorted. Well, at least he wasn't the only one suffering now.

He pulled out a book from the bottom of a pile and riffled through it, sighing in relief when no Richards appeared. Kade did the same, and they resumed their research in a less eventful fashion, with the occasional pause when Liam received a request for a sigil.

They managed an hour and a half before Kade got too restless. He was a fast reader, but clearly wasn't enjoying it. There were three days until the full moon, and Liam wondered how worked up Kade would get. Would he be able to sit still at all?

They'd woken up to another awkward and supremely unsatisfying morning plastered together, but after they got past that part, Kade was fun to hang out with. Yes, he was a complete pervert, but Aran was too, and Liam grudgingly liked hanging out with him.

He was laid-back and easy to talk to. He was also sinfully attractive, with his long, wavy hair that Liam certainly did not want to run his fingers through and his full lips that were not tempting Liam to kiss them. His looks and muscular body had done nothing to alleviate their morning situation. Neither had his distractingly wholesome scent. If anything, he smelled better than before. There was a smoky note to his scent that seemed to be growing stronger. It made Liam fantasize about trailing his nose along Kade's neck and breathing him in.

But he would not be doing that.

It did make him wonder though... How was Kade handling his inability to smell? Everything Liam had read and learned about shifters indicated scent was a huge part of how they experienced the world. Having that suddenly taken away must have been disorienting. How much did that play into the way Kade acted around him? If he could smell Liam's magic, would those moments when his instincts seemed to take over be fewer? Would he still crowd into Liam's space and stroke hands over his neck, or would the harsh scent of magic remind him this had been a mistake?

And more than that, if his sense of smell returned, would it help him ward off whatever lingering trauma he had from the decay spirit possessing him? It was clear he hadn't fully dealt with that, and scent was so tied to memory. Could they use it to keep Kade grounded in the present when there wasn't a window nearby to crack?

But that was all theoretical. It wouldn't affect anything with Kade in his current condition.

Liam shook himself and focused on the book in front of him. His mind had wandered, and he couldn't even blame it on Kade feeling restless. Though as they sat there, Kade got progressively more antsy, but just when Liam was about to suggest they take a break, the shop's doorbell rang.

Kade jumped up.

"I'll get it," he declared, sounding ecstatic, then sprinted toward the door.

Anything to avoid research, Liam supposed. He went back to his reading.

Time slipped by as it always did when he was immersed in a book. It was a good fifteen minutes later when he finished, and Kade hadn't returned. Liam sensed him—a vague, shimmering amusement winding through his presence.

Why wasn't he back? Was something happening in the shop?

Liam was considering checking on him when Kade strode through the door, grinning and pleased with himself.

"We should practice!"

Liam shot Kade a suspicious look, but followed him to the floor below.

Just the thought of using his magic, of channeling Kade's energy, sent a frisson of arousal zipping through his body. Things would get embarrassing if his dick started associating workrooms with sex.

Not that they'd been having any.

When Kade dramatically opened the door for him, Liam blinked inside.

In place of the candles he'd set out two days before, there was a row of...

"Are those—"

"Candles," Kade said brightly. "I thought you could use some new ones."

Liam looked closer. They were indeed candles. Candles shaped like realistic dicks. A whole line of them in every skin tone imaginable, from dark to light.

Despite himself, he snickered. "Did they have to drip

white wax over the tips?"

"Obviously. It's the attention to detail that makes them a masterpiece."

Liam raised an eyebrow at him. "Do you really want me to light those?"

Kade paled, realizing that would mean watching a dozen dicks slowly melt from their tips down to their balls. "I did not think this through."

Liam bit back a smile. "Okay then. Let's get started."

They tossed the fireball as a warm-up, and Liam marveled at how simple it was to connect to Kade's energy through the tether, even when they weren't touching. Without Kade's hands on him, he didn't have unfettered access to it, but that was to be expected. From what he'd read about transactional bonds, the mage had an easy but limited ability to use the shifter's energy.

If transactional bonds were like this, how over-whelming must a true bond be?

"So..." Kade lobbed the fireball at Liam. "You think some mage somewhere knows what we're dealing with?"

Liam caught the ball. "You can't tell me this has never been faced before. Aran found a pack in California we think was attacked by something similar, but we haven't confirmed what. There might be more cases. The only reason Aran heard about them was because the mage who'd tried to save that pack had done her apprenticeship with the teacher he's studying under. So again, it's about the line of magical knowledge. If we weren't connected to that teacher, we wouldn't even know that much." He tossed the fireball back before continuing.

"Our knowledge is so scattered, but if we gathered that information and made it available to everyone, we might not be in this situation. We wouldn't have to hope we received the right training from our teachers. We'd have the collective experience of all the mages in the world at our disposal, no matter our area of study."

"Why hasn't anyone done that?"

"Presumably for the same reason shifters haven't. Tradition. Mages are reluctant to embrace technology—a handful of tech mages aside. And I do get it. To some extent, entire fields of magic have been rendered almost obsolete by technological advances, and that's likely to continue. But maybe if, twenty years ago, someone had established an archiving project and digitized our records, Elijah could have typed 'evil decay spirit' into a search engine and had answers. There'd be no resorting to trial and error like we're currently doing."

"You figured out how to trap them though. That has to be a solid start."

"But we don't have a clue what they are or how to destroy them. We've used binding contracts to contain the spirits in those boxes, but that's a temporary fix."

"How do you destroy a binding contract?"

"You don't destroy them. They must be fulfilled. Oaths have to be honored. That's the whole point. They're not supposed to be something you can easily get out of."

"Right, but few absolutes exist in this world. If there was one you had to break, how would you do it?"

Liam couldn't imagine any situation where he would want to break a binding contract. "A person's oath should be their word. If they swore to do something, they should do it."

"I get that you would never do it personally, but what if someone were forced into a contract and needed out of it?"

"I don't believe a binding contract would work if

someone signed it against their will. The magic binds the spirit of their oath."

"I'm pretty sure the spirits didn't consent to being sucked into boxes."

"Oh." Liam frowned. "True." He missed the fireball Kade tossed him. It fizzled out midair as Liam lost his concentration and the magic and energy flowing between them faltered.

How would he destroy a contract? He'd never researched it. They hadn't put any conditions on the bindings in the boxes. If they did, could they fulfill them? And what would happen to the spirits? Normally, binding contracts released a person from their oath after it was fulfilled. That was no good. They couldn't risk the spirits being released.

Binding contracts were impossible to destroy by physical means. Chucking the boxes into a fire would do nothing. But could they be destroyed by magical ones if enough energy was put into it? That brought him back around to what would happen to the spirit if the contract was destroyed.

"What are you thinking?" Kade asked.

It was just an inkling of an idea. Liam hesitated.

"Dude, I sensed your brain spinning. You can't not give me something after that."

Liam wasn't thrilled about sharing a theory he hadn't supported with research yet, but he shrugged. "Hypothetically—and I cannot stress enough how hypothetical this is —I'm wondering if we can destroy the boxes and the spirits with them. Elijah wasn't able to destroy the decay spirit itself, but if it's trapped, maybe that would contain it so it could be destroyed."

He paused, and Kade waited while he considered it.

"I honestly don't know," Liam said after a minute. "There are books on binding contracts in the library, some of which have been archived, but I'm not sure they have anything about destroying contracts. It's just not done. We can check into it, but to make it work, I bet it'd take a ridiculous amount of magic, and it'd need to be done individually. I don't love the idea of having to trap the spirits one by one, then destroy them one by one. But if that's the only option, I guess we'd have to do it."

"Do you want to test it out?"

"Not with as little control as I have over your energy, and not with as half-baked as my theory is. We'd need a plan for how to keep the spirit contained if it gets released while we're attempting to destroy it, and we should be certain I can control your energy before we try that kind of spell. We can't risk setting a spirit loose."

Kade scooted forward. "Then let's learn how to control it and destroy these things."

He was oversimplifying the situation and skipping about a dozen steps, but Liam reached out to him.

Like every time before, the moment they touched, Liam was caught in an all-consuming blaze. But after the initial thrill swept through him, he realized he was adjusting to it. It still filled him so full, still made him long to give in to the pull between them and let his magic take over, let Kade and his wolf take over. Get pinned down and fucked until he couldn't think anymore.

He took a deep, steadying breath and centered himself in the midst of that lust and euphoria. It crackled and sparked around him, but it didn't devour him.

Anytime he used Kade's energy, it felt like they were being dragged toward each other, like they needed to get closer. Like the bond or the tether, or both, were demanding it, trying to lure them into deepening it no matter how ill-advised.

Did transactional bonds constantly try to push people together? Was there always this urge to touch and be touched? Did people who expected a loveless arrangement feel this pull? Were they able to deny it?

In the accounts he'd read of transactionally bonded mages, they had sex with their mates frequently, even if they disliked them. Apparently the sex was too good to pass up. This had to be why, but none of them had mentioned how heady the pull was. It threatened to consume his entire being, like he and Kade, their bodies entwined, could burn brighter and hotter than the sun.

For the hundredth time, he reminded himself that was a horrible idea. He trained his eyes on the candles across the room. Not that they helped him keep his mind off things he shouldn't be thinking.

He channeled a trickle of Kade's energy, shaping it into a thin thread, then cracked it like a whip.

Every single candle caught alight.

Kade grinned. "That was amazing, but could you put them out before... well, you know."

Liam chuckled and extinguished the flames before reluctantly dropping Kade's hand.

"Thanks," Kade said wryly. "Really didn't think that through. But that felt more controlled."

"I'm getting the hang of it. How much will your energy increase over the next couple of days?"

"A lot."

"And I'm assuming you'll get more instinctual and hornier as well?"

"Yep. Ideally on the full moon, all I'd be doing is running and fucking to get that extra energy out."

Liam repressed a shiver. "Given how intoxicating your energy is at its current level, we should consider holding off on practicing for a bit, then pick it up again after that."

"That's probably for the best." Kade didn't sound happy about it, but they wouldn't do anyone any good if they ended up fucking while they practiced.

"Okay," Liam said, standing. "Let's get back to work."

Kade stood as well. "Ah, research. The only thing less enjoyable than blue balls."

Liam snorted and shook his head.

They made their way upstairs, where the piles of books they hadn't read kept getting smaller and smaller.

It wasn't until after dinner that the message arrived, but Liam should have seen it coming.

MILES

Ah, Liam, what were you doing in the workroom today?

LIAM

I CAN EXPLAIN.

ARAN

Sure you can.

ELIJAH

What's going on?

Liam started to type, but Aran and Miles were faster, flooding the chat with pictures. Aran's were positively pornographic—his fist wrapped tight around a candle, his mouth opening over one as he leered at the camera, two candles with skin tones close to Liam and Kade's frotting against each other.

He should have hidden them before he and Kade left for the evening.

Elijah replied with a string of emojis, all wide eyes and raised eyebrows.

LIAM

KADE BOUGHT THEM.

ARAN

Is your better half in the habit of buying you dicks?

LIAM

He is NOT my better half!

I am not half of anything!

MILES

I hate that I'm typing this, but why did Kade buy you dick-shaped candles?

LIAM

For practice!

ARAN

Practicing what?

LIAM

Oh shut up.

You remember I basically have to relearn how to use my magic, right?

It's good, by the way.

Thanks for asking.

After the full moon, we can help with the spirits again.

ELIJAH

And you needed the dick candles
because...?

LIAM

I didn't need dick anything!

This was him getting back at me for the
book covers from yesterday.

Oh.

Right.

Thanks for the literal porn, Aran.

Because that's super helpful when we can't
get off for three weeks.

ARAN

First, you're welcome. Second, you
absolutely need dick something. And third,
this can't stand unanswered. What's your
plan?

LIAM

My plan?

ARAN

How are you going to respond? You gave
him porn; he gave you dicks. What's your
next move?

LIAM

I suggested romance covers.

YOU gave him porn.

MILES

I have an idea.

And then Miles outlined a plan that proved he had
spent too much time with Aran over the last few years.

ELIJAH

You used to be so sweet!

ARAN

My baby is all grown up. *sheds proud tears*

He sent a link.

ARAN

They have overnight shipping. Send them to the house tomorrow and we'll take care of the rest.

ELIJAH

Why did you have that link ready so fast?

And why do you know about the overnight shipping?

ARAN

A fuckboy never reveals his secrets.

ELIJAH

You say that like you don't tell us all your secrets.

LIAM

In explicit detail.

Repeatedly

ARAN

Should I recommend my favorites?

The NOs were quick and emphatic.

ARAN

But seriously. I can't believe you're agreeing to this. I like this Liam. Victor may have stretched Elijah's channels, but damn, Kade has loosened you up. Whatever he's doing to you while you two are alone all day, tell him to keep doing it.

ELIJAH

Could we stop talking about my channels already?

LIAM

He isn't doing anything to me!

ARAN

He's definitely rubbing off on you.

LIAM

He isn't rubbing off on me!

In any way!

He added that second line because he knew where Aran would attempt to take the first. Not that the clarification stopped Aran.

ARAN

That's a shame. He's fucking hot. He should rub off on you. You need to get on that. Literally. That is one beautiful dick.

Liam narrowed his eyes at his phone. Did that mean... No. He wasn't going to ask.

ELIJAH

Wait. You've seen Kade's dick?

Well, it was nice of Elijah to ask for him.

ARAN

Of course. What do you think his profile
picture is on the forums? There's a reason I
didn't recognize his face. While you were
being so warmly welcomed home, I thought
Kade looked familiar, but he put his clothes
on too quickly for me to be sure. Plus, I'd
only seen him hard, so...

Oh god. Liam was bonded to someone who had a dick pic for his profile on a secret supernatural porn site. How was this his life?

MILES

I'm asking this against my better judgment,
but does that mean your picture is...

Nope. Never mind. Don't answer that.

ARAN

What else would it be?

Hold on. I'll show you.

There was a second flurry of NOs in the chat.

ARAN

Your loss.

The lighting on it is perfection.

Liam ignored him. He had no desire to dwell on how many people had seen Kade's cock. Or the fact that he'd barely glimpsed it himself.

Instead, he spent ten minutes putting in the most distracting order of his life. He winced at the cart total and shipping costs. He might have gone a little overboard, but he hit the Checkout button anyway. The dick candles couldn't have been cheap, and it wasn't like Liam went out much. He had money for this.

A short while later, Kade walked in and sent him a look. "What are you planning? I can feel you're up to something."

His curiosity was a tangible thing. It brushed against Liam like a cat, but he just hummed innocently.

"Alright," Kade said. "Keep your secrets. I'm guessing I'll find out soon enough."

Yes. Yes, he would.

ELEVEN

For the second day in a row, Kade woke to find himself grinding against Liam, against an ass that felt like it was made for him to do just that. The desire to sink into Liam burned through him, some ghost of a scent haunting him from his dreams.

It took effort to still his hips, to stop the slow roll of his body, to release the iron-tight grip of his arm wrapped around Liam's chest, and flop onto his side of the bed.

"God, I wish I could fuck you. Not fucking you for three weeks while you're in my bed should be a miracle that gets me canonized," he grumbled. His dick throbbed in protest.

Liam rolled onto his back as well. "I don't know. Your self-control feels more evil than saintly. I've never been so wound up in my life." He scrubbed a hand over his face. There was a tent in the blanket draped over him, and Kade's gaze fixated on it.

He wet his lips and swallowed. He couldn't taste anything, but fuck, Liam looked delicious.

"I can't tell what you're thinking," Liam said. "But

you're staring at my dick and thinking *something*, and I'm smart enough to put two and two together."

Kade forced himself to stare at the ceiling. "Should I sleep on the floor?"

"Honestly, I'm not sure it'd matter. Besides, your dick is like an alarm clock with how regularly it wakes me up."

Liam didn't seem like he'd appreciate an alarm cock joke, so instead, Kade said, "Alright. Talk to me. Tell me the least sexy parts of your job."

"You want to hear about ancient library books?" Liam eyed him doubtfully.

"It's better than obsessing over how much fun it'd be to pin you down and fuck you. So yeah. Please bore me?"

"You're not helping when you talk like that. How is this not you at your horniest?"

"We all have our talents. You have your researching and multiple language speaking and spell creating, and I have the ability to turn the mundane dirty." Kade leered to emphasize the point.

"You and Aran both. But okay. What would you like to know?"

"Anything. What about this archiving project of yours? How does it work? Give me the most boring minutia you can think of."

"Oh." Liam lit up. "No, that's not boring, not even close. There was so much I got to learn!"

He launched into a detailed explanation of how he'd set up the project, his eyes shining as he described consulting with a tech mage to develop a magically enhanced scanning program.

Kade wasn't able to follow the more technical aspects— something about mining information, even from books in languages that weren't commonly spoken anymore, and putting it into a searchable database that Liam hoped would be automatically translated someday—but Kade didn't need to understand the details to know how passionate Liam was about his project.

Liam's hands moved constantly as he spoke, his gestures animated. In Kade's mind, his presence glittered with excitement. His morning-rough voice washed over Kade, relaxing him, making him want to listen to anything and everything Liam cared to say.

This project of his was something he'd dreamed of doing since he was a teenager. He'd done extra work during his apprenticeship to make it happen. Kade couldn't relate. He still wasn't certain what he wanted to do with his life. Or rather, what he could do while he was Victor's second. It had never been said officially, but he'd always felt like taking that position had been expected of him from the day Victor was born. Trying to imagine a different path... Well, there was no real point to it.

Instead, he focused on Liam. On how he'd roped his friends into helping him by sending them crates of books to scan, on how the elderly librarians were supportive, if a bit baffled by the magic he was using. How it'd take years to get the library archived, but he knew the effort would be worth it.

Eventually, it was enough for Kade to cool down, though his wolf made it known it was not pleased with this situation.

They got up and got ready, heading downstairs for breakfast before driving to the shop. It was only the fourth day, but Kade felt it becoming routine. It would be so easy to make this a habit, for the rest of his life to look like these mornings.

Ideally with less sexual frustration.

But that wasn't happening. Liam had an entire library of books waiting to be archived. There was no happily ever after here.

With the full moon approaching, Kade's wolf was rising closer to the surface, unhappy that they hadn't truly staked their claim on Liam, hadn't proven to him how good they could be for him. How much he'd enjoy belonging to them, how much they needed him to claim them in return.

That restlessness made his attempts at research more difficult, especially now Liam had decided it was a bad idea for them to practice magic, and Kade was going insane.

Liam was right though. Practicing magic was too seductive. This close to the full moon, it was playing with fire, and not in the casual, 'tossing a ball of it around' way they'd been doing. He could easily see it getting out of control—neither of them remembering they weren't supposed to be doing what they were doing, that they shouldn't be grinding against each other and trading kisses until they came, Liam hot and hard under him, his hands exploring every inch of Liam's body.

Across the small table, Liam's head hit the book open in front of him. He groaned. "Could you stop that? I can't concentrate."

He lifted his head and thunked it onto the book again. He was a jumble of frustrated desire, and that made Kade's wolf want to growl. Their mate needed to get off. They should give him that, give him everything he could ever ask for.

Liam let out another groan. "The full moon is going to kill me, isn't it? Death by someone else's blue balls. The first death of its kind."

Kade snorted. "Sorry. Can't help it."

"Okay." Liam sighed, standing up. "This isn't working. What's there to do around here?"

"Nothing."

"There has to be something. Tour-guide me. Show me the sights."

"There is literally nothing."

"Pretend you're on the local tourism council. What would they suggest I do?"

"Go elsewhere?"

Liam rolled his eyes and grabbed his backpack, putting a few books inside. "Nowhere has nothing. There's always something. Even if the residents think it's nothing. So take me there. Show me all the nothing this area's got."

"There's a touristy ghost town about an hour and a half from here with a bunch of preserved buildings? We could get there by lunch, wander around for a while, and be home in time for dinner."

"Perfect. You're less horny when you're driving. Hopefully getting up and being active will help you, and I can get some reading done on the way."

That was... better than nothing. He'd rather be driving than researching any day of the week, and this late in the year, it was unlikely there'd be many people there, so his protective instincts shouldn't get triggered. This might work. If he couldn't run, driving was the next best thing.

Liam spent the journey immersed in a book, relaxing more as he was able to get work done. His phone buzzed a few times, and he made the sigils, then immediately went back to reading.

They were down to the smaller spirits, and it was taking them longer to find and identify them, which meant longer between Liam getting requests for sigils. That had to indicate this was almost over.

Liam's contentment helped ease Kade's nerves, his presence soothing.

Kade was sensing more of his emotions. Even without having sex, the bond was deepening. It wasn't the same as a true bond would be. It was more of a general impression than anything, but it seemed like it could go so much deeper, and Kade was having difficulty remembering why he didn't want that.

He reminded himself Liam wasn't his mage. That was a shame. They could have had fun together, but Liam would never be happy out there. He had his archiving project to finish.

The parking lot near the ghost town was thankfully empty when they arrived, no tourists in sight. Kade had been to this place several times and never found it impressive. While it was well-preserved, there was nothing special about it. There were dozens of these gold rush towns scattered throughout the mountains, and Kade had visited them all. Liam was fascinated by it though, and it was impossible not to view it in a new light.

The air was brisk with the promise of winter, and the hills surrounding the town gave it a rugged beauty. Being outside in the cool weather took the worst of the edge off, and Kade breathed easier.

"During summer, they have guided tours and do re-enactments," Kade said. "There are a lot more people."

Liam shook his head. "I prefer it this way, with no one else here, like we're in some frozen moment in time. It's nice they're keeping it preserved. This snapshot of a few years of history. Besides, I have you to show me around, don't I?"

"In that case, are you ready to get on your knees and see god?" Kade smirked, his eyes raking down Liam's body.

Liam gave him a flat look.

"There's a church," Kade explained.

"I figured."

"I'm just saying, if you'd like to receive the body of Christ—"

"Nope."

"What if I lay hands on—"

"Pass."

"But it'd be a religious experience."

"I'm sure it would."

"This is the kind of commentary you'd never get on an official guided tour."

Liam cracked a smile like he couldn't help it. "I mean, you did give me a nice long ride, so horny tour-guide me to your heart's content."

He led Liam through the church and the schoolhouse, its rows of weathered desks waiting for students who'd never return, then showed him the old hotel, with its wooden facade and now-empty rooms. They wandered through the abandoned buildings that lined the dusty main street. A few were locked, their contents kept behind glass, but most they could enter. The occasional sign explained the town's history in bits and pieces. Liam was drawn to those, nodding thoughtfully as he read.

After they'd been through the buildings, they stopped by the meandering creek that ran along the length of the town and stood there for a few minutes, listening to the babbling of the water.

A car door slammed in the parking area, followed by the boisterous voices of a family, and Kade twitched.

Liam laughed. "I take it that's our sign to leave."

It was ridiculous, but Kade couldn't handle strangers around Liam right then. His pack was bad enough.

They walked back and got into Kade's car.

"Ready for another long ride?" Kade asked.

Liam pulled out a book from the bag he'd packed, grinning. "Absolutely."

The drive home was filled with a companionable silence. Anytime Kade had gone on a road trip with Victor, he'd gotten the impression Victor was counting down the minutes until he could return to the pack. With Liam, it wasn't like that. It seemed as if he'd be content to curl up in the passenger seat and let Kade drive anywhere he wanted to go, as long as he had a few good books with him. If someone like Liam had been in their pack, maybe the extent of Kade's travels wouldn't have been measured in the distance he could drive in one day. That would have been nice.

The moment Kade opened his bedroom door after dinner, he knew someone else had been in there. He couldn't smell it, but somehow he *knew*. It was merely a feeling, a certainty that someone had been in his space.

He stood and sensed the room, letting his awareness touch everything, checking if anything had been disturbed. He'd been paranoid when they'd arrived at the shop, expecting some sort of surprise from Liam, but nothing had come of it.

Apparently he'd just needed to wait a little longer.

On instinct, he walked over to his dresser and paused. Anticipation shivered through their bond, telling him he was getting warmer.

He placed his hands on the top drawer and hesitated again. Liam was bright and shimmering, and Kade could sense him holding his breath. Part of Kade wanted to make him wait, but he didn't have the self-control or patience for that. After the last few days, his already limited supply was at an all-time low.

He slid the drawer open and willed himself not to react.

What should have been a drawer full of his underwear had transformed into something quite different. A dozen slips of silk and lace had replaced the usual cotton. From shiny black to fire red and a few deeper jewel tones, the underwear was artfully placed in his drawer, laid out like a display in a high-end lingerie shop.

He had to keep from raising his eyebrows at the sight. So this was what he got for ordering Liam those candles. Liam must have had them delivered to the house so his friends could switch them out while Kade and Liam were away. Kade wondered what they'd done with his regular underwear, but he wasn't about to ask. There was no fun in that.

He grabbed a red pair, more string than fabric, then glanced at Liam.

Liam was watching him, waiting for his reaction. He must have felt Kade's surprise, but Kade wasn't giving him more than that.

He gestured toward the bathroom with the hand holding the underwear. Liam's eyes followed its vibrant arc through the air. "I'm going to shower, unless you need to get in there."

Liam's expression was the epitome of disbelief and shock. "No? I'm good?"

Kade stepped inside the bathroom and closed the door

behind him. Only then did he give the lingerie a proper look.

It was designed for men, but for all it purported to be underwear, it would not be covering much. The sheer fabric would leave little to the imagination. And, he realized, it would technically be classified as a jockstrap. Damn if that didn't give him mental images of men's locker rooms that were significantly more interesting than normal.

This had not been expected. Not at all.

He stripped off his clothes, started the shower, and got in, brainstorming ideas for payback. It was a welcome distraction from how turned on Liam felt in his mind. Something to focus on instead of storming out of the bathroom and doing a whole list of things that would not even remotely qualify as playing nice.

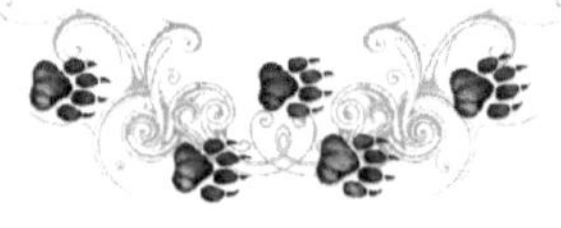

CHAPTER

TWELVE

Liam stared at the bathroom door for a solid five minutes before his brain came back online.

His phone buzzed with a new message, jolting him out of his stupor.

ARAN

So how did your wolf take it?

LIAM

He didn't really react?

Just grabbed a pair and went to shower.

I spent a couple hundred dollars on sexy underwear…

And I think he's just going to wear them?

ARAN

I'm not seeing a problem with that. Sounds like money well spent.

LIAM

This didn't go as planned.

Just change them back.

For the sake of his own sanity.

ARAN

> It's because you ordered the tamest ones they had. I mean, did you not see the pair that looks like a glittery fire hydrant complete with a hose?

The underwear he'd purchased were plenty racy. The thing Kade had picked was completely open in the back. Liam was about to respond that he had no desire to spend money on sparkly dick hoses, but then the shower turned off, and he found himself staring at the door again.

What was he even expecting? For Kade to parade out in nothing but string and a few square inches of sheer fabric?

Not that he wanted that. No. Not at all.

Kade walked out of the bathroom, toweling his hair dry. His worn sweatpants hung low on his hips, but his tank top covered any potential straps that might be peeking out.

"Are you..." Liam's brain was too scrambled to finish the question.

Kade's grin was more than a touch wicked. "Only one way to find out." He hooked a thumb in the waistband of his sweats, pushing them down a fraction of an inch.

There were things Liam was not capable of handling. Seeing Kade in a minuscule scrap of fabric whose entire purpose was to titillate, not cover, was high on that list.

Liam snatched his night clothes off the dresser, sensing Kade's amusement as he fled to the bathroom.

He really hadn't thought this through.

That fact was reinforced when, in the morning, Kade hummed contemplatively over the selection in his drawer, holding up several before choosing a silky black pair and taking them into the bathroom to change.

Liam didn't know which was more distracting: Kade wearing those, or him screwing with Liam and going commando under his jeans. Both options were their own kind of torment, designed to test Liam's self-control, and he only had himself to blame.

Well, himself and Miles. And Aran. He could always blame Aran.

Once at the shop, it became obvious they weren't getting anything productive done. Kade was too restless for that. The ripples of discontent that inundated Liam made him feel ready to crawl out of his skin.

Whenever Liam did manage to focus on the book in front of him, he was interrupted by the mental image of Kade strutting around in black silk. And very little of it, at that.

But even if he could have concentrated, it wouldn't have mattered. They had a dozen books left, the pile pathetically tiny compared to the mountains of discards.

It didn't help that practicing magic seemed guaranteed to end with him getting fucked. Not being able to jerk off or use magic was bad enough; not being able to read was a *Twilight Zone* hell created specifically for him.

They were barely an hour into their disastrous attempts at research when the doorbell rang. Kade cringed and stood.

"I'll get it."

Liam cocked an eyebrow at him, but didn't say a word.

When Kade returned, he was holding a package. Liam eyed it suspiciously. It was small; surely it wasn't another dozen dick-shaped candles.

"Do I want to know?"

"Probably not. It seemed like a great idea last night, but I clearly didn't think it through."

There'd been a lot of that going around lately.

Liam's curiosity got the better of him. "Okay, show me."

Kade slid the package across the table, not meeting his gaze. "I was planning to offer it to you as dessert after lunch."

Liam ripped open the tape and peeked inside. His eyebrows climbing, he pulled out a plastic box containing a sucker that was not meant for children. "Are you implying it would be a bad idea for me to suck on something dick-shaped right now?"

Kade groaned. "I did say I hadn't thought it through."

Yeah, that was pretty damn apparent. Even Liam's restraint wouldn't hold if Kade sucked on this.

He slipped it back into the packaging and stood, walking over to the kitchen cabinets to hide it behind the glasses. Not that he was counting on that to keep him from dwelling on it. If Kade's new underwear had taught him anything, it was that out of sight was *not* out of mind.

He glanced at Kade. "Any other nearby ghost towns?"

Kade snorted. "Like, eight."

Which was how Liam ended up, for the second day in a row, reading in the passenger seat as Kade drove over an hour to visit a different historical ghost town. Though he got through fewer books this time—driving wasn't helping Kade much.

If this was Kade twenty-four hours before the full moon, they'd never survive tomorrow.

While the ghost town from the day before had been a tourist attraction, the one Kade brought him to today was a world apart. Kade drove up a mountain to get to it. The road was narrow and winding. Liam avoided looking out the window at the plunging drop inches from the wheels of the car, with no barrier between. The ruts and bumps did nothing to help his reading.

When they reached the parking area, there were no other cars. That was a relief. With as twitchy as Kade felt, Liam thought it was best for them to avoid people.

The previous town had been out in the open, surrounded by barren hills. This place was overrun by nature. There were no beautifully preserved buildings here; it was all ruins and remnants, piles of wood and sketchy outlines of foundations with trees growing inside. The structures that still stood were crumbling, some half-collapsed and the rest ready to fall over in the next storm.

Liam would never be an outdoorsy person, but he found he didn't mind the hike. The air was rich with the scents of the forest and decaying wood, and there were gorgeous sights everywhere he looked.

Ahead of him on the path, Kade turned back to him, an eyebrow raised, and Liam realized he'd been staring at Kade's ass. Not the wisest life choice, given the fallen trees strewn across the trail.

"Sorry." He winced.

Kade leered. "Don't let me stop you from enjoying the view."

Liam shook his head, and they continued their journey through the forest.

There was no map, but Kade guided him around. The ruins were scattered out here, not clustered together like yesterday. And while there were signs, most were faded, with some utterly illegible.

One of the few buildings that appeared structurally sound was a cabin with a half-legible sign that explained it was the home of the town's last resident, who'd died about fifty years ago.

"It reminds you how quickly history can fade," Liam said. "Less than half a century and the forest has already reclaimed so much of what happened here. Another fifty years, and there might only be traces left."

Gazing over the area filled him with sadness, but also determination. He couldn't save this town from the inevitable march of ages that stole away parts of their history, but there was knowledge he could preserve for generations to come. He could leave behind something more than ruins that would be consumed by the forests of time.

He looked over and found Kade watching him intently, a low ache coming through their bond. Desire, maybe, but it didn't feel sexual—at least not entirely.

Kade stepped closer to him, his wolf showing itself in the amber flare in his eyes, and all Liam smelled was that warm, smoky scent. He let it fill his lungs, and Kade did the same, leaning in and inhaling, his presence heating.

They were alone in a forest, and it was giving Kade ideas.

Liam wet his lips and swallowed, the sound loud in the quiet nature surrounding them. His heartbeat kicked up and his breathing accelerated. He forced out a long exhale.

"My plan to make you less horny isn't working."

Kade's hands settled on Liam's waist and pulled him closer.

"Will shifting help?" Liam's voice quavered. "You said running helps on the full moon. It'd be safe for you to shift here, right? There's no one around, no spirits out here."

"You want to see me shift?" Kade asked in a low rumble.

"If it will help?"

"Honestly?" Kade whispered in Liam's ear. "At this

point, I doubt anything short of fucking you will help." He inhaled again and let the breath out with a sigh.

Liam shivered, his stomach clenching with desire. That was... not what they were supposed to be doing out here, and if Kade pushed him, Liam might forget why.

Thankfully, Kade took a step back. "There's a lookout point with a bench farther up the mountain. You could read there while I run."

Liam nodded and followed Kade.

The view was spectacular, a stunning scene of trees and mountains, but it wasn't what held Liam's attention when he sat down.

Kade pulled off his shirt and tossed it onto the bench. Liam's eyes traced over his chest, following every line of his abs, and Kade smirked, basking in the heat of Liam's gaze.

Slowly, he popped the button on his jeans.

"You're going to..." Liam trailed off as Kade unzipped. Because yes, of course Kade was stripping right there while Liam watched, the thrill of it singing in his veins.

Shifters weren't shy when it came to nudity, but that didn't prepare Liam for dealing with it in real life.

Kade inched down his jeans, and Liam's breath hitched. He was unable to tear his eyes away.

Oh, fuck. Kade was wearing the black underwear. If they could be called underwear. They certainly weren't doing much to contain his half-hard cock. Dear god, why had he thought buying those was a good idea? Did he have some hidden masochistic streak he'd never noticed before?

Kade slid his thumbs under the strings that were, against all odds, holding the fabric up and toyed with them.

Liam's lungs had forgotten how to function. He wasn't sure which was worse: Kade shimmying the black silk down, or the moment he finally pushed them off, revealing himself fully.

Liam swallowed. That truly was a beautiful dick.

Kade tossed the slip of silk on top of his clothing and stood there, naked, letting Liam's gaze roam over every inch of him. And there were a fair amount of inches.

"You..." Liam cleared his throat. "You should... shift. Run. Relieve some of that... energy."

The smug smile Kade gave him said he knew damn well he wasn't the only one who needed relief, but he didn't push it. Instead, he shifted.

Liam gasped as his transformation echoed between them—a tingling pleasure-pain like nothing he'd ever experienced. He'd seen the shift a handful of times, and it never ceased to amaze him, but to *feel* it? He didn't have words to do it justice.

Kade stalked forward, coming closer until Liam could stroke a tentative hand over his soft fur.

A rumble reverberated in his chest, startling Liam, though it wasn't a threatening sound.

"Okay." He exhaled. "Maybe you should stay a wolf. When you're in this form, it's easier to remember the reasons we shouldn't have sex."

Kade huffed, like that might not be true for him. In Liam's mind, he burned with lust, and Liam got the impression his wolf side was less willing to behave.

But Kade shook himself and turned away from Liam, heading out into the forest.

Even with Kade gone, concentrating wasn't easy, but Liam got some reading done.

An hour later, Kade returned, panting. He was still a tangle of instinct, but the edge had been taken off. His desires were there, but softened by the pleasant haze of exertion.

That didn't prevent him from dressing slower than he'd stripped though. Sweat glistened on his skin as it cooled in the late autumn air. Liam didn't even try to look away.

They hiked to Kade's car, then headed home.

Liam blinked. No. Not home. To the pack house.

By the end of the day, he'd only made it through four books, but he was chalking it up as a win since they hadn't jumped each other in the skeletal remains of a long-abandoned bank. Or a log cabin. Or on the bench.

They both deserved sainthood for that.

Waking up to Kade's dick digging into his ass was not new; the untamed presence in his mind, on the other hand, was a first. There was a slow deliberateness to the rhythm of Kade's hips, not the half-asleep motion it previously had been. This was a purposeful drag—the kind that left zero questions about how pleasurable Kade would make this if they gave in.

But this wasn't Kade. No, this was all his wolf.

There was a fierce possessiveness to the way Kade's hands were gripping him, and Liam found it impossible not to rock his hips, to meet that instinctual grind. The moment he did, Kade was on him, rolling him onto his stomach, pinning him to the bed as he rutted against his ass.

Liam moaned. He'd been craving this, though he'd prefer less clothing to be involved.

Kade leaned in, trailing his nose behind Liam's ear,

inhaling deeply. A growl resounded in his chest, and Liam's eyes threatened to roll back into his head.

This might be what Kade wanted now, but he would regret it after the moon had passed. Liam had to be the responsible one here.

"Kade?"

He got another rumble in reply.

"Kade?" He tried again.

Kade gripped him tighter.

This wasn't working. Liam reached behind him and threaded his fingers through Kade's long hair, tugging lightly to get his attention.

Kade scraped his teeth down Liam's neck and over his bite mark. Pleasure shuddered through Liam, momentarily distracting him from his annoying impulse to do the right thing.

He yanked harder on the strands. "Do you actually want to do this, or is it the moon talking?"

For a second, he doubted he'd gotten through, but then Kade tensed up, and Liam felt him struggling to suppress his wolf.

The minute it took stretched out, but eventually, his human side clawed its way forward.

He flopped off Liam, scrubbing a hand over his face. "Shit. I'm so fucking sorry I keep doing that."

Liam turned over to lie on his back next to him. "It's fine. Are you alright?"

"You're the one who keeps getting mauled. Why are you asking if I'm okay?"

"How many times do I have to tell you I'm fine?"

"I just hate that I keep losing control, especially since this is all me and my wolf's fault. At least when the spirits possessed me, I could blame it on those evil bastards."

"Ah. About that... Elijah doesn't believe we were possessed. He said the decay spirit had hooks in you, but when he captured the lust spirit, it didn't have any in us. He thinks it was affecting us and feeding off us, but it hadn't possessed us yet. Maybe it was too weak to do that?"

A tidal wave of Kade's emotions swept over Liam, and he worried he'd triggered another panic attack, but Kade breathed through it.

"We weren't possessed?" He sounded as if the wind had been knocked out of him.

"Doesn't seem like it."

"That makes this a hell of a lot worse." Kade let out a bitter huff.

"Still not our fault. We weren't in control. If we had been, neither of us would have done this."

A chilly morning breeze gusted through the open windows as they lay in silence. The longer they did, the more Kade's scent invaded Liam's senses. It surrounded him, stroked over him, filled him. He could get high off it.

"Do you wear cologne?"

Kade shot him a confused look. "Shifters generally don't. Those scents are extremely harsh and chemical-y smelling. It's one of the most annoying things about humans—how they douse themselves with that shit. Walking through the perfume and makeup section of any department store is torture."

"Then a bodywash or something?" Even as he asked, he knew that wasn't right. Nothing in Kade's shower smelled remotely similar to him; Liam had checked. "If you're not wearing anything, there should be some way to bottle your scent. You smell so good. Like a summer bonfire?"

Kade frowned. "I don't smell like that. A summer night, yes, but it's wheat fields under the full moon."

"No, there's a smoky note to your scent. I didn't notice it when we first met, but it's definitely there." A thought hit him. "Wait. I read about bonds and scents. What did the book say? That when two shifters bond, their scents combine? Does it work the same with mages and shifters? Is that what this is? Am I smelling *me* on *you*? Do I smell smoky? Is that my fire affinity?"

"You'd have to ask someone else." Kade's gruff tone didn't cover the slink of his distress through Liam's mind.

Fuck. He'd stepped in that one. "Sorry."

"It's fine."

Right. Because that wasn't exactly what Liam said whenever he didn't want people to worry about him.

It seemed better to drop it, so he rolled out of bed, went into the bathroom... and froze, his hand hovering over the light switch.

In the mirror, his tattoos shimmered faintly, visible in the darkened room.

He'd heard of this before, but only after rituals that used a large amount of shifter energy, and he hadn't used any for days.

Staring at himself, he pulled his shirt over his head. He hadn't properly examined his tattoos since this had happened. He'd always been decently powerful; his tattoos had begun to creep over his shoulders during his apprenticeship. That had been impressive enough, but now, this hint of a glow showed how much farther they'd spread. A pattern spiraled out from the bite mark and over his right pec, and when he turned, he caught a glimpse of it sweeping across his shoulder blade.

It wasn't close to Elijah's, but it was still a significant increase from what he'd had before, and he couldn't deny that he liked the look.

Why were his tattoos glowing though? That was weird. It had to be the extra energy from the full moon in Kade's system and, by default, in Liam's as well.

He hadn't read anything about this in the books discussing mages transactionally bonded to shifters, but it seemed like something they would have mentioned.

Were Elijah's tattoos doing the same? And if they were, what did that mean for Liam and Kade?

His experience so far had been lining up with the accounts he'd read. While he had easy access to Kade's energy, he couldn't tap into its entirety unless they were touching. He sensed Kade, though not in the all-consuming way Elijah described. But this? This was making him question his assumptions. What he and Kade had was miles apart from what Elijah and Victor had, but things still weren't adding up.

Was there something in between a true and a transactional bond? Or was this the bond deepening? He'd been feeling more of Kade's emotions. Perhaps sex was only one method of strengthening the bond. Could using Kade's energy have the same effect?

He frowned. If that were the case, he shouldn't use it, as tempting as it was. Kade had said the deeper the bond, the more it could hurt a shifter when it was severed, and Liam would rather not cause Kade pain just because he enjoyed channeling his energy.

Or maybe he was overthinking it and this happened to all mages bonded to shifters. But overthinking was what he did.

He'd ask Elijah at breakfast and go from there.

Not for the first time, he wished there were better records of mage-shifter bonds.

He flipped on the light, and the bright bulbs drowned out his tattoos as he picked up his toothbrush.

When he exited the bathroom, dressed and ready for the day, Kade was lying in bed, giving no indication of moving anytime soon.

"I'm grabbing breakfast. I'll see you down there?"

He didn't get a response, but the moment his hand touched the doorknob, he was unceremoniously pressed into the door by a growling Kade.

"...or not?" Liam said.

It took Kade a beat to pull himself together, though 'together' still involved keeping Liam pinned against the wood.

"Sorry, but if you leave, I'll hunt you down and haul you back here. I'm not sure I can stop myself."

Liam liked the mental image that conjured up more than he should admit.

"I can't let you out of this room today. The idea alone is driving my wolf feral. It seems willing to not fuck you, though it thinks we're being stupid about that, but it doesn't want you outside or around anyone else in exchange."

"Is this... normal?"

"Newly bonded couples usually spend their first full moon, uh..."

"Screwing like very wolfy bunnies?" Liam supplied.

"Something like that." Kade chuckled, the gust of his laughter ghosting over Liam's neck, making him shiver.

"So no research trip to the shop today?"

"Ah. No. I don't think so."

Liam sighed. "That's fine. I just wish you'd given me a heads-up yesterday so I could have brought the remainder of the books and some of my own."

He only had two with him, and they wouldn't last long if he had nothing to do but stay in this room.

But if it made things easier on Kade, he'd do it.

His stomach growled, protesting the idea of missing breakfast. "Can you leave, or should I check if Elijah is willing to make deliveries?"

"I'll bring you whatever you want," Kade said, his voice rough, and it almost felt like he was talking about more than food.

It took another minute for him to detach himself from Liam. Once Liam was clear of the door, Kade slipped out to get breakfast.

Liam sat on the bed, took out his phone, and pulled up the group chat.

LIAM

So...

Bit of a complication.

Kade's wolf doesn't want me to leave the room today.

ARAN

Ooh. Sounds like someone is going to have fun.

LIAM

Decidedly not.

I only have two books with me.

ARAN

You really need to realign your definition of fun.

ELIJAH

Victor's super unhappy I'm out of our room.

He feels about ready to throw me over his shoulder and carry me back to bed. It's AMAZING. I'm seeing how long it takes him to break.

ARAN

THAT'S the kind of fun I'm talking about.

ELIJAH

But seriously, Victor has forbidden the pack from running in the forest tonight.

It's understandable, but the whole pack's antsy.

MILES

I'm assuming that means it's better if we don't go out there today?

ELIJAH

Probably. The remaining spirits are small. They can wait another day before we trap them.

At our current pace, we'll get them all by Tuesday or Wednesday, and then we'll focus on figuring out where they came from and how we can destroy them.

LIAM

While you guys are at the apartment, can you finish up the books on spirits?

It's the shortest stack on the table.

There are six left.

ARAN

I figured you would have gotten through the rest yesterday. What have you been doing?

Liam ignored that comment.

MILES

Um. Speaking of. Another thing I'll regret asking, but...

What's with the package in the cabinet?

Liam winced.

ARAN

What package?

There was a pause, and Liam pictured Miles explaining what he'd found to Aran. He waited for the inevitable.

ARAN

Oooh. Yeah. What's with the ~package~, Liam? Is that why you couldn't get through the books? Too busy sucking on that delicious hardness Kade has been feeding you?

Yep. There it was. Time for a topic change.

LIAM

Hey, Elijah, are your tattoos glowing?

ELIJAH

Yeah, faintly. I didn't realize they did that.

LIAM

Me neither.

ARAN

Are you telling me you both are so full of metaphorical shifter dick that your tattoos are glowing even when you aren't using magic?

ELIJAH

Yep.

ARAN

Damn.

LIAM

Am I wrong to think that's weird?

I don't remember reading about this.

Maybe I should research it?

ELIJAH

Ah, sure. You could do that.

I have faith you'll figure it out sooner or later.

Liam nodded at his phone. Yeah, he would. The answer had to be in a book somewhere.

ARAN

Can I have this sucker?

MILES

Oh god. Please no? I don't need to see that.

LIAM

Yeah, no.

It's not yours.

ARAN

Fine. I'll leave it for you. Kade would much rather have you suck it anyway.

We'll take care of the final few books while you two have your hands full dealing with your shifters. And I don't mean that figuratively.

Liam sighed and closed the app. Elijah would be having a lot more fun "dealing with his shifter" than Liam would with Kade.

His gaze landed on the bookshelf. There were only travel photobooks on it—one for virtually every country in the world and a dozen for the US—organized north to south within their continents. The librarian-adjacent part of him approved of that. Most people would have gone with alphabetical, if they'd bothered to organize them at all. Having them by continent was pleasing to him, even if it didn't provide him with additional reading material.

He wandered over and flipped through a book on Greece, with its glossy photographs of blue-domed churches, ancient ruins, and charming streets, then slid it back onto the shelf. It was beautiful, but not what he was looking for. Hopefully Kade's willingness to bring him things extended to searching the house for any books lying around. Liam could read on his phone if he had to, but he preferred physical books when he had the option.

Assuming he was able to get any reading done. With as wild as Kade was feeling, it seemed unlikely.

He collapsed onto the bed and stretched his arms up, his hand bumping into something under Kade's pillow.

Blinking, he pulled out an e-reader.

Well, this was more promising than the bookshelf. He'd known Kade had been dodging the question with that "Do I look like a reader?" answer.

Before he could turn it on, the bedroom door opened.

"Hey. Do you have anything on here I can—"

Plates clattered onto the dresser, and then Kade was pinning him down and yanking the e-reader out of his hand.

"Apparently not," Liam said. "What do you have on there?"

"Nothing." Kade reached over and put the e-reader in his nightstand drawer.

"Ah, yes. The classic empty Kindle under the pillow. If I had a dollar for every time I found one of those."

Kade didn't seem to be listening. Instead, he stared at Liam, his gaze intense, his eyes flashing. He felt more wolfy than human again. His dick dug into Liam's hip while his fingers brushed over Liam's scalp.

"You should grow this out." The growl behind his words promised things Liam did his best to ignore. "Then I'll have something to grab onto."

Liam scoffed. He said that like they'd be doing activities that justified hair grabbing. "You're overestimating how much my hair can grow in two more weeks."

That jarred Kade's human side into taking control, and he jerked back. "Sorry."

"It's going to be a long day, isn't it?" Liam groaned. "And night."

"Long and hard," Kade agreed dryly. "Literally."

This was going to suck.

A voice in his head that sounded like Aran added, *And not in the fun way.*

Liam mentally resigned himself to a day of sexual frustration with not nearly enough reading material to get him through.

THIRTEEN

This sucked, Kade thought. And not in the fun way.

He'd had an idea or two about what his first full moon bonded might be like. Sexless, restless, and bored was not it. He was going insane, and Liam wasn't doing much better. Some of it was the echo of Kade's emotions, but the majority of his frustration was from being trapped in a room with nothing to learn or do.

Kade had scrolled through the entire internet on his phone in an attempt not to maul Liam. Because he'd already done that. Multiple times. And he kept trying to convince himself he didn't want to do it again.

But *fuck*, he wanted to do it again.

He'd worked out after breakfast to get rid of some of his excess energy. If running was out of the question, hundreds of sit-ups and push-ups and an hour-long plank might help.

Except Liam's gaze had dragged over his body as he watched Kade over the top of his book, and that made things so much worse. Made Kade want to remove his shirt so Liam could get a better view of his muscles as they glistened with sweat.

Yet another terrible idea.

It was almost a relief when lunch rolled around and he could use it as an excuse to step outside, though he felt like an even bigger ass because that relief was his alone.

Downstairs, Elijah was sitting in the living room, working on his laptop, looking smug and pleased with himself. No other pack members were in there; everyone was giving him a wide berth.

Kade found Victor in the kitchen, making lunch, his movements a tense, predatory prowl.

"He's enjoying this," Victor grumbled as he ripped a head of lettuce to shreds. "He's waiting to see how long it takes me to break."

"And you're not breaking because...?" Once Victor broke, they'd have significantly more fun than Kade and Liam were.

"Because I have self-control, and he said I wouldn't make it past noon."

There was still a half hour to noon. Given how tightly wound Victor was, Elijah might have been onto something. But if anyone could suppress their wolf on a full moon, it was Victor.

"How do you keep your wolf tamped down?" Kade asked.

Victor grimaced. "Years of practice. But when it comes to Elijah, I should have listened to it from the start, so maybe you should listen to yours too. What's it telling you about Liam?"

"My wolf is confused because it thinks we're bonded."

"You are bonded."

"No, not really."

Perhaps that was why he felt anxious when his thoughts wandered to Liam. His wolf knew they weren't bonded—not properly, not permanently. Liam didn't want this, but his wolf thought it just needed to prove itself, to prove they'd be a good mate for him, that they'd take care of him and do everything they could to make him happy.

"Take your own advice," Victor said.

Kade's brow furrowed. "What the hell does that mean?"

"You'll figure it out." With that, Victor snatched the chicken Caesar salad he'd made off the counter and stalked away, heading back to Elijah.

Kade returned to his bedroom, food in hand, then froze as he stepped inside.

He inhaled, frowned, then inhaled again.

The faintest hints of summer greeted him, but not what he was used to, not what he was expecting. Summer, yes, but with other elements mixed in.

Liam had said there was a smoky note to his scent, and when Kade took in another lungful of air, he caught a ghost of that. It was frustratingly light, just a whisper of breath over his skin, but it was there, teasing him with a presence he couldn't quite grasp, flickering in and out of his perception.

He'd suspected Liam had been smelling their combined scents, and now he was sure. It seemed unfair that Liam could smell them better than Kade.

Being able to smell *something*, no matter how faint, was a nice change, but he wanted more. He wanted his enhanced sense of smell back, wanted to know how he and Liam smelled together.

"Everything okay?" Liam asked from where he was

propped up against the headboard, reading on his phone. He'd finished the two books he had with him hours ago.

Kade shook himself and brought Liam his food. "Yeah, all good."

Liam didn't call him out on the blatant lie, though it was clear he didn't believe him.

The day dragged by, the longest of Kade's life. Had the moon ever been this slow to rise?

Having Liam to himself was easier than letting people get near him, but at the same time, being alone with him, in the same room as him, getting the occasional confusing whiff of their scents mingling... It was maddening.

Kade's wolf hadn't felt this wild since he was a teenager. It was like he'd lost control over his ability to shift, like he might sprout claws and fangs at any moment. And what was worse, Liam sensed it, sensed how wound up and feral he was becoming.

If the spirits hadn't been lurking in the forest, he would have shifted and run under the moonlight to work off some of this energy. That wasn't happening tonight.

He paced his bedroom and held back a growl, resisting the urge to go over to where Liam was sitting and... But he couldn't do that either.

Liam was pretending to read, but his gaze was a delicious weight on Kade's skin, and it did nothing to calm his amped-up instincts.

With a sigh, Liam set his phone aside and gestured toward the bookshelf. "Where do you want to go?"

Kade hummed noncommittally, then made another lap of the room.

Liam scoffed. "Don't give me that. You don't collect books about every country in the world if you aren't interested in visiting a few."

"I had a bookshelf and figured I should get some books to put on it. They seemed like they'd look nice."

"You bought a bunch of expensive photobooks for aesthetic reasons?"

"Maybe I enjoy the pretty pictures."

"Fine. Then which has the prettiest?" Liam got up and pulled two books off the shelf.

Kade wanted to flinch. He had those arranged the way he liked them.

That sentiment must have transferred through their bond, because Liam narrowed his eyes at him. "I work at a library. I know exactly how you have these organized. Now stop pacing, come here, sit down, and tell me where you'd go."

Kade found himself obeying. They sat on the floor with their backs against the bed, peering up at the bookshelf.

"You've heard of those around-the-world tickets?" Liam asked, and Kade glanced at him before nodding. "East or west?"

"West," Kade answered without hesitation.

"Okay. Seattle first. I want to visit my teacher and family, and you'd probably have fun in the clubs there."

Kade didn't say that if they were together, he'd have zero desire to go clubbing. He'd rather take Liam out for the cliched Space Needle dinner, or go to Kerry Park and watch the moon rise over the city skyline. Instead, he leaned forward to snag a book on the West Coast of the United States and flipped it open to a panoramic view of Denali National Park. "Then up to Alaska. We have some remote areas around here, but I want to see truly untouched wilderness."

Liam grabbed a book on Japan. "Aran has family in Shizuoka. They might be willing to show us around."

And then they were off, planning a ridiculously lavish journey, the likes of which Kade had never let himself consider taking before. They arranged the books around them as they did, a line forming along the floor—one stop after another, all the sights Kade had seen in books but couldn't imagine visiting in person.

He was still restless, still longed to shift, to run, to fuck Liam until they were both out of their minds with pleasure, but this was as good a distraction as he could ask for. Liam sat beside him, traveling through the world one book at a time, going through Asia, swinging down to Australia, up Africa to the Middle East, over to Europe, and back to the Americas. Then they traveled in the opposite direction to hit some of the countries they'd skipped, because there'd been no backtracking once they'd started going west, and sometimes that meant sacrificing visiting one destination for another before moving on. Debating where to go, why country X instead of country Y, and what they'd do there helped him ignore his baser instincts.

As they planned, the scent in the room grew stronger— a Polaroid coming into focus, blurry but revealing itself with each breath. Smoky and warm and relaxing Kade further.

When they were finished, they had two lines of books, two around-the-world trips—one going west, one going east. Kade wanted nothing more than to go on either. On both. It didn't matter as long as it was with Liam.

"Why do I get the feeling you don't share this part of yourself with people often?" Liam asked. "Does your Kindle have travel memoirs on it?"

Kade shrugged, uncomfortable. "I've lived my entire life in the middle of fucking nowhere. I hauled Victor on a couple road trips when we were younger, and sometimes we'd head to nearby cities, but that's about it. Even a night away was too much for him. He used to do it when he was a beta; he'd never do it as alpha. I have no clue the amount of effort it would have taken to get him to go further from the pack than that, and he was the only one who'd even consider it."

"You can't go by yourself?"

He could; he'd just never felt like he should allow himself to have that. "Victor was raised to be alpha, and I might not technically have been raised to be his second, but there was an unspoken expectation that I would be. Those lessons were driven into me as a child. Support the alpha, support the pack. There was never a point where I could leave for any extended period. Once Victor took over, I needed to be here, helping him. Before that, there was everything with his father. It was always something. And now, there's the spirits. I can't abandon the pack when it's like this."

"When it's over?"

"Maybe, but no one here wants to go with me, and I don't want to travel solo. Wolves are pack animals by nature. Besides, I'm second-in-command. Being gone a night is one thing. A week? A month? How could I do that?"

"I can understand not wanting to travel alone. Like I said, my parents were fond of family trips. Occasionally we'd sneak Elijah along with us. And during our apprenticeships, the guys and I would take road trips whenever our studies allowed it. So I can't imagine traveling on my own either. I know some people prefer it, but for me, it's something you do with family and friends. Sharing those memories is what makes them special. But solo or with friends, it'd be amazing to see the world."

Liam tilted his head back, staring up at the ceiling, his

neck exposed as he continued. "There's disparate magic spread throughout the world. Every family and mage line has their own practices. How my family does magic differs from how someone in Asia or South America might do it. My parents never had enough money to take us overseas. Not that we were poor by any means, but with four kids— five, with Elijah—international travel wasn't happening. But I'd love to go abroad. To learn the various practices and preserve them before they die out or something happens to them. To make that knowledge available to people who can't afford the airfare. The more we know, the stronger we are. Same goes for how interconnected we are."

"Wolf shifters are the same. Our connections—to other pack members, to nature, to neighboring packs—make us stronger. Where did you go with your family?"

"Before my siblings were born, when we were living in Louisiana, basically all over the South and up the East Coast."

Kade relaxed as Liam's words flowed over him, as he told stories of his family trips, when it had been just him and his parents, and then later, when he'd spent most of his vacation time chasing after his younger siblings, making sure they weren't getting into trouble.

There was a passionate spark in Liam's dark eyes whenever he talked about something he'd learned, his hands gesturing as he spoke. It was fascinating to listen to him, to hear how recounting his childhood memories seemed to tease out his accent, but part of Kade's mind was wandering through the itineraries arranged before them.

What would it be like to have the freedom to do either of those trips, let alone both? To leave the pack and wander the world with Liam as he learned anything and everything his heart desired, then come home with him, curling up in bed together to rest and relax for a month or two before doing it again with a new set of places to see.

He inhaled deeply, his eyelids fluttering shut at the summery scent filling the room. His scent. Their scent. No longer a fuzzy, nebulous thing, an image blurred with motion. Instead, it sharpened to distracting clarity. A late summer night infused with fire and woody smoke. The moment before a pack run, the bonfire crackling bright in the dark, anticipation hanging heavy in the air, as full as the moon.

Liam smelled right, like he was meant to be Kade's. Like Kade was meant to be his. The combination of them was euphoric, everything Kade had ever wanted.

Unable to suppress the instinct, he filled his lungs with Liam, with *them*. His wolf surged forward, rumbling its approval. It had known when Kade had not.

Liam's story faltered.

Kade trailed his hand down Liam's neck, and he leaned closer, running his nose along Liam's skin and inhaling like Liam was the room's sole source of oxygen. He let out a shuddering exhale.

Damn, Liam smelled so good. So perfect. And more than a little turned on.

He rested his hand over Liam's bite mark and dug his fingers in. Liam groaned, his scent spiking with arousal. He'd been half-hard most of the evening, as had Kade, but now Kade smelled it on him, and he craved more. How much better would Liam smell without his clothes in the way, when he was fully hard and leaking precome, when he was wrapped around Kade's knot?

Kade growled, drunk on the scent of him.

His bed was right there, and he had so much extra energy. It'd be a shame if they didn't put it to proper use.

Liam let out another groan, but it was more of a frustrated sound than one of pleasure. His hand came up, and he yanked on Kade's hair.

"Your wolf seems to have taken over again. Remember the whole 'not a good idea to deepen the bond' thing?"

"Fuck being good," Kade said, his voice a deep rumble. "Let me show you what a wolf shifter can do on a full moon. I'll make you feel better than you ever have. Just say the word, and I'll have you begging for my knot."

Liam shivered.

"You want that, don't you? Last time doesn't count. This time, I'll get you warmed up and ready, so when I'm stretching you wide, all you'll feel is ecstasy. And then after I've made you come, I'll grind on you until I milk you dry."

Liam forced out a breath. "You'd regret it in the morning."

Kade was pretty damn sure he would not. He dropped his hand to Liam's knee, then slid it up the inside of his thigh toward the bulge in his pants. Liam caught his wrist before he got anywhere interesting.

"*Kade.*" Liam's voice was tight. "I'm trying to do the right thing here, but I'm not a saint."

"Then don't be one."

"Okay," Liam said, breathy and low. "You want to fuck me? I want explicit consent from both sides of you. Give the human side full control. If human Kade can look me in the eye and make me every filthy promise wolf Kade just did, we'll talk."

That seemed fair. Kade's wolf sank below the surface.

Kade inhaled.

Liam's scent was all around him, all over him. So fucking perfect, so entangled with his.

What the fuck?

Liam wasn't supposed to be his mage. Kade wasn't supposed to find him immediately after Victor found his. It should have taken a while. He'd spent hours mapping out the various scenarios. Their first meeting, how he'd sweep his mage off their feet. It shouldn't have played out like this.

But after smelling them together, it was impossible to deny. The way their scents had mixed was divine.

This was why his wolf had kept sniffing Liam, why it couldn't stop breathing him in. It had been able to register something the human side of Kade could not, some pheromone that went deeper than scent that had let it know.

Not that his wolf knowing made this any better.

He'd spent the last few days joking around with Liam. Playing stupid pranks on Liam. Being entirely too casual with him. Thinking he was hot and kind of funny and enjoyable to hang out with, but obviously they weren't compatible. That wasn't how he was supposed to treat his mate, not even close. And this sure as hell wasn't how he'd intended to get bonded to someone. He should love and cherish them like they were the most precious person in the world, do romantic shit for them, tell them he loved them, take care of their every need.

But Liam didn't want to be tied to a pack. To be tied to Kade forever.

They were so different; Kade couldn't blame him for that. Even without that goddamn spirit, he couldn't fathom how they'd make this work. No one would think they were meant for each other.

But their scent. Fuck. Anyone who smelled them together had to realize—

His fucking pack. Those bastards. They'd known for

days and hadn't bothered to mention how Liam's scent fit perfectly with his. Instead, they'd let Kade continue to screw things up royally. He'd thought they'd been judging him at their pack dinners, but that wasn't it at all.

He was going to kick Victor's ass for this. Some closest-thing-to-a-brother he was. How could he not have told Kade something this important?

But if he and Liam were supposed to be like Victor and Elijah, why wasn't their bond working the same way? He sensed some of Liam's emotions, and Liam did have some access to his energy, but not to the same degree.

True bonds didn't feel like this.

Maybe they weren't meant to be together after all and he was convincing himself they smelled compatible when that wasn't the case. His sense of smell had come back online, but it might still be fucked up.

This wasn't how shifters were supposed to experience their scent mixing with someone else's. It was intended to be gradual, and he'd planned to savor the whole process. That first note of developing attraction, their scents slowly blending as they got closer. Traces of his future mate teasing him, lingering on his clothes after they'd touched, mingling until there was no question about their compatibility. And then, when they finally did bond, their scents would combine in that sublime way that came from a true bond.

He'd missed all of those stages and had been blindsided by his scent completely, utterly, blissfully entwined with another.

This was too overwhelming. Too confusing.

Liam snorted. "Considering how freaked out you feel, I'm going to assume that's a solid no on the sex."

It wasn't a no—not even remotely—but how could Kade explain that?

"On the plus side," Liam said, "at least we only have to deal with this for one full moon."

That hit Kade like a blow to the chest.

Liam raised an eyebrow at him. "You alright there?"

Kade nodded. He was a little numb, a bit nauseous, and a whole lot shell-shocked. "Yeah. I'm fine." The faintness of his voice exposed that for the lie it was.

Liam looked skeptical, but he let Kade play it off. "We should have the spirits captured before the new moon."

"I guess we can only hope that happens," Kade gritted out.

Liam's presence lit up in his mind. "What did you just say?"

"Let's hope we get this done before then."

"No. How you said it before. 'Only hope.'" He stood up and grabbed a sweater. "Jesus fucking Christ. I'm an idiot. I have to go to the shop. If your wolf isn't okay with that, find a way to get it to be."

Kade had no idea what was going on other than the fact that their bond was glittering with Liam's excitement.

Liam tugged his sweater over his head and changed into pants so fast Kade couldn't appreciate the show. He grabbed his bag and gestured for Kade to hurry.

"Come on. I will leave without you, even if it means stealing your damn car and driving myself."

Kade dropped his sweats and pulled on jeans, but Liam wasn't paying attention. He was too absorbed in checking something on his phone.

It was early morning, a hint of dawn on the eastern horizon as they exited the quiet house and got into his car.

Liam radiated determination.

For all that he was driving, Kade was just along for the ride, but his curiosity about what he'd discover when they got to the shop helped distract him from this fucked up situation. He'd have to face this revelation later, but for now, he focused on Liam's impatience as they sped toward town.

FOURTEEN

Liam let himself into the apartment with his spare key, and Kade followed him inside. Miles sat up in the bed, blinking at them, groggy and confused. Aran did the same from the floor.

"What are you guys doing here?" he asked, his voice sleep-rough, but Liam ignored him and headed straight to the stacks of books.

God, how had he not put this together? He was a dumbass.

"He's had a light-bulb moment." Kade shrugged. "But he's refusing to tell me until he gets confirmation."

Liam already had his confirmation though. Lady was perched on the books he'd brought for his personal research again, glaring at him.

"I take it I'll be needing those," he said to her. She let out a short, disgruntled trill before stretching her way off the pile leisurely and sitting beside it, her eyes accusing him of being ridiculously slow.

He shuffled through the books until he found the one he wanted.

"I'm an idiot," he announced as he leafed through the pages. "I should have made the connection before. It's so obvious."

He located the entry he was looking for, only reading halfway through before nodding. He pointed to it. "Here. This has to be it."

"And for those of us not fluent in... is that Greek?" Kade asked. In Liam's mind, he was a buzz of emotions—that catlike thread of curiosity, but this time strung tight with tension. It was the clearest Liam had sensed him when they weren't touching, but he couldn't concentrate on that, not now.

"Oh, right. Sorry. It's Ancient Greek."

Kade and Aran stared at him expectantly, while Miles was slowly reading the passage, a furrow between his brows. He knew enough Modern Greek that he'd understand the gist of it.

"This book is about Greek myths with possible mage or shifter origins," Liam said.

Miles cocked his head. "Pandora's jar?"

"I thought it was a box," Kade said.

"In the original, it was a jar," Liam explained. "That got mistranslated in later retellings, and it became a box. But we've literally been trapping evil spirits in boxes for days."

Kade frowned. "We're fighting Pandora's jar?"

"What's this part here about tainted magic?" Miles asked. "I'm missing something in the translation."

"Okay." Liam needed to start from the beginning to get everyone on the same page. "Mages who cause harm with their magic—forcibly draining a shifter of their energy, taking more than they need, using dark magic, things like that—it causes their magic to become fouled. It makes it unclean. It's impossible to use that kind of magic for anything good. For healing, for most spells, honestly. It's unbalanced, and the more tainted their magic becomes, the more it affects the mage. They can poison themselves with their own magic."

"And that leads to evil spirits in a jar, how?" Aran asked.

"The mage who wrote this had a theory about the Pandora's jar myth. She thought a family of mages had a spell that let them siphon the taint off their magic, or at least enough that they could continue to use their magic normally. Basically, it would skim off the filth and corruption. But it wasn't a one-time solution. They had to keep doing it, and that filth couldn't be destroyed. It had to be stored."

"In a jar?" Kade asked. "That someone opened?"

"I think it fits." Liam flipped the page to a list of the contents of the jar. "Here. There are *nosoi*: personifications of plagues and diseases. *Phthora*: rot, decay, and putrefaction. That was probably the first spirit Elijah trapped." A shiver of memories twisted through their bond, and Liam rushed ahead before Kade fixated on it. "Pretty much everything I've made a sigil for is listed here. Negative emotions, environmental problems, illnesses, and more."

"That would be extremely forbidden magic," Miles said. "No one should be able to do that. If the mage council knew about it, it'd be outlawed immediately."

Liam doubted anyone willing to do this would care about the mage council's rules. "Theoretically, if the author is correct, it was a single family doing it."

Maybe some compartmentalization of knowledge wasn't so bad after all.

Aran's eyes narrowed at the page. "So they scrape off the taint, store it in a sealed, warded container, and when it gets released, it turns into everything corrupt and evil in the world, and they use that as a weapon. Release it on some unsuspecting pack. That would explain what happened to the California pack I found. In which case, it's not just one jar. If there are two—that pack and here—there might be more."

Liam winced. Who knew how many of these jars existed? The book had no information on how tainted the magic had to get before a mage could siphon the corruption off, or how much was needed to fill a jar. There could be dozens of these things waiting to be let loose.

"Whoever is behind this... their magic must be so twisted and corrupt." Miles's face was pale and drawn.

"It has to be Victor's father and that evil fucking bastard of a mage who owned the shop before Elijah. As revenge for Victor overthrowing and exiling his father and for getting the mage council to punish that asshole," Kade said with a growl.

That seemed the most likely scenario, though Liam hoped for Victor's sake that his father wasn't involved.

"But why like this?" Miles asked, gesturing at the book. "Why go through all this when they could target Victor directly? This seems like so much more effort."

"Alphas get strength from their pack, just as packs get strength from their alphas." Kade's tone was grim. "Want to make an alpha too weak to protect their pack? Weaken the pack first. Hunters would love it. They wouldn't need to take down shifters one by one. Once the pack was weakened, they could take them all out, if the spirits didn't do the job for them."

Those words hung heavy in the air, oppressive and painfully true. If Elijah hadn't captured the decay spirit, Victor's pack would already be dead.

Kade finally broke the silence. "You're thinking this...

jar, or whatever, was opened on our territory? So we should search for a container of some sort to prove it?"

Liam considered it before answering. "It might not need to be *on* your territory. The spirits start small and grow as they gain strength. They have to gather energy before they become personified. I don't think wards would pick up bits of emotion floating through them unless they were keyed to block it. What ward would stop a wisp of sadness from getting through? At least not until that sadness had strengthened to the point where it could cause harm."

"But if they release them outside the wards, how do they guarantee they attack the pack?" Kade asked.

"If I had to guess? It's shifter energy. Shifter energy is attractive to mages. It feeds our magic. If the spirits are some corrupt byproduct of magic, it stands to reason they might also be attracted to it and feed off it."

"That would explain why the decay spirit was the first to get so strong," Aran said. "Sadness wouldn't feed off the pack wards, but a spirit of corruption could latch on and eat away at them while the rest passed through to find better energy sources."

Kade's brow furrowed. "If the wards don't stop it, or wouldn't have stopped it before Elijah reinforced them, are there spirits outside our wards?"

Liam jerked his head up and glanced at Miles and Aran.

Miles hurried to his bag and took out his map. When he returned, he held it out for them to see. Victor's territory comprised almost the entirety of the map, with a dozen or so spirits still roaming it—small things, little smudges. Nothing was outside the territory. But then...

"Did Elijah spell the maps to look for spirits on Victor's territory, or simply to look for spirits?" Liam asked.

Miles and Aran shook their heads. They didn't know either.

"We need a bigger map," Liam said. "Kade, can you message Victor and Elijah and tell them our theory?"

Kade pulled out his phone to do that.

"There has to be a map of the surrounding area with the pack territories marked out somewhere in this place," Aran said.

Miles nodded. "Worst-case scenario, we'll run to a gas station and grab a local map."

They headed downstairs to rummage through Elijah's office.

After a minute, Kade followed. "Elijah says there's a map in the storage room on the second floor. The one he hasn't completely organized yet."

When they'd moved Elijah into the shop, it had been an absolute wreck. The mage council had forced the previous owner to leave without notice, multiple enforcement mages showing up to send him on his way and supervise him packing his belongings.

The storeroom had shelves lining its walls—overstock and various magical supplies filled every inch of them. While the room wasn't a complete disaster like the last time Liam had been there, it was far from the well-organized chaos that sprang up around Elijah. The fact that Elijah had managed to organize the shop as much as he had in a year while running the business was impressive enough.

The four of them scattered and poked through the boxes. Liam cracked open a wooden crate and blinked at the dozens of glass vials inside. Most were empty, but a few held a single dried flower each. He pulled one out and examined it. The petals were white and in a shape that should have been familiar, but he couldn't place it. The box gave off a soapy-peppery scent.

Liam's curiosity got the better of him. "Aran, what kind of flower is this?"

Instead of the quick answer Liam expected, Aran frowned. He took the vial and turned it around in his hand. "No clue. Hey, Miles, have you ever seen a flower like this?"

"If you don't know what it is, I definitely don't. How do you not know?"

"Eh. I'm better with wood. Twigs and berries, I'm all over. Anything with a nice, long stamen, really. But seriously, I have no idea what these are."

Kade snorted, but before he could say whatever perverted comment was about to come out of his mouth, his phone vibrated, and he answered the video call, holding it so they could see.

"Did you find it?" Elijah's voice scraped like sandpaper.

"Well, well, well." Aran smirked. "It's nice to know someone had fun last night."

Even from across the room, on that little screen, it was clear Elijah had been thoroughly fucked. His hair was a mess, and dark marks littered the pale skin of his neck.

Elijah wisely ignored Aran's comment. "Look for a file box on the bottom shelves. It's full of old paperwork I need to sort through. There's one in there, if I'm remembering correctly. Victor's gone downstairs to grab a map for me too."

Miles ran over to the box and began to dig through it. As he did, Aran asked, "Hey, Elijah, what's with this case of white flowers?"

"Oh, those. No fucking idea. I was assuming someone was buying them regularly, given how many empty vials there were, but no one has requested any. I kept meaning to check with you, but it's been so far down my to-do list. You saw how messy that asshole left the shop."

"Do you mind if I take a few? I want to figure out what they are."

"Knock yourself out."

Aran pocketed two of the vials, and Liam was sure he'd have the flower identified in no time.

"Victor's back with a map," Elijah said. "I'm going to do the spell on my end. If you can't do it on yours, I'll show you when I'm done."

"Sounds good," Liam said.

"Got it," Miles called out, holding up a map.

They stepped into the workroom, and Miles spread the map out on the floor while Aran grabbed a vial of ash from the more organized of the two storerooms.

A string of curses came through the phone, and Liam looked over, but when Kade flashed the screen at him, it was nothing but a ceiling.

"You seeing what I'm seeing?" Elijah asked.

"Give us a minute," Liam said.

Aran dumped the ash on the map, and Liam reached out, Kade's hand finding his. He ran Kade's energy through the ash, then stared at the map in horror.

Victor's territory was mostly clear; that wasn't the problem. It was the rest of the map that was making him sick, making his chest feel tight. No, making *Kade's* chest feel tight. He squeezed Kade's hand and heard him take a breath, the pressure around Liam's lungs easing, but he couldn't tear his eyes away from the map to check on him.

The ash had pooled over what Liam had to assume were the other two local territories, now teeming and swirling with ashy masses within their borders.

"Fuck," Aran said.

Liam couldn't agree more. They'd been too focused on Victor's land.

"Okay." Elijah paused, pulling himself together. "So this means it's absolutely attacking the other packs."

"What are they being affected by?" Miles asked. "There seem to be large spirits over both territories. The one closest to town is jagged and spiky, and the second is hazy."

He was right. The predominant spirits on both covered a disturbing amount of land, but smaller spirits also darted underneath.

"Niall was acting super paranoid when I saw him last," Elijah said.

"Same here," Victor agreed from off-camera. "He wouldn't show me his back and kept looking around like he expected someone to attack him. And I haven't been able to reach Grant since he sent me that message. Something about sleeping. He seemed tired the last time I saw him, but that was over a month ago."

"Alright," Elijah said. "The remaining spirits here can wait. These are more urgent. They're even bigger than the decay spirit. We'll make two large boxes as quickly as we can. Two very fucking large boxes. The spirits do condense when they're trapped, but not enough that I want to try to get these into the boxes we've been using. Let's meet on the main road outside Niall's pack wards, since his territory is closer to town. It'll take you about thirty-five minutes to drive there. Hopefully we can have the boxes ready and arrive around that time."

"And then what?" Liam asked. "If they're paranoid, will they let us help?"

Elijah grimaced. "We'll see."

"Okay, we'll meet you there."

Miles and Aran rushed upstairs to get ready, with Liam and Kade close behind.

This was so much worse than he'd thought. They'd arrived knowing they needed to help Victor's pack, but now three packs were in trouble, and the spirits they'd been facing were tiny in comparison.

"If Elijah struggled to trap the decay spirit, will he be able to trap these?" Aran asked as he stripped out of his night clothes.

"If anyone can do it, Elijah can," Miles said.

"And if not," Liam added, "we're here. We can feed him our magic to help."

It had to work; they didn't have a choice.

Miles and Aran put on fresh clothing. Kade hadn't glanced at them once as they'd undressed, which was foolish on his part, Liam had to admit. They were both nice to look at. But Kade was a jumble of emotions, too distracted to notice as he fell into his memories.

They weren't standing close enough for Liam to reach out and squeeze his arm, so instead, he pushed a sliver of magic at Kade through the tether.

Kade's head swung toward Liam, his eyes wide.

Liam caught his gaze, hoping to get his question across without asking it.

Are you okay?

They were about to face massive spirits, more powerful than the one Kade had been possessed by. That would shake anyone, and Kade had more reason than most to be shaken.

As they stared at each other, Liam sensed Kade's presence settle, determination taking over. Kade didn't want to let these spirits control him, not anymore. He wanted to defeat them.

Good. They couldn't do this without him.

Liam turned to see if Miles and Aran were ready. They were both standing there, eyebrows raised.

"You just had an entire silent conversation, didn't you?" Aran asked.

"No." Liam scoffed. "Of course not. It's not like we're Elijah and Victor." He exited the apartment and descended the stairs.

Wait.

They had, hadn't they? Huh. That was weird, but their bond did seem to be getting deeper. He'd have to talk to Kade about that later and ensure there wouldn't be any problems when they severed it.

They piled into Kade's car and sped toward Niall's territory while Liam wondered what awaited them.

When the spirit of decay had gotten large enough, when Elijah had been a genuine threat to it, it had possessed Kade and manifested itself physically, creating golems to attack the people trying to stop it. Would they be attacked by monstrous creatures as well? Were the packs possessed by those spirits?

He opened his codex and started to sketch a sigil for paranoia. For the other, he had to guess what the spirit might be. If Grant had looked tired and sent a message about sleeping... Insomnia, perhaps?

He wasn't sure, but he'd have it prepared just in case.

FIFTEEN

Going from zero sense of smell to having it fully restored in one day was messing with Kade. Everything seemed extra potent—Liam more than anything. The scent of *them*. He couldn't get over it. And while that was throwing him off-kilter, it wasn't the only thing he needed to acclimate to.

Kade was far more accustomed to magic than the average shifter, but three mages in one confined space was a lot, even for him, even with one of them having the best scent to ever walk the planet. His nose itched, and regardless of his other reasons for it, he would have wanted the windows cracked open. Thankfully, despite the chilly morning air whipping into the car, the mages didn't ask him to roll them up.

Aran and Miles weren't horrible. They smelled better than he would have expected with them not being pack, but nothing like Liam did. Their scents were too sharp to be truly pleasant.

He was using that train of thought to distract himself,

but a lot had happened in the last few hours, and he hadn't managed to wrap his mind around any of it yet.

When he had a moment to himself, he needed to decide what to do about Liam. About the fact that Liam smelled like they were meant to be together. But they had more pressing issues to deal with first.

It was early morning when he parked just short of Niall's pack territory. Victor and Elijah weren't there yet.

Kade got out of his car and walked to the wards, holding up his hand to sense them better, then yanked it back. He hadn't touched them, but he still felt unclean, like he'd brushed up against a cold, slimy thing.

He forced himself to inhale, and when he did, Liam's scent stroked over him. The vice-like bands around his chest loosened a fraction, enough to let him breathe.

"There's something very fucked up happening with these wards," he said, glancing over his shoulder.

The mages approached, only to have the same reaction as he had to the wards. He sensed Liam recoiling in disgust.

"What the hell could do this to wards?" Aran asked.

"I've never felt magic this corrupt before." Miles scraped one palm over the other as if he were brushing off the filth he'd gotten so close to touching.

"The spirit must be in the wards." Liam squinted at the invisible barrier.

"If it's in the wards," Kade said, "it's probably in Niall, if not the entire pack."

The wards were strong though. Solid. Wards like these usually weren't set to prevent people from entering unless they meant to do the pack harm, but Niall's made him think they were locked down so no one could get in. He didn't want to test that theory though—that would require touching them, and there was no telling what that would do to him.

Tires crunched over the gravel road behind them as Victor's SUV pulled up.

Victor, Elijah, Rick, and Will got out and joined them.

"The wards are severely corrupted," Liam explained.

Elijah raised his hand to the wards and released a small amount of magic into them. The spirals of purple were consumed by a churning blackness that then faded away.

"I called Niall and Grant multiple times," Victor said. "No answer from either."

With a grim set to his lips, he brought his hand as close as he could without touching the wards, then pushed a substantial burst of energy into them—a clear message, one alpha to another, letting Niall know he was there and they would be talking.

It wouldn't take long for Niall to show up.

Kade leaned against his car and took in Victor and Elijah's state. He snorted.

Elijah had been thoroughly mauled, and Victor, for all the seriousness of the situation, looked pretty damn pleased with himself. He also didn't seem to be able to stop stealing touches or to let Elijah get more than an arm's length away.

Kade tried not to envy that. Tried not to think about spending a night lost in Liam.

Rick stood next to Kade and tilted his head toward Victor. "Right?" He mimicked Victor's gruff tone. "'Everyone stay in your rooms. No running in the forest.' Uh-huh. Must have been a real hardship for them."

"He wouldn't have made it fifteen minutes on a pack run," Will added.

Victor shot him a flat look. "What did you last your first full moon bonded? Five?"

Aran's eyes raked over Elijah. He then gave Victor an approving nod. "Good job, Alpha. I've never seen him this well-fucked before."

Victor's expression was obnoxiously smug and self-satisfied.

"Don't encourage him. After last night, I'm going to have come leaking out of my ass for days." Elijah cringed as he realized what he'd said, then sighed and shrugged.

Kade grinned. It was nice that he was getting used to the lack of secrets in a shifter pack. Either that, or Victor had fucked the filter right out of him.

Victor leaned in and said under his breath, "You can return the favor tonight."

Elijah looked significantly more mollified.

"Ugh, I didn't need to know any of that about your sex life," Liam said with a groan.

Rick chuckled. "At least you can't smell it. Be glad you don't have shifter senses." He winced, glancing over at Kade. "Sorry, man."

"Oh, I can smell it. My sense of smell is back."

A bright flare of shock stampeded through the bond, and Liam's head swiveled toward him, his eyes wide. The surprise dimmed to a dull ache, something raw to it, like betrayal. And fuck, Kade kept messing this up, didn't he? He should have told Liam after he'd gorged himself on Liam's scent, not just announced it to everyone like he couldn't be bothered to tell Liam directly.

"Is it now?" Victor asked. His smirk wasn't even mildly repentant.

Kade glared at him.

Fuck him. Kade wasn't the only one messing this up, and they'd be talking about it later.

There was a rustle of leaves, and a lone figure emerged from the forest.

Niall's second-in-command, Pierce, stopped on the road, not crossing the wards. He glanced toward the pack house, then back at them.

"You shouldn't be here." His words were a whisper that Kade had to strain to hear, and his face was pinched and tight. "You should leave before Niall comes."

"What's going on?" Victor asked, and Pierce flinched, checking behind him again. Victor lowered his voice. "What's happening to your pack?"

Pierce's dark eyes were wild as he tried to take in everything at once. He looked so different from how Kade had always seen him—self-assured and confident, a natural to become alpha when Niall was ready to retire.

"You came to my shop around the beginning of last month. Why?" Elijah prompted.

Pierce shook his head, attempting to clear it. "Something... something's *here*. In our territory. It's been here for months. Growing. Getting stronger. Watching us. It's affecting Niall. Affecting all of us. And I can't... I don't..." He rubbed at his temples, his breathing accelerating.

Miles took a step forward, but Elijah held out a hand. The motion drew Pierce's attention. His gaze darted around their group, landing on the mages one by one. He zeroed in on Aran, his eyes flicking over the tattoos on his exposed forearms.

"You're a mage. You're all mages. He won't like that. You should get out of here before he arrives. I don't know what he'll do if he sees you." Pierce kept his voice to a harsh, hurried whisper.

"Let us help you," Elijah said.

"I convinced him to go to you for help, but then you smelled like Victor. He decided you were in on it. Behind it. He's so certain Victor wants our land, but I don't know. Everything's so confusing. And now you have four mages."

He jerked upright. His face was wiped free of any emotion, and the twitching nerves melted away.

"They're here," he called out, the proclamation answered by the sound of feet and paws on gravel.

A few seconds later, Niall appeared around the bend, almost his whole pack behind him, some in human form, some as wolves.

As they fanned out, Pierce took his position next to Niall, quiet and cowed.

Kade stepped up beside Victor. He'd known this could be bad, but their packs had lived side by side for decades. Seeing Niall's pack like this had been beyond his imagination. For them to be so militant and ready to fight. Their wolves flashed in their eyes, a feral warning. They stayed on their territory, but Kade got the impression they were merely waiting for the signal from Niall to attack.

"Why were you testing my wards?" Niall snarled at Victor.

"If you'd answered my calls, I wouldn't have needed to," Victor countered, his tone cool, but tension radiated from his body.

Niall's gaze landed on Elijah, then swept over the rest of them. He sneered. "I knew you were working together, but I hadn't realized you'd taken so many mages, Victor. You've been busy, but I'm not letting you take my land too."

Taken? That was one fucked up word choice.

"I don't want your land," Victor growled. "We're here to help you."

Niall scoffed. "You and your little harem of mages are going to *help* me? Sure."

That comment caused the mages to bristle, and Kade with them.

"What right do you have to keep four mages?" Niall asked.

"What the *fuck*? Excuse you?" The way Aran was holding his hands made Kade think he was preparing to throw something nasty at Niall.

"I am not *keeping* anyone," Victor said. "They're here as guests of my pack; they're helping us."

Niall sniffed the air. "You've already bonded two of them. Why didn't you take the other two last night?"

Rage rushed through Kade. The implication made his skin crawl more than the wards had. He'd known Niall his entire life. This was not the man Kade had met on countless occasions. He smelled wrong in a way Kade couldn't describe, but that had his throat closing up when he tried to think about it. He inhaled carefully, picking out Liam's scent from those around him.

"Give me one," Niall said casually, "and I'll forgive your attempt to intrude on my land."

Kade was striding forward before he could stop himself, but Victor grabbed his arm.

"They're people, not things to give." A warning rumbled in Victor's tone.

"You don't need them all. The only reason you could want four mages for yourself is so your pack can take over."

"I'm not after your territory." Each word was bitten out.

"Prove it. I'll take that one." Niall pointed to Aran, eyeing his tattoos. "He looks powerful."

Pierce blanched, and Miles gripped Aran's arm, though

it seemed more to hold him back than to keep him safe. A cold fury burned in Aran's eyes.

If Victor didn't kill this asshole, Kade would like the honor.

Elijah placed a hand on Victor's arm. "It's the spirit talking."

Victor nodded, the movement tight, before addressing Niall again. "We aren't here to fight you. I'll call you tomorrow, and we can discuss this then."

Kade wanted to punch Niall in the face, but Elijah wasn't wrong. This was the spirit affecting him. Niall wouldn't be like this otherwise. Fighting him would do nothing. They needed to take care of the spirit, but that wasn't happening now.

He caught Pierce's gaze, hoping to telepathically convey something remotely like *contact me.*

They'd never been close, but they were the same age and had gone to school together. If Pierce could trust anyone in their pack, Kade hoped it'd be him.

They backed away from the wards and got into their cars, driving down the long, narrow driveway until they reached the main road.

Liam's phone buzzed, and he answered it, putting it on speaker.

"Well," Elijah's voice said cheerfully, "that was supremely fucked up."

Kade snorted.

"I realize he's possessed," Aran said from the back seat, "but man, that fucker seems like he'd make excellent fertilizer."

A chorus of agreement came from the phone.

Kade's grip tightened on the steering wheel, and Liam glanced at him. Kade shook his head slightly. He was fine.

That comment hadn't been directed at him, so he wasn't going to dwell on it. They had more important things to deal with than his issues.

"Okay," Elijah said. "We'll have to figure out what to do about him. If we can get onto their land somehow and capture the spirit, it should bring Niall and his pack to their senses. But first, let's see how Grant's pack is doing."

"Maybe they aren't as affected by the spirits on their land," Miles said.

Kade would not put money on that.

"Who's the guy with the arms?" Aran asked.

Liam screwed up his face. "Pretty sure they all had arms, Aran."

"You know which one I meant. Everyone here knows which one I meant."

Kade firmly agreed. Pierce's arms were a work of art. The kind you'd want pinning you to a mattress as he fucked you.

"Pierce," he explained. "We were the only shifters in our grade."

"You ever?" A leer colored Aran's tone.

Liam paged through his book, though he'd already drawn both sigils they needed.

"Nope. He's tragically straight. White picket fence with two-point-five kids written all over him. But he's a good guy, even if he's too good for my personal preferences."

"The hottest ones always are. But he seemed... not completely insane?"

"He wasn't acting like himself, but definitely more normal than the rest."

"Do you still have his number?" Victor asked over the phone.

"Yeah. I'll send him a message after we check on Grant's pack. Whether or not he'll respond is another matter."

"Might as well give it a try," Elijah said. "If he convinced Niall to seek help before, maybe he can do it again."

Kade didn't have much faith on that front, but he also didn't have any better ideas to offer.

Elijah continued. "Alright. It's a twenty-minute drive from here to Grant's territory. Let's hope their giant-ass spirit isn't affecting them in a way that'll prevent Grant from accepting our assistance."

They ended the call, and Kade kept driving, following Victor's SUV and hoping their luck was better with this spirit.

When they arrived at the entrance to the Lucas pack territory, Victor pulled to a stop. Beyond his front bumper were the pack wards. They were invisible, but where they stood was stomach-sinkingly apparent. A hazy wall of fog stretched before them, cutting visibility to nearly nothing. Everything on the other side of that barrier looked surreal.

Liam cursed, and in the back seat, Aran and Miles leaned forward.

Was that the spirit, or just its effects? What could a spirit that size do? What would happen if Kade crossed those wards? Would it be the same as the decay spirit? Would it fill his lungs until he couldn't breathe?

No. He inhaled Liam's scent. This was not the decay spirit. He wouldn't let it control him.

"I hope Elijah brought one hell of a fucking box," Aran said.

They got out and watched as Elijah examined the wards. He didn't touch them, but it didn't matter once he tested them with his magic. Swirls of purple spread out from under his palm, followed by more in a steady flow. Elijah wrenched his hand away, shaking it out.

"*Fuck*. It's so desperate for energy, it's trying to leech my magic. This is a day or two from collapsing."

Victor put his own hand against the barrier, ripples of silver flowing into the wards, but he pulled away too. "Grant's alive, but I've never felt wards this weak, so I don't know how much longer he will be."

"Will they let us through?" Liam asked.

Elijah studied the wards. "With as depleted as they are, I don't think they can stop us, and we don't have any ill intentions. It might not be a pleasant trip through them though."

"Can we trap it from here?" Miles cocked his head.

"We can try." Elijah gestured to Rick and Will, who grabbed a chest-sized box out of Victor's SUV and brought it to where he was standing.

Kade took the opportunity to send Pierce a quick message.

KADE

Hey! It's been forever. We should catch up. Call me when you can.

He hoped it was vague enough that it wouldn't get Pierce in trouble if Niall saw it, but given the timing and how paranoid Niall was, he doubted it. He wasn't holding his breath for Pierce to reply.

"So what are we dealing with?" Elijah asked.

"Let's go with insomnia," Victor said. "Not sleeping is the only clue we have."

Liam showed Elijah the sigil he'd sketched, and Elijah knelt beside the box, transferring it inside. Victor stood behind him, cupping the nape of his neck as Elijah activated the seal.

Kade smelled the magic stirring around them—pack magic, soft and familiar, welcome after a decade-long absence.

Wisps of smoky fog lapped over the edge of the barrier like they were considering pooling in the box, though they kept getting pulled back inside the wards.

Elijah narrowed his eyes, then did something that caused the hair on Kade's arms to stand on end. He sensed Elijah channeling the pack's energy, and the magic surrounding them spiked, the air heavy with it.

Liam inhaled, surprise sparking through their bond.

More tendrils of fog were tugged closer to the box, but they didn't flow inside. Elijah dropped his magic and stood, Victor's hand sliding down to his waist.

Aran whistled softly. "I know I joke about your channels being stretched, Elijah, but fuck me, that was crazy."

Miles nodded. "I think my ears popped from the pressure change. Did you double your strength? Triple it?"

Elijah looked a little sheepish, a little pleased. His gaze darted to Victor, a soft smile on his face. "I'm not sure yet." But then he returned his focus to the issue at hand. "Not that it makes a difference. I can't get a hold of the spirit."

"So that's not the spirit itself," Liam said. "We're only seeing its effect."

"Yeah, but there's more to it than that. The way it isn't latching on feels different than with the anger spirit."

"Wrong sigil?" Liam's brain was churning, attempting

to find a solution to the problem they'd been presented with. Kade could do nothing but watch as the mages sorted it out.

"Maybe. It also feels anchored to the pack, to their territory."

"Could you sense what it is?" Aran asked.

"I wasn't getting any emotion from it." Elijah paused, considering. "Possibly an echo of fear?"

"How is it tied to the pack?" Miles asked.

"From what I experienced with the decay spirit, it was hooked onto the pack and had to be removed from them to trap it properly."

"So we need the pack alpha, or access to the pack's energy," Liam said. "Then you can extract it from their bonds."

"Which means finding Grant, and there's only one way to do that."

They looked into the pack territory, into the thick fog that waited there. It would affect them; it might try to possess them. They'd be defenseless. There'd be no avoiding it.

Kade swallowed, his heart rate kicking up. Liam reached over and wrapped a hand around his wrist, the gesture oddly casual, almost instinctive, like he just knew what to do, what Kade needed to distract himself from the crushing pressure on his lungs.

"Do we drive?" Liam asked.

"That's probably the best idea," Elijah said. "The longer you're affected by these things, the worse their effects on you seem to become. So maybe if we drive, it'll be better."

Aran huffed. "Unless the spirit causes road rage and we end up crashing into a tree."

"We need to risk it."

"You can't ward us or something?" Rick asked the question that had been running through Kade's mind.

"I can't ward living things. I can put wards *around* them, not *on* them. But those wards would be stationary—they wouldn't move with us. I could try that protection spell again though. It didn't seem to do much to stop the decay spirit from affecting the pack, but it didn't hurt."

"Worth a try," Victor said.

Elijah's eyelids slid closed, and magic poured through the pack bonds, sparkling and incandescent. Kade had felt this before. It had done nothing to mitigate the effects of the spirit that had possessed him.

When Elijah opened his eyes, his gaze caught on Aran and Miles, and he winced. "Shit. That spell depends on pack bonds."

"And we're not pack," Aran said wryly. "No worries. We'll be fine without."

"Sorry."

Aran shrugged. "Our fault for not getting kno—"

"Should we test it?" Liam asked, cutting Aran off.

"Should we?" Elijah glanced at Victor.

"I'll do it," Kade said.

Everyone whipped their heads toward him, but all he saw was Liam and his concerned expression. Kade met his stare. He needed to do this. He needed to prove these spirits couldn't control him, that he wasn't afraid of them.

After a moment, Liam nodded. "I'll go with you."

Elijah frowned. "I don't think that's a good idea."

Kade turned to him. "We need to know what effect this spirit will have on us before we all go in there."

"He's right," Victor said to Elijah, though he didn't sound happy about it. He grimaced as he looked at Kade. "If you feel anything amiss, cross back immediately."

"Will do." Kade walked up to the barrier, his heart pounding. Liam came to stand by him, the fog inches in front of them.

God, why had he volunteered to do this? It was the stupidest thing he'd done in his life. He wasn't certain he was breathing, but then, no one else around him seemed to be either.

Liam's hand came up to rest on his arm. He was a ball of nerves, but as determined as Kade.

They stepped across the border.

The wards washed over them, stealing his energy, stealing Liam's magic. He'd never felt a confused ward before, but this one seemed exactly that. It wanted to block them from entering because the pack was too vulnerable to face outsiders, but also wanted to allow them in because they were there to help.

What resulted was a fraction of a second stretched out, like he was being both pushed and pulled, but then they were through.

Kade exhaled a sigh, only for his breath to catch as he was surrounded by thick fog. He inhaled shallowly, expecting to be overcome by that choking, drowning sensation, but he wasn't.

Liam squeezed his arm, and they stood there, waiting for something, anything—a stray emotion, a sign of illness—but nothing seemed wrong.

"Are you feeling anything?" Elijah asked.

"No, I feel totally normal," Liam replied.

Kade nodded his agreement. Whatever the spirit was, it wasn't affecting them like the others had.

"Any clue what it is?" Miles asked.

Liam shook his head. "I've got nothing."

"Come back over," Elijah said.

"Passing through those wards is unpleasant. Can someone bring Kade's car across instead?"

"We should go in the same car," Victor said. "I don't want us to get separated in whatever that is."

They piled into his SUV, leaving Kade's car and the first box behind. They'd brought two, so they had one more shot at this. Then they drove over the border and picked Kade and Liam up. Will and Rick crouched in the back with the box. Kade squished onto the bench seat with Liam, Aran, and Miles. Liam and his scent were pressed against him.

Elijah spun in his seat. "Now that you're all in here, I should be able to put a ward around the back seats to protect you."

"What about you?" Liam asked.

"I've never warded a car before and have no idea how the electronics will react if I run a ward through them. I'd rather not find out the hard way that brakes can't function through wards."

"Just exclude me," Victor said. "There are no control systems in your seat."

"No. I'll ward everyone but us."

Worry twisted Liam's face. "If you're not warded, I don't want you to ward me either. That's not right."

"Not to interrupt this beautiful, sacrificial moment," Aran said. "But I think it's too late for that."

Traces of fog had filled the vehicle.

They eyed each other, but no one was feeling any effects.

As Victor drove, an eerie silence settled over them, everyone's senses on high alert.

Out of the corner of his eye, Kade saw something running through the foggy forest. He snapped his head over, but nothing was there.

Liam raised an eyebrow at him.

"Did you see that?" Will asked Rick, pointing behind them.

"Are there..." Miles trailed off, frowning out the window.

Something moved outside, but again, when Kade tried to catch a glimpse, it was gone. He stared into the forest, but the trees were flickering, jumping from one spot to another. "Is anyone else seeing the trees move?"

"I don't think they're moving," Elijah said. "I think our perception of reality is shifting around us. Like a dream."

"Like a fucking nightmare, you mean," Aran said.

"Could that be it?" Elijah asked Liam.

Liam pulled out his codex, but then froze. Panic clawed at their bond as he began to frantically flip through the pages. "I can't... Why can't I read?"

Kade gripped his wrist, his fingers sliding against Liam's skin. "It's not real. You can read."

Liam pressed his eyelids shut, forced out a breath, then opened them. He looked at the book and sighed in relief. "I can read." He sketched a distorted sigil for nightmares as they neared the pack house.

When it came into view, Kade's stomach plummeted at the sight that greeted them. He sensed that same emotion roiling through Liam.

The entire Lucas pack of just under twenty members was outside the house. They were waiting for them, like they were ready for a fight. But unlike Niall's pack, they were gaunt and sallow, their eyes glassy with dark circles smudged beneath, their postures slumped.

"They look like zombies," Aran said.

Kade had never seen wolf shifters so weak and wretched before, so close to death. Even at his worst,

Victor's father hadn't been this bad. Grant's pack was wasting away. Had they slept or eaten in days? In weeks?

Victor put his SUV in park. "Everyone stay inside until I give you the all-clear."

He slowly got out, and Elijah copied his actions. Victor sent him a look across the front seat, but Elijah answered with a cocked eyebrow that said Victor was losing his mind if he expected Elijah to stay in the vehicle.

Their movements were measured and deliberate, and they left their doors open, like the sound of them shutting might startle the pack into action. They kept their hands in plain sight, though Kade didn't know how that would make a mage less dangerous.

They approached where Grant was waiting in front of his pack. He was trying to stand steady, trying to protect his pack members, but he swayed on his feet. They were all there, from the oldest to the youngest, including Grant's ten-year-old son, Remy.

A vision flashed in Kade's head. Oliver on the night they'd battled the decay spirit, his tiny body heaving as he vomited up something black and foul, something caused by the spirit infecting their pack bonds because of Kade.

Kade ached with the instinct to protect, to fight off whatever this was, to help these weakened shifters, though it was impossible for him. He couldn't fight this, not on his own.

Victor and Elijah stopped a few feet from the SUV, keeping enough distance between them and Grant that it wasn't threatening.

"You're on my territory uninvited," Grant said, the words slurred to the point Kade barely understood them even with the open doors.

"We want to help you," Victor said. "What happened to your pack?"

Grant's gaze sharpened, locking on Victor. "Don't sleep. They can't get you if you don't sleep."

"So it is nightmares," Liam said. "They haven't been sleeping to avoid the nightmares, but I doubt it matters."

As if proving his point, Aran jerked, inhaling sharply, then cursed. "Nope, nope, I'm fine. Just had that weird-ass feeling like you're literally falling as you doze off. But I'm good."

"Hypnic jerk," Miles replied, but his attention was trained on Grant's pack.

Victor took a step closer to Grant. "We can help you, but you have to let us."

Behind Grant, Remy teetered where he stood, his eyes rolling into his head as he collapsed to the ground.

Before anyone could react, Miles was climbing over Aran and throwing open his door.

"*Miles*," Liam cried, but Miles wasn't listening. He jumped out, and to Kade's horror, Liam followed with near shifter-like speed.

Kade threw himself out of the SUV and raced after them, managing to grab Liam before he passed Elijah and Victor. He got an elbow to the sternum for his efforts as Liam struggled to break free from his hold and go after Miles, who rushed past Grant, into the midst of his pack. He fell to his knees next to Remy.

Grant and his pack responded sluggishly, but no pack would stand for an unfamiliar mage racing toward their weakest member. They began to stagger closer to Miles.

"Oh Jesus fucking Christ." Elijah dropped to his own knees, pressing his hands to the ground. "So glad we all stayed in the SUV."

A ward sprang up around Miles and Remy, snapping into place a second before Grant reached them. Grant growled, partially shifted, his claws out and scraping against Elijah's barrier, but it was far too strong for him to do more than scrabble at it.

"Miles," Elijah yelled, "I know you're not an idiot, so what the fuck are you doing?"

"He needs help!" Miles rolled Remy onto his back. He pushed up his sleeves and placed his hands against the kid's neck. Sweeping lines of light blue glittered across Miles's arms. He mumbled to himself, but then, over Grant's snarling, he said, "I don't think he's slept for weeks, and he hasn't eaten much either."

The rest of the pack milled about, distressed, unsure what to do.

Victor grabbed Grant and yanked him back from the barrier, an arm wrapped around him. "He's healing him."

Grant thrashed, clawing at Victor.

Victor shook him. "*Look.*" He put his alpha authority and power into that word. "He's saving your son."

It took a beat to sink in, but Grant sagged in Victor's hold. In Kade's arms, Liam did the same, and Kade reluctantly let him go.

Elijah maintained the ward around Miles until Remy stirred and sat up, confused and drained, but no longer seconds away from death.

When Elijah released the barrier, Victor let go of Grant, who fell beside his son and Miles, then pulled Remy into his arms.

"Can I try to heal you too?" Miles asked, tentatively holding his hands out.

Grant hesitated, but nodded.

The amount of trust that showed floored Kade. Not

many alphas would allow an unknown mage to touch them, to heal them. But he supposed after what Miles had done, he might have won Grant's loyalty for life.

Miles's hands settled on the sides of Grant's neck, and Grant stared at him intently, like Miles was an anchor grounding him, his eyes becoming more focused as he breathed deeply.

After a few moments, Miles dropped his hands, shaking them out, his brown irises glowing a vivid blue. Grant's gaze didn't leave him, and Miles seemed caught in the scrutiny.

"Sorry. I can't do more than that. You need sleep and food. That's not something I can heal."

But Grant shook his head. "It's better. Thank you."

Kade exhaled. Grant still looked haggard, but more like himself.

Grant stood, offering his hand to Miles to help him up. He clutched his son to his side, though Remy was starting to squirm.

"*Dad*," he hissed, and Grant relaxed his hold, but didn't let him go.

Grant turned to Victor, exhausted but lucid and in control. "What the hell is going on?"

Victor waved to Aran, Rick, and Will, and they piled out, coming to stand behind him. Grant watched them warily but seemed to recognize they weren't a threat.

"Evil spirits are attacking our territories," Victor said. "All of this was caused by them. How long has it been since you've slept?"

Grant frowned, his eyes growing distant. "I... I don't remember."

"What happens when you sleep?" Liam asked. "Nightmares?"

Grant shuddered and swallowed thickly. "They're bad. You know you're dreaming, but you can't wake up. All your worst nightmares, chasing you down."

His son shivered and pressed closer to him. Grant's arm tightened around him.

Kade refused to think about his worst nightmares—they'd been haunting him for over a week.

"We can capture it, but it's tied to your pack," Elijah said. "We can't get rid of it without access to your energy and pack bonds."

Grant studied him, expression wary, but then he inhaled. "You two are bonded?"

"Yes." Elijah and Victor said that word as one. It held both pride and happiness.

"I told you to go see him when he first came to town, didn't I?" Grant's tired voice was threaded with amusement.

Victor rubbed his neck, looking abashed, and Kade suppressed a grin. Apparently Victor had been the only one who hadn't realized how obviously meant for each other he and Elijah were.

"I'm glad you figured it out." Knowing they were bonded seemed to relax Grant further. "Okay. Whatever you need. I want this thing off my territory."

Victor gestured for Rick and Will to grab the chest, and they got to work.

This time, Kade vowed to himself, he'd be on the right side of the battle they were about to face.

SIXTEEN

Liam stared into the forest as Elijah prepared the spell. The trees surrounding them kept shifting, changing shape and position with each blink. Grant's territory didn't look real, like the world itself was no longer solid or tangible, reality consumed by a twisting haze of feverish nightmares.

They needed to work fast and capture this spirit before it affected them too much. It was so strong that Liam worried they might not be able to trap it at all.

"Liam," Elijah said.

Liam shook himself, bringing his notebook over to show Elijah the sigil he'd made for nightmares.

Elijah transferred it to the bottom of the chest. "Can you feed me Kade's energy? I don't know if Victor's and Grant's will be enough."

"You can't use Grant's," Miles said. "At least not much. He has barely any left. You'll have to be extremely careful."

Elijah grimaced. "Then I'll definitely need Kade's."

Liam nodded. "I'm better at controlling it now. I should be able to feed it to you."

"Can you channel Grant's?" Elijah asked Miles. "Whatever amount is safe. I need that connection to the pack."

"I can. It'll just be a trickle though."

As a healer, Miles was excellent at handling delicate spells. Healing often required a light touch and precise use of magic. If they could only use a small amount of energy from Grant, he was the best one to do it.

"I'll make it work."

"You said the decay spirit created golems. Do you think this one will too?" Liam asked.

"I seriously hope not, but I doubt we're that lucky."

"Grant's pack should be inside then, ideally with a ward around them. They can't protect themselves, and we can't do it for them while we're trapping this thing." Liam hated leaving them vulnerable to whatever might come at them.

They looked over at Grant, and he nodded.

"Everyone inside," he ordered.

There was some hesitation, but his pack members followed his command, shuffling inside. Liam was almost surprised they made it without assistance.

A distressed expression crossed Miles's face.

"You can't heal them all," Elijah said. "I know you want to try, but I need you here. It's the best thing you can do for them."

Miles wasn't happy about that, but he didn't protest.

With everyone inside, Elijah set a quick ward around the house. "Aran, can you provide cover?"

"I'll do my damnedest." Grim determination radiated from Aran as he surveyed the forest.

"Okay." Elijah knelt by the box. He unbuttoned his shirt and tossed it aside, leaving him in his undershirt with more of his skin exposed for them to touch. "Let's do this. Victor?"

Victor didn't have to be told what to do; he stood behind Elijah, a hand resting on his neck.

Liam placed one hand on Elijah's shoulder, then held his other out to Kade, who took it. The connection between them opened effortlessly.

On the other side of the chest, Miles gestured for Grant to kneel, and Liam realized he was doing it because he didn't think Grant would be able to stand as he used his energy. His left hand settled on Grant's neck, and then he copied Liam, his right hand on Elijah's opposite shoulder.

Aran stood next to Rick, and Will took up position a few feet away, though he could do little against the spirit on his own.

Liam swallowed. He didn't even have to do the hard part—that was all Elijah. He was merely a conduit, but his heart thundered in his chest. They couldn't fuck this up. Too many lives depended on them.

Elijah inhaled deeply, his shoulder rising under Liam's hand. He exhaled, then activated the seal.

The moment he did, something tilted, the earth falling off its axis, and Liam plummeted, tumbling endlessly with nothing around him as he plunged down and down and down, nothing to do but dread the inevitable landing.

Kade squeezed his hand, and Liam jerked, sucking in a shaky breath.

No. He wasn't falling. There was solid ground under his feet.

He opened himself to Kade's energy and it filled him, crackling inside him, burning so brilliant and beautiful. He spun that energy with his magic, though a word like spun implied it took effort; this required none. It was effortless grace, as natural as breathing, as familiar as the rhythm of his heart. He offered that radiant thread to Elijah, and

Elijah grabbed it, weaving it into his own power. Then Elijah did the same with the trickle of Grant's energy Miles fed him, before channeling it into the seal.

The seal glowed painfully bright, shining into the sky, latching on to the spirit.

Liam's pulse skyrocketed as he looked up and saw the spirit pooling there, a murky fog growing denser and more ominous by the second. Within the haze, ghastly figures darted in and out—eerily grotesque creatures from the darkest corners of the imagination, unspeakable things that slithered and lurked, their presence a bone-deep chill that shivered through his body.

He was submerged under polluted water. It filled his lungs as he gasped for air. Bands of panic tightened around his chest, and his insides burned from the chemical filth as it stripped him of his control, as it corrupted him from the inside out, suffocating him with decay.

But he forced himself to breathe, to push past the feeling until the polluted water receded and he resurfaced. He felt Kade inhale. Their hands clasped each other, their grip tight to the point of pain—a stinging anchor he could focus on, a desperate lifeline to reality.

The seal wrenched the spirit toward the box, and the nightmares came at them faster, bombarding them until nothing made sense, until everything was a surreal horror that would never end.

Trees twisted and contorted, morphing into ravenous creatures that towered over them and reached out with their branches to take and devour. He was adrift in a maze of shifting illusions with no way out. His mind reeled, and Elijah pulled harder on the magic and energy being fed to him.

Liam offered Elijah everything he had, everything Kade

had. More energy than he'd ever handled, more magic than he should have had the capacity to use. It scorched through his system like wildfire, both painful and divine.

Sweat poured off his brow, stinging his eyes. This level of power wasn't sustainable.

His body dissolved under that fiery onslaught, every cell of his being seared away, but Kade gripped his hand, reminding Liam he was still there, still whole, still himself.

He knew this wasn't right. It wasn't real. But it was difficult to remember that when his feet were floating off the ground and the laws of gravity no longer applied.

But Kade's hand kept him tethered to the earth.

The dirt below him opened, sucking him under, crushing him, but he clawed his way back to the surface.

He lost track of the number of nightmares that assaulted them in wave after wave of every fear they had.

Bridget stumbled out of the forest and collapsed, covered in blood. She tried to crawl toward him, her eyes wide and terrified, begging him for help, for him to go to her, to remove his hand from Elijah's shoulder and save her. He dug his fingers into Elijah's skin and refused to let go.

Spiders and snakes and worms slithered and skittered over him. The pack house went up in flames, Grant's pack screaming in agony, trapped inside. Dark shadows fell across them, bringing with them a terror so deep it stole Liam's ability to scream.

But none of that was really happening. Liam focused on Kade's grip.

The door to the house creaked open, and a woman emerged, her gaunt body and glassy eyes incongruous with her floating movements and the deadly clench of her hand around Remy's throat, her claws out, digging into skin.

"*Fuck*," Elijah breathed, and it took Liam a moment to realize why.

The woman wasn't changing. She was real. As was Remy.

Other pack members followed, swaying in her wake, too confused to do anything to stop her.

"She has to be the one the spirit infected to get its hooks into the pack," Elijah said, his voice strained. He continued to reel the spirit in.

"Remy!" Grant struggled to stand, but his legs weren't cooperating, his energy almost depleted.

Miles stepped forward, but Elijah's hand seized his wrist.

"I need his energy to do this," Elijah gritted out.

Miles looked between Elijah and the kid, his expression torn.

Liam's chest ached. They had to capture the spirit for this to be over; none of them would be safe until they did, but that didn't mean he could ignore the blood trickling down Remy's throat. It didn't make it an easy choice.

The woman's hand scraped across Elijah's barrier, nails on a chalkboard, hazy gouges left by her claws.

"Will," Elijah called out, "can you get the kid?"

"Yes." Will marched toward the house.

"So much for protecting the pack." He dropped the ward.

The world hung suspended for one drawn-out second.

Then, the golems came. Nightmare creatures—gruesome and hideous—closed in on all sides. They shambled through the forest, yet Liam knew that no matter how fast he ran, they'd gain on him. They flickered in and out of existence, never remaining in one place for long, coming closer, closer, closer.

Chaos exploded around them as Grant's pack scattered, running for their lives, as sluggish as they were.

Kade crowded into Liam, tugging him against his chest like that would shield him from the monsters bearing down on them. His heart hammered against Liam's back, matching the frantic pace of Liam's own. Their bond was flooded with the instinct to protect Liam, the desire so fierce that Liam's breath hitched.

Grant pulled Miles to his knees and wrapped himself around him as well, though his gaze was fixed on his son. He was so out of it that Liam doubted he'd processed what he was doing. Of the two of them, Miles was far more capable of protecting Grant than the other way around.

Victor stayed standing, but he projected the threat of violence to anyone who dared get too close.

"Aran," Elijah yelled.

"On it!" Aran crouched, pressing his palms to the ground, Rick's hand landing on his neck.

Around them, roots sprang up, grasping at gnarled legs. Most of the creatures guttered out, only to reappear elsewhere, but a few were caught, struggling to shake off the roots, clawed hands tearing at their flesh to get free.

There was too much happening. Liam couldn't follow it all. The monsters stalked Grant's pack despite Aran's attempts to capture them. Will squared off against the possessed woman.

"We need to finish this," Elijah shouted over the screams and shrieks. He yanked on Liam's magic, and Liam hissed at the burn of it. He felt disoriented as he was inundated by a torrent of Kade's energy, as it swept through him and into Elijah.

The spirit was above them, and Elijah dragged it down, racing the creatures drawing nearer to the pack members.

The woman knocked Will off his feet, her hand still around Remy's neck, but Elijah kept feeding their energy and magic into the seal until nothing was left in the sky. Then he meticulously removed the hooks that had been sunk into the pack.

As he worked, the woman shuddered and fell, releasing her hold on Remy, and one by one, the golems began to disappear.

When he was done, the spirit was pooled in the box, a surreal haze that flickered and jumped in those confines. Elijah slammed the lid shut, and wards flashed around the box, sealing it closed.

Everyone collapsed, panting.

Liam slumped forward, winded and exhausted. Kade stayed draped over him as they sank onto their knees, his arms holding him tight, a warm, soothing presence that Liam melted into. Kade's breathing was harsh in his ears, his body shaking as he clung to Liam. Sweet relief sang through their bond, and Liam's eyes slid shut as it washed over him.

"*Please*," Grant said, a broken whine, and before Liam could turn his head, Miles was on his feet, unsteady from the magic he'd used, but running to where Remy's crumpled body lay. Grant tried to drag himself forward, but he was too weak.

Miles's hands landed gently on the boy's neck as he healed him again. "He's okay," he called out. "He'll be fine." Grant seemed close to sobbing with relief, but it was clear he wanted to go to his son.

When Miles was satisfied with his work, he crawled over to the woman who'd been possessed and healed her as well, though Liam couldn't see any visible injuries on her.

Then he looked at Will, who was battered but sitting up. Will waved him off. "I'm already healing, but thanks."

Miles frowned like he was about to argue, but then his gaze caught on another shifter.

"Aran," Liam said. "He isn't going to stop."

Aran went after Miles, grabbing him before he reached the shifter. Miles fought to get away, but Aran pinned him to his side.

"Yes, yes, I know. You're a very feisty kitten." Aran hauled Miles toward the chest. "But we can't have you burning yourself out trying to heal everyone. I used the least magic, so I'll check them over, and anything urgent that I can't handle, Rick will bring to you. Deal?"

Miles sagged in his arms, and Aran deposited him beside Grant.

"Hey, Alpha Silver Wolf Daddy, make sure he doesn't hurt himself and I'll bring you your son."

Liam huffed. Only Aran would give someone such a ridiculous nickname directly after a battle.

Grant squinted up at Aran, unsure how to take him, but he wrapped a trembling hand around Miles's wrist, like he fully intended to keep Miles right there. His face was pale and he swayed as he sat, but there was resolve in the way he nodded to Aran, who did as promised, gathering up Grant's son and bringing him over, where he was immediately tucked against Grant's side.

Miles turned, taking in Grant's exhausted state and wincing. "I'm sorry. I tried to use as little as I could."

Grant shook his head. "It was willingly given. You could have taken more if you needed to."

Miles pressed his lips together, frowning. "No. I couldn't have."

They caught their breath as Aran checked Grant's pack

for serious injuries. The members who had scattered into the forest staggered back into the clearing now that the threat had passed.

Liam pushed himself to his feet, and with Kade's help, walked to Victor's SUV. He retrieved one of their maps, grimacing when he saw it. Kade flinched, but there was no instinctual fear response, no tightening panic around his chest.

Grant's territory was no longer almost completely black, but capturing the larger spirit had revealed dozens hidden underneath. More than a few were as large as some of the biggest on Victor's territory had been. He brought it to show the rest of them. Kade was still plastered to his side, but Liam had no desire to put distance between them.

"They can't stay here." He held the map out.

Considering how weakened the pack was, they needed a safe place to heal and recover, and this wasn't it.

"Their wards are also shot to hell, and those can't be reset properly for another month," Elijah added.

"You and your pack are welcome to stay with us," Victor said. "Until these spirits are cleaned up and your wards are reset."

Grant hesitated, and Victor tried to reassure him.

"You've helped my pack before. I know I can trust you. I hope you can trust us in return."

"It's not that I don't trust you, but leaving my territory..."

"I understand. We'll help you get back on it as soon as possible."

Grant looked conflicted, but said, "Thank you."

"How are we getting them to Victor's?" Liam asked.

"We can drive." Grant's voice was rough.

"No, you fucking cannot," Miles said sharply. "None of you are in any state to drive."

Grant blinked at him, clearly surprised at being overruled on his territory by someone he'd met less than an hour ago.

Elijah snorted. "If you have cars, we'll drive them. I think we're fine for that." He glanced at Miles, who narrowed his eyes and looked around before nodding.

"Okay, so you'll come with us, and we'll discuss things further after you've gotten some food and rest," Victor said.

"After *a lot* of food and rest," Miles corrected.

"What he said," Victor amended solemnly.

They managed to get the entire pack bundled up, though many of them seemed so out of it that they had no clue what was going on as Liam helped them into cars. They'd have to return for clothes and other belongings, but those could wait. It was more important that they were somewhere safe where they could sleep.

They picked up Kade's car on their way out. During the entire drive to Victor's, one thought played on repeat in Liam's mind.

Once they were at the pack house, they got Grant and his pack settled into spare bedrooms—more per room than Liam would have believed possible, but Kade assured him there was enough space since they could sleep in their wolf forms on the floor.

Liam then turned to Kade and said the most cliched line in the history of cliched lines. "We need to talk."

SEVENTEEN

K ade's heart drummed a deafening rhythm in his ears as he followed Liam to their room.

No, it was *his* room, not *their* room. For his own sanity, he needed to remember that.

"We need to talk" was such a relationship thing to say, but he was trying not to overanalyze it.

Everything that had happened in the last few hours had left his head spinning. Realizing how compatible he and Liam were despite their differences, discovering what the spirits might be, finding out their neighboring packs were overrun by them, and facing one that large. How did he begin to process it all?

When they got inside, Liam turned to him, his expression nervous. In Kade's mind, his presence jittered.

He inhaled like he was about to speak, then startled. "*Oh.* First. Your sense of smell returned?"

"Ahh, yeah. Last night. Sorry. I should have told you."

"So... Could you smell me when you were... uh... smelling me?"

That was a very polite way to put what Kade had done

to Liam, how he'd feasted on his scent. There was no use hiding it.

"Yes."

"The scent of my magic doesn't bother you?"

Not even remotely. "You're bonded into the pack, so your magic smells like pack magic." Among other reasons it didn't bother him in the slightest.

"Oh, I hadn't thought of that. I suppose it would." Liam winced, then squared his shoulders. "About that. About our bond..."

Kade refused to get his hopes up. It was doubtful this was going where he wanted it to go.

"I think we should keep it," Liam said. Kade's eyebrows rose, and Liam hurried on, starting to babble. "I'm aware that's not what we agreed on. But don't worry. I don't mean forever. Just for now. Because this morning? Elijah needed all the power I could give him. I wouldn't have been able to do that if we weren't bonded. Or at least not to that extent. And we still have to face the spirit on Niall's land, which will take as much energy to capture, if not more. And who knows what will happen after that? We need to be as strong as possible, and that means keeping the bond. I know, I know. I can sense you're unhappy about that. You must be as eager as I am to get rid of it, and I understand, but if this isn't finished before the new moon, we should stay bonded until it's over."

Unhappiness was only one of a dozen things Kade was feeling—elation that he could keep this longer, dread that it would make the severing more painful, and everything in between.

Liam was reading some of his emotions, but wasn't parsing what they meant, and that "as eager as I am" was keeping Kade from contradicting him. All he was getting from Liam was the anxious jangling of nerves.

But the bond did make them stronger. Insanely so. The amount of energy Liam had channeled from him should have left Kade exhausted and depleted, but it hadn't. They were more powerful together, and they needed as much strength as they could get. Regardless of what was happening between them, the best thing Kade could do for his pack was keep the bond until they were positive they'd taken care of the situation.

Liam's face twisted into a poorly concealed grimace, like he thought Kade would reject the idea flat out, but Kade couldn't do that. Even if it was a false hope, he could pretend there was a chance they'd stay bonded long enough for Liam to realize how right it was.

Kade nodded. "I think that's for the best. After we get this worked out, we can decide what to do from there."

Liam exhaled, his shoulders sagging with relief. "Hopefully it'll be done within the next two weeks, but with the way things are going, I doubt it."

"The sooner we defeat these spirits and whoever is behind them, the better."

That was the closest he could get to agreeing with Liam. He did want the spirits gone, but he also needed to figure out what to do about Liam and the sudden revelation of how compatible they were.

Which reminded him...

"Now that we've settled that, I need to talk to Victor."

Kade reluctantly left the room that was saturated with their scent.

Victor wasn't difficult to find. He was sitting at the small table in the kitchen with Elijah and glanced up as

Kade stalked toward him. "I take it you want to kick my ass?"

"Very much so." A growl laced through Kade's words.

Elijah snorted. "You guys have fun."

Kade and Victor headed outside.

"Do I get to explain why before you kick my ass?" Victor asked as they turned to face each other.

"Sure, but that's not changing anything. Why the fuck didn't you tell me?"

"Because it's *you*."

"What the hell is that supposed to mean?"

"I know you. For all you fuck around, you're weirdly romantic about true bonds. Don't pretend you didn't want that moment when you realized it yourself. I'd bet the fucking pack house you've wanted that for years. Someone else telling you wouldn't have been the same. I thought your sense of smell would return sooner, but if I'd known it'd take the better part of a week, I still wouldn't have told you. I wouldn't have taken that realization from you, and I wasn't letting the pack do it either."

Kade huffed in frustration. As much as he hated to admit it, there was something special about experiencing it himself, realizing it himself. Learning about it secondhand would have felt like a spoiler.

It also pissed him off that Victor had guessed the stupid romantic notions he held about getting bonded.

He knew it took time to recognize true compatibility—scents needed to mingle first. But he'd figured it wouldn't take long, and then he'd treat his mate like they were the most precious person in the world. He'd make them feel special. He wouldn't pin them down in the forest and fuck them, creating this mess of a bond.

"It sucks it happened how it did," Victor said, following

Kade's train of thought. "Things would have been a lot easier if he'd come to visit Elijah in a month or two, but that's not the case. And no, before you ask, it wasn't until afterward, when your scents were thoroughly mixed, that I noticed. Obviously the circumstances aren't ideal, but even if it comes with an ass-kicking, I don't regret my decision."

Kade ran a hand through his hair and paced away from Victor, then back.

Everyone in the pack had known. Their damn gossipy pack had kept their mouths shut for almost a week. They'd probably all had aneurysms over repressing the urge to meddle, but they'd done it. For him. Because Victor had made it clear they shouldn't.

"Fuck you." He glared at Victor. "I can't kick your ass when you're being irritatingly reasonable and shit."

"Never stopped you from trying when we were kids."

"You were never reasonable when you were a kid. This is an entirely new thing you've started. Clearly Elijah's doing."

Victor grinned.

He was such a dick. And not the fun kind.

A thought hit Kade.

Dicks.

Oh fuck.

He cringed and buried his head in his hands. "The first present I gave him was a bunch of dick-shaped candles," he said in a horrified whisper. "And then a dick-shaped lollipop. Our grandchildren are going to ask how we met, and I'll have to tell them an evil spirit played matchmaker, and then I wooed him with dick-shaped presents."

"You're already imagining grandkids?"

"We won't have them if I keep giving him presents shaped like dicks."

"And what has he given you?"

"...Porn and sexy underwear."

Victor snorted out a laugh. "See? Match made in heaven. Besides, anyone meant for you is basically required to enjoy a variety of dick-shaped things."

Kade blinked at him. "That sounded like something I'd say."

"Someone has to pick up the slack. Should I embrace my inner Kade and say you better hope he likes dick-shaped things because your face is dick-shaped?"

"Oh, fuck off. I'd never say something that lame." Kade shoved him, and Victor pushed back.

"Give me four or five hours and I'll make you a list of all the dumb-ass shit you've said over the years."

Kade scoffed. "Lies."

They stood in silence as Kade processed everything.

He huffed, his shoulders slumping. "I didn't think it would be any of Elijah's friends."

Victor raised an eyebrow.

"Grandma June," Kade said. "Once, when we were alone, shortly before she passed, she had a vision that I'd also end up with a mage, but it'd take a while. So I figured it couldn't be one of Elijah's friends. It seemed too soon after you two getting together."

"You never told me that."

"You're one to talk when it comes to hiding things. We still need to discuss the real reason you didn't trust your wolf when it came to Elijah."

"Oh, no. This is about your issues, not mine."

"Fine. But don't think for one second we aren't going to deal with your shit eventually," he said, pointing at Victor before deflating. "I didn't tell you— didn't tell *anyone*—because I'd seen you get teased about it for years, and I don't know... I wanted something of my own. A secret little piece of the future just for me. Plus there was the whole 'taking a while' thing. What if I told everyone and it didn't happen until I was fifty?"

"That 'it'll take a while' might have meant it would take a while for you to become aware of it."

"Maybe? Or maybe she was getting the general impression of this fucked up situation. She never would have imagined one of us bonding a mage in something other than a true bond."

"But you do have a true bond."

"Do I? Because it sure as fuck doesn't feel like it. I can sense his emotions to some extent, but it's nothing like you and Elijah."

"You can smell how compatible you two are now. The entire pack can, and Elijah says it's written in Liam's magic too."

"Then why is the bond so weak?"

"How does it feel when Liam uses your energy?" Elijah asked.

Kade spun around to see him descending the porch steps. He'd been so focused on Victor, he hadn't heard Elijah slip outside.

Elijah shrugged, reading his surprise. "Since it appeared no ass-kicking was happening, I decided I might as well join you. But seriously, how much access does Liam have to your energy?"

Kade frowned. "When we're touching, he can access all of it, but when we aren't, it's sort of a light flow."

"Consent," Elijah said.

"What?"

"The reason your tether isn't like ours. Consent. You

were under the influence of the spirit when you bonded. Neither of you were consenting."

"I was more than willing to have sex with Liam."

"Finish that sentence."

"What?" Kade asked again.

"There's more to that sentence. Would you have had sex with Liam in the forest when you were supposed to be doing something to protect the pack if you weren't affected by the spirit?"

"Of course not, but in a different situation, I absolutely would have."

"But it wasn't a different situation. You couldn't fully consent, not while the spirit was affecting you. I'm not sure about bonds, but from the mage side, tethers require consent to work properly. If Liam doesn't have full access to your energy, that might be why. He didn't have your full consent."

That seemed logical. Kade looked at Victor. "Would that affect the bond? I know transactional bonds don't have the same level of emotional transfer as true bonds, and I've been assuming that's why I'm not sensing him completely. That it's distant and muted because it was similar to a transactional bond."

Victor cocked his head. "I've never heard about how non-consensual bonds feel, other than that they can be used to steal control of a mage's magic. Not that you forced the bond on him, but that's the closest thing I can think of. Maybe the best parts of a bond don't happen unless it was consented to by both parties?"

Kade's stomach sank. "So I fucked up my chance."

"What do you mean?" Elijah's gaze bounced between Victor and Kade.

"We can't bond the same person twice," Kade

explained. "If our bond is messed up, it's not like we can sever it and get a redo."

"Liam should be able to reset the tether between you if you're both willing. That might fix it?"

Whether it would or not, in reality, it didn't matter. "Liam doesn't want the bond. Why would he fix it when he plans to sever it as soon as this is over?"

Victor stared him down. "Have you given him any indication that it could be something more than temporary?"

"No, because he doesn't want to be a pack mage or be trapped here. He has a job he loves and a life on the East Coast, and unlike Elijah, that's not changing. He wouldn't want to live in the middle of nowhere for me." He glanced at Elijah. "Liam would never stay out here, right? Would he be happy in some little rural town?"

Elijah shook his head. "I wish he would. I'd love to have him here. But unfortunately, no. I can't imagine him living here permanently. I think he'd be fine being here occasionally, but definitely not full-time. He needs to constantly be learning new things, and that's not possible here. Not to the level he requires."

"See," Kade said to Victor. "I can't leave; he won't stay."

Victor snorted. "Why can't you leave? There are packs on the East Coast. Pretty sure you're even related to one. Do you honestly think I'd keep you here if that's what you had to do? If you need to leave to be with him, then you need to leave."

Kade's mouth dropped open. It took him a minute to respond to that. "But I'm your second."

"Don't get me wrong, I want you here, but only as often as you want to be here. No more, no less. I'd miss your obnoxious ass more than you'll ever get me to admit. But I'm not going to be the reason you can't be with him."

Something inside Kade loosened at the permission Victor had given him. He didn't have to be chained there; he could go wherever Liam wanted or needed him. Part of him ached at the idea of leaving his pack, but the rest was certain Liam could be his pack too.

But that lovely sentiment aside, he couldn't let a comment like that slide. "How would you run this place without me?"

Victor waved him off. "I can replace you."

"Fuck you. I'm irreplaceable. No one could do as good a job as I can."

Victor scoffed. "Katrina would run circles around you. She'd make a killer second."

Kade wanted to be offended, but Victor was right. He was being right an annoying amount today.

"So are you done thinking of reasons this can't work?" Victor asked. "Are you going to stop denying it?"

Kade sighed. "He smells so good. Fucking perfect. I don't want to sever the bond. I want to see where this goes, but I don't know. It feels like karma that I ended up with a bond like this after everything I did to you two."

Victor growled. "I thought we were past this shit. If I'd been possessed and had attacked you, would you be saying I didn't deserve Elijah?"

"Fuck no."

"So why are you saying it about yourself? Give yourself a break. You deserve happiness as much as we do. One shitty run-in with a spirit didn't change that."

"But—"

"No. I told you to take your own advice, and I meant it. Get your head out of your ass. You and Liam smell like you should be together, and until you discuss it with him, don't assume it can't happen. If there was zero possibility of him wanting to be with you, I don't think you'd be as compatible as you are."

Kade wished he could believe that, but he still worried there had been a mistake. Were scents ever wrong?

"You should show him the attic," Elijah said.

Victor chuckled. "Yeah, you should."

Kade's brow furrowed. "Why would I do that?"

He got the parallels between this and him making Victor show Elijah the attic, but everything up there had been destined for Victor's mage. That didn't apply this time.

Elijah's expression grew mischievous. "You should have your *Beauty and the Beast* moment. It makes a mage rather fond of the person who shows them." He exchanged a warm, knowing glance with Victor that left Kade longing for that kind of connection.

"Plus," Elijah continued, "Liam really likes books, and there are a lot of them up there. He might find something useful. I've only looked through things briefly. Once Liam was finished with the books he brought, I was planning to have him go through it, and Aran and Miles took care of the last of his books yesterday."

Resolve built inside Kade. He could do that. He'd show Liam the attic, and then they'd go from there.

Victor smirked. "Hey. I'm starting to see your face again."

Kade did the emotionally mature thing and flipped him off.

But he needed to know something if he was doing this. They couldn't avoid the pack and Liam's friends forever. They had to help.

"How can you stand Elijah being away from you and letting people get close to him?"

Victor shrugged. "It's what I need to do for the pack. I focus on that. It doesn't stop the instincts, but it mitigates them. You managed just fine today. I'm assuming because your attention was on the spirits? On saving Grant's pack?"

Kade paused, then nodded. Although he hadn't been happy they were around so many people or that Liam had been in danger, he'd known it was what they had to do.

"So the next time you have the urge to drag him to your room because someone breathed in his general vicinity, concentrate on what you need to do," Victor said.

"Also, the overly possessive feelings are super hot, especially when he's worked up and ready to haul me to bed. Liam will grow to appreciate it too." Elijah sent Victor a heated look that made Kade think Victor's self-control wouldn't be holding out long after this conversation.

He rolled his eyes. "Oh, go fuck already."

"Same to you," Victor shot back.

"Yeah, same to you," Elijah said. "You have my permission to be your perverted self around Liam and court the absolute hell out of him. And I know I don't need to give you the 'if you hurt him' speech, because you won't. But if you hurt him..." He held out his hand, and a ball of fire sprang up over it. He grinned at Kade—a pleasant threat.

A smile twitched at the corner of Kade's mouth. "Fair enough."

He had no intention of hurting Liam. If anything, it'd be the other way around.

With a nod to Victor and Elijah, he went inside the house and up the stairs.

When he got back to his room, Liam was passed out on their bed, the night of no sleep and the morning's magic use catching up to him.

Kade sat beside him and just breathed, letting Liam's scent—their scent—wash over him.

They smelled so right together. So perfect.

He didn't want to give this up. There were so many things he longed to do. Pull Liam close, wrap himself around him, bury his nose in the crook of his neck and drown in his scent. But he didn't; he restrained himself. For now.

Their to-do list felt endless—catching more spirits than ever, determining how to destroy them and who was behind them, getting Niall to let them help him, and more —but none of that would stop Kade from trying. If he didn't do that much, he'd regret it.

No matter how this had begun, he wanted to keep it, so he was going to do everything he could to convince Liam they were meant for each other.

He'd make this into the perfect love story he'd always dreamed of if it was the last thing he did.

EIGHTEEN

iam woke, momentarily disoriented by the abundance of light and the lack of Kade's dick digging into his ass. He hadn't realized how used to the latter he'd gotten over the last few days.

A drawer slid shut, and he rolled over. Kade was propped up against the headboard.

"Morning," Kade said.

"What time is it?" Liam asked, his voice rough from sleep.

"Ten past three."

Liam winced. "I only meant to close my eyes for a minute or two, not multiple hours."

"Grant's entire pack will be out until tomorrow, and there's not much we can do about Niall at the moment."

Liam got out of bed and stretched. Kade could say that, but he'd still wasted the better part of a perfectly good afternoon.

A little groggy, he shuffled into the bathroom, splashed water on his face, and got ready for the rest of the day.

When he reentered the bedroom, Kade was standing

with impeccable posture, projecting an oddly formal air, though he was in his usual t-shirt and jeans. Liam raised an eyebrow at him. Why did he look nervous?

Kade cleared his throat. "If you would be so willing, may I request your permission to allow me to escort you somewhere?"

Liam furrowed his brow in confusion. "What now?"

"Would you kindly bestow upon me the honor of accompanying me elsewhere in our humble abode?"

What was Kade doing? Besides freaking Liam out.

Kade tried again. "It is a lovely afternoon. Perhaps we might take this opportunity to experience a short promenade."

Liam stepped into Kade's personal space and squinted up at him. "Are you okay?" he whispered. "Did something happen? Blink twice if you're being held hostage."

Though Kade's posture remained ramrod straight, he was clearly flustered.

"And why are you being so stiff?"

"I merely wish to obtain—"

"No, no, no. If you're the real Kade, the only proper answer to a question about being stiff is some terrible line." Liam put his palm on Kade's forehead. Nope, no fever.

Kade's shoulders slumped. "I want to show you something I think you'll like."

"Something you think I'll like that requires you to be stiff?"

Kade sighed. "Please come with me?"

"You want me to come with you?"

The smirk that crossed Kade's face made him look like himself again. "You know I do." He winked, and Liam rolled his eyes, secretly relieved Kade had dropped whatever had come over him. Kade not cracking dirty jokes seemed as wrong as Aran passing up an easy innuendo. Not that he'd tell either of them that.

Kade led him upstairs into a dark attic. Liam was about to ask why when Kade turned on the light, and the question fled his brain as he stared in awe, trying to take everything in at once.

The attic was large, lit by a single bulb hanging from the middle of the ceiling, but the numerous shelves and chests crammed into the space made it feel cozy. There were things that demanded his attention everywhere, from bookshelves stuffed with ancient volumes and trinkets to dressers with drawers hiding unknown wonders. The air was so saturated with magic that it stroked against his skin. It was foreign and old, but not unwelcoming, and for all that he would classify it as 'foreign,' there was a familiarity to it as well. Hints of Elijah's magic were laced throughout, but it was more than that. It felt like Kade's energy, the pack's energy, but entwined with magic. It glittered with the balanced perfection Elijah's spells now did.

He looked at Kade in question.

"This is from our pack mages," Kade explained. "The books in here go back hundreds of years, if not further than that. Victor and Elijah thought you might be able to find something useful that could help with the spirits."

Liam wandered around the room, taking in the bookshelves, chests, and dressers. Everything was so haphazardly placed on the shelves. There was no order to it, and while a heavy layer of dust had settled on most of the furniture, the books and other items showed signs of more recent handling.

He frowned. "When's the last time someone went through this?"

Kade grimaced. "Elijah has been up here, but before

that, we had to move everything to ensure that asshole mage didn't get his hands on it. Rick and Will asked me to help. We boxed it up and entrusted it to Grant for safekeeping. We didn't bring it back until after Victor's father was exiled, Victor was in firm control, and that bastard was no longer in town. We didn't worry about organization though. Just packed it up as fast as we could without damaging it, and when we unpacked it, we had no clue where things should go, so everything got put wherever it would fit."

Liam nodded. It was too much to ask for a cache of books like this to be organized in a manner he'd approve of.

"Why are you showing this to me now?"

Kade glanced away. "You had books we needed to go through, and Victor and Elijah suggested I bring you up here today."

Liam narrowed his eyes, but didn't call Kade on his evasiveness. He wasn't answering that question fully—something he did a lot—but Liam had more important matters to take care of. There were so many grimoires up there. Who knew what they held?

His gaze landed on a pile of books and vials and miscellaneous things on the floor. While the whole room was in disarray, that was the worst of the clutter. He walked over to it.

"I assume that was in the chest Elijah used to capture the decay spirit. Rick or Will must have dumped out the contents before they brought it to the clearing."

For once, mentioning that spirit and what had happened that night didn't seem to be causing Kade anxiety.

Liam sat in front of the pile and started to sort through it, setting the jars and vials upright. Nothing had been broken, though his breath caught when he found a vial of wolfsbane. That was not something he would have guessed he'd find in a pack house. There were four books mixed in with the mess.

He paged through the first. It was full of botanical drawings, the paper yellowed by the centuries, a multitude of notes scribbled in the margins. While it wasn't the type of book he preferred, Aran would love it. He'd have to check with Elijah and Victor, but it felt like something Aran should have. He set it aside.

The second book was modern looking. He doubted it was more than twenty years old; an outlier in the attic. When he turned to the first page, he nearly laughed. In a script that was elegant if shaky with age, there was a note that almost felt like it had been addressed to Miles.

Our family doesn't have a history of healers, but these are the handful of healing spells we've developed. For obvious reasons, they're geared toward wolf shifters. There's plenty of room for more to be added.

The book contained spells meticulously transcribed from elsewhere, including marginalia written in a variety of colors to help differentiate the various writers, and there was indeed room for additional spells. Grinning, he set that book on top of the other.

Even more curious, he picked up the third book. It was a hefty volume, leather-bound and not particularly old, a few hundred years at most. The fourth book beneath it was the second of the matched pair.

He opened the cover and his eyebrows shot up at the single word on the title page.

Index

Index of what?

He turned the page, and his eyes widened at the contents listed there.

Untitled Grimoire of Ward Magic—p. 7
Illusions and Glamours—p. 10
Collected Incantations for Elemental Control—
p. 12
Untitled Book of Ritual Circles—p. 15
Binding and Protection Runes and Related
Spells—p. 18
Untitled Spellbook of Hexes and Curses—p. 20
Blood Magic Rituals—p. 23

The list continued. Hundreds of entries. He looked at the nearest bookshelf, at the index, and then back. Were all of these books indexed here? It wasn't digital, but still.

He flipped to page seven.

Title: Untitled Grimoire of Ward Magic
Description: A comprehensive history of our family's wards and related magic
Appearance: Brown leather, leather cords, dating back to the early 1600s
Contents:

The list took up three pages. The final spells were written in different hands, updating the table of contents started decades earlier.

Cradling the book in his lap, he reached forward and opened its twin, wondering if there were books listed in it too. There weren't, but that didn't mean it wasn't an index. Instead, each page consisted of a drawing of some type of magical object, complete with a summary of what was known of its history and use.

"Did you—" he started to ask, glancing at Kade, only to find him leaning against a wall, engrossed in a book, a soft smile on his face. "Kade?"

Kade jumped and hid the book behind him, like it was a reflex.

Liam cocked his head. "What are you reading?"

"Ah. This is..." Kade winced, looking embarrassed. "It has the accounts of how the mages in our family met their mates."

"What?" Liam didn't care that the word came out as a half-strangled squeak. "You have historical records like that and never told me?"

God, how many times had he babbled about his theories on mage and shifter history to Kade? How he wished he had access to books that covered the period before the abductions. Kade had known this book existed. He'd found it and settled in too quickly for that not to be the case. But he hadn't told Liam.

Guilt squirmed through their bond. "It's pack history,

and I didn't think... Well. You know?" Kade gestured at Liam.

Liam's gut tightened. "Oh. Yeah." He wasn't pack. He didn't have any right to know pack history.

"But I should have reali—" Kade shook his head. "I should have asked Victor sooner."

He came over and sat next to Liam, holding out the book for him to see. It was small and one of the oldest books there, its cover worn and faded, but well cared for. A protective spell was wrapped around it, and all the other books, and Liam itched to examine it. They put similar spells on the books in the library, but what they used to preserve those didn't begin to compare to this.

"I've read the entries I can. None mention what happened pre-abductions. Like here," Kade said, flipping to a handful of pages toward the back of the book in a handwriting Liam was already starting to recognize. "This is my grandparents' story. They met when they were six. Grandma's mother came to visit our pack mage—our great-grandmother. Grandma and Grandpa spent the entire visit fighting and calling each other names, but after she left, Grandpa declared they'd get bonded when they were older. Twelve years later, she showed up to do her apprenticeship with our great-grandmother and never left. The story before that is our great-grandparents', and so on. But I can't read the oldest ones, so there could be something there."

He handed the book over, and Liam marveled at it, perusing it backward into history one generation at a time. Each entry was written in a more antiquated style until he hit the first dozen, which had all been recorded by the same hand in Old English. They were prefaced by a paragraph with more subtext than words.

Owing to recent happenings, circumstances necessitate the preservation of a faithful chronicle of our history. What is set down hereafter is all that can be recounted of how the wolves and mages of our pack came to be bonded.

Liam read the words over and over, finally tearing his eyes away from the book to glance at Kade. "This was started during the abductions, but the initial chunk of entries is from before that."

Kade's shock was evident. "Seriously? I didn't know it went back that far. What does it say?"

Liam skimmed the first story. "This one. This is from well before the abductions. From when your pack was founded?"

Kade nodded. "That's in our oral history. Our pack was formed when there was a dispute over who would take over leadership. There were two betas, both equally strong, both with support from pack members. They fought, but neither could bring themselves to concede or kill the other, so the pack split. The larger group stayed on the pack territory; the smaller group left. We're descendants of that smaller group. Our history says they searched for new territory and wound up on what was essentially the land of a family of mages, though, I mean, not as strictly defined."

Liam leafed through the pages. "The first handful of shifter-mage pairs came from..." He trailed off as he read.

"Came from?" Kade prompted, and Liam shook himself.

"Sorry, I can't get over finding something like this. But I think I was right about historical interactions between mages and shifters. If mages suddenly discovered a pack of wolf shifters uninvited on their land today, there would be so much suspicion, but there's none of that here. The mages weren't happy the shifters were trying to establish their pack on territory the mages were holding as neutral, but it seems like annoyance rather than distrust."

"Our history says mages joined our pack after we stumbled onto mage territory, but it doesn't give many specifics beyond that. The details have been worn away with time. Mainly, it focuses on the first bonded pair. The fact that our pack alpha, almost immediately after founding the pack, had a true bond with a mage is seen as fortuitous. It set the course of our pack. It's why we've had so many true-bonded shifter-mage pairs."

"This has more..." Liam's words faltered as he scanned the next page.

"More?"

"Uh, yeah. More. There's some of that high heat you were looking for." Liam's cheeks warmed. "This couple, the fourth entry, bonded during a sex ritual, and there are significantly more details than I would have expected to be passed down a few generations to be recorded in this book."

"It's not like you can hide sex in a wolf shifter pack. Especially if there's bonding. What happened?"

Liam translated the entries to Kade, starting from the beginning, when the new alpha and the head mage had argued over territories and borders until they'd... come to an agreement.

Kade listened with rapt attention as Liam gave voice to the tales in the book. Liam's index finger skated over the pages, and Kade's eyes followed along like he was trying to understand the language he couldn't read. Liam hadn't realized he was doing it until he reached the couple that had done the sex ritual and glossed over it.

"Oh no," Kade said, amusement in his tone. "That entire page you just breezed by did not say, 'And then they did a ritual and bonded.' You skipped too many words for that."

Liam tried not to squirm.

"Read it to me." Kade's voice dropped lower, taking on a gravelly note.

Liam swallowed. "They'd been circling each other for a while, not quite courting, but the pack agreed their scents were compatible and they should start. On the night of the full moon, the mage wanted to try a certain ritual, but needed someone to do it with."

"Ah, that classic pickup line. 'I need some supplies for this ritual. Mind if I borrow your dick?'"

Liam snorted. "The shifter was very neighborly and more than willing to lend a helping—"

"Dick?"

"Yep. During that kind of ritual, the shifter isn't supposed to move or touch the mage."

"Sex rituals operate under stripper rules? The mage can touch you; you can't touch the mage?"

"Obviously it's different for bonded pairs, but otherwise, yes. However, in this case, it seems like the shifter's wolf was too close to the surface to behave, and they both forgot what they were supposed to be doing and ended up bonding instead of completing the ritual."

"Is that it?" Kade's smirk was knowing as he pointed to the final paragraph on the page.

"Fine. It says, 'The sounds of their vigorous coupling and bonding rang joyous through the territory. Until the breaking light of dawn colored the horizon, their repeated amorous congress was known to all by sound and scent and, to a few most daring, by sight. They emerged from the forest with marks of passion on their bare skin and swiftly sequestered themselves for the traditional period of conviviality with such ardor that none in the household could sleep for a fortnight.'"

"Well done, my however-many-times-great-grand-relatives."

Most of the stories in the same hand weren't quite so lurid, though a number did sneak in lines about melting together or attending the service of Venus or riding below the crupper, and a memorable one noted that a particular couple spent a month 'clicketting like foxes,' which had made Kade huff out a laugh.

The subsequent stories were considerably less discreet. Apparently when recounting one's own bonding, the mages felt zero compunction about divulging salacious details, and Kade had a sixth sense for knowing precisely where those parts were, regardless of the language they were written in.

"You missed these two paragraphs," he said, and Liam cringed.

"Um, those paragraphs? They start with 'As his knot began to swell inside me...' and get more graphic from there. Do you really want me to read that?"

For a moment, he thought Kade might say yes, but in the end, he groaned. "No. Not while I can't do anything about it."

He didn't call Liam on abridging the racy parts after that, though his curiosity shimmered between them. It was almost enough to make Liam read even the most explicit paragraphs out loud, but he didn't.

Each entry specified how the mage and shifter had met. Many were acquaintances of the mages already bonded to pack members. Often there was initial suspicion of the pack, and shifters in general, but slowly it was overcome. As mages and shifters grew further apart, Kade's pack always managed to have at least one true-bonded mage, usually mated to the alpha.

Liam was reaching the point where Middle English was transforming into modern English, the last entries Kade hadn't read, when one stopped him cold, his words catching in his throat as his eyes raced down the page, a furrow forming between his brows.

"What is it?" Kade asked.

Liam finished the entry before answering. "This mage theorizes that the amount of mage blood in your pack makes your energy different from other packs. When a shifter and a mage have a child, that child will generally be a shifter, right?"

"I guess? That's how it's worked in our pack. It's the same with shifter-human pairs. The shifter side wins out more often than not."

"Her theory is that blood is still there. Even if the shifter can't use magic like a mage would, that link to magic doesn't disappear. Basically, she believed it acts as an amplifier. It makes any connection easier and stronger, and it increases exponentially as compatibility increases. So on one end, an average mage with zero compatibility with a shifter from your pack would find it easier to use their energy than that of a shifter not of your bloodline, and on the other end—"

"Victor and Elijah? Stupidly compatible from the start. Ridiculously, insanely strong together."

"Exactly." Liam paused, considering. "Are Rick and Will your blood relatives, or did they join the pack more recently?"

"Distant relatives, but yes. They have mage blood in them."

Liam pulled out his phone and sent a few quick messages to the group chat.

LIAM

Hey, Miles, Aran.

How easy is it for you to use Rick and Will's energy?

You don't need blood to make a connection, right?

As he waited for their answers, he thought it over. Even before they'd bonded, using Kade's energy had been effortless. Not to the extent Elijah had described channeling Victor's, but it had been far more accessible than he'd anticipated. How much mage blood was required to have that amplifying effect?

"Is your pack related to any others? Was there another split in your history?"

"No. No other splits. We occasionally have a member go off to join their mate's pack, like new members join ours. There are a small handful of packs we consider sort of cousin packs."

"But none have the same history with mages your pack does?"

"Not that I'm aware of. Honestly, the ones we're related to the closest are probably Grant's and Niall's packs. We've lived side by side on good terms for a hundred-plus years. There was bound to be some mating between the packs."

Liam's phone vibrated, and he brought up the group chat.

ARAN

Surprisingly easy. Way easier than the few
shifters I worked with during my
apprenticeship. No blood needed.

MILES

Same here. It's been nice.

I was worried I wouldn't be much help
capturing the spirits, but I've been able to
do more with Will's energy than I expected.

Thinking about what Kade had said, Liam sent another question.

LIAM

How was Grant's?

There was a long pause before Miles answered, the three dots appearing and disappearing multiple times.

MILES

He was so depleted, I'm not entirely sure. I
was concentrating on not using too much
of the little he had left.

But it did seem easier to connect to his
energy than normal, and yeah, no blood
needed for me either.

Interesting.

"Are you related to Grant?" he asked, and Kade shrugged.

"Very distant cousin, I believe."

Liam's mind swam with the possibilities. If he was correct and mages and shifters had formed true bonds more often in the past, and if this mage was also correct about mage blood and shifter energy, then they were stronger together. The closer they were, the more they mixed, the stronger they became.

As far as he knew, transactionally bonded mages and shifters rarely had children, so ever since the abductions and everything that followed, the mage blood in shifter packs would have become more diluted, making shifter energy harder to use. And from what he understood, shifters found pack magic less offensive smelling, which got them accustomed to the scent of magic in general and allowed them to be closer to mages, making it more likely for them to be in a position where they'd end up bonded to a mage.

It spiraled. Whichever direction it went, it spiraled. The further apart they got, the fewer reasons for them to be around each other, causing them to get even further apart. But the opposite had to be true as well. If more mages and shifters bonded, if their magic and energy intertwined again, what would they be able to do? Would it be like the pre-abduction times he'd only glimpsed in his research? Would they stop living as two completely separate groups?

He looked up to find Kade watching him, grinning.

"What?" Liam asked.

"Whatever your brain is doing, it's like a light show in my head." Kade's voice was a gentle caress.

"I think we're meant to be together," Liam blurted out.

Kade's eyes widened, bright shock flashing through their bond. "What?"

"I mean, not us." Liam rushed to clarify. "*Us.* Shifters and mages. I think Elijah and Victor are what we're meant to be."

He surveyed the room with a fresh perspective. There were hundreds of books in there, each written by mages who had been close to shifters most of their lives. What would he discover in them? Given this book's explicitness, he doubted the rest had censored themselves.

"Are there books about sex magic in here?"

Kade tilted his head. "Why would I know that?"

"Because you knew about this book? And it has plenty of sex in it? I figured you'd located every single book dealing with sex. Like you have some sex book radar."

"But it's not just—" Kade cut himself off. "I haven't gone through the grimoires. Grandma showed me this book specifically. She told me to make sure Victor's mage, and other mages connected to the pack in the future, wrote in it. After she passed, I kept track of it to do that."

Liam thumbed to the last entry—Kade's grandmother's —and the empty pages that followed. More than enough room for Elijah and anyone who came after him. "We'll get Elijah to write his and Victor's story in here."

He returned the book to Kade and grabbed the index. At least someone in this pack had known how to catalog books.

It took scanning through the table of contents, but eventually he found what he was looking for.

Title: Untitled Book of Sex Magic
Description: Various sex magic spells and rituals
Appearance: Green leather quarto with gilded decoration, dating back to the 1850s

The contents list had Liam's eyebrows rising.

Kade, reading over his shoulder, whistled softly. "Damn. I had no idea mages could be so... inventive. Is there any spell you can't make into a sex ritual?"

Evidently not. Liam cleared his throat, his gaze darting around.

"Let's find this book of yours." Kade stood and offered his hand to Liam. When Liam took it and their skin touched, he shivered at the warmth of Kade's presence in his mind.

It was not his book, but he didn't bother correcting Kade.

After some searching, they found it, and Liam opened the cover, only to slam it shut again.

Kade snickered. "Nice. That was no Richard Knotz screencap, but for a book written in the nineteenth century, that did not look like Victorian sensibilities."

"Good to know you had some skilled artists in your pack." Liam cracked the book open.

Yeah, there was no avoiding the illustrations, but he had a question, and it didn't take much skimming to answer it.

"Yes!" He pointed to a page. "This is exactly what I wanted!"

"Pretty sure that's what the mage in that drawing is saying too."

Despite himself, Liam chuckled. "No, not that. Do you remember when I mentioned that book with the vague line about how sex rituals were best suited for incompatible shifters and mages? And how I thought it was warning that there might be consequences if compatible couples did them?"

"Other than getting carried away mid-ritual and ending up bonded?"

"Well, that too. But no, this says that if a highly compatible shifter and mage exchange a lot of magic and energy, there is a possibility it will forge the start of a tether, whether it's intended or not. And until that tether is properly established or severed, it's unstable. It warns that if the pair is compatible, the mage needs to be extra careful with how they sever the tether at the end of the ritual. This aligns with what I was thinking happened to Elijah and Victor. We even made a bet about it, and he totally owes me. The next three times my mother tries to set me up, Elijah has to run interference. Though, I suppose it'll be harder to collect the winnings now that we'll never be living in the same state."

A sharp stab of unnamed emotion came through their bond, but Kade's face was carefully neutral for a beat before he leered at Liam.

"Any chance anything else in this book could be enlightening?"

"Sorry. We won't be needing this."

"That's too bad. The illustration on page fifty-three seemed like something worth exploring."

"I'm not that flexible." Liam's cheeks burned at the confession.

"I am."

Jesus fucking Christ, the mental image that painted.

To distract himself, Liam cast his gaze around the room. "I've been going about this all wrong, looking in the wrong places. I've been trying to archive the library's books, but those books are what the council allows in the library. The real knowledge is in places like this, in family libraries scattered throughout the world. This is the stuff I should be archiving and sharing so we can learn from each other and not be constrained by limited information. Would Victor let me archive this? When everything is over with the spirits? Maybe if I start with this collection, other mage families would be willing to share theirs. My family would, for sure."

"You'd have to ask Victor and Elijah. If the books reveal private information about the pack, Victor might not want those made public, but I don't see why you couldn't do the rest."

That seemed fair. The book on how the mages and shifters in their pack had bonded was important, but it was also pack history, and he could understand Victor being reluctant to share that.

"So do you think there's anything in here that will help?" Kade asked.

"Only one way to find out." Liam walked to the index. "Let's see what there is about binding contracts."

K ade stared at his phone, more than a little shocked to see the name on the screen. It had been over a day, and he hadn't thought he'd get a reply.

"Everything okay?" Liam asked, glancing up from the book they'd pulled from the attic for his research.

"Pierce replied." Kade opened the message.

> **PIERCE**
>
> Yeah, man, it's been forever. We should catch up one-on-one. How does tomorrow sound?

He was playing along with Kade's casual tone, like their packs hadn't been moments away from fighting the last time they'd seen each other.

"He's willing to meet up?" Liam's surprise flared bright through their bond. "Would he try to trick you?"

"The Pierce I knew in school? Never. The Pierce who's affected by some evil spirit of paranoia? No idea. But also, don't we need someone from their pack if we're going to do anything about what's happening to them?"

"I'm pretty sure there's no getting around that." Liam didn't sound happy, but there was nothing else to do.

Kade typed out his response, hesitated, then hit send.

KADE

Name the time and place, and I'll be there.

"Let's go find Victor and Elijah," he said.

Liam shut his book, and they headed downstairs.

They found Victor and Elijah in the office. Victor was sitting at his desk, with Elijah standing beside him and Grant in the chair across from them. Grant still looked exhausted—dark circles were smudged under his blue eyes, and he was thinner than Kade had ever seen him—but sleeping for the better part of a day and some food had made a difference. His enhanced shifter healing had kicked in, and he no longer appeared hours from death.

If their recovery was like Kade's, it'd be about a week before Grant and his pack regained their full strength, but they'd get there.

"Good," Victor said as they walked in, "I was just going to send you a message. Grant wants to help us defeat these things, and we need a plan."

"I can help with that," Kade said. "Pierce contacted me."

Victor cocked an eyebrow. "Okay. Let's get Grant up to speed first, then we'll decide what to do about that. Liam, can you explain the spirits to Grant?"

Liam launched into a brief, for him, explanation of his theory about the spirits. Kade leaned against the wall, enjoying the sight of him lighting up like he always did when he discussed his research.

"Pandora's box, or jar, or whatever? Isn't that a myth?" Grant asked.

"Should werewolves and wizards be calling anything a myth?" Liam countered.

Grant dipped his head in acknowledgment. "Fair point."

Victor then gave Grant a rundown of everything that had occurred on their territory. How the decay spirit had affected them and how Elijah had captured it. How his friends were there to trap the rest and destroy them.

He glossed over Kade's role in their battle against the spirit, but that wouldn't benefit anyone but Kade.

"The decay spirit possessed me," Kade said, interrupting Victor.

Victor assessed him for a beat, then explained the situation to Grant.

Kade sensed Liam's concern brush against him in his mind, checking he was alright. While he wouldn't go that far—*alright* was a ways off—it was information Grant needed to know. Kade was done holding everyone back.

"That's what happened to Jessie?" Grant asked. "Why she attacked Remy?"

"Yes," Elijah said. "Miles confirmed there are no traces of the spirit left in her. Kade..." He looked over, and Kade nodded. They needed to be on the same page. Elijah continued. "The spirit that possessed Kade decayed him from the inside out, but according to Miles, the nightmare spirit didn't have the same effect on Jessie. He believes the spirits with physical effects cause the most damage to the people they possess, but he wants to check her again when she's awake. And he suggested we keep her under observation in case there are any psychological effects. At minimum, PTSD is likely."

It figured, Kade thought. Of course he'd stumbled into one of the worst spirits.

Grant took everything in, then asked, "Who set them loose on our territories?"

Victor grimaced. "We don't have confirmation, but the most probable suspects are that fucking bastard of a mage who owned the shop before Elijah. And my father."

There was a hint of sorrow in Grant's expression when he replied. "For your sake, I hope your father isn't involved. But that mage, I believe it. He always smelled wrong. Why though?"

"I thought it was revenge for me taking over the pack and running them out, but that was when we assumed the spirits were only infesting my territory. Now that we know they're attacking your pack and Niall's too, it doesn't feel as personal anymore."

That statement hung in the air. If they wanted revenge against Victor, why would they attack Grant's and Niall's packs? It had to be something bigger, didn't it?

"It's possible they got caught in the crossfire," Liam said. "The spirits seem attracted to shifter energy. They might have been let loose outside Victor's territory, with the knowledge they'd be drawn inside, but given how close your territories are, some spirits might have gone in the wrong direction. Though, if they'd wanted to avoid that, they could have released the spirits on the side of Victor's land farthest from yours and Niall's."

"So someone is targeting all three packs, or Grant's and Niall's packs are collateral damage," Elijah said.

Kade didn't like either of those options.

Liam looked at Grant. "How did the spirit affect your pack?"

Grant's eyes went distant, and he shivered. "It started

this summer, but none of us realized what was happening at first. A few of us were having nightmares. Then it spread to everyone, and the nightmares kept getting worse. It was harder to wake up from them. Harder to tell when we were awake and when we were asleep."

Liam's voice was gentle when he spoke. "They seem to feed off us, off any living thing, plants included. So the more nightmares you had, the stronger it became, allowing it to create even more nightmares."

"That aligns with what we experienced."

"You tried to warn me at the grocery store the last time I saw you," Victor said. "You knew something was going on with Niall."

"The week before the nightmares started, I found him testing our wards. He was acting strange. Very twitchy. I thought he was trying to take over our territory. I wanted to warn you, but I was also unsure whose side you'd be on, and you seemed fine."

"You didn't go to anyone else for help?" Elijah asked.

"With Niall? No. There aren't many people willing to get in the middle of a territory war. With the nightmares? Honestly, I wondered if they weren't caused by my pack being stressed about Niall, since it corresponded with his more aggressive behavior. But when it got really bad, I didn't know who to trust. It was impossible to sort out what was real."

There weren't many shifters who'd eagerly ask for help. Asking revealed weakness, and it was better to hide that lest it be exploited. Kade doubted Victor would have gone to Elijah if he'd had any other options.

Grant's brow furrowed, then he looked at Elijah. "Did you contact me? To see if I needed help?"

"No. I wish I would have though."

"I swear..." Grant pulled his phone out and opened his call history. There was a series of private numbers calling him, starting a month earlier and stopping a week ago. "My battery went dead. I was too out of it to charge it. That message I sent you, Victor, is the last thing I recall doing with it. But before that, I kept getting these blocked calls. I vaguely remember answering one."

He scrolled through the list, and sure enough, one had connected for about five minutes.

Kade's eyebrows rose. "Who was it?"

Grant shook his head. "It's a blur. I have this fuzzy memory of them asking if I needed assistance from a mage. But the timing was too suspicious, so I turned them down. That's all I remember."

Elijah's phone buzzed, and he checked the notification. "Aran and Miles are here. Can they join us?"

Victor and Grant nodded, and Elijah sent a quick message to his friends. A minute later, they walked into the room. It was a tight fit with the seven of them in there, the alphas sitting and the rest standing around the desk.

Miles's gaze immediately found Grant, and he walked up to him. "How are you feeling?" He held out his hand, and Grant inclined his head, giving him permission.

Miles rested his palm against Grant's neck, his eyes glowing blue as his magic scanned Grant's body. Kade's nose twitched. It wasn't that Miles's magic reeked; it just wasn't the scent of pack magic. Though Kade was still too relieved that his sense of smell had returned to be bothered by it.

But what he found interesting was that Grant didn't flinch at the scent. Miles dropped his hand, his fingers flexing.

"You're healing well. I don't sense any issues that more food and rest won't take care of. How's your pack?"

"Recovering. Everyone here is feeling better, and our two members currently living away from us—Aiden and his mate, Zayn—are doing alright. They'd been suffering from nightmares too, but it didn't seem as bad for them, and they were blaming it on stress from grad school. I sent them a message this morning, and they confirmed they didn't have any nightmares last night."

Distance from one's pack could dull the connections between them, stretching the threads of energy that bound them together thin. That might have created a buffer between Aiden and Zayn and the spirit, but not enough to fully insulate them from its effects.

"Would you mind if I checked everyone over after this?" Miles asked. "Especially Jessie, Remy, and the younger, weaker members."

Grant studied him before saying, "I'd appreciate that."

Miles seemed relieved, and he stepped away. Grant's eyes followed him before he faced Victor again.

"You can help clear these spirits off my territory?"

"I can't, but they can." Victor gestured to the mages.

"We'll help you." Elijah cocked his head at Liam. "The bigger spirits need pack energy to capture. What about the smaller ones?"

Liam shrugged. "I'd guess it's only the spirits hooked into the packs, but that's just a theory. We'll have to test it."

Elijah considered that, then looked at Grant. "Either way, we'll need shifters from your pack to guide us. We may also require their energy. Ideally, it'd be you and your betas helping. Whoever's the strongest. Particularly for the largest spirits."

Miles opened his mouth to protest, a concerned expression crossing his face.

"After Miles clears everyone for it," Elijah amended.

That seemed to mollify Miles. "Given the rate Alpha Lucas is healing, he should be fine after a few more days of rest. That'll allow his energy reserves to replenish themselves to the point they'll be safe to use for magic."

"Whatever you need. I want these things off my land."

"We'll make it happen," Elijah said, "but it'll take a while since we have to track them down and identify them one at a time."

Kade frowned. "Don't we know what they are now though? What did you call them, Liam? Nosoi?"

"That's only the diseases and sicknesses. There are other categories, not just physical. Emotional, moral, environmental."

"Can you trap them by category?"

"I..." Liam faltered, thinking it through before he spoke again. "I have no idea. We can try? We'd still need to see them for the binding contracts to latch on, but if the general categories work instead of naming them specifically, we wouldn't have to make a sigil for each one."

We. Right. Like anyone there but Liam was capable of doing what he'd been doing.

"That would be extremely helpful," Elijah said. "When we tracked down the smallest ones, we had a difficult time figuring out what they were since they weren't large enough to affect us. We thought we'd have to wait until they grew stronger to identify them. If we could capture them by category, it'd save time and effort."

"I'll see what I can come up with. Maybe I could design a set of seals that encompasses all four categories and..." Liam trailed off.

Kade sensed Liam's brain slotting things together, clicking pieces into place. He felt like he was seconds from wandering out of the room to grab his sigil codex.

Clearly used to Liam not finishing his thoughts when he got like this, Elijah looked back to Grant. "We'll give it a try, but if it doesn't work, we'll do it the same way we did here."

"Can you reset my wards as well?" Grant asked.

Victor growled, and every head in the room turned sharply toward him. Kade snorted. Somehow, it was reassuring that Victor didn't have complete control over his more wolfy instincts when it came to Elijah.

"Sorry." Victor winced. "I'm aware that was an overreaction, but that ritual was intense."

Elijah chuckled, patting him on the arm. "I only want to do intense rituals with you. Besides, I don't think I even could do them with anyone else. I'm not positive I know how *not* to use your energy. It mixes so easily with my magic. I'll have to practice until I can guarantee I can keep them separate when needed."

"Why's that a problem?" Kade asked.

"Because I doubt Grant wants wards made with at least as much of Victor's energy as his own."

That made sense. No alpha would feel comfortable with that.

"Ah," Grant said. "I trust Victor, but yeah. I'd rather not have wards made with Mills pack energy."

"So there's no need for you to get all growly," Elijah told Victor. "Your energy is keeping me from doing anything intense with another shifter at the moment."

Victor smirked, pleased with himself.

"Don't look so smug about that, you ass." Elijah's words were warm and fond.

"It's that big metaphorical shifter knot keeping you full

of his energy like I theorized," Aran said. "There's no room for another shifter dick to get into your channels."

Elijah slapped a hand against his face. "Do you still think Kade is worse?"

"Yes," Victor replied without hesitation.

"Hey!" That was uncalled for. Kade didn't use dick analogies during important meetings. Often.

"Do I want to know?" Grant asked.

"No," Liam, Elijah, and Miles said in unison.

"Okay then. I suppose this metaphorical... shifter anatomy means you can't do it either, Liam?"

The other mages burst into laughter.

"Oh, shut up," Liam snapped.

Grant glanced at Kade in confusion, but Kade couldn't provide much clarification. "Something about him setting a ward that failed to block a cat?"

That only confused Grant more.

"In all fairness," Elijah said, "when he's using Kade's energy, his wards aren't half bad. But no, you don't want Liam doing it."

"I can do it," Miles offered.

Elijah seemed surprised, and Kade bit the inside of his cheek to keep from grinning. Miles doing an intense ritual with Grant sounded like a wonderful idea.

"I'm slightly better at wards than Aran," Miles said quickly, trying to justify himself. "Though neither of us is anywhere near Elijah's level. But I can use Alpha Lucas's energy, and it will save us from Aran talking endlessly about the size of the shifter dick he took a night-long pounding from."

Grant sat up straighter. "Wait. It's that kind of ritual?"

"It isn't." Elijah sounded exasperated. "Well. It could be. If you both consent to that. But no, we're talking about metaphorical dicks. Still. Because apparently dick metaphors can be used in every situation."

"Like all the best dicks, metaphorical shifter dicks are highly vers," Aran said.

Kade huffed out a laugh and exchanged a decisive nod with Aran.

"*Anyways*," Elijah said. "Moving on. Miles can reset your wards on the next full moon, which means we've got a month to get everything else taken care of. In the meantime, we'll clear your territory of spirits. But that leaves us with three other problems. Who's behind this, how to destroy the captured spirits, and what to do about Niall."

"I'm researching the second," Liam said. "No solid theories yet, but I'll keep you updated."

"I'll leave it to you."

Kade's phone vibrated, and he opened the message.

PIERCE

Tomorrow at noon? Where the three territories meet?

That was deep in the forest, almost as far from Niall's house as Pierce could get.

Liam leaned over to read the screen. "Is that safe?"

Probably not, but Kade was convinced he had to do it anyway.

"Pierce replied," Kade told the group. "He wants to meet tomorrow."

"Alright," Victor said. "We'll meet him then."

"No. He said one-on-one."

"I don't want you meeting him alone. I don't want *anyone* near that pack alone."

"I'll go with him but hang back so Pierce can't see me. Our bond isn't as strong as yours, but if something goes wrong, I should feel it." There was no question in Liam's voice. He would be going. Kade reminded himself that offer held no deeper meaning.

"That's better, but I'd still like someone else with you. What if it's a trap and he brings his entire pack with him?"

"I can chaperone them," Aran said. "I have the least to do here anyway."

Liam shot Elijah a look Kade could only interpret as 'Please, no.'

But Elijah shook his head. "He's right. I'll be making more boxes, and Miles needs to monitor how Grant's pack is healing and learn the ward ritual."

Liam sighed. "Fine. I will subject myself to hours with these two for you. Oh, also. I was correct about your tether with Victor. It started during that ritual because you two are so compatible. After this is over, you're helping me avoid the next three dates my mother tries to arrange with whatever 'nice young man' she bumped into at the store."

Kade kept his face neutral, but Victor's and Grant's gazes weighed heavy on his skin.

Elijah's eyes darted to Kade, then back to Liam. "If I need to, I will."

"Okay," Victor said. "You three will meet Pierce. Kade, get as much information as you can out of him and try to get him to help us capture the spirit. Grant, are you sure you want to be involved? This could get messy."

"If you're helping us, I'm helping you. We seem to be connected in this, and none of us will be safe until the threat is eliminated. Whatever my pack and I can do, we'll do it."

"Hopefully Pierce feels the same. If he'll help, what do you need?" Victor asked the mages.

"We'll need his permission to enter their territory,"

Elijah said. "He should be able to let us through their wards, but won't Niall sense that?"

"He will, but if we do it as far from their pack house as possible, that should give you an hour to capture the spirit. Will that be enough?"

Elijah grimaced. "It'll have to be. Even though the nightmare spirit was stronger than the decay spirit, having Liam and Kade's combined power offset that. If I've got access to energy from the three of you plus Pierce—four mages, two alphas, and two seconds-in-command—it should be doable. And if all goes well, once that spirit is off their land, they'll be more reasonable."

Kade didn't love the idea of capturing something so massive while a hostile pack was bearing down on them, but that seemed like what they'd have to do.

"What if we do it on the new moon?" Liam asked. "Given its size and the fact that we're fairly certain it has hooks in the pack, it might help. If it's tied to pack energy, it might be at its weakest then, but would it endanger their pack further if we waited that long?"

"They didn't appear unhealthy," Miles said. "Not like Alpha Lucas's pack, though—"

"You don't need to use my title. Call me Grant."

Miles looked flustered, but continued. "I don't know what the spirit is doing to them mentally, but physically, they should be fine. Plus it'd give Al—Grant plenty of time to recover."

Aran tilted his head, thinking it through. "It'd be a trade-off. The spirit would have another two weeks to feed off the pack's paranoia, and our shifters would also be at their weakest."

"It might be worth the risk," Elijah said. "We can use the downtime to clean up Grant's territory, then tackle

Niall's after that. And most of his pack will be in their house that night, right?"

"That's generally protocol on a new moon," Victor said. "There'd be less chance of someone being close to us when we start. Anyone willing in my pack can guard us."

"Same with mine," Grant said.

"Kade, see if you can get Pierce to agree to that."

"Will do, Alpha."

"But if anything about the situation feels off, get out of there."

"Absolutely." Kade would haul Liam away the moment he sensed danger.

"Which leaves one problem." Elijah's lips tightened. He was obviously less than thrilled to be broaching the subject.

"My father called me and told me to call him back when I was ready to ask for help. Should I do that now?" The reluctance in Victor's words was easy to hear.

Kade winced, knowing how much that would cost Victor and that they couldn't trust anything his father said or did.

Silence fell in the room.

Finally, Grant spoke. "Do you have proof it's your father?"

"No, but there doesn't seem to be anyone else. Just him and that fucking mage."

"Can we deal with them right now?" Aran asked. "Do we have the resources? If we need to clear the spirits off Grant's territory and prepare to break into Niall's, can we afford to split our focus to a third area and try to determine what's going on with Victor's father? It'll take us the majority of the two weeks to get the worst of the spirits off Grant's land. Wouldn't it be better to take care of the imminent threats, get Niall's pack sane and safe, then face whatever that mage is doing as a united front?"

"That assumes they won't attack us while we do all that," Liam said, his worry gnawing at Kade's mind.

"Do we want to divert our attention from the actual problems we know the scope of and can address in order to deal with a theoretical problem we lack information on? We don't know where they are or if they're working with anyone else, and there are no clues to help us figure those things out. We can keep an eye out and watch our backs, but if they were going to attack, wouldn't they have done that already?"

"That's the assumption we've been operating under," Elijah said. "We've been concentrating on the spirits from the beginning because they're the most direct threat to the pack and we don't have any true leads, just suspicions. I think it's better to ensure the packs are safe, then track down whoever the fuck is behind this and make it so they can never do it again."

Victor rolled his shoulders, clearly uncomfortable. "I'd rather focus on the direct threat, but you shouldn't trust my judgment on that."

Elijah placed a hand on his shoulder and squeezed. "That's my vote too. Once Niall is on our side, the spirits are captured, and all three packs are healthy, then Victor contacts his father and we try to find that mage."

Kade agreed. If Victor's father truly was behind this, he wasn't eager for that confrontation. There was no way Victor fighting his father again wouldn't end in death for one of them.

That settled, they finalized their plans, and Grant led Miles off to see his pack. Liam, Elijah, and Aran left to make more boxes for the spirits they'd be trapping on Grant's territory, leaving Kade alone with Victor.

"Time to deal with my shit?" Victor asked.

"Why didn't you tell me?"

Victor sighed. "Because I was ashamed of myself. Of my wolf. Of my lack of control. That asshole mage. I knew he smelled wrong, but my wolf wanted to let him use us. To let him do anything he wanted to us. If he had suggested it, my wolf would have bonded him then and there. Hell, it would have been happy letting that bastard tether himself to us—no reciprocal bond necessary."

"That doesn't sound like you, Victor. You wouldn't do that."

"That night, I would have."

"But you didn't. He must have used magic on you. Put a spell on you. Something."

"No. I would have smelled active magic. He wasn't using any. It was my wolf."

"If you were in your right mind, you wouldn't have even considered a transactional bond, or whatever the fuck he was after."

"You weren't there. You didn't see how out of control I was. How much my wolf wanted it."

"I don't know how he did it, but he put some spell on you. I'm going to need proof to believe otherwise." Victor started to protest, but Kade didn't let him get a word out. "That's why you were avoiding magic? Why you didn't trust yourself around Elijah?"

"I still don't trust my wolf around magic, but I trust Elijah and his friends. Beyond that..." He shrugged.

"And you honestly thought this was your fault?"

Victor cringed.

"Well, I hate to break it to you, but it isn't. The world doesn't revolve around your broody ass."

"I should have stopped it. Should have guaranteed that bastard would never get near our pack again."

"You aren't responsible for his actions. Or your father's actions. Their shitty behavior is their own."

"But—"

Kade cut him off. "Elijah was right. If you'd told me this sooner, I would have kicked your ass until you regained some sense. None of this is your fault. And whatever you think, your wolf can be trusted."

Victor pulled a face. "I don't—"

"Oh, shut up. What did you tell me yesterday about being possessed? If I'd been the one that asshole had targeted, would you blame me for this entire situation?"

"Of course not."

"So give yourself a fucking break. Your head hasn't been wedged up your ass since you and Elijah bonded. Don't cram it back in there now."

Victor snorted. "Such loving advice. Really enjoying your delicate handling of my shit."

"I can still kick your ass if you prefer."

"The only way you could kick my ass is if I let you."

He wasn't entirely full of shit—it had been a good decade-plus since Kade had come out of one of their sparring matches victorious. That didn't mean he had to admit it. "Big words. Wanna prove it?"

Victor rolled his eyes. "No. I will try not to... How did you put it? Cram my head back up my ass?"

"Excellent. Elijah will appreciate it. It'd be terribly hard for him to fuck you like that."

"Why are you my cousin?"

"Because the powers that be decided to bless you with my presence?"

Victor huffed. "More like cursed."

They settled into silence until Victor spoke again.

"Be careful tomorrow. I'm okay with you running off to be with Liam, if that's what you need to do. I'm not okay with losing you any other way."

That hit Kade harder than he would have expected. "I will."

"And keep Liam and Aran safe. I didn't like how Niall was looking at them yesterday."

That made two of them. Niall had been talking about the mages as if they were things to be possessed, and it creeped him out.

"I will," Kade said again with conviction. He'd keep them both safe, no matter what he had to do.

"So..." Aran fell into step beside Kade as they hiked toward the area where they were meeting Pierce. A nice, neutral location, if more secluded than Kade would have preferred. "I heard you couldn't come up with a decent innuendo about Liam being an archivist."

Behind them, Liam groaned. "I told Elijah that in private."

Aran scoffed. "Like the four of us have ever kept secrets from each other."

Liam grumbled, but didn't refute it.

"I mean," Aran said, "the glove jokes alone."

"Could we not do this?" Liam asked.

"Oh, no. Mr. KnottyWolf69 here and I have been friends for too long. I was under the mistaken impression that he was better than that. If he wants to get his shifter dick—metaphorical or otherwise—all up in your channels, he needs to prove himself worthy."

Liam sputtered. "He doesn't want to do any such thing."

Aran side-eyed Kade, raising a brow, and Kade tried not to squirm.

"And how does coming up with bad pickup lines make him worthy or not?" Liam's question interrupted Aran's knowing look.

Aran waved his hand dismissively. "Because I'm aware of how much you love my brand of humor, and I need to ensure your shifter is capable of a good dick joke no matter the circumstances. Someone who can't make a naughty librarian joke about you isn't up to my standards."

"I'm not a librarian!"

"Hey!" Kade said. "Any other job, and I wouldn't have had any problem."

"Prove it. What if he were a plumber?"

"Too easy. I'd ask about laying pipe."

"Baseball player."

"Are you serious?"

"True. The jokes about the bases alone. Flight attendant."

"Join the mile-high club."

"Cashier."

"Check him out."

"Priest."

"Get him on his knees and make him see god. You aren't even trying to challenge me."

"Politician."

"I'd get his opinion on my poll, then stuff his ballot box."

"Not bad. Farmer."

"Offer to plow his field."

"Lawyer."

"Ask him if he'd like to see my briefs."

"Firefight—"

"OH MY GOD. STOP IT!" Liam's cheeks were taking on a pink tint. "Why are we friends? This is why I can't take you anywhere, Aran."

"Aww." Aran looked over his shoulder at Liam with a wicked smile. "Admit it. You love me."

"Things that will never happen."

Aran looped an arm around Kade's shoulders, leaning in to stage-whisper, "He says that, but I know the truth. He's going to pretend he doesn't enjoy you talking about dicks, but deep down, he loves it. Like, one hundred percent, he'll deny it, but he's totally the type to get all hot and bothered if you tell him every dirty thing you want to do to him."

"*Aran.*" The warning in Liam's voice was clear, but Kade sensed him squirming through their bond.

Aran paid him zero mind. "Words and information are a total turn-on for him. So use that to your advantage."

A ball of fire whizzed between their heads. Kade reflexively snagged it out of the air as Aran jumped away from him.

"Dude!" Aran spun to face Liam. "Not cool! You singed my hair with that thing."

It had been quite close to their faces.

"I wasn't aiming to hit you with it. But stop hanging all over him and saying shit like that."

"Interesting choice of which complaint came first there." Aran smirked and turned away, only to freeze when he saw the ball of fire in Kade's hand. It'd dimmed, but it was holding on. "...What?" he asked eloquently.

Kade felt the urge to hide the fireball behind his back, like it was a secret meant for him and Liam.

"Oh." Liam deflated. "That's how we've been practicing so I can get used to his energy. He has some of my magic in his system and can sustain the fire. If I feed him more magic, the flame will get bigger."

"Seriously? Do that. I want to see."

Kade cleared his throat. "Um. No."

"Yeah, no. We're not doing that in front of other people."

"Ooh. Is this the finger stretching Elijah was talking about?"

"What now?" Kade asked.

Aran leaned closer again, though he didn't touch Kade this time. "Apparently he needs to transfer his magic into you when he stretches you open."

Kade's eyebrows attempted to climb to his hairline. If it felt good when Liam did it through the tether, how much better would it be if his fingers were buried in Kade's ass? He swallowed, his gaze darting over to Liam.

"Uh," Kade managed to say, "I'll remember that."

His brain had already latched on to the thought so thoroughly that he doubted it would leave even if he wanted it to.

Aran seemed satisfied with the chaos he'd caused, and the rest of the hike was uneventful.

As they neared the territory border, Kade paused. "You guys wait here. It's far enough away, and the wind is blowing in the right direction. He shouldn't be able to smell you."

They weren't thrilled about it, but they stayed there, and Kade finished the hike on his own, passing through Victor's wards as Pierce stepped up to Niall's, though he didn't cross that boundary. Probably for the best. Niall would feel that and question why Pierce had left their territory.

Pierce's gaze bounced around the forest. He cast a quick look behind him as well. "You're alone?"

"Yes. We want to help you."

"Niall won't trust you. He's been ranting nonstop about how unfair it is that you have four mages."

"We don't have four mages. Victor and Elijah are bonded. The rest aren't part of our pack."

Pierce breathed in deeply, his eyes narrowing. "But you're bonded to one of them. It's a true bond, isn't it? Why are you lying about that?"

He was too suspicious for half-truths. Kade needed to be honest, even if that meant talking about this. "It's complicated. Yes, it's a true bond. Or it should be. It's fucked up. He doesn't want it."

"But you do?"

"Only if he does."

Pierce inhaled again, frowning. "Why do you smell like the other mage too? The one with the tattoos."

"We're friends. I've known him for years. Met him on MateHub's forums."

Pierce's expression was still pinched, but his shoulders relaxed a fraction. "No one would lie about something that stupid."

"Hey, don't knock Richard Knotz just because you're too straight to appreciate his awesomeness."

"You... haven't changed since high school, have you?" Pierce asked, but it seemed to set him at ease. He cast another look behind him, then inched closer to his pack's wards. "What's happening?"

Kade pulled out the map he'd tucked in his back pocket and unfolded it. Victor's territory was relatively spirit-free —just a handful of small ones zipping around—while Grant's had dozens of spirits of various sizes roaming over it, and Niall's was almost completely covered by the spirit of paranoia.

Pierce stared at the map. "What are those?"

"Evil spirits are attacking our packs. All of them, not just your pack. The mages are here to help us. We've trapped most of the spirits on our territory, and we're helping Grant clean up his. But we need to be on pack territory to capture them, and we need pack energy to do it."

"Niall will never agree to that."

"It doesn't have to be him."

Pierce flinched. "What would I need to do?"

"The mages want to capture the main spirit affecting your pack on the new moon. You'd need to let us into your territory. Preferably out here, so we can get the spirit captured before Niall brings the pack to attack us. And one of the mages would need to channel your energy."

Pierce narrowed his eyes, studying him. "That will fix my pack?"

"Once the spirits are trapped, they no longer affect people, but Grant's pack needs time to recover from what their spirit did to them. Yours might be the same."

"What happened to your packs?"

"Our worst spirit was decay. It corrupted our wards before Elijah fixed them. When it couldn't feed on the wards anymore, it spread to the plants and animals, then our pack. For Grant's pack, it was nightmares. What about you? When did you notice something was wrong?"

"One day, this summer, when Niall returned from a patrol, he seemed different—paranoid and controlling. And it's only gotten worse since then. He doesn't trust anyone. Not even his betas or me. He's using his alpha command almost constantly to make sure we follow his orders. When someone doesn't do what he says, he lashes out. At first, it was just him, but now, the other betas are acting the same. Our pack members are terrified of Niall and what he might do to them. We keep looking over our shoulders, expecting to see him there."

As if to prove his point, he glanced behind him again.

"It's affecting the other betas, but not you?"

"It comes and goes. When I'm away from Niall, it's better. I can sort out which thoughts are mine and which are… I don't know. Foreign?"

"If you aren't prone to feeling a certain emotion, it seems easier to identify the ones that aren't your own."

In school, Pierce had always been a genuinely nice guy. Kade didn't think he'd had a paranoid bone in his body.

Pierce squeezed his eyelids shut and steadied his breathing as he tried to gather himself. When he opened his eyes, he nodded. "I'll help you if that's how I can save my pack. I'll meet you here at midnight on the new moon. But don't contact me again. Niall checks our phones."

Kade nearly sighed with relief. "We'll see you then. Stay safe. Try to keep your head straight."

"I will." Pierce checked his surroundings once more, then slipped into the forest behind him.

Kade did sigh then. They had to hope Pierce could hold out for two more weeks. He walked back to where Liam and Aran were waiting.

"How'd it go?" Liam asked as soon as he saw Kade.

"He's definitely affected by the spirit, but he agreed to our plan."

"Can we trust him?" Aran asked.

"I don't think we have a choice. Let's head back to the pack house."

"Actually," Liam said, "can we look around a bit? That area out there, it's the neutral land between the three packs, right?"

"Niall's is straight ahead, and Grant's is to the north." Kade gestured to both.

"And it's possible to get there without triggering any of your wards?"

"It'd be a pain in the ass to hike between the wards, but yeah. You could do it if you knew the area."

"So if someone wanted to open a jar of evil spirits that would affect the packs equally, this would be the best place to do it?"

"It would. What are we searching for?"

"A jar would be traditional, but it could be a box or any kind of container."

They crossed into the unclaimed territory and started to search. As they did, Kade told them what Pierce had said.

"If Niall was the first possessed, that can't be good," Liam said. "If the spirit had alpha energy to feed it from the beginning, it must have gotten powerful fast."

"Hey!" Aran called from a few feet ahead of them. "Over here."

Kade followed Liam to where he was standing. In the underbrush, a clay jar lay on its side. It was covered in symbols, and Kade had no clue what they meant. "Is it empty?"

"I don't know," Liam admitted.

"Even the smallest spirits were visible. Just little balls of light," Aran said. "And I don't see any around here."

"Still, I'd rather not risk touching it."

Kade inhaled, catching a whiff of a scent he'd never wanted to smell again. "It's faded from months out in the elements, but that's got the same reek to it as that asshole mage."

Liam snapped half a dozen pictures with his phone, though he stayed well away from the thing.

"This supports my theory, but beyond that, it doesn't help us much." He slid his phone back into his pocket.

"You don't think the spirits will crawl into that jar if we ask nicely?"

"You never know," Aran said. "Stranger things have happened."

Liam shook his head. "I'll stick with Elijah's boxes. Let's get back home and tell everyone what we've found."

Kade's heart skipped a beat at Liam calling the pack house *home* so casually.

If only Liam wanted it to be his actual home.

TWENTY

Hiking through the forest fell firmly in the category of things Liam never would have thought he'd get used to and maybe even enjoy. He'd rather be inside with his books, but this wasn't the worst way to spend a day. Once in a while it might be nice, provided there were no spirits involved. He'd had enough of spirits to last him a lifetime.

Kade led him through the forest as they tracked down one of the small spirits remaining on Victor's territory.

It was a bright, clear day, but the weather was chilly and the trees were mostly bare. The looming threat of winter hung in the air, and Liam was glad he'd packed a heavier coat. Unfortunately, it seemed like he'd be there for that thick six to seven inches Kade had promised him.

Of snow. And nothing else.

With each step he took, two wooden boxes clattered in the bag he'd slung over his shoulder. They were already marked with the new catch-all sigil he'd created. Now to see if it worked.

In Liam's mind, Kade felt steady. Liam had been

worried hunting down more spirits might set Kade off, but apparently, after facing the massive spirit on Grant's territory, these minuscule things weren't causing him to panic. That was good. Kade seemed to be getting over the worst of his encounter with the decay spirit.

Liam had been able to read Kade's emotions with increasing ease since they'd captured the nightmare spirit. That had to mean their bond was deepening. Maybe it had something to do with the amount of Kade's energy he'd channeled to help Elijah? That was the only thing that had changed.

"When I use your energy, does it deepen the bond?" Liam asked, and Kade looked over his shoulder at him in surprise.

"I don't know. Possibly?"

"You mentioned sex does. Anything else?"

"Sex is the big one." Kade continued hiking.

Huh. His presence seemed to be trying to slither away from Liam. "But there are other things?"

Evasiveness wriggled into discomfort. He didn't want to talk about this, did he? Liam was too curious to let the subject drop.

"What are they?"

Kade shrugged. "A bond deepens as the relationship develops and the couple gets closer, as they become more open to each other. Usually, that involves sex, but it doesn't have to."

"So any kind of intimacy, physical or emotional?"

"Yeah."

"In that case, using your energy might be creating a sort of magical intimacy?"

Kade halted on the trail and turned toward him. "Does it matter?"

Liam frowned. "You said the deeper the bond, the more painful it could be for the shifter to sever it. So if channeling your energy deepens the bond, I shouldn't be using it except when we absolutely need it."

The twisting, shifting sensation coming from Kade had to be unease.

"Listen," he said, "I'm going to do what I need to do to help my pack, and that includes letting you channel as much of my energy as necessary. If that deepens the bond, it deepens the bond. I'm hoping this doesn't end in a painful severing ritual, but if it does, it'll still be worth it."

He stared at Liam like he was about to add more to that, but then a colorful ball of light whizzed past them. They jumped, their heads whipping in the direction it had gone.

"What was that?" Kade asked, checking the map and pointing to where they were. "Was that a spirit?"

Sure enough, a tiny mote of ash was bouncing around the area. No foreign emotions were affecting Liam, but the spirit was so small that he doubted its effects could be felt more than a few inches away from it.

They took off after it, running until they found it again.

Liam tilted his head and stared in confusion.

The spirit zipped around unpredictably, darting through the trees like it had too much energy to contain, resulting in a rainbow of neon streaks and electric sparks. It didn't appear evil so much as hyperactive—a giddy kid on a sugar high.

"No, seriously," Kade said. "What the fuck is that?"

Liam had no clue, but that made this the perfect spirit to try the new seal on.

He pulled a box out of his bag and held it open in front of them. He didn't need to ask; Kade was already stepping up beside him, resting his palm on the back of Liam's neck.

Liam breathed through the surge of energy that came with that contact. God, how could a simple touch feel so exquisite? But he couldn't get distracted. He did his best to ignore the heady lure of Kade's energy and got to work.

He activated the seal inside the box, the sigils lighting up and latching on to the spirit.

Considering the size, there was more resistance than he would have expected in comparison to the spirits they'd trapped before, but it worked. The colorful spirit was sucked into the box, where it ricocheted off the sides.

Liam snapped the lid shut, Elijah's wards flaring to life. Since he didn't know what the spirit was, he wrote a description of it on the box. That would have to do.

But more importantly, the binding seal worked. Their lives had just gotten a hell of a lot easier when it came to cleaning up Grant's territory and the remaining spirits on Victor's. Liam didn't have to be on call to make a sigil whenever anyone identified a spirit. Since these sigils weren't as accurate in naming the spirits individually, they seemed to require more magic to capture their target. He'd make specific sigils for the largest spirits on Grant's territory to keep Elijah from overexerting himself when he trapped them, but the smaller ones could be captured with this seal.

And on the plus side, while Kade's energy was still intoxicating, after the amount he'd used while capturing the nightmare spirit, it did seem like he'd become accustomed to its potent effects. He could probably use it without jumping Kade.

Probably.

Kade smirked like he was reading his thoughts. "You're getting pretty used to taking just the tip."

Liam snorted despite himself. "Yeah. Now let's find another one of these things so I can take it again."

In his mind, Kade glittered with amusement.

They could do this, but he'd keep his use of Kade's energy to just the tip as often as he could, and only when they were dealing with the spirits. That way severing their bond wouldn't be more painful for Kade than it had to be.

"Are you sure you want to help us clean up Grant's territory?" Elijah asked as he wove a ward around another box.

They were in the workshop they'd been using to make the boxes. It was a cluttered room filled with the scent of cedar wood and sawdust. A sturdy workbench sat against the wall, and a stack of lumber was piled in the corner. Saws and sanders and things Liam couldn't name were scattered throughout, and underneath everything, the memory of magic lingered, whispers of spells cast years ago.

"Positive," he said. "We've got this. We've practiced. I won't get lost in his energy. I was fine when I fed it to you while you trapped the nightmare spirit, wasn't I? We can do this. We can help."

"Alright. I trust your judgment, but be careful."

"Stop stealing my lines."

Elijah rolled his eyes. "Right. Because only you get to tell people to be careful."

"Exactly."

Elijah studied him. "You aren't staying here and

working on whatever your theory is about destroying these things?"

"I can do both. We can come with you during the day to capture some spirits, and then I'll figure out how to destroy them in the evening."

Those were big words—he still wasn't certain destroying the spirits was possible—but he wanted to do both.

For whatever reason, that answer amped up Elijah's scrutiny.

"What?" Liam asked.

"I never thought I'd see the day you'd pick the practical over the theoretical."

"I'm not. Kade will get restless if he can't help."

Elijah raised an eyebrow. "Speaking of Kade. Have you looked closely at any of the magic you've done with his energy?"

Liam hadn't, not really. It hadn't occurred to him. He didn't cast spells that often beyond protections for books and the like. Most of the work he'd done with Kade's energy didn't last long enough to be studied. No one examined the magic woven through a fireball before they threw it.

Elijah read his answer in his hesitation. "You should."

"Why?"

"Liam, I love you, and you are the smartest person I know, but you're kind of an idiot sometimes. Do a spell with Kade's energy—something you've done before that requires craft and skill to cast—then look at it closely. Look at the threads. Then we'll talk."

"Fine, I will."

He understood what Elijah was implying—that there was some level of compatibility between him and Kade—

but most of the ease with which he could use Kade's energy was likely due to the magic in the pack's blood.

Besides, he didn't see why it mattered. Their bond wasn't the same as Elijah and Victor's, and even if it was deepening, they were severing it once this was over. He didn't want the life Elijah had here. He'd never be happy with that, so there was no point. Compatible magic and energy or not, he wouldn't be staying in Lost Creek forever.

Liam had been sure they could do this, but his nerves still jangled as Kade drove up to Grant's pack house shortly after noon the next day, following a car driven by Grant's second, along with his beta and one other member of his pack. Miles and Aran were behind them, bringing up the rear.

He stared at the map of Grant's territory in his hand, at the spirits teeming over it. These weren't the little things he and Kade had trapped yesterday. There would be no avoiding their effects when they captured them.

But they had this, he told himself. They wouldn't get caught up in a spirit again.

They parked their cars outside the pack house and got out.

Elijah, Victor, and Grant were waiting for them. They'd left earlier that morning to attempt to trap the spirits without pack energy.

As they walked up, Elijah said, "Good news and bad news. We don't need pack energy for the small and medium spirits, and while we haven't tried a larger spirit yet, I think Liam was correct. Only the spirits that have hooked themselves into pack members require access to pack energy. But, like he said, the new seals use more power. It'll cause more of a strain on your magic."

"But we can do it?" Miles asked.

"You can, but stick with the smaller spirits until you've got the hang of it, then work your way up from there."

Liam had no desire to argue about that. He would not be making the same mistake of rushing to trap a large spirit when there were enough small and medium-sized ones to keep them busy for days.

"Okay," Elijah said, "Grant, you and Miles should work together so he can get used to using your energy before he resets your wards."

Grant's gaze landed on Miles, and he inclined his head.

"Then, to keep power levels as even as possible, your second should go with Aran." Elijah gestured to the no-nonsense-looking woman who'd driven the lead car out to the territory.

"Be careful with how much of her energy you use, Aran," Miles said. "Grant's pack is still recovering."

"Will do." Aran grinned rakishly at her. While he was what Liam would classify as extremely gay, he would also happily flirt with anything that moved.

She stared at him flatly.

Liam almost laughed. Aran wouldn't be getting much of a rise out of her either.

"Your beta can go with Liam and Kade, and your other pack member can come with Victor and me."

Grant nodded again. "Sounds like a plan. Let's go in separate directions and meet up here in about three hours so we can get back in time for dinner. I don't want anyone out here at night."

Everyone headed out along different paths.

Grant's beta, Aiyana, was a woman in her late thirties, nearly as tall as Liam, her black hair flowing loose around her shoulders.

She took them south, pausing to study the map Elijah had given her. "Should we go after this little guy first?" she asked, pointing to a shimmering squiggle Liam had to assume wasn't far from where they stood.

"Sure. Let's steer clear of these two." Liam motioned to the largest spirits on their quarter of the map. "Those, Elijah will have to take care of."

Aiyana led them deeper into the forest.

Though Liam didn't want to admit it, there was comfort in having someone else around. They wouldn't lose control, but having a backup made him worry about it less.

"How long have you two been together? Last I remember, Victor's pack didn't have any mages, and now it's got two."

There was a sharp burst of emotions from Kade, and Liam exchanged a glance with him. They should have known Grant's pack would have questions.

"Ah," Kade said. "A little over a week."

Aiyana winced. "Oh, it sucks these spirits are interfering with what should be some of the best days of your life. My mate and I didn't leave our room the first week we were bonded. But I guess you can make it up afterward. Something to look forward to."

Liam forced out an awkward chuckle, his embarrassment mixing with Kade's. There would be no making anything up. "That's what Elijah and Victor will be doing, and I bet it'll be for longer than a week."

He was saved from having to elaborate further about himself and Kade when she said, "It should be around here."

When they finally found the spirit, it was a shadow that bent any light that hit it, distorting their view of the plants beyond. Once again, Liam had no idea what it was, but capturing it didn't take much effort. The lack of pack energy wasn't a huge detriment.

"That... didn't seem bad," Aiyana said. "I'm guessing they get harder to capture as they get bigger?"

"Exponentially so," Liam said. "This was too small to affect us."

"Well, this is the next closest." She tapped an ashy smudge that hovered over the map. "Do you want to try it, or should we avoid it?"

It wasn't large by any means, but it was a sizable step up from the day before. It was also scarcely moving.

Liam would rather not be utterly useless. If they could only handle the smallest of the spirits, they wouldn't be much help. He looked at Kade and got a shrug in return. "Let's try it."

While they tracked it down, Liam couldn't stop himself from asking a question he'd had for the last few days.

"I am fully aware what I'm about to ask will sound sexist and that this is a terrible way to preface a question, so I shouldn't even ask," Liam said.

"Are you going to ask about our pack's second and beta both being female?"

Liam cringed. "Yeah, sorry. I've just never heard of a pack with two women in positions of power, but in all fairness, I haven't worked with packs often."

"It's decently rare still and depends on culture and tradition. Long ago, it was normal to have female alphas and betas in relatively equal numbers, but we're talking a thousand-plus years ago. A lot of things became unbalanced back then."

That fit with what Liam had gathered from his reading.

"Until recently," she continued, "it's been more common to have male alphas and betas, but that's changing in some packs. Grant isn't the type to feel peer pressure from dead alphas, so he picked the best people for the job. Niall is more traditional, which is why all his betas are male."

"Victor's father was similar," Kade said. "But we've had female alphas in the not-so-distant past, and Victor won't give a shit about gender when it comes time to replace any of us."

That made sense. The mage council was also predominantly male. There was a chance that would even out when those old bastards died, but they certainly weren't giving up power before then.

Aiyana checked the map. "It's still a ways off. Shall we take a break here?"

"Yeah, that sounds—" Liam cut himself off, blinking. There was a furrow between Kade's brows.

Their hesitation confused Aiyana.

"Normally, are you fond of taking breaks?" Liam asked.

She frowned. "No. There's generally too much to do to take breaks."

"You know how you asked if the bigger ones were worse? Well, you're about to find out. If you're experiencing any weird cognitive dissonance, it's because you're in the trail of a spirit. It's affecting us. Amplifying emotions that aren't necessarily our own."

"Laziness?" Kade asked.

"Or something like it."

"Got it," Aiyana said. "Pay no attention to the sudden urge to play a mindless game on my phone. So do we keep going in this direction, or is it better to circle around?"

"We keep going," Liam said. "But if it gets overwhelming for any of us, we'll move on to a different spirit."

They forged ahead, and lethargy sank into Liam's bones. It would have been so easy to sit, to lie down, to close his eyes for a minute and relax. But he knew that wasn't him talking, no matter how much effort each step required, no matter how tempting it was to rest for a moment.

When they came upon the spirit, it was the only patch of fog in the forest, making it impossible to miss.

It was a languid, drifting thing in a gauzy gray, enveloping the trees, slowing the world around it to this tedious sluggishness that weighed down Liam's limbs as he reached into his bag and pulled out a box. He had no energy, no will to do anything. It'd be so much nicer to lie around and do nothing.

But he couldn't do that; he had a job to do. And this was one hell of a way to stop him from doing it. He flipped open the box and activated the seal as Kade's hand found his neck.

The seal latched on to the spirit, but then that resistance kicked in, a drag that slowed the spirit's capture, making it harder to haul the spirit into the box. Making him wish for a break from this tiring work.

He opened himself up to more of Kade's energy, gasping as it filled him. It flooded into him, stretching him full. He channeled that energy, funneling it into the seal, using it to yank the spirit forward.

The fog oozed, congealing in the box—a lazy, hypnotic swirl. He was so sleepy. He never wanted to move again...

Kade reached forward and closed the lid.

Liam shook himself. That hadn't been exceptionally

difficult, but he wasn't ready to try anything bigger than that.

"This is going to be unpleasant, isn't it?" Aiyana asked.

Liam and Kade snorted in unison.

"That was our reaction too," Kade said.

They captured another spirit—a churning yellow ball of light that had no noticeable effect on them—and then it was time to head back to meet everyone.

Liam checked his map and was surprised when a large spirit to the east started to shrink.

"Hey, look at this." He showed the spirit to Kade. "Did Elijah and Victor go east?"

"No, they went north. Isn't that the direction Miles and Grant went?"

"If so, Miles must be getting the hang of using Grant's energy. I wouldn't have expected him to go after something that size."

It was bigger than Liam would have attempted, but from how it was steadily shrinking, Miles wasn't having any issues with it. The area to the north was missing a couple larger spirits as well. There were still dozens roaming free, but they'd made a dent.

They were nearing the pack house when Kade froze, pressing his eyelids shut as he inhaled deeply. The hair on Liam's arms rose as Kade's presence shifted in his mind, becoming more alert, sensing danger beyond the spirits surrounding them—something more imminent, something that was making Kade's heart beat faster, and Liam's in time.

When Kade opened his eyes, he asked Aiyana, "Do you smell that?"

She copied his actions, then looked at Kade, anger

clouding her face. "That's not the scent of any of these four mages." There was a displeased growl in her voice.

"What?" Liam asked. "You're smelling another mage?"

"Two, I think," Kade said.

"And shifters," Aiyana added. "All wolves, not from our pack or Victor's. Four of them?"

"At least. They aren't from Niall's either."

Liam glanced around like he was expecting them to jump out of the trees, but Kade shook his head. "It's been a day, maybe two. I think they've already left, but that doesn't make it less concerning."

"Is it the previous shop owner and Victor's father?"

"Not that I can smell, but one of the mages has the same taint to his scent as that bastard did."

"The other doesn't?"

Kade inhaled again, his shoulders tense. "Not that I'm picking up. It's abrasive, but I wouldn't call it corrupt." He looked over at Aiyana, and she nodded in agreement.

"Definitely foreign magic. And the shifters' scents are... muted? Or concealed with magic?"

"They're subdued in a way I've never smelled another shifter's scent before," Kade said. "Let's get everyone and bring them here."

"Wouldn't Grant have sensed someone intruding on his land?" Liam asked, hurrying to keep up with Aiyana as she sped toward the pack house.

"If he was paying attention, maybe?" Kade said. "If it happened at night, while he was asleep, with how out of it he was and how weak his wards are, I highly doubt it."

They arrived at the pack house first.

Aiyana paced as they waited for everyone. "Why the hell was someone on our land?"

Liam had no answers to give her.

When Miles and Grant returned ten minutes later, Grant was less than pleased to hear Aiyana's report.

"I didn't feel anything," he said, "but the wards are shot. The only reason I noticed you guys passing through them today was because I knew you were coming."

He seemed ready to storm into the forest and hunt down the scents, but he restrained himself, waiting for the other groups.

Miles stood beside Liam and watched Grant join Aiyana's pacing.

"Did everything go alright? Were you able to use Grant's energy without any problems?" Liam asked.

"Uh, yeah. It was fine. No problems here." His cheeks were stained pink.

Before Liam could say anything else, Aran appeared with Grant's second. Aran's gaze immediately zeroed in on Miles, mischief in his eyes. He walked over and tossed an arm around Miles's shoulders.

Grant glanced at them, then away. He stopped his pacing to fill his second in on what was happening.

"*Miles,*" Aran said. "I saw the size of that spirit you captured. I didn't realize you could take something so big that easily. Don't tell me your channels are getting a good stretching too. How's Alpha Silver Wolf Daddy's energy treating you?"

If Miles had looked embarrassed before, it didn't begin to compare to his expression now. He pushed Aran's arm off him. "Why do you keep calling him that? He's barely started going gray."

"I mean, Alpha Soon-to-be Silver Wolf Daddy seems on the long side, but then again, I'm guessing that'd be fitting. So... how did that alpha energy treat you?"

"He's still recovering!"

"So no stretching yet? It's just been the tip?"

"Liam's made that joke," Kade said cheerfully. The traitor.

Both Aran's and Miles's heads wheeled toward Liam.

"*Liam* has?" Aran asked as he stared Liam down.

Liam's cheeks heated. "So what? I made *one* dick joke. It's not a regular thing."

"You've made significantly more than one," Kade said, and Liam hoped his glare promised pain and punishment, but Kade only seemed amused by it.

Aran looked Kade over. "How on earth did you get the stick out of his ass long enough for him to tell a dick joke?"

Kade smirked. "Oh, he totally makes dick jokes. You just have to warm him up first."

"What are you doing to warm him up?"

"Not that!" Liam said. "Not whatever you're implying!"

"I mean, I was assuming he asked you nicely. What did you think I was implying?"

Aran had not been thinking that. No way.

Liam huffed. "It isn't appropriate to be talking about this when there were intruders on Grant's territory after the full moon."

"Are they here now?" Aran asked.

"No."

"Is there anything we can do about it in the next five minutes?"

"No."

"Then I'm going to continue to make dick jokes. I'll get serious when I need to be serious. And until then, I want to hear all about Alpha Silver Wolf Daddy's massive—"

"Oh, look, Elijah and Victor are here," Miles said. "Time to get serious."

Aran gave him an unimpressed stare, but listened as Kade and Aiyana ran through what they'd sensed.

Aiyana led them back the way they'd come. Grant grew more agitated, and tension crackled around them as they followed the scent away from the pack house. It was faint, but the wolf shifters agreed it was two mages and at least four shifters.

As they got farther from the house, they stopped twice for Elijah to capture spirits that were blocking their path, but that just made Liam wonder. If someone had been on Grant's territory, how had they avoided the spirits affecting them? With as many as there were, it seemed like an impossible task, and considering how straight the trail was, they hadn't been going around them.

"Okay," Elijah said as they hiked, "if Victor's father and the previous shop owner weren't in this group, we have several potential scenarios on our hands. One, they're working with this group, which means we're not dealing with two people, we're dealing with at least eight, including three or more mages. I don't love that idea. Or two, this is a separate problem. Which means we have two enemies we have to worry about. That's also not great. Or, I guess, best case, these are the people behind the spirits and Victor's father isn't involved. But that means we have zero leads as to their identity."

Yeah, Liam didn't like those options either. "These must be the same people who contacted Grant, and if so, we have to conclude they knew Grant and his pack were weakened."

What would these interlopers have done if the pack had been here during their unwelcome visit? Nausea clawed at Liam's gut, and Kade's unease echoed through their bond.

They made it to the edge of Grant's territory and passed through his wards, the ghost of them prickling across

Liam's skin, then followed the scent to the main road, where it disappeared. They couldn't track them beyond there.

Grant snarled in frustration.

Elijah squinted down the road. "They had to have known how weak the wards were. Were they waiting until Grant's pack was so weakened they wouldn't put up a fight? And if so, what were they planning to do? They didn't smell like hunters, right? So why sneak in?"

Given the state they'd been in, they wouldn't have been capable of protecting themselves against mages or shifters with ill intent.

"Maybe someone was after my territory after all, just not Niall." Grant's tone was low and dangerous.

"Would your father try to take control of Grant's pack?" Elijah asked Victor, keeping his voice gentle.

Victor grimaced. "He was always ambitious, but he wanted to make our pack powerful, not take over others. Or at least, not before that mage came along."

"Whoever's behind this—Victor's father, that mage, someone else—they must be after something. They have to have a purpose," Elijah said, then looked at Grant. "I mean no disrespect by this, but is there a reason anyone would want your territory? The land itself. What good would it do them with these spirits on it? Unless they have a more efficient way of capturing the spirits than we do, it seems like a lot of work to take over someone else's territory. Or is there anything valuable here they'd be after?"

Grant frowned, then shook his head. "There's nothing I can think of. I love my territory, but it's no different from Victor's or Niall's. It's no different from the unclaimed territory around here. If they wanted land, they could claim any of that."

However Liam looked at it, the other option was so much worse. "If it's not the territory, it has to be the pack. It's not common, but mages do work with hunters sometimes."

"But not with hunters *and* shifters," Aran said. "I can't imagine they'd be using shifters to attack another pack of shifters."

"There are cases where they've set packs against each other," Kade said. "Start a pack war, let the packs weaken themselves, then swoop in and kill the survivors."

Elijah cocked his head. "Aran, that pack you found in Southern California. You assumed they died?"

"I didn't see any bodies, but I also didn't stay in their territory to search for them. No one has heard from them since. It seems likely they're dead. Two dozen shifters don't disappear into thin air."

Elijah made a noncommittal noise.

"You believe they were abducted?" Liam asked. "But why? And how do the spirits play into it?"

"It could be what we were thinking before," Kade said. "If they weaken the pack, the alpha included, they could grab them all at once."

"But to what end? What would they do with an entire shifter pack?" Liam wasn't sure he wanted to know the answer to those questions.

"I have no clue," Elijah said.

That was the constant state they'd been in since this had started.

Victor pressed his eyes shut. "Alpha energy. That's what that bastard wanted from my father. His energy, the pack's resources."

Liam inhaled sharply, and they stood in silence.

"That's the most logical theory we have," Elijah said eventually. "But with the state Grant was in, alpha or not, these mages wouldn't have been able to get much energy from him."

"Shifters heal quickly." Miles spoke in the quietest of whispers, like the implication in his words was too horrible to speak aloud. "Even as close to death as Grant was, he'll be back to full strength in a day or two."

"Jesus fucking Christ," Aran breathed out.

"Weaken a whole pack with the spirits until they can't protect themselves when you abduct them. Wait until they've recovered their strength... and then drain them?" Elijah's pale skin blanched stark white.

Liam's stomach heaved. Kade's emotions were a whirlwind that raged between them.

"No shifter would consent to that," Miles said.

"With as corrupt as their magic is, and with their ability to scrape that taint off, I'd bet anything these mages don't care about consent," Elijah said.

"It's some twisted inverse of the abductions. Instead of a shifter pack abducting and forcibly bonding a mage so they can control the mage's magic, it's mages abducting a shifter pack and forcibly draining them to use their energy." Disgust dripped from Aran's tone.

Liam swallowed down the bile in his throat. He hoped their theory was wrong, but as sickening as that plan was, it did fit. "So the question isn't 'what would they do with an entire shifter pack?' It's 'what would they do with an entire shifter pack's energy?'"

They headed back, night falling as they neared Grant's pack house, everyone lost in their own thoughts, turning that question over and over and finding there were no reassuring answers.

Even with as unsettling as the day's revelations had been, a certain amount of relief radiated off Kade as he drove to Victor's territory. They'd done something to help. Something that wasn't reading through dozens of books and finding zero answers. They hadn't been a burden to the pack; they hadn't let the spirits take them over. Kade had needed that, needed to prove himself, and Liam knew he'd made the right call. There was plenty of time for him to do research in the evening.

And, he realized, he'd needed it for himself too. To prove that he could handle Kade's energy, regardless of how tempting he might find it.

In total, they'd captured a dozen spirits that day. Things would get more challenging after they'd taken out the bulk of them and finding the remaining ones became more time-consuming, but he was confident they'd get it done.

His biggest concern was the people behind it. How could they stop them? Too many lives were on the line here. Too many shifters were vulnerable to their attacks. As much as Liam wanted to return to his archiving project, he wouldn't be able to do that until this situation was resolved. Until everyone was safe.

They arrived late for dinner. With the addition of Grant's pack, calling it a full house was an understatement, but they were making it work. The two packs crowded around the dining room table and spilled into the living room.

It was fascinating to watch the dynamics between

them. They were on friendly terms, and both packs were doing their best to accommodate each other, but Grant's pack hadn't settled in. While they'd be there for a month, Liam didn't know if they'd ever feel comfortable. They were grateful for the help, but this wasn't home.

The only members who seemed truly at ease were the youngest.

Oliver was glaring at Remy when Liam and Kade entered the bustling dining room.

"Nuh-uh," Oliver yelled. "Elijah is the coolest!"

Remy pulled a face, his annoyance clear. "Miles is way cooler."

"Miles smells funny!"

"*Oliver*." Katrina sounded long-suffering. "How many times do I have to tell you we don't talk about how mages smell?"

"But, Mama, he said Miles is cooler than Elijah. No one is cooler than Elijah! Smelly mages are not cool!"

"Miles doesn't smell!" Remy took offense on Miles's behalf. "He's awesome! My whole throat was ripped out of my body, but he healed it!"

Grant winced, and Miles looked equally distressed.

"I threw up so much icky black stuff it filled the most hugest ocean! And then Elijah built a wall IN MY HEAD! Miles can't do that! So Elijah is cooler!"

"*Okay*," Victor said, cutting their debate short. "I'm glad we're all getting along."

Members of both packs seated around the table chuckled.

"They've been like this all day." Katrina pinched the bridge of her nose.

"Sorry. I thought we'd talked about how to be a good

guest." Grant put a large hand on his son's shoulder, though that didn't end the boys' stare-off.

"Nope, your son isn't the main instigator."

Liam grinned. They had been arguing over everything imaginable since Remy had recovered enough to be out of his room, though the awesomeness of Elijah and Miles did seem to be a favorite topic of discussion. The injuries they'd suffered from the spirits grew with each iteration of their arguments.

Kade edged closer to him. Whatever satisfaction he'd been feeling in the car was rapidly dissolving into twitchy discomfort, though it took Liam a moment to realize why.

There were too many people too close to him. Kade had been getting better about it, but having dozens of people crammed into the room—half of them not being pack— was getting to his wolf.

Liam leaned toward him and said under his breath, "It's a bit chaotic in here, and I want to get some reading done. Would you mind if I grab food and eat in your room?"

The pure relief that washed through their bond staggered him.

"I'll grab us something and bring it up," Kade said, then slipped into the kitchen.

When Liam wrenched his eyes away from him, he was greeted by knowing smiles on the faces of every adult present. It took all his willpower not to clarify that he was not using 'reading' euphemistically. Even Elijah was giving him a look Liam felt the need to deny. Having a quiet meal in Kade's room didn't justify Aran's smirk. Liam supposed he should be thankful there were kids around, otherwise who knew what Aran might say.

But whatever. It wasn't a lie. He did want to read, and it was chaotic in there. He was itching to get back to his research. There were so many interesting books in the attic. There had to be information in one of them that he could use to destroy the spirits.

Thankfully he didn't have to stand there long, repressing the urge to explain himself. Kade reappeared in no time, balancing an impressive amount of food on a tray as he herded Liam up the stairs.

As soon as the bedroom door closed behind them, Kade relaxed.

"Do you need to…" Liam trailed off, gesturing at himself.

"Do you mind?"

Liam didn't mind nearly as much as he should have. "Go for it."

Kade placed the tray on his dresser and stepped close to Liam. He brought his hands up to Liam's neck. His fingers and energy stroked over Liam's skin. "Sorry."

"No problem." Liam sounded breathier than he would have liked. He refused to let his eyelids flutter shut.

"There are so many people in this house." Kade leaned in and inhaled. His exhale came out shuddering and relieved.

Liam swallowed as Kade's palms slid down his arms, then back up to his neck. How would it feel to have him do that in a way that wasn't quite so respectful? If his hands wandered to places that hadn't been deemed in bounds?

Kade's face was so close to his, kissing him would only take the slightest movement of his head. And fuck, he wanted to know how Kade kissed. Purely for research. Scientific curiosity, and nothing more.

But Kade pulled away and cleared his throat. "Sorry. I thought I was getting better control over that instinct."

"No, it's fine."

It wasn't fine. Kade's smoldering need to touch Liam only fueled Liam's desires. But acting on that was a bad idea, he reminded himself as Kade got them tucked into dinner. A thoroughly unappealing idea. No merit to it whatsoever. No matter how good Kade's hands felt on him.

After they ate, Kade propped himself up against the headboard next to Liam and scrolled through his phone as Liam read a book on binding spells and seals. But Kade felt... not restless, exactly. Liam thought it might be the lingering buzz of arousal causing it, but after a while, he recognized the problem for what it was. There was something Kade wanted to do.

"You can read on your Kindle. I won't tell if it's a secret."

Kade looked flustered, then said, "It's impossible to keep secrets in a shifter pack."

Liam scoffed. "First of all, clearly it's not. You just can't tell anyone. And second, you keep deflecting anytime the subject of you reading comes up. You don't flat-out lie, but you aren't telling the truth either. So what do you have on there?"

Kade shrugged.

Liam narrowed his eyes at him. "You want books with high heat and manchest covers, and occasionally, you talk like you're from some overwritten bodice ripper. I lived with avid romance readers for years. If your Kindle doesn't contain at least one trashy romance, I will never do magic again."

With a sigh, Kade deflated. "Almost entirely romance. Some trashy, some not. With travel guides mixed in."

"Why are you keeping that a secret? It's not a big deal. Now, if you didn't read at all, I'd question your sanity. I don't understand people who don't read. And I can't say

I'm eager to read the books my mother does, but there's nothing wrong with them."

"Have you met my pack? Do you honestly think they wouldn't roast me to hell and back for reading fluffy rom-coms?"

"It's not like you hide your viewing preferences."

"But porn is just sex. Before DickHunt, there were no genuine feelings on MateHub. Romance is different. Yes, there's often porn, but it's more than that, and I'd get so much shit if they found out. Especially because... I, uh, read mostly paranormal romance."

"Well, obviously my mother does too. And my sister, apparently, which worries me because she's too young to be reading the things I presume are in those books. But why 'especially because' it's paranormal?"

"Why would my pack tease me for reading about throbbing knots and fated mates?"

"Ah, yeah. True. But isn't it completely inaccurate? I believe most of the books my mom reads are written by humans. Their portrayals of vampires, shifters, and mages can't be right."

"A few are disturbingly accurate, and I have to wonder about those, but most aren't even close. That's part of the fun though. It's a fantasy. It doesn't need to be realistic. Some of the plots are so ridiculous you have to love them. Like sweater shifters."

"...Sweater... shifters?" Liam's brain was not wrapping itself around the combination of those two things.

"You know, 'Usually, she wears him. Tonight, he wears her.'"

"Um. No."

"It's this series that went viral last year. *Embraced by the Sweater Shifter, Cupped by the Bra Shifter, Flossed by the Thong*

Shifter, Knotted by the Tie Shifter, and more. There's one for pretty much every piece of clothing you could imagine. Super inclusive, if a bit stereotypical. The tie shifter is MM, as is *Supported by the Jockstrap Shifter*. That one's adorably wholesome. *Moved by the Flannel Shirt Shifter* is FF, and there are holiday novellas like *Stuffed by the Stocking Shifter* and *Fingered by the Mitten Shifter*. The first book in the series is *Embraced*. It's about a young woman who discovers her big fluffy sweater is secretly a big hard alpha sweater shifter."

"Alpha… sweater… shifter?" What world had Liam stumbled into? What was this conversation? "Like Victor? But a sweater?"

"Nah. It's more the mistaken human concept of 'alpha.' Victor is too soft to be an alpha sweater shifter."

Liam's brain had given up. All words had fled in the face of this new reality. His mouth opened, then closed, then opened again.

Kade laughed. "Yeah. That's everyone's first reaction, but they're oddly addictive. And it makes it even better when you find out the series was written by Y. Jesus."

Liam was still unable to produce a sound.

"There are rumors the MateHub Originals division is planning to adapt *Embraced*."

"Oh god, no." Liam regained his ability to speak as a horrific realization hit him. "I'll never hear the end of this if it comes out. Aran would not shut up about that *Howling Heats* thing. He was raving about men in corset vests for an entire month."

"*Howling Hearts and Hidden Heats*," Kade corrected. "It's so hot. Not as good as the book, of course, but they did a great job with it. Really respected the source material. You should watch it if you haven't."

"I'm not one to watch... uh, *that.* Or any video-based media."

"I've got the book trilogy if you want to borrow it."

"I'll pass, thanks."

"Your loss."

"And I'm devastated by it. When did you start reading romance?"

"Six or seven years ago? I was reading it ironically at first, but I found I actually liked it. Unironically. I'm aware I've got a reputation, and it is well earned. *Very* well earned."

"I'm channeling Aran here to comment about you putting in a lot of hard work to get that reputation."

"And from time to time, the hard work gets put in me."

Liam groaned. "Yeah. I walked into that one."

Kade got quieter as he said, "I don't know. Sleeping around is sort of... meaningless? Don't get me wrong. It's fun, and there's not much else to do around here. But there's nothing special about it. There's no connection. Reading romance—even cheesy, overwritten, instalove romance—is a nice reminder there's more than that. I like seeing people find that perfect someone they have a soul-deep bond with, and it's even better when I get to play the meddling friend in real life."

"And I'm sure Elijah and Victor appreciate your meddling, regardless of what they might claim."

"Damn right."

"But seriously, while you'll never convince me to read it, I won't judge you for it either. Read whatever you want."

Kade stared at him for a beat, grinned, then pulled his Kindle out of the nightstand drawer.

Which was how Liam found himself in bed with Kade, Kade reading on his Kindle while Liam perused the book on binding contracts. The warm, contented hum coming from Kade made a soft smile play on Liam's lips. He couldn't help but think this was the ideal way to spend an evening.

It was thrilling to have access to uncensored books. In more ways than one. He still wasn't used to how casually these mages referred to sex magic with their mates. He'd lost count of the number of times he'd read something to the effect of, "This spell has excellent results if done while knotted." Okay then, good to know.

Two hours later, after he'd finished the book, he shut it and let out a sigh.

Kade arched an eyebrow at him in question.

"There are two other books from the attic I want to read, but after that, I'd like to experiment with destroying the spirits."

"I'm in. Whatever you need."

Liam's determination grew. They could do this. They'd eliminate these spirits and make the land safe for the packs again.

The next three days followed the same pattern. Cleaning up Grant's territory in the morning and afternoon, then returning to Victor's house for dinner and retreating up to their room. To *Kade's* room. Kade read while Liam did research. Every now and then, a distracting wave of lust would roll through their bond, but for the most part, Kade being immersed in his books helped Liam concentrate.

After Liam had read through the remaining books

they'd pulled from the attic, he sketched out his theories on how they might destroy the spirits.

Generally, mages didn't break binding contracts, but it seemed like they could be destroyed with the right amount of energy. There'd been enough information about it in the books that he was optimistic they could accomplish that much. The trick would be containing the evil spirit within the binding spell while it was being destroyed.

As Liam listed the supplies he'd use—the herbs and stones that would aid his magic—then sketched the sigils and runes he'd need and the circle he'd draw, Kade was less focused on his Kindle than he had been on the previous nights. He kept glancing at Liam's notebook.

"Should we go to the shop tomorrow instead of Grant's territory?" Kade asked, and Liam jumped in surprise as the silence was broken.

He paused, unsure how to answer that, but Kade understood his hesitation. "No, it's okay. As long as I'm doing something to help, I don't care what it is. Just don't make me read a bunch of old grimoires again, please?"

Liam snorted. "Deal. No more grimoires for you. Unless we need to research sex magic."

"Now that is research I would eagerly do." Kade's grin held a wicked delight that promised things they'd already agreed not to do. "But sex research aside, I am fully capable of sitting there and attempting not to maul you as you use my energy for your experiments."

"Okay. Let's tell Elijah and Victor the plan, but we don't have to go into town if I can find what I need in the attic. If there's something I can't find, Aran and Miles can bring it on their way out. It feels like, in the past, there was a lot of magic used in that workshop where we've been making the boxes. Would we be able to use that space?"

"Yeah. Grandma used that as her workroom years ago, but her things got moved to the attic after she passed. You can use it, and we can move some of the machinery out of there so you have room to work."

"That'd be amazing. Hopefully it won't take much experimenting to destroy these spirits."

Even as he said it, Liam knew it was a long shot, but he was looking forward to trying.

The following morning, Victor's pack helped Kade move everything out of the workshop while Liam rummaged through the attic for supplies. He loaded up his bag and headed downstairs, finding Kade in the near-empty room.

"Perfect," Liam said, and Kade winked at him.

"I know I am."

Liam did him the favor of not rolling his eyes.

Kade stood off to the side, watching Liam work.

On the floor, Liam drew a circle in chalk and added candles to the compass points along with a handful of stones—obsidian for cutting ties, smoky quartz for letting go of the past, onyx to promote closure. Then he sprinkled a mixture of rue, mugwort, and black pepper flowers over the candles, herbs selected for their associations with breaking hexes, ending phases, and severing unhealthy bonds. Last, he placed tiny bundles of yew between the candles to symbolize the ending of a cycle.

He walked over to the workbench—now devoid of all its chisels, clamps, and hand tools—and grabbed a sheet of parchment. The base enchantments for a binding contract weren't complicated, but once they were set, he glanced at Kade.

"The spirits are bound inside the boxes by something similar to a binding contract. I don't know if we can destroy the spirits alone, but I'm hoping with the spirits being trapped by the binding spell, if we destroy that spell, it'll take the spirit with it. So first, I'm attempting to destroy a basic binding contract—the contract and the spirit of the oath with it. I'll increase the difficulty from there, but I need something we can test."

"Does it have to be an emotion? How would we test an emotion?"

"No. It'd be easiest to have you swear not to do something simple, then try to do it."

"How simple? What about not saying a particular word?"

"Yeah, that would work."

"What if I swear not to make any dick jokes until you release me from the contract?"

"Sure, but I won't want to destroy that contract. I'll just try to get Aran to swear the same thing."

"Aw, but think how sad I would be if I couldn't tell dick jokes."

"You'd survive," Liam said, deadpan, but he wrote the terms of the agreement on the parchment. Kade Mills, Mills pack second-in-command, would not be allowed to say dick or cock or any slang with the same meaning, tell any form of dick joke, or use any euphemisms for the duration of the contract, until Liam agreed to release him from his vow.

"Damn. Did you have to be so thorough with those terms?"

Probably not, but where would the fun be in that? "We want to prove it works, right?"

Liam grabbed a ritual knife and pricked his finger, dripping blood into the glass inkwell he'd found in the attic. Kade bit his own thumb, adding his blood to Liam's, and Liam dipped his pen into the inkwell. The nib pulled the blood up, leaving spotless glass behind.

They signed the contract, their signatures drying to a dark crimson. Liam pressed his hand to the paper and sealed the contract with his magic, glowing lines spiraling out from under his palm. He then raised an eyebrow expectantly at Kade.

Kade opened his mouth, but no words came out. A furrow formed between his brows as he struggled to speak.

After a few moments, he huffed. "I realize this was my idea, but it was a stupid fucking idea. I don't like this at all."

Liam chuckled. "What's wrong? Got something on the tip of your tongue? Or is it deeper than that? In your throat? Is your mouth stuffed full of it?"

Kade looked utterly unimpressed, and Liam couldn't help himself.

"You know," he said nonchalantly, "mages work with wood frequently. There's such a wide variety with so many fun uses. Each one is magical in its own way. I'm fond of hardwood. It gives spells a little extra thrust. But softwood can be wonderful too. And I mean, the range of colors alone. From pale birch and maple to a nice dark ebony. They're all great, don't you think? There's nothing quite like holding a rod of hardwood in your hands while you work your magic. Particularly if it's got some girth to it. You can feel its power pulsing, ready to erupt if you handle it right."

"If I kill you, will this contract be nullified?" There was no heat behind Kade's words.

"Nope. You'll be stuck like this forever."

"What?" Kade's expression was aghast, and Liam laughed.

"Oh, come on. I could never keep up with you and Aran when it comes to innuendos. Let me enjoy this for once."

"You want to enjoy—" That sentence was cut short, Kade's mouth silently working. He looked like he was dying to say something, but had to settle for glaring instead. "I'll have to tell Aran you said that."

"Please don't."

"It can be our little secret. Just get this damn spell off me?"

It really did feel wrong for Kade to be unable to say ridiculously perverted things. Liam sensed how uncomfortable he was, how his skin felt too tight, how that restriction made him want to squirm. So he rolled up the contract, stepped into the circle, and sat down in the middle. He waved Kade over to join him as he studied the contract before setting it on the ground and reaching out to Kade.

Kade's hand slid into his, and their fingers entwined. The rush of Kade's energy was as exhilarating as ever, but after multiple days of working with it, Liam felt more grounded as he used it. It was still intoxicating, but the aphrodisiac part of it was easier to ignore now that he'd become familiar with it.

He placed his other hand against the floor, and the lines of chalk began to glow, the candles lighting. He channeled as little of Kade's energy as possible, weaving it together with his magic, then directed that power at the contract.

Binding contracts were written on spelled parchment so they couldn't be easily destroyed. Fire and water would not damage the paper.

Liam poured Kade's energy and his magic into the contract.

Slowly, the paper ignited. It smoldered and burned red-hot, the scent of charred ash permeating the air, and Liam pushed more energy into it, the pressure in the room building until it reached its breaking point.

Heat exploded outward from the center of the circle, making his breath catch. When he looked down, the parchment was gone.

Kade blinked in surprise, but then his shoulders relaxed.

"Damn, I haven't felt a release that satisfying since the last time I—"

"*Okay*. I take it your vocabulary is no longer restricted."

Kade tilted his head from side to side like he was assessing himself, then rattled off, "Cock, dick, penis, arousal. Turgid length. Pulsating tumescence. Throbbing manstick. Meaty—"

"I'm so glad that worked," Liam said wryly.

Kade leered at him. "Admit it. Your life wouldn't be complete without my skillful and loving use of dick."

Liam ignored Kade and considered his options. He wasn't prepared to tackle the spirits yet. He wanted to be absolutely certain he could destroy a more complex contract before he tried anything with the spirits, but this was a good start.

"Let's see what else we can make you not do."

Kade groaned, but said, "Whatever you need."

TWENTY-ONE

The icy brush of Elijah's wards swept over Kade as he followed Liam into the room where they'd been storing the trapped spirits. Dozens of wooden boxes were stacked along the walls. The room itself was heavily warded, so if something were to happen and the spirits got out of those boxes, they couldn't escape into the pack house.

It was impressive to see all the spirits they'd captured, all the work they'd done. Most of the boxes were the ones that fit on the palm of a hand, but a few were larger, and the two chests were there as well—one freshly made and one Kade remembered from his childhood. He swore the latter radiated a malice that squeezed his lungs. He inhaled deeply, getting a good hit of Liam's scent, then turned away and scanned the labels on the boxes.

The spirits from Victor's territory had specific labels, while those from Grant's contained a lot of question marks. For the stronger spirits, there were guesses as to what they might have been, otherwise, they had descriptions of what they looked like and how they acted.

Liam placed his hands on his hips and stared at the boxes. "What should we try first?"

They'd been experimenting with destroying various binding contracts over the last few days, Liam's skill and confidence growing until he was ready to move on to a spirit.

"It should be small," he said. "In these boxes, they've been cut off from their source of energy, but the larger ones might somehow maintain the strength they had, which would likely make them harder to destroy."

Kade nodded.

"Ideally," Liam continued, "we should pick something that won't cause too much damage if it does get free and escapes the workroom."

That made sense. The last thing they needed was a spirit escaping while they were attempting to destroy it, especially if it was roaming free so close to the pack.

"Would it be better to do this outside?" Kade asked.

"That would be safer. I'd rather have it escape into the forest than the house, but also, it's getting cold. I could cast a heating spell in the area to warm it up while I work, but those take a fair amount of magic to maintain for any extended period, and I'll need most of my magic for this."

"Should we do it here instead of in the workroom? Inside Elijah's wards?"

Liam considered that, then grimaced. "No. When a spell backfires, unpredictable things can happen, and I don't want to take any chances in here."

"So the workroom it is, but we find the most innocuous spirit we've captured so far."

"Exactly."

"At least we aren't lacking options."

It was a hard decision to make. There was no way in hell

they were touching the lust spirit, that was certain, but everything they'd trapped was nasty in its own right. Though, Kade supposed, it was probably too much to ask for a spirit of happiness to be mixed in with the shit they'd captured.

In the end, they settled on annoyance and took the box to the workroom.

Kade helped Liam scrub the floor clean, then watched him draw a new circle similar to the last, with a smaller circle in the middle where the box would be placed.

"The outer circle will hopefully help keep the spirit contained if it does escape," Liam explained. "It's not remotely close to what Elijah could do, but it should slow it down."

He finished his preparations with many of the objects he'd been using while breaking the binding contracts, then added more, explaining their symbolism to Kade. Black tourmaline to expel negative energy, wormwood for exorcism and protection, and hyssop for purification. The sachets of oak, ash, cedar, and elder—each selected for its ability to protect from, ward off, or banish evil spirits—had Kade biting his cheek to keep from asking Liam if he'd enjoyed handling all that wood. Liam eyed him suspiciously as he placed the little bags around the circle, like he knew exactly what Kade wasn't saying.

They sat facing each other, the box between them. Liam drew intricate sigils on it with charcoal, starting on its top and then sweeping down the sides until the design flowed onto the floor. Each sigil was beautiful and unique, a tiny piece of art meticulously copied from his notes.

Liam held his hands out, palms up, and Kade placed his over them. He nearly sighed at being able to touch Liam again. It had only been a few hours since he'd woken up wrapped around Liam, but it had still been too long. It was always too long.

Magic fluttered against his skin, an electric hum Kade wanted more of. He wanted that feeling against his entire body as they moved together. The tattoos on his chest kindled to a pleasant, warm tingling, but he shook himself and tried to focus.

He sensed Liam opening himself up completely to Kade, and energy surged out of him and into Liam, like it belonged to Liam as much as it belonged to him, like it wanted to fulfill Liam's every request and desire. But as soon as it filled Liam, it flowed back, now woven with Liam's magic, making Kade impossibly stronger because of it, then it swirled into Liam again.

Liam let out a shaky exhale. He'd been keeping his use of Kade's energy to just what he needed, but Kade would willingly give him everything. Liam never took this much. Only with the nightmare spirit had he used more, and they'd been too distracted by the horrors around them to feel the full effects.

Liam's breathing accelerated, his heartbeat pounding loud enough for Kade to hear, but he had control. Kade sensed that too, sensed how confident Liam was becoming that he could handle Kade's energy, that he could work with it and not be carried away by it, not lose himself in it. Even as arousing as it was, as pleasurable as the rush between them felt.

How someone channeling his energy could feel better than most of the sex he'd had, Kade couldn't begin to fathom, but it was bliss like he'd never experienced before. Once more, his mind wandered to what it would be like to have Liam using his energy as he moved in Liam, knotted Liam, or as Liam fucked him.

"It's difficult to concentrate when you're thinking whatever it is you're thinking," Liam said. "And I really need to concentrate to do this."

Whoops.

"Sorry. Can't help it, but I will attempt to keep my thoughts semi-PG."

"Appreciated." Liam shifted how he was sitting, and Kade carefully didn't think about how turned-on he smelled. That wouldn't be PG in the slightest.

Liam gathered himself, then began.

Kade watched in fascination as the sigils and circle sparked to life; a subtle illumination that increased in intensity as Liam fed more magic into the spell. The box itself started to glow—a red-hot ember in a fire.

Magic was thick in the air, to the point Kade felt like he wasn't breathing oxygen anymore. Every breath was nothing but magic and energy, their entwined essence filling his lungs.

Liam kept working, sweat beading on his brow. He poured energy into the box, and it grew brighter and brighter, blindingly so. It seemed as if no more magic or energy could be contained in such a small object, that it had to be destroyed under the weight of it all.

For one moment, the world narrowed down to that box.

Then, it exploded.

It struck Kade like a blow to the chest, the force of it knocking him back, his hands slipping out of Liam's. The air was punched from their lungs as the box shattered, sending shock waves through the room. He was tossed to the edge of the outer circle, blinded and disoriented, his ears ringing. He blinked, trying to regain his sight. His awareness of his surroundings returned one sense at a time.

The iron tang of blood, both Liam's and his own, hit

him first. Splinters of wood had left stinging cuts on their skin. Their harsh gasps echoed loudly off the walls, and the afterimage of the explosion faded enough to allow him to see Liam. He'd been flung to the other side of the circle. His sweater was torn and ripped. Blood dripped from a gash on his cheek.

When Liam's eyes focused again, his attention wasn't on Kade; it was on the space between them.

Kade wrenched his gaze away from Liam, and when he did, he cursed. A ball of light hovered in the circle. It pulsed, turning from a pale yellow to a harsh orange with each throbbing beat.

His movements sluggish and slow, Liam dragged himself from where he'd been sprawled and grabbed a spare box. After he activated the seal inside, the spirit was trapped easily. He slammed the lid shut and latched it, then collapsed to the floor, panting. He rolled his head over to look at Kade.

"Are you okay?"

"Yeah. You?"

"Fine," Liam said, though his voice was reedy. He huffed. "Well, that clearly didn't work. We need to figure something else out, but I don't have enough magic right now to try anything on this level again."

Kade had no doubt about that. Liam had used quite a bit of his energy. If he did another spell like that, it would leave Kade's reserves lower than was advisable. Kade didn't love the idea of letting himself get that drained unless it was absolutely necessary.

"I've never had a spell backfire that spectacularly before." Liam pushed himself up to sit, looking shaken.

"What went wrong? I mean, apart from the exploding."

Liam's brow furrowed. "I don't know, but if I had to

guess, it would be that the connection between the box and the spirit was too weak to bind the spirit while the box was being destroyed."

"Can you bind it more securely?"

Liam paused, considering that, then said, "I'll have to. The main difference between the binding contracts we were experimenting with and this is that the contracts use a signature of blood to bind the oath into the contract itself. It seals it into the paper. However, with the boxes, the seal binds the spirit to them like a suction cup. *To* the box, not *into* the wood. So when the box is destroyed, the spirit is able to escape."

"Can you seal the spirits *into* the box?"

"Not with how they're currently in there. Maybe..." Liam squinted at the box like it would give him answers.

Kade sensed him moving pieces around in his head, slotting them together, until there was a flickering spark. Not quite a light-bulb moment, but the start of one.

Liam reached into his pocket and pulled out his phone. "I'm sending Aran a message. He recently did this thing with infusing his magic into water. I wonder if..." He paused, typing furiously, and Kade was left hanging, waiting for the second half of that sentence.

Finally, Liam glanced up. "Oh, sorry. We think it might be possible, if we know what the spirits are, to infuse them in blood, then use that blood to sign a contract in the name of that spirit and destroy it. It'll be a pain in the ass and too many steps, and it wouldn't help with the spirits we never identified. Plus it'll take a ridiculous amount of energy, so we'll have to do them individually, but maybe that will work." He didn't sound convinced.

"Do we have any other options?"

"I'll keep trying to think of something, but for now, this

is all we've got." Liam was a snarl of frustration in Kade's mind.

"You okay?" Kade asked.

Liam gave him a tight smile. "I'm fine."

Right. Of course he was fine. He was always fine.

Kade pushed himself to his feet with a groan. "Well, I'm exhausted, and if there's nothing else we can do here, I could use a change of scenery."

"A change of scenery?"

"Yeah. Grab a book. I want to go for a drive."

Liam looked ready to protest, but Kade cut him off.

"Can you do any more magic today? Whether working on this or capturing spirits?"

"No." Liam sighed. "If I'm going to try something like this tomorrow, I shouldn't."

"Perfect. Then let's go."

Liam felt vaguely unsure about the whole thing, but after they got cleaned up, he picked out two books and settled into the passenger seat as Kade pulled away from the house. In minutes, he was engrossed in whatever grimoire he'd gotten from the attic, the sharp edge of perceived failure softening into a gentle contentment.

Kade drove aimlessly along rural highways, managing to double the journey to Lost Creek and timing it so he was pulling into a little parking lot as Liam finished his book.

Liam blinked like he'd forgotten where he was, then leaned forward and read the wooden sign on the building in front of them.

"Lost Creek Library?"

Kade shrugged. "In case you're feeling homesick."

"Contrary to what some people might say, I do not actually live at the library. I have an apartment."

"Which are you at more? The library?"

"Define more."

"I'm taking that as a yes."

Liam side-eyed him, but didn't argue.

Inside the library, it didn't take them long to wind through the handful of shelves.

"You were only exaggerating slightly when you said this place was a single half-full bookshelf of farmer's almanacs, weren't you?" Liam kept his voice to a library-appropriate whisper.

"I submitted an anonymous suggestion that they needed a gay paranormal romance section, but for some reason, it hasn't materialized yet. My fingers are still crossed it'll show up."

"One shelf of almanacs, one of children's books, one of local history, and one exclusively for gay manchests?"

"It's important to have balance in the world, and they certainly wouldn't be the first books in here about plowing."

Liam snorted. "I'm sure they'd contain many tips on how to plant your seed." He winced. "I didn't just say that."

"Of course not. I heard nothing about emptying a big sack full of seed and spreading it all over. You'd never say anything of the sort."

Liam was fighting back a smile, their bond shimmering with amusement.

They exited the tiny building, and Liam took a deep breath. "Thanks. I didn't realize how stressed I was getting. It's been so frustrating that I haven't found anything directly related to how to destroy these spirits."

"We'll figure it out. Even if it means me reading hundreds of boring books with zero spice in them, we'll figure it out."

Liam's determination seemed to solidify. "We will, and

I'll do my best to save you from the horrors of spiceless books."

Kade grinned at him. "And if you decide you'd like something spicier than your usual—"

"I'm still good, thanks."

"And it's still your loss."

The drive home was peaceful. Liam read the second book he'd brought, and Kade took the time to mull over their situation.

Liam was kind of amazing. He was intelligent and good-looking and smelled so achingly perfect, but Kade didn't have a clue how to make a move on him.

This differed from anything he'd done before. This mattered. He couldn't use any of the moves he usually did —he didn't want Liam to think it was just about sex. Realistically, he knew they needed to talk. He'd had the urge to strangle more than a few characters who refused to confess to their love interest for so long it became painful. Miscommunication was high on his list of the worst tropes ever. But he'd also hate to make Liam uncomfortable.

What if he laid his heart out, and Liam wasn't interested, regardless of what their scents said? It wasn't like mages cared about scents. And then they'd have to stay bonded for another month or more, while Kade continued to fall pathetically, helplessly in love with Liam, and Liam had no desire to stay in a relationship with him. Plus, Liam was so focused on destroying the spirits, and Kade shouldn't distract him from that.

He realized he was making excuses and catastrophizing, but that didn't mean he knew what he should do. He dwelled on it the entire drive and still had no answers by the time he pulled up to the pack house.

After dinner, instead of their new nightly ritual of

reading in bed, Liam disappeared with his friends to hash out the details of their next step.

Although they were in separate rooms, Kade felt Liam lighting up in a way he'd come to associate with Liam creating things, the brightness of him working on a theory.

Kade couldn't imagine how dull his own head would be without that spot of light inside him.

TWENTY-TWO

Aran grinned at Liam as they walked into the pack house's workroom. "Sooo, how are your channels feeling? Nice and stretched?"

Liam rolled his eyes. "Yep, and getting more stretched by the day."

"Good to hear it. I wouldn't expect anything less from Kade." He glanced behind them and gave Kade a thumbs-up. "Keep up the excellent work. Liam is so much more fun now that he's bonded to you."

Kade seemed unsure how to respond to that, and Liam shook his head in exasperation. While he couldn't say he was thrilled to have Kade and Aran in the same room, he was glad Aran was there. Hopefully together they'd get this to work.

Elijah and Miles would continue to clear Grant's terri-tory of spirits while Aran helped Liam for a day or two. They'd gotten most of the medium-sized spirits and were down to a few large ones that only Elijah could tackle and a bunch of small ones that were a pain to find in the forest.

"That book you gave me on plants has been fascinating," Aran said as they got to work resetting the circle and preparing the room. "I've never read anything like it, but I don't know how useful it'll be for me. Most of the spells require shifter energy, and that's not to mention the notes from multiple generations helpfully adding things like, 'For utmost potency, prepare this herb whilst knotted.'"

Yeah, Liam hadn't gotten over that yet either. He'd been devouring as many books from the attic as he could. They were filling in the blanks and supporting his theories about mage-shifter bonds in the past. He still hoped, after this was over, Victor would allow him to archive them.

The books were an amazing find, but some of the more explicit marginalia led his mind into spiraling fantasies of what it would be like if Kade bent him over a workbench, fucked him, then knotted him. How he'd get any work done after that, Liam had no idea. He could only imagine attempting to brew a potion with shaky hands as Kade ground into him, trailing kisses over his bite mark, a hand sneaking down to stroke his cock, to get him hard again as they—

From where he was leaning against a wall as they worked, Kade cleared his throat, and Liam blinked back to reality to find Aran smirking at him.

Aran didn't look away as he said, "So, Kade, would you be up for—"

"Your blood or mine?" Liam asked, cutting him off. He didn't need to know what Kade might be up for.

Devilish glee glittered in Aran's eyes for one moment before he sobered. "I'll do it this time. We'll see if it works, then go from there."

The supplies were still on the workbench from Liam's previous experiments. He'd already prepared a basic contract, the parchment waiting for the finishing touches, so Aran grabbed a knife. He pricked his finger and drops of his blood splattered into the inkwell.

Liam passed over a mixture of finely ground herbs that Aran sprinkled into the blood as Liam drew a circle on the wooden tabletop.

With a careful hand, Liam dipped a pen into the blood until the inkwell was clean glass again. He drew the binding sigils at the bottom of the contract, and Aran flipped open the lid of the box, beginning to channel his magic, feeding it through the blood on the paper and reaching out to the spirit.

The spirit was pulled from the box, and the blood took on an odd glow as it absorbed the spirit. Liam finished writing the final sigil of the binding contract.

Aran released his magic, and they stared at the paper, holding their breath, but the spirits stayed firmly attached, the sigils flickering. The soft yellow pulsed into sharp orange, almost appearing to move on the page.

They eyed each other and shrugged.

That much seemed to be working. Liam exhaled. Now for the tricky part.

"I want you to stay in here," Liam told Aran. "If this backfires, you need to trap the spirit. Don't check on us; get the spirit. We can't risk it escaping."

"I can do that."

Liam stepped into the center of the circle, and Kade came over and sat across from him, holding out his hands.

"Here's to no unexpected releases," Kade said.

Liam snorted. He really was surrounded by far too many perverts, but he took Kade's hands.

Kade's energy filled him, bringing with it the exquisite burn of being completely full, the lurid temptation of letting it consume him, the guilty delight of using so much of it. Then he channeled that energy and his magic into the contract, like he had with the box and the binding contracts before it.

As he flooded it with magic and energy, the parchment began to glow until it was red-hot, and still he poured more energy into the paper, putting all his strength and effort into it.

The spirit resisted his magic, resisted Kade's energy, but slowly it started to lose ground, started to be washed away in the tide of power scorching through the contract until it was nothing but ash and soot held together by the memory of the parchment alone.

Sweat poured down his brow. His breathing grew labored, and his heart raced.

He could do this. They could do this.

It just needed a little more.

He pushed an extra burst of magic into the spell.

There was no explosion this time.

When it finally gave, it imploded. The contract was sucked out of existence, only a dusting of ash remaining.

The sudden lack of force caused Liam to collapse forward, and Kade did the same. They sat there, panting, their heads almost touching.

Liam glanced around and sighed with relief when he saw no trace of the spirit.

They'd done it. He was exhausted, but they'd done it. He wouldn't be able to do more than one of those a day, if that, but they had something that worked.

Aran walked over. "That was fucking impressive. But I can't do that, and neither can Miles. If that's what it takes, you and Elijah will have to do them all."

Liam grimaced. Given how many spirits there were and the fact that even Elijah would be limited to one or two a day, it'd take them a month to destroy them all, and that was before they captured the ones on Niall's territory. If this was their only option, they'd do it, but it was a shitty option.

He opened his mouth to say as much, when out of the corner of his eye, a light flickered. Yellow, then orange. He turned, but nothing was there.

"Did you guys—" He didn't have to finish that sentence. Their heads jerked to the side, and they cursed at what they saw.

The tiniest speck of light floated around the room, pulsing a brighter orange and growing steadily as Liam's annoyance at his inability to defeat these fucking things increased.

Aran ran to the workbench to grab a box. It didn't take much for him to recapture the spirit, but that didn't make the situation any less frustrating.

Liam groaned as Aran snapped the lid shut. "What the hell are we going to do?"

"We'll figure it out." Kade sounded as tired as Liam felt, and for the first time since this had started, Liam truly doubted whether or not they ever would.

Kade reached over and squeezed his shoulder, looking him in the eye. "We'll figure it out," he said again, with more determination and certainty behind his words than Liam was capable of mustering.

Liam sighed and nodded. "We'll figure it out."

He'd think of something that would work. He had to. There was no other choice.

But over the next week, as they waited for the new moon, everything they tried, every increasingly convoluted, overly complicated plan he came up with, every single idea he had, failed, one after another. Each drained him and

Kade of their magic and energy, but with no results to show for it.

Yet somehow, Kade's belief in him remained unwavering, and that made Liam want to keep trying, no matter how disheartening his failures were. And no matter how exhausted he was at the end of the day, settling into bed with Kade and reading their vastly different books was more comforting than he ever could have imagined.

TWENTY-THREE

The night was dark, the forest quiet as they gathered outside the pack house one hour before midnight. With no moon visible in the sky, the stars shone brighter than usual. The weather had taken a cold turn, and an icy gust blew through the trees, making Kade glad he'd grabbed a jacket.

Next to him, Liam shivered, though he was bundled up in a winter coat. Kade resisted the urge to pull him into his arms and warm him up.

Unease settled over him as he flanked Victor, standing before their assembled pack members. Grant and some of his pack were there too. With the four mages, there were nearly two dozen members in their party.

"After we cross through the wards," Victor said, "we'll have maybe an hour before Niall's pack arrives, but assume it's less than that. Establish a perimeter around the mages and get into the positions we've discussed. Any questions?"

They shook their heads. This was just a reminder; they'd been through it before.

Elijah took over. "The likelihood of the spirit affecting

you is extremely high. These things leave trails relative to their size, and this one's could be covering the entire territory. If so, you'll feel paranoid from the moment you step across the border. Keep that in mind. Remember that you trust your partner, no matter what the spirit is telling you about them."

They'd been paired with someone they trusted with their life, in the hopes that it would help to remind them they didn't need to be suspicious of their partner. But given how strong the spirit was on Niall's territory, it seemed unlikely that would hold out for long.

"Also," Elijah continued, "the larger spirits hide smaller ones underneath them, so there may be other spirits affecting you as well, depending on what's nearby. If you see any, whatever you have to do, don't let them touch you."

Kade swore a few members of their pack glanced at him before returning their attention to Elijah.

"When we first cross, we'll quickly capture any spirits in the area so we don't have to worry about them as we work, but we need to trap the spirit of paranoia as soon as possible. It could take longer than an hour, and once we start, it'll increase its effects on us. The last two spirits we fought created golems to attack us. I expect this will do the same. Monitor your thoughts and emotions, and focus on which are yours so you don't let the spirit overwhelm you."

Through their bond, Liam's nerves jittered. This wasn't something he would ever choose to do. He was more comfortable with his books than this kind of potential physical confrontation. Regardless of how his affinity was traditionally used, Liam would never feel at home in the middle of a fight. But he was trying to project the aura that it was fine, he was fine, no one should worry about him. It made Kade long to pull him close for a different reason—to comfort him as well as warm him, though he doubted Liam would appreciate that.

He was also unsure how comforting he could be. It wasn't like he could say everything would be alright. This spirit was massive, the pack whose land it was on was hostile, and their alpha was insane from its effects. They had a plan, but how could it hold up when so many variables were at play? They didn't know how the spirit would affect them or what it would do when they tried to capture it, and they didn't know how much time they had until Niall's pack showed up or what they would do when they got there. He couldn't blame anyone for being nervous about that. Hell, he was nervous, and part of his desire to pull Liam close was simply because the one thing keeping him from freaking out about the size of the spirit, about what that spirit might do to them, was Liam's scent. He wanted to bury his nose in Liam's neck and inhale deeply to anchor himself, to use it to keep his lungs working, to keep the bands of panic from squeezing his chest.

The fact that a good chunk of their pack was outside the house on a new moon didn't help. They were at their weakest that night; it made them vulnerable to attack. His instincts screamed at him to herd everyone inside, tuck them in, and protect them. Considering the tight expression on Victor's face, he was fighting that same urge.

But they needed to do this. The new moon was the whole point of them doing it tonight, after all.

Grant wasn't faring any better than Victor. He appeared to be restraining himself from physically hauling his pack to safety. After two weeks of eating and sleeping properly, they looked healthy again, no longer gaunt and seconds from passing out. Grant was the imposing figure Kade had always remembered him being—a solid bulwark in the looming chaos.

They finished their final preparations, and the mages called light into their hands, though each was unique. Liam's was the familiar fire Kade had grown so used to. Elijah's was a soft glow, while Aran's was a bioluminescent green. And when Kade glanced over at Miles, he blinked at the radiant light in his hand, a little ball of sunshine. Between the four of them, it was bright enough that Kade hardly required his enhanced senses to see.

Their group headed out, Victor and Elijah leading the way with Grant behind them. Kade and Liam followed, then Rick carrying the chest they'd made for the spirit. Liam had carefully transferred the sigil for paranoia into it earlier that day, checking it multiple times to ensure he hadn't messed it up. The rest of the packs trailed after them.

They'd barely been hiking for ten minutes when Elijah's footsteps faltered. He pulled up short, gasping. Victor spun toward him, his senses on high alert, feeling whatever Elijah was.

"What is it?" Liam's concern burrowed into Kade.

Aran and Miles walked up from where they'd been farther back in the line.

Elijah turned, his eyes wide. "Someone's trying to break into the shop. There's pressure against my wards, an unfamiliar magic working on them."

Kade's brow furrowed. That couldn't be a coincidence. Someone breaking into the magic shop on the new moon, when no one was there and they were about to confront Niall's pack.

"Do you think they'll get in?" Liam asked. "Your wards are pretty impenetrable."

"They aren't giving yet, but they won't hold out forever, not if this mage knows what they're doing." He paced a few steps, running fingers through his hair. When he came to a stop, Victor's hand rested on the nape of his neck, attempting to comfort Elijah and ease his distress. "Fuck. I should have reinforced the wards. If I'd used Victor's energy, I could have made them stronger, and it wouldn't even be a question."

"No one expected this, Elijah," Liam said. "It's not your fault for not reinforcing them."

Aran and Miles made noises of agreement.

"Whether or not it's my fault, it doesn't change anything. There's still a mage trying to get into my shop."

Kade grimaced. He understood that all too well. Not being at fault didn't prevent the consequences of someone's actions.

"What do you want to do?" Victor asked.

Elijah winced. "As much as I hate to say this, my shop doesn't matter. It's just stuff, and Lady can take care of herself. Capturing the spirit on Niall's land is more important."

"Are you sure?"

Elijah nodded.

"If we leave now, we might catch them," Aran said. "And we have to assume they're involved in this. It might help us figure out what's happening."

"Or we miss them and lose our chance to get Pierce to assist us. If they break into my shop, they break into my shop. Even if they steal everything in there, if we can get this spirit off Niall's land, that's what we have to do." He didn't look or sound happy about it, but he was right.

"What if we split up?" Miles asked.

Elijah shook his head. "Given the spirit's size, I don't

think I can do this without all three of you. Not in the time we have."

"What if we send a few pack members instead?" Kade disliked the idea, but the mages needed to be there, as did Victor, Grant, and himself. Their pack members didn't.

"No," Elijah said firmly. "I'm not sending any shifter off to face mages without magical backup. Especially on a new moon."

Kade exhaled, and Victor did the same.

"There's no good solution here." Elijah's voice was tight. "But we've got to do this. So let's go."

They continued their hike, pausing just inside Victor's wards, facing the neutral area between their territories.

It was ten minutes to midnight. Pierce should be there soon.

As they waited, Elijah paced, a furrow between his brows. He was agitated, restless like a wolf shifter on a full moon, unable to stand still.

Liam studied him. "Are you going to be able to concentrate?"

"If I'm doing something, I'll be okay. Right now, all I can do is sense them battering the wards." His movements were sharp with his growing frustration.

Time stretched out, each second passing with painful slowness. The forest was silent around them, with the usual nocturnal creatures long since scattered in the presence of the wolf shifters.

The only sounds were the crunch of Elijah's steps and the wind whistling through the bare branches of the trees. It was frigid with the oncoming winter, making their breath fog, and Liam shivered, his coat not protecting him entirely from the cold. For a second time that night, Kade had to resist warming him with his body.

No one spoke as they stood there, shifting their weight from foot to foot. Elijah's restlessness was seeping into the packs, fueling their desire to move, to do something. The feeling of being powerless to stop this had Kade's foot tapping against the ground. His wolf—subdued by the new moon—prowled with discontent.

Kade gazed at Niall's territory. Nothing looked wrong. It appeared as it always had, no different from their own. But if he got closer, the proof of how misguided that impression was would crawl against his skin, leaving him repulsed by its foulness.

He tilted his head up toward the stars that glittered between the branches, searching for patience and finding he had none.

Pierce had been perpetually early when they were in school, while Kade's relationship with punctuality had been more casual.

He should have been there.

Kade exchanged a glance with Victor and Grant. They'd interacted with Pierce enough to know he wouldn't be late under any normal circumstances. There were no good reasons for him not to be there.

Elijah grimaced. "They're getting through."

"Do we need to go?" Victor asked.

"At this point, we won't make it. They'll get through before we get there. It'll be too late." His tone was laced with resignation, and he started his pacing again.

It was five past midnight, and there was no sign of Pierce.

Victor leveled a look at Kade. "You know him best. Is he coming?"

"He said he'd be here and isn't the type to make

promises he doesn't intend to keep, but he's also affected by the spirit, so can we really predict how he'll act?"

"Could he be working with whoever's behind this?" Aran asked. "You can't tell me it's a coincidence that they did this tonight, when we're supposed to be meeting him way the fuck out here."

Kade had no answer for that. He didn't want to believe Pierce would be involved, but these spirits made people do things they'd never do of their own volition.

"The mages are working with shifters," Liam pointed out.

"We were the ones to suggest the time and place," Elijah said. "And his pack is being affected like ours were. I can't imagine him endangering them for... What? Power?"

Aran shrugged. "Or the spirit is making him do it."

Kade hoped that wasn't the case.

"Alright," Liam said. "We know we've got a group of mages and shifters who are probably behind the spirits that have attacked the pack lands. We know spirits are affecting Niall's pack and that mages are breaking into Elijah's shop. We don't know why they're doing that or how Niall's pack is connected, though we can speculate. What's our most pressing issue?"

There was no hesitation in Elijah's reply. "Saving Niall's pack. Which means we wait. If Pierce doesn't let us through the wards, things get even more complicated. I can't break through those wards without Niall feeling it and getting everybody out here before we've captured the spirit. We need to give this as much of a chance as we—" He cut himself off with a sharp inhale. "Fuck. They're through." He pressed his lips together, and Victor's hand settled on his shoulder and squeezed.

"Can you sense anything about them?" Miles asked.

"It's an unknown mage. If I had to guess, there's shifter energy involved. Not many mages are capable of getting through my wards on their own."

Kade didn't love what that indicated about the strength of the mages they were up against. He took out his phone and checked the screen. Ten past midnight. "Should I contact him?"

"If he set us up, I'm a no on that," Aran said.

"Maybe there's another reason he isn't here," Miles suggested.

Kade wasn't sure the other possible reasons were any more reassuring. Niall might have discovered his plan, or the spirit might have made him too paranoid to trust them.

"We have to risk it," Elijah said.

"Is there something you can send that won't cause an issue if it's intercepted by Niall?" Liam asked.

Kade couldn't think of anything. "If Niall sees it, I doubt what I write will make a difference. But I'll keep it casual."

He typed out a quick, "Hey, man, what's up?" The reception was nonexistent out there; it'd have to wait until they were somewhere with a signal again.

They waited another hour, everyone growing more restless as they did, but Pierce didn't show up. Then they hiked back home. Elijah strode with determination, on a mission to get to his shop.

When they reached the house, most of the pack members went inside while Kade, Liam, Victor, Elijah, Grant, and the other mages formed a caravan to head into Lost Creek.

Liam was a ball of worry in Kade's mind as he drove.

"We'll figure out who did this," Kade said.

"Of course we will. But that doesn't mean I'm not going to worry about it."

Victor, in the lead car, set a pace that got them to town in far less time than usual. As they pulled up to the empty shop, the door stood ajar, its handle wrenched off.

Elijah was out of Victor's SUV before it had come to a complete stop, and Victor sprinted after him a second later, shouting, "Elijah! Wait!"

He didn't pay Victor any mind, though he did pause at the threshold and put up a hand, sensing what lay inside.

Kade got out and hurried up the sidewalk with Liam, everyone else following them.

"I don't feel any magic," Elijah said. "Except what they used to break the wards. I think it's safe."

He ducked inside, and Kade heard a string of curses. Liam dashed after him, Kade on his heels.

The shop was nothing but destruction. Its normal state of semi-organized eclectic clutter had been marred and vandalized. Shelves were tipped over, their contents spilled on the ground. Broken glass and splintered wood littered the floor, forcing them to pick a careful path through the room.

As Elijah made his way to his office, a few lights flickered on—lamps that had previously resided on shelves and tables, now knocked over but working, while others were smashed beyond repair.

Kade breathed in. "It's the same mages from Grant's territory. One corrupt, one not."

"Yes," Grant agreed. "And at least four shifters. Maybe the same four. They still have that weird, muted scent."

Once again, Kade was relieved that Victor's father wasn't in the group.

Elijah reached the open door of his office and entered the small room. From what little Kade could see, it was a wreck.

A cold rage simmered in Elijah as he emerged, an icy, dangerous edge to his voice as he spoke. "I know I chose not to come here. Protecting the pack was more important, but fuck, I'm going to kill whoever did this."

"I'll help." Liam's tone was dead serious. He crouched, extricating a battered book from the debris and brushing it off.

His eyes took on an orange glow, and the pleasant warmth of his magic pulsed in Kade's chest as he placed a spell on the book that made its pages ruffle and its cover shimmer. When the light around the book faded, he set it on a toppled shelf and stood, his face grim. "What do you think they wanted?"

"My ledger and inventory list are in the office, but given how ruined everything is in here, if they took something, I'm not certain I'll be able to tell."

He glanced around, his gaze landing on the door in the back corner of the shop that led to the stairs. "They definitely went upstairs. I never leave that open. Let's see how bad it is up there."

The second-floor workroom itself wasn't trashed. There wasn't enough in the room for that. But Kade smelled the shifters and mages, and the two storage room doors were thrown open. Inside, they were as destroyed as the shop had been.

Aran stalked straight into the larger one, stepping over boxes and sorting through the mess. "I bet I know what they took. Why they broke in."

How could he tell?

"What is it?" Liam asked.

"Those flowers. The crate they were in, it isn't in here anymore."

Elijah did a quick check and didn't find anything either.

"Why would they go through all this effort for less than a dozen dried flowers?"

Aran shook his head. "I've been trying to determine what it is in the evenings, but every identification spell comes up blank, which means it's something new. The only thing that had any sort of resonance with it was moonflower. So it's a moonflower hybrid, but I don't know what it's crossed with or what it does. Not yet."

They exited the storage room, and Elijah headed to the third floor.

"I have another layer of wards on my apartment," he said over his shoulder. "I didn't feel them touch those."

The door was closed and locked, and when they let themselves in, everything was as it should be.

Lady sat on the dining room table, her tail thumping with annoyance, her expression saying, 'About fucking time you got here.'

Elijah walked over and scratched her behind the ears. "Are you okay?"

Kade didn't understand why he was worried if she'd been in the apartment. Obviously she was okay. They hadn't been in here.

Liam must have felt his confusion because he explained it to Kade. "Locked doors don't stop her if she wants to go somewhere."

He raised an eyebrow, but Liam shrugged. "We have no clue how she does it."

Lady flexed her paws, her claws coming out. Each was tipped in red. Kade inhaled, getting the faint scent of blood. He'd never seen a cat look quite so pleased with itself before.

"You are the best cat ever," Elijah told her, and she gave him a flat, unimpressed glare. "Guys, can you?"

He didn't say what, leaving Kade even more confused, but the mages knew what to do, leaping into a flurry of activity. Victor and Grant seemed equally unsure.

"I'll get a map." Miles ran out the door, his footsteps light as he descended the stairs.

"I've got the candles." Aran grabbed a couple off a small table on the other side of the room.

"Liam?" Elijah asked as he headed out of the apartment.

"On it," Liam called after him. He cleared everything off the table except the cat, then took the piece of chalk Aran handed him.

As he drew a circle on the tabletop, Aran set two candles on opposite sides of it, and Liam lit them with a snap of his fingers.

A few seconds later, Miles came back with a rumpled map and spread it out over the circle. Then Elijah returned, holding a smooth tiger's eye stone and a knife.

He placed the stone in front of Lady, then used the dull side of the knife to delicately flake the dried blood off her claws and onto the stone. When he was finished, she jumped to the top of the refrigerator and regarded them haughtily before cleaning herself.

Elijah pricked his finger and added a drop of his own blood to the stone. It mixed with the flakes, then somehow sank into the glossy brown-and-gold surface. He laid the stone on the paper, rested his hands against the table, and closed his eyes.

The scent of magic filled the air as Elijah did something to the stone. It started to wiggle, then circle around and around, but after a moment, Elijah grimaced, removing his hands from the table. The stone stopped.

"Not enough blood?" Liam asked.

"No, they aren't on the map."

Kade frowned. That map showed hundreds of miles around Lost Creek. Even if they'd left directly after breaking through the wards, they couldn't have driven outside its bounds.

"How could they have gotten farther than that?" Victor asked.

"They didn't," Elijah said. "The spell isn't locating them because they aren't traceable."

"They're untraceable? How?" Kade asked.

"There are a couple of possibilities, but most likely they're behind some kind of ward that protects them from notice."

"So they're somewhere around here," Victor said. "But hidden."

"Exactly."

"Well, fuck." Kade didn't like that at all.

"It's fine. We have their blood. There's no time limit on this spell. We can try again. And when they leave whatever protection they're hiding behind, we'll locate them."

"If you leave the map here, Aran and I will try in the evenings," Miles said.

There was a bright flash through the bond, and Kade glanced at Liam.

"Actually," Liam said, "hold on. Here. Take the map."

Elijah picked up the stone and map, and Liam wiped away part of the circle with a towel from the kitchen before writing over it.

"*Oh,*" Elijah said as he watched. "Will that work?"

Liam shrugged. "Only one way to find out."

"Will what work?" Kade asked, but they weren't paying any attention to him.

Elijah set the map back down and the stone on top of it. He pressed his hands to the table and the stone began to move, but at a slower pace than before. This was slow, lazy spirals and circles sweeping over the map. When Elijah pulled his hands away, the stone kept moving, slithering along, rasping over the paper.

"Nice." Elijah was clearly impressed. He then explained what they'd done to the shifters in the room. "He made the spell continuous. Or, well, continuous until it runs out of the magic I fed it, so it should last for a day or so. Basically, it'll be constantly searching and should eventually lock on to the signature of whoever broke into the shop."

"We'll feed it more magic until it does," Aran said.

"What happens if they leave and then go inside their wards again?" Victor asked.

Liam squinted at the map. "I'm not positive. It might stop over the area they disappeared, waiting for them to leave. In which case, we'll know where their hideout is."

Kade pulled out his phone. His message to Pierce had been sent, but remained unread. "If Pierce contacts us in time and we trust him, can we try tomorrow night?"

The four mages exchanged glances.

"It'd be better than waiting another month for the next new moon," Elijah said. "The bigger issue is whether or not Pierce is compromised, or if Niall suspects he was helping us. But that's not going to change whether we do it tomorrow or a week from now."

"If Pierce can't help us, what do we do?" Victor asked.

"I'll have to sort out the best method to get through the most clamped-down wards I've ever seen around a pack territory, and then we'll have to do this as fast as we can. It's not something I've looked into, though the ward book does have a few spells that might work. I should also practice how quickly I can do it beforehand. The last thing we want is for it to take me so long that they arrive and are waiting for us."

Kade hated the idea of delaying longer than they already had—Niall's pack had been under the influence of the spirit for months—but they couldn't rush it if they wanted to do it right.

"What would we do about the spirit though?" Liam asked. "If it has hooks in the pack, what good is breaking into their territory if we don't have someone inside to help us capture it?"

"Either way, we have to try." Elijah's expression was grim.

"What do we do until then?" Miles asked.

Elijah sighed. "I don't like this, but I think we need to keep doing what we've been doing. When we get their location, we'll scout the area and hopefully figure out who we're up against. But until that happens, let's finish cleaning up the spirits on Victor's and Grant's territory, and I'll work on plans to get into Niall's. On the full moon, Miles will reset Grant's wards as planned."

Miles's eyes darted to Grant, then back to Elijah.

"I have two of those white flowers that I've been using for testing." Aran pointed to some of his belongings. "I'll keep working on it until I find out what the hell they are and what the fuck they can do."

"I'm still working on destroying the spirits. No luck so far, but we'll keep experimenting." Liam's frustration prickled against Kade's senses. "And in the meantime, I'll start cleaning up the shop since there are only so many tests I can do on any given day without depleting myself and Kade."

"Some of our pack can help get the shop cleaned up," Victor said. "At the very least, they can sort through the worst of the mess to find what's salvageable, repair the damaged shelves, and build new ones."

"My pack can help too," Grant offered. "They'll be relieved to have something to do."

"That would be appreciated," Elijah said. "I can't deal with it on top of everything else, but Liam can give you instructions on what to do."

Liam nodded. "I'll take care of it."

With that settled, they headed downstairs and got into their cars. The first hazy tint of dawn stained the horizon.

On the drive home, Liam looked over at Kade. "You don't think Pierce would set us up?"

"If he was in his right mind, and it was his choice, he would have helped us, absolutely. So either the spirit got to him, or Niall did. Considering Niall's behavior, I don't know which is worse."

"Will he reply?"

Kade had no idea. "We'll have to wait and find out."

That was an answer he knew no one would be happy with.

TWENTY-FOUR

"What if Elijah puts a ward around the contract before you destroy it?" Aran asked as he sifted through the broken jars and dried herbs that had been spilled onto the floor. Most of it was too contaminated to be saved, but he was managing to salvage some. Liam knew he wouldn't want to waste it by simply sweeping it up and throwing it away. Aran was no more capable of doing that than Liam was of tossing out a book.

"We can try, but I can't see that helping." Liam placed a protection spell on a grimoire he'd pulled out of the mess before continuing. "It might contain the inevitable explosion, but I think the result would be the spirit getting trapped inside that ward after the contract was destroyed."

They'd been brainstorming as they tackled Elijah's shop, though nothing they'd come up with seemed likely to destroy the spirits. Liam was making mental notes of things to try. Eventually something had to work. At least it offered a distraction from the other problems they were facing. It had been a full day, and they hadn't heard from Pierce. They had no clue what was going on with him or his pack, and that lack of knowledge haunted Liam—a looming specter hanging over him as he cleaned the shop. How much danger was the pack in? Were they a threat?

"Too bad that fertility spell Elijah tried on the rot spirit wasn't effective. I'm sure Kade would kindly assist you with that."

"What now?" Kade asked as he righted one of the larger shelves that had been knocked over, his curiosity glittering through their bond.

Liam huffed. "It wasn't a fertility spell. It was a—"

"*Four seasons ritual*." Aran's tone was teasing. "Uh-huh. You could still try it. Maybe a sex ritual is exactly what this needs."

"I keep telling him that," Kade said, "but he won't even let me read the sex ritual books."

"I've got some you can borrow."

"We don't need any sex rituals," Liam rushed to say before Kade could accept Aran's offer.

Aran snorted. "Sex rituals are always needed. But fine. If we're back to the boring pre-Kade Liam, maybe we ask Lady if she can destroy these things. She seems to know what's up."

"What do you suggest? We hold her out in front of us like she's a newborn lion cub and cross our fingers the spirits bow down to her?"

"Do you have a better idea?"

"Literally anything that wouldn't involve our immediate demise. Anointing her forehead alone would guarantee instant death."

"I was thinking of lining up a bunch of books and seeing which she'd choose, but your version sounds more fun."

The fact that Liam was considering it as an option didn't bode well for the situation they were in.

He gently dusted off another book before placing protections on it. He'd done this spell hundreds of times; it came as naturally as breathing to him. Every book in the library was protected by it. The tomes in Elijah's shop were in private circulation though, and while most had some form of protection on them, none were as strong as the library's.

He set the book on the pile with the others, then paused. His brow furrowed, and he blinked at the spell on it before picking up the previous grimoire he'd done and studying it too.

This spell... It looked nothing like the library spell he was so familiar with. That was precise work, methodically applied. This was something completely different. It was art. It wrapped around the book, each page painted with magic—a delicate filigree with the strength of steel, protection that would withstand anything thrown at it.

"Everything alright?" Kade asked, and Liam jumped, setting the book aside.

"Yeah, I'm fine." That might have been more convincing if he hadn't sounded winded.

Kade raised a questioning eyebrow, and Aran side-eyed him.

"I remembered I need to check something in the sigil codex." Liam stood, hurrying toward the staircase. "I'll be right back."

It wasn't a lie, not entirely. He did want to check the codex, but not for something in it.

Once he was in the apartment, he grabbed his bag, pulled out the codex, and examined it. He'd cast this protection spell himself—it had been some of his best work—but compared to the ones he'd just done, it looked like a feeble attempt by an amateur.

Exhaling forcefully, he reached for the spell with his magic, watching it flicker and change as he reset it, the standard library protection spell transforming into something so much more, so much stronger. His breath caught in his throat.

It wasn't to the same level as the magic Elijah did with Victor's energy, but it was close. Far closer than Liam had ever believed it could be, more beautiful than any magic he'd ever done. This wasn't the mage blood in Kade's family making his energy easy to use. This was special.

Lady leapt onto the kitchen table and glared, her tail thumping against the wood.

"I'm... I'm an idiot, aren't I?" he said, and she trilled in reply.

"You kind of are."

He startled again, swinging his head around to find Aran leaning casually by the door.

Aran grinned at him. "I hope you enjoy having your channels stretched, because it seems like that's how they're supposed to be."

Liam opened his mouth to argue. Even if his magic and Kade's energy were compatible, did that mean anything? He had no desire to stay there, and Kade couldn't leave. There was no future in that.

Before he could respond, Kade entered the room. "Are you sure everything's alright? You feel unsettled."

That was the understatement of the year. Unsettled didn't begin to describe him. His thoughts were messier than Elijah's shop. Out of all the things he'd been worried about happening while he was in Lost Creek, this hadn't crossed his mind. How did a person stumble into a true bond with a shifter?

"I'm fine. Let's get back to cleaning up the shop."

Kade didn't call him on the lie, but he did give him a skeptical look, and his disbelief seeped into their bond.

Aran's expression was wry as Liam passed him and headed downstairs.

What the hell was Liam supposed to do with this information? It upended everything he knew about the world. Everything he'd *assumed* he knew. But given what had happened to Elijah, maybe he shouldn't make assumptions.

Out of the corner of his eye, he watched Kade work. Were they really that compatible?

Yes, Kade was attractive, but most shifters were. Yes, Liam was attracted to him, which was a rarer distinction, but attraction and compatibility were two different things. Did compatible magic and energy automatically mean he and Kade were compatible too?

Kade glanced over, and Liam quickly looked away.

On paper, Elijah and Victor wouldn't have seemed right for each other, but somehow, they worked. No one would think he and Kade were a good fit, yet he also couldn't deny how much he enjoyed the time they spent together.

A month ago, he would have said he had no interest in sharing a bed. He'd rather have his bedroom to himself so he could read in peace. But it was becoming difficult to imagine reading in bed without Kade next to him. Waking up without Kade wrapped around him. And that realization freaked him out. He wasn't used to relying on someone; he always strove to be as independent as possible.

Kade's concern brushed up against him, but he didn't pressure Liam; he let him have his private freak-out for the rest of the afternoon and into the evening. He didn't bring it up until they were in bed, Liam curled up with a book from the attic, all its spells suddenly taking on a whole new dimension as he realized he could do every single one of them if they kept this bond.

"If I ask you what has you freaking out," Kade said, a whisper of sadness in his words and in Liam's mind, "are you going to say you're fine?"

"Probably," Liam admitted.

"Okay. But when you're ready, I hope you'll tell me."

Liam swallowed and nodded. He would. He just needed to process it first.

Liam threw himself into cleaning Elijah's shop, like eradicating the disorder there would help excise it from inside him as well.

Between him, Kade, Aran, and a handful of shifters from both Victor and Grant's packs, they had it ready for business far quicker than he would have expected. It was early afternoon on the fourth day after the new moon, and there was nothing left for them to do. The other shifters had headed out, leaving Liam alone with Kade and Aran.

He stood behind the counter and gazed around the shop. The shelves were emptier—too much of the inventory had been damaged beyond saving—and they'd stay that way until Elijah could restock them. It wasn't high on his to-do list though. He hadn't bothered opening the shop in weeks. Liam was certain he'd have it up and running again after this was finished, but Elijah's priorities were no longer focused on making the shop profitable, so he didn't seem upset by the potential loss of sales and customers during the downtime.

A sense of satisfaction filled Liam at completing this task, but now that it was taken care of, he didn't know what to do. His theories on how to destroy the spirits were half-baked at best, and he wasn't sure how to handle Kade. And those were only a fraction of his worries—of *everyone's* worries.

Kade checked his phone, frowning at the screen.

"Still no reply?" Liam asked.

"Still unread."

Liam grimaced. That couldn't be good.

Elijah and Miles had spent the last few days hunting down the spirits that remained on Victor's and Grant's territories. They were so small that they were hard to find in the forest, but they didn't present much of a threat. The spirits on Niall's land were another matter altogether. They were growing larger, the ash over his territory on the maps darkening with each day. Whenever Liam saw it, anxiety constricted his chest and sent his stomach churning. What was happening to the pack trapped inside Niall's wards, surrounded by those spirits?

There'd been debate over whether they should be worried for the pack or about them. Miles's primary concern had been their health. They hadn't seen them in weeks. The pack might have been incapacitated by the spirit. Aran seemed convinced they were plotting something, while Elijah thought there was a chance they'd become too paranoid to go outside their territory, fearing the mages would attack them if they showed any sign of weakness. Liam found it easiest to worry about all of it.

No matter how he looked at it, the conclusion was the same. The longer they waited, the worse it would get. That didn't mean they had a solution though.

"Do you think we'd see anything if we scouted around their territory?" Aran asked.

Kade shrugged. "The wards seem to be concealing whatever's behind them, but we might be able to sense if the barrier is weakening. That would point to the pack getting weaker."

"Beats sitting around, waiting for someone else to make a move."

Liam had to have misheard that. "What? No. If they notice us, it might provoke them."

"We'd need to avoid touching their wards, but we should be able to get close without them realizing we're there as long as we're careful," Kade said.

Liam stared at him. "You can't honestly think this is a good plan."

"Aran's right. Do we want to wait around for them to attack us? Or for the mages to do it? We might find something that will help."

"Elijah and Victor won't allow that. It's too risky."

It was Aran's turn to shrug. "Let's ask them tonight."

"Okay..." Liam doubted they'd get the go-ahead. It was a terrible idea. But if they got approval, it would give him another job to do besides failing to figure out what to do about the spirits and failing to figure out what to do about Kade.

TWENTY-FIVE

A sharp wind blew through the trees, biting at Kade's skin. It wasn't often they made it to mid-November without snow, but he didn't miss it. This hike was challenging enough—they didn't need the added complication of wading through drifts.

Kade led the way, with Liam and Aran following close behind. The neutral area between the pack territories was some of the wildest the forest had to offer. There were no natural paths here. Instead, they scrambled over rocks and carved through underbrush. As they wove between gnarled trunks, their steps rustled the thick bed of fallen leaves beneath their feet.

From time to time, they strayed into Victor's territory, and later Grant's, when the land was too unforgiving for the mages to traverse, but they attempted to stay outside the pack wards as much as possible. If they were going to find any signs of someone else patrolling or indications of what was happening on Niall's land, it would be in this unclaimed area.

But there'd been none. No broken branches, no tracks in the dirt, no scents in the air.

"Ugh." Liam's whole body shuddered as he passed within a foot of Niall's wards. His repulsion twisted through their bond. "These things make my skin crawl."

Kade grimaced in agreement.

Victor and Elijah had grudgingly approved this scouting expedition after an extended debate over whether or not they should accompany them. In the end, it was decided Elijah needed to continue working on ways to break pack wards quickly and the three of them could go provided they absolutely did not, under any circumstances, touch Niall's wards. Kade wasn't going to argue over that. Whenever he got too close, a warning buzzed through him, prickling down to his bones, screaming at him to stay away. The wards might have been invisible, but there was no question where the barrier lay, no chance they'd accidentally brush against it.

Niall's land was suspended in eerie stillness on the other side, deceptively peaceful, no spirits in sight. A glance at their map proved otherwise. It teemed with ashy streaks.

"Okay," Aran said. "We've been hiking for nearly two hours and haven't seen a damn thing. I'm bored, and it's so cold my balls are trying to retreat into my body. So, I need a distraction. Kade. Accountant."

"Please, no." Liam pinched the bridge of his nose.

"Oh, that's easy," Kade said. "I'd appreciate his assets."

"Or C if he wants a P in his A?"

"That works too. Your turn. Pharmacist."

"Could we not?" Liam asked, but Aran ignored him.

"Obviously we'd get Rx rated."

"But over the counter can be fun too."

"It can. Computer programmer."

"Of course I'd be getting into his backend."

"*Guys*," Liam said, exasperated.

"What?" Aran grinned at him. "Would you rather we rank our favorite MateHub scenes?"

Liam groaned. "I'm never going anywhere with both of you ever again."

Kade inhaled, about to respond, but then froze, his senses suddenly on high alert. He scanned the area. It appeared undisturbed, but when he took another deep breath, the ghost of corrupt magic invaded his lungs.

Liam and Aran had stopped as well and were looking at him in question, but Kade closed his eyes and concentrated on that reek. Foul magic polluted the air. This was different from the stale scent that had lingered in Grant's territory; this was fresh. Two mages and at least two shifters.

They were nearing the part of Niall's land that ran parallel to a narrow county road. If these unknown mages wanted to check out the territory like they had with Grant's, this was a good balance between remote and accessible.

"Mages," Kade explained, his voice low. "Possibly the same two. And shifters. I think they're still here."

Liam and Aran exchanged a glance, their expressions concerned.

"Do we continue?" Liam asked.

"Fuck yes, we do." Aran's tone was resolute. "We need to know who these bastards are."

Kade couldn't have agreed more.

The three of them gathered closer together as they proceeded. They crept through the trees, each step placed with precision. Tension coiled around them.

Kade's heart thundered; his muscles bunched. Every

instinct he possessed demanded he get Liam out of there, get him to safety. He did his best to ignore the impulse.

Icy gusts scattered the corrupt scent of magic like loose leaves, but they weren't far from the source. The mages and their shifter accomplices were just up ahead.

He signaled for Liam and Aran to halt so he could close the final distance on his own. Neither listened.

They crouched and inched forward until four figures were visible through the dense growth. Kade had never seen any of them before. Two shifters flanked the mages, both with the gaunt, worn look Victor's father had taken on after he'd started to let that bastard mage drain his energy regularly. Their scents were muted in that odd way Kade didn't understand.

The two mages were facing Niall's wards, their hands raised, sensing the barrier. One was older, his hair a mix of black and gray. The reek of tainted magic hung around him like a noxious cloud. The other mage was younger. He couldn't have been much past twenty, perhaps an apprentice, and while his magic was harsh, it lacked the foul scent of darkness.

Kade strained to hear their conversation, their words snatched away by the wind.

"...too strong..."

"...wait until..."

The shifter closest to the older mage leaned in and whispered something that stilled the mage's movements, a deadly calm washing over him.

He stepped away from the wards.

"We're heading out." His voice was quiet but authoritative, and as one, the four of them turned toward the road.

Before Kade could do anything, Aran pressed his hands

to the ground. The scent of his magic spiked, and the trees around them stirred.

The mages and shifters spun around. One shifter lunged at them.

Liam leapt up, putting himself between the shifter and Aran. The warmth of his magic bloomed in Kade's chest as he called a fireball into his hand and lobbed it at the shifter, not aiming to hit him, but a clear warning shot.

The shifter didn't flinch. Kade cursed and sprinted past Liam to intercept him.

"*Stop*," the older mage barked, halting the shifter mid-step as if he'd used alpha command, though that didn't cut off the shifter's growls.

The older mage slipped a hand into a satchel that was slung over his shoulder and said, "Ward."

Annoyance marred the younger mage's face, but he raised his hands in front of him, his fingers moving like he was weaving threads in a tapestry. His eyes glowed purple, and a moment later, a transparent wall of magic was sweeping toward them.

"What the fuck is that?" Aran asked from a few paces behind Kade.

It slammed into Kade first—as frigid as the darkest winter night, stealing his breath. It rolled over him, leaving him shaken and chilled to the bone, but unharmed. He pivoted on his heel and saw Liam running forward and Aran dashing off to the side.

The magic didn't hit Liam—it curved and enclosed him in a dome.

Something whizzed past Kade's head, carried by a wind of corrupted magic, and he took a step toward Liam, toward that strange wall of magic that had trapped him.

There was a flash of brilliant white, and the wards

solidified as Kade's fist connected with the barrier. It didn't budge.

His gaze locked with Liam's wide-eyed stare for one heartbeat, but then something inside the ward exploded.

A silvery fog billowed in the dome, blocking Liam from Kade's view.

But he felt him.

Felt his lungs filling with smoke.

Felt him choking.

Coughing.

Struggling to breathe.

Kade battered at the ward, scrabbled with ineffective hands, scraped against it with his claws. Panic inundated him. He had to get to Liam. Something was wrong with him. More than not being able to breathe. This went deeper.

The forest groaned. Trees creaked and came to life, and Aran's magic flared again.

Kade wrenched his eyes away from the barrier and saw the mages and shifters fleeing as roots shot up to snare their feet. They dodged branches that lashed out, snagging their clothing. They struggled and fought through it until they disappeared among the trees.

"*Fuck.*" Aran hurried over. "I can't control trees I can't see."

Kade had zero fucks to give about that. Liam was still trapped. Still felt *off* in his mind.

He turned back to the barrier. The smoke inside had cleared enough to reveal Liam on his knees, shaking hands braced against the ground as he coughed, then took in a rattling breath. The sight of him barely eased Kade's nerves. He didn't know what was happening to Liam or how to help. Frustration ate away at him, mocking his uselessness.

"Go after—" Liam's words were interrupted by a coughing fit.

"Oh, shut up," Aran said. "Like hell I'm leaving you here. What happened? What did they hit you with?"

"Artemisia," Liam said, then coughed so hard it had Kade pounding against the ward before he realized what he was doing.

Aran gently pushed him away. "That won't do anything."

Kade knew that, but he couldn't just stand there. Liam needed help. He snarled.

Aran placed a palm on the ward. "This is well made, but there isn't much power behind it. I bet that fucking kid could make wards only Elijah could break, but this I can handle. He must not have had time to set it properly."

He crouched and pressed his hands to the ground. Roots slithered up from the earth and wrapped around the base of the ward. It flickered and shimmered, and the roots grew thicker, like they were feeding off its energy.

"It'll take a bit for the roots to leach off enough energy for me to break it," Aran said. "You might as well sit."

Kade pushed against the barrier and swore it gave a fraction, but when he did it again, it felt as solid as before.

Liam looked up at him, his eyes watery from coughing. He gestured for Kade to sit. "I'm—"

"Don't even think about saying you're fine," Kade said, and Liam's surprise sparked through their bond. "Artemisia?" Kade asked Aran, the word finally registering. "Is that the shit that keeps you from using magic?"

Aran's expression was grim. "A certain variety of it, yes. I've never heard of a mage using it offensively before. Most won't touch the stuff."

That was it. That was why Liam felt off. He couldn't access his magic.

The fog had dissipated completely, and Liam seemed to be catching his breath, his cough subsiding, though Kade still needed to get inside that barrier.

An eternity passed before Aran stood, the roots he'd summoned sinking back into the ground. He rested his hands against the dome, his eyes narrowing as he focused on sending a pulse of magic into the ward.

It shattered, the remnants of magic falling away, and Kade rushed to Liam, dropping to his knees beside him. Liam didn't resist as Kade pulled him into his arms and ran his hands over him.

"I'm fine." Liam's voice was wrecked, so rough he sounded nothing like himself.

Kade didn't believe him for one minute. He skated his hands up to Liam's neck and froze when they brushed against skin.

Liam's magic wasn't moving under his fingertips; it didn't respond to his touch.

Liam was not fine. Not even remotely. Kade sensed how uncomfortable and unsettled he felt.

"How long does this last?" Kade asked.

"Depends on the dose," Aran said. "It usually wears off after about twenty-four hours, but if Elijah has any on hand, I can use a spell to help draw it out of Liam's system. That'll speed things up considerably."

"Then let's get to the pack house."

Liam shook his head. "We should go after them."

"No. That's not happening."

"Yeah," Aran said, "I'm with Kade. We aren't chasing down dangerous mages when you can't use magic. Besides, if they're intelligent at all, they're long gone. They probably had a car waiting, and we do not."

Liam seemed about to argue, but then he deflated. Kade helped him up.

The journey back to Victor's territory was rougher. Liam was unsteady on his feet, his mind fuzzy from the effects of the herb and the adrenaline crash after their confrontation with the mages. Kade had to restrain the instinct to pick him up and carry him home. Liam wouldn't appreciate that, and Kade was trying not to push him, trying not to freak him out more than he already was over the last few days.

He was fairly certain Liam had realized they had a true bond, but he clearly needed time to process it. Kade had sworn to himself that he'd give Liam space to do that, but goddamnit, that promise was difficult to stick to when his wolf wanted to comfort their mate, to wrap him in his arms, to keep him safe and care for him.

Once they got to Victor's territory, they followed the regular paths.

Aran sent a message to Elijah, and as they neared the house, Elijah's reply came through. He didn't have any of that particular variety of artemisia in the shop, and he didn't believe there was any in the attic.

"That's not surprising," Liam said. "Who'd keep something on hand that can do this to them? But I'm fine waiting it out."

Kade didn't call him on that either. "Wolf packs generally don't keep wolfsbane around, but Grandma did. Apparently she could use it to cure wolfsbane poisoning if necessary." From what he understood, only mages could do that, so packs without mages kept it as far from themselves as possible.

Aran nodded. "It's basically the same spell I would have done on Liam if Elijah had some of the right artemisia. It's a like-to-like thing. You aren't healing the mage or shifter, just removing the poison so it can't do more damage."

That made sense, and for shifters, once the wolfsbane was out of their system, their enhanced healing would kick in and take care of the rest.

"Honestly," Liam said. "I'm kind of glad Elijah doesn't have any. I've done enough coughing today."

Kade frowned, not following.

"It comes out the same way it went in," Aran explained. "If you inhale it, you have to exhale it. If it's ingested, it gets thrown up. If it's in your blood, you bleed it out."

Liam grimaced. "So the chances of it not bringing on another coughing fit are exactly zero. But that doesn't matter. Did you recognize those shifters or mages?"

"No," Kade said. "They aren't from around here."

"If they're waiting for the wards to fail, they aren't allied with Niall's pack." Each word sounded like it'd been dragged over gravel. "And if they need the pack to be weakened before they attack them or capture them or do whatever they do to them, they must not be strong enough or have enough people to take on an entire pack. Those are both good things."

"But we still haven't discovered who they are or where their hideout is," Aran countered. "I'd wager any amount of money that the blood we're tracking is from a shifter who wasn't with them today."

"That younger mage's scent wasn't corrupted," Kade said. "Is it because he's young? Does it get worse as you get older?"

Liam cocked his head. "He might not have done

anything too terrible yet. But considering who he's working with, it seems like only a matter of time."

"That ward he did," Aran said. "It moved. I didn't think that was possible."

"Same. We'll have to tell Elijah."

It wasn't long before they could do that. Victor and Elijah were on the back porch, and Elijah bounded down the stairs to meet them the moment they emerged from the forest.

"Are you okay?" Elijah asked. "Yes, yes, I know you're fine. Beyond that?"

Liam huffed. "I just need some time to recover."

Elijah shot Kade a look. "Can you keep him in bed until he does that?"

Aran cackled. "Do you even have to ask?"

"I don't need to be in bed!"

"That'd be more convincing if you didn't sound like you've been deep-throating sandpaper," Elijah said.

"I can't use magic, and I coughed a lot. That doesn't mean I need to be confined to bed."

"I'll bring you any book you want from the attic," Kade offered.

Liam paused, eyeing him.

"As many as you want."

When Liam didn't immediately protest, Elijah clapped his hands. "Perfect. That's settled. Liam gets a day in bed reading."

"But I should be—"

"Nope. We're done for the day. We'll pick things up tomorrow."

Liam grumbled, but let Kade herd him up to their room. He felt frustrated, though Kade didn't need their bond to know that—they were all frustrated. Not that they could do anything about it. They had to wait. Wait for the artemisia to leave Liam's system, wait for Elijah to figure out a quick way into Niall's territory, wait for the stone to stop so they could find the hideout. Wait, wait, wait. Enough waiting to test anyone's patience.

Kade hovered until Liam climbed into bed and grabbed the book on his bedside table.

"Can I get you anything? Something to eat?"

"No, thanks. My throat can't handle food right now."

"Something to drink? Tea? Soup? Broth?"

"I'm not sick. You don't need to bring me chicken soup in bed."

But what if he wanted to?

"Are you going to be able to relax and read if I don't let you bring me something?"

Well, Kade was feeling called out. If he answered that truthfully, would Liam think he was fussing too much? "Umm..."

"Okay. Tea, please? And if you must, soup for dinner."

Kade fought back a grin and slipped out of the room.

Maybe a little waiting wasn't so bad after all.

TWENTY-SIX

Liam wouldn't wish artemisia poisoning on anyone. Even if he had gotten a day of reading out of it. Reading and Kade bringing him everything he could possibly want, often before Liam realized he wanted it.

Not having access to his magic had left him empty, his entire body aching from the lack. It had been like his magic was hovering on the edge of his vision, disappearing when he turned to look. As the artemisia's effects had begun to fade and his magic had returned, it had remained elusive, on the other side of glass, a fraction of an inch from his fingertips, but impossible to grasp. It'd been late afternoon the following day before he could use it, and the first contact had been blissful relief. Feeling his magic, feeling Kade's energy—he'd been whole again, and it had shaken him how thoroughly he'd missed both, how much he needed both. He wasn't sure he'd feel like himself without Kade's energy in his system anymore, without Kade's presence in his mind, without Kade reading in bed beside him every night.

He had to decide what to do.

Part of him wanted a few more days of cleaning. It had kept him somewhat occupied. He didn't even have the distraction Aran presented since he'd switched his focus to testing the white flower, though he was having the same amount of luck as Liam was with the spirits. Never in Liam's life would he have believed he'd be missing Aran and all his inappropriate jokes.

Instead, he was alone with Kade. Stupidly attractive, apparently ridiculously compatible Kade.

Kade, who sensed that Liam needed time and space and was doing his best to give him that, as much as the bond allowed. Who was sweet and funny, even though he told almost as many dick jokes as Aran did. Who longed to travel the world, but had too many responsibilities here to do that.

Liam glanced up from his book to where Kade was sitting against the wall opposite him in the pack house's workroom. Aran had given him three books on sex magic, and Kade was reading them with far more interest than any of the books on spirits. He'd nod thoughtfully, an occasional thrill of arousal sparking in their connection, and Liam refused to let himself think about what it would be like to do any of those spells with Kade. To have Kade's energy flowing through him as Kade—

No. No. No.

He wasn't going there. No matter how attractive he found Kade or how intoxicating his energy was. He wasn't being logical when he thought about things like that, and he needed to be logical right now.

He returned his attention to his own book, though he couldn't concentrate on the words on the page.

Would he want a life with Kade? Certainly not here. Or,

maybe, not here more than a few months out of the year—preferably the months without snow. Spending more time with Elijah would be nice, and the pack seemed amazing. He'd love to see what they were like when this situation wasn't hanging over their heads.

The more he considered it, the more he loved the idea of traveling the world to gather all the knowledge he could and make it accessible to as many people as possible.

Would Kade want a life like that? Them traveling together, with Liam working on his archive while they explored the places Kade had dreamed of visiting?

There was so much Liam had to learn. The fact that he hadn't figured out these damn spirits yet was proof of that. Everything he didn't know about shifters would fill volumes, just about bonds alone. He'd recognized there was more to them after what had happened between Elijah and Victor, and since then, it had continued unfolding. He still didn't comprehend the full scope of them.

Which brought him back to his main question. What did it mean to be compatible?

"Do shifters—" he started, then cut himself off. The realization that this might be an awkward conversation to have with Kade caught up to his curiosity a second too late.

Kade looked up from *The Joy of Sex Magic*, which couldn't be remotely academic given the warm buzz of his emotions. He cocked an eyebrow at Liam. "Do shifters...?"

Liam repressed a sigh. He might as well ask. Not knowing would drive him crazy. "Do shifters have multiple people they're compatible with?"

Kade closed the book and set it aside, immediately alert and attentive. "Yes and no. Like we were talking about before with shifter energy and magic, it's on a spectrum. Take Victor, for example. No one else in the world could be as compatible as Elijah is with him. But if he and Elijah had never met, Victor might have found someone compatible enough. They would have developed feelings for each other and had scents that combined fairly well. They would have bonded and had a connection between them. It just wouldn't have been as intense."

"So you have a choice? You don't have to be with one specific person to be happy?"

It felt like Kade was choosing his words carefully as he answered. "Not everyone is lucky enough to find someone as compatible as Victor and Elijah are. They can be happy without that level of connection, but I think anyone who finds something like that would be a fool to let it go." His eyes didn't leave Liam's face, and the scrutiny made Liam want to squirm, but he pressed on.

"You can tell based on scent? Not just if people are compatible, but how compatible?"

"It isn't an exact science, but generally, yes, we can. The way Victor and Elijah's scents combine is on a different level from an average, decently compatible pair. Saying their scents are complementary isn't an adequate description. Together, they're almost transcendent. Our grandparents were similar. I've only ever smelled one combined scent that was better than either of those."

Kade was expecting him to ask the question that hung between them, but Liam wasn't ready to do that. Not yet. He had plenty of other questions though. "Do people ever have compatible scents, but then don't work out?"

"Not that I've heard of. If they aren't a good match, their scents would clash."

"But some shifters ignore that, right? Or don't care? Otherwise, transactional bonds wouldn't exist."

"Yeah. There have always been arranged marriages for

alliances and, more recently, the transactional bonds with mages. Our pack has never done that though."

Liam breathed in, catching hints of Kade's scent, *their* scent, on his clothes, on his skin. He was dancing around this. He should ask. But did it matter? Whether or not they were compatible, did he want this? Whatever it was? He'd never imagined himself with a shifter. He'd hardly imagined himself with anyone at all. It had never been a priority. He had future plans, but he'd never pictured himself in a long-term relationship. Hell, he'd never even dated. Not seriously. The closest things he'd had to relationships were the ones Aran had labeled "academically stimulating arrangements," and those didn't require exploring what sharing his life with someone might entail.

Kade studied him, still waiting for a question Liam was certain he could already answer. The workroom stretched wider than usual, heavy silence blanketing the distance between them.

If he asked, would the answer change anything?

"Let me take you out," Kade said, his voice low and smooth.

"What?"

Kade stood and prowled over to where Liam sat, then reached down. Liam took his hand out of habit, and Kade hauled him to his feet but didn't step back, didn't let go of Liam's hand. His energy hummed against Liam's skin. He leaned closer and inhaled in a way that answered any unspoken question Liam might have had about their scents, his wolf flashing in his eyes, a hint of a rumble in his chest. "Let's go for a drink."

Quiet confidence radiated from Kade, just a step away from cocky. Not to the point where he'd transformed into the type of guy Liam automatically disliked in clubs, but sure enough in himself that he exuded the promise of a good time, if Liam would allow it. He was the Kade Liam had gotten to know, but with a heat banked in his gaze that had Liam's breath hitching, something dangerous and hungry about him that wasn't entirely his wolf.

This didn't seem like the smartest move while Liam was still confused.

"I don't drink. I hate how it makes my head feel."

"It doesn't have to be alcohol."

"I haven't figured out how to destroy the spirits."

"Do you have a spell you want to try?"

Liam sighed. He really didn't.

"Will staying here help you think of something new?"

He was loath to admit it, but probably not. If inspiration was going to strike, it would have done so by now.

"Then let me take you out," Kade repeated, so close that Liam felt the heat of his body, that tempting warmth.

Liam wondered if he was being foolish to agree, but when he nodded, the pleased gleam in Kade's eyes made it hard to regret the decision.

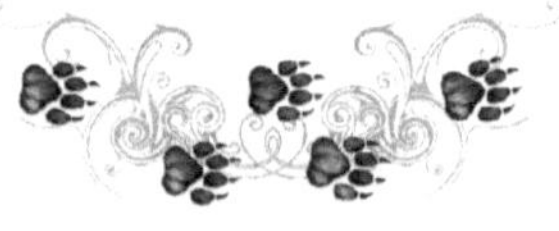

Kade drove them to a local bar. If there was one thing Lost Creek wasn't lacking, it was bars. Considering there were fewer than ten thousand people in the town, Liam wouldn't have expected such a selection.

Inside, the lights were dim and the music would make it difficult for anyone to overhear their conversation.

Kade ordered a beer and water, passing the latter to

Liam, then gestured at a pool table in the corner. "Do you play?"

"I haven't in over a year, but I can." Pool was all about calculations; he'd always been decent at lining up shots and working out the ideal angles to hit the balls.

But that didn't prepare him for how Kade played. He swore Kade had to be deliberately provoking him by bending over the table to take his shots, even the ones that didn't call for it, from the side of the table Liam was on, like he was making sure Liam got the best views of his ass he could offer. He stood in the line of sight of Liam's shots, his jeans tight enough that Liam had no doubt which way he hung. And Kade knew he was looking too; it seemed to encourage him.

"Okay," Kade said as Liam lined up his next shot. "Two truths and a lie. I've never been more than a day's drive from Lost Creek. I've never gotten higher than a B on a report card." He leaned in and continued under his breath. "And I've never had sex on a pool table."

Liam missed his shot.

"What?" he asked, standing quickly, though that brought him closer to Kade.

"Two truths and a lie. You have to guess which isn't true."

"I'm familiar with the rules. But why?"

Kade shrugged. "Maybe if I distract you with other puzzles, your subconscious will do what it did with identifying the spirits, and you'll solve it."

That seemed unlikely, but Liam could play along.

"The middle one. It makes the most sense that you'd hide the lie in the middle." Plus, whatever image he projected, Liam knew Kade was smart.

Kade grinned, still too close for Liam's sanity. "You think I haven't had sex on a pool table?"

Liam swallowed, doubting himself until Kade's smile grew wicked.

"Wanna help me fix that?"

Liam shivered.

"Your turn." There was a low growl behind Kade's words, and all Liam could picture was himself getting bent over the table, hands scrambling against the baize as Kade pounded into him from behind.

But then Kade stepped away, and it took Liam a minute to process that he hadn't meant it was Liam's turn to have sex on a pool table. He wet his lips as Kade bent over and took a shot, sinking the eleven in the far left hole.

"I'm... uh, closer to Elijah than my blood siblings. I secretly do like Aran. I helped Miles research his final project for his apprenticeship."

"Miles?"

"Yes. Though you aren't allowed to tell Aran."

Kade chuckled, sinking another ball. "Wouldn't dream of it." He circled around the table for the follow-up. "I like eggplant. Especially big purple ones. I like cucumbers; they're so nice and firm in your hand. And I like thick, meaty sausages."

Liam wasn't laughing at that. It wasn't funny. "I know you're fond of meat, so not that. Eggplant?"

"Why?"

"Because last time, the lie was second."

Kade snorted. "Are you going to guess the first one is also the lie next because you think I'll put it there to try to outsmart you?"

"Maybe."

"Your turn." He sank a third ball, then looked at Liam expectantly.

"I met Elijah—"

"Nope. I let that slide once. This should be about *you*, not you via your friends."

Liam opened his mouth to protest, then paused. That did seem fair. He considered what to say.

"The first time I used magic on my own, I set fire to the curtains in my bedroom. When I was a teen, I was convinced I was developing foresight for about a week." He inched toward Kade, his cheeks heating. "During my apprenticeship, I studied some sex magic. Hands-on. Literally."

Kade raised an eyebrow at him.

"What? Yours were dirty."

"I have no clue what you're talking about. My last one was about food."

Liam scoffed. "Sure it was."

Kade aimed his shot, drew back his cue, then cut his follow-through short as he straightened abruptly. The ball veered off course, missing its target.

"With who?" he asked.

"You have to guess which isn't true," Liam teasingly parroted back at him.

"The first one. You always had a stack of books on your bedside table. Even as a kid, you never would have done fire magic near them. With who?"

Liam blinked in surprise at Kade's confidence and accuracy. "Ah... another apprentice. I was curious. So was he."

"Not a shifter?"

"No. I barely worked with any shifters before you."

That seemed to please Kade. He lowered his voice to

say, "You know those books Aran lent me? One mentioned using shifter energy during sex magic is better than—"

"Your turn." Liam knew what it was better than. *Everything.* He didn't need a book to confirm that theory for him.

Kade shot him a sly look, but let it drop. "PE was my favorite subject in school. My favorite trope to read is fated mates. I fantasize about leaving my pack."

"Leaving your pack."

"My favorite subject was art, actually. Not that I was any good at it, but it was fun messing around with whatever supplies they gave us. PE, on the other hand, requires us to constantly suppress our natural abilities so we aren't suspiciously fast or strong."

Liam frowned, but before he could ask, Kade was moving on, not giving him time to think about the third statement being true.

"Let me give you an easier set. My favorite DickHunt scene is *Celebrating the Exclusive Contract.* I would happily be the meat in a DickHunt sandwich. I have Richard's merch, but have never used its... most famous feature."

"Most famous feature?"

Kade leaned in. "It has a fully functioning knot."

Oh. There were toys like that? Okay. Well. Kade seemed romantic enough for that particular scene to probably be his favorite. While Liam hadn't watched it yet, he'd be willing to bet that much. But if Kade did want to be in a... sandwich, surely he would have tried that feature. "The second one?"

"They're the hottest stars on MateHub, but I've never been into threesomes. Plus, Richard would kill me."

"But you haven't—" Liam snapped his mouth shut. He shouldn't ask. Instead, he aimed for the seven... and failed to sink it. When he straightened, Kade was right there, his breath fanning Liam's ear.

"I wanted to save that for my mate. Feeling my knot expand in them and the echo of that through the bond. How tight and hot they'd be clenching around me. How full I'd made them feel. Our bond connecting us as pleasure built, until there was no separating us."

Liam remembered how that had felt. What would it be like without the spirit affecting them?

Kade inhaled deeply, his eyelids drifting shut, but then he pulled back. "No toy could live up to that. Not even Richard's."

He went to take his shot, and Liam tried to convince himself that the space between them didn't bother him.

They stayed at the bar longer than Liam would have expected, and it did end up distracting him from his failure with the spirits and from everything else they didn't know, but it absolutely didn't distract him from his thoughts of Kade. Not with how Kade kept getting close before pulling away. With the provocative options he gave Liam to choose from.

Liam was almost regretful when they called it a night.

He assumed it would be a one-off evening, but they did the same the next night and the night after that.

They'd try some experiment on a spirit that was all but guaranteed to fail, or Liam would research until even he was sick of it, and then they'd head out to a bar.

He wasn't sure what Kade's intentions were. Their evenings together felt like dates, but were they? He didn't want to ask. At least not until he decided whether he wanted them to be dates. That didn't stop him from enjoying them though, even if they weren't offering any brilliant insights into destroying the spirits. They weren't helping with their other problems either. Niall's pack was still in danger, and those mages were still out there.

And as the full moon drew nearer, Liam realized they had another problem on their hands.

Kade was growing restless, his energy more potent and rousing when Liam used it. His wolf prowled with an untamed hunger that permeated their bond.

Kade's wolf craved things, and Liam could sense it, could sense how frustrated it was that Kade wasn't acting on its desires. Liam was finding it harder to deny that he wanted those things too.

He'd thought the last full moon had been as bad as it would get, that he'd be able to resist that temptation. But with Kade getting more worked up with each passing day, Liam was starting to doubt that, and it wasn't even the full moon yet.

Kade's phone vibrated as they left the bar, and he dug it out of his pocket. A jolt of shock flashed through him so suddenly, it caught Liam's breath. He looked at Kade.

"What is it?"

It took Kade a moment to tear his gaze away from the screen. "It's Pierce. He's asking to meet tomorrow."

"What?" Liam's eyes wanted to pop out of his skull. "Are you kidding? It's been nearly two weeks, and he wants to do it *now*? The full moon is in two nights."

Kade held up his phone to show him the message.

"Nope. No way," Liam said. "I know Elijah is struggling to figure out how to break into the wards fast enough, but we can't trust him, and I don't think we should attempt to capture a spirit with hooks in a pack so close to the full moon."

Kade grimaced. "He's a good guy."

"A good guy who could be so messed up by a spirit that he isn't aware he's not being a good guy."

"Let's see what everyone else thinks." Kade sent off a quick message, and they drove to the pack land, Liam tapping his foot against the floorboards.

Pierce had to be setting them up, right? Why else would he have waited so long to contact Kade? Trusting him seemed like a mistake on all fronts.

When they'd assembled, most of the group agreed with him.

"Yeah, fuck that," Aran said. "This is beyond suspicious. He likely set us up so we couldn't get to the shop while it was being broken into, and now he's setting us up again."

"But why would he do that?" Miles asked.

Aran shrugged. "The spirit?"

"Or his alpha found out and he hasn't been able to contact us."

Liam shook his head. He knew Miles was giving Pierce the benefit of the doubt, but they couldn't trust him.

"If Niall found out," Elijah said, "we're fucked. Every option is shitty here. If I try to break through their wards, they'll arrive before we capture the spirit. If we agree to meet with him, we might be left in the middle of nowhere while someone does who knows what somewhere else."

"Or he shows up with his pack ready to fight." Aran's tone was tense.

"That too. And even if this isn't a trap, I'd rather not do it directly before the full moon because Miles needs to reset Grant's wards, and he should be conserving his magic over the next few days."

"If it comes down to it, my pack can wait another month." Grant clearly wasn't thrilled about it, but saving Niall's pack was the more critical issue.

Elijah blew out a breath and exchanged a look with Victor, some silent communication passing between them, then he turned to Kade.

"See how he reacts to meeting on a different day. If he insists on tomorrow, there's something going on. Say we'll meet him exactly one week before the new moon. That'll give Miles about a week to recover from resetting the wards, and any effect the moon has on the spirit's strength should be decreasing by then."

"But regardless of him insisting," Liam said, "there might still be something going on."

Aran nodded in agreement.

Liam watched Kade type a message and hit send. They stared at his phone, but the reply wasn't immediate.

"I don't like this," Liam said.

Elijah grimaced. "None of us do. But we don't have a choice."

Liam wished he could argue with that. They needed someone in Niall's pack to help them, and Pierce was their best bet.

Kade's phone buzzed. He opened the message and read it aloud.

PIERCE

Same time, same place. Don't contact me
again.

An uneasy silence settled over the room until Elijah
finally broke it.

"If anyone has a better plan, I'm all ears."

Liam had nothing, and neither did anyone else. Dread
pooled in his stomach, cold and heavy. Kade's hand rested
on the small of his back, offering what comfort he could.

He'd do this if he had to, but every cell in his body was
certain it wouldn't end well.

Liam walked around the clearing in Grant's territory. It was
hours from moonrise, but Kade was already a jittery ball of
energy. He attempted to push that sensation away and
concentrate on the task at hand.

He marked out a circle larger than the one Miles would
be drawing after he was finished. This wasn't a difficult
spell, but it would require a fair amount of magic.

Only Miles, Grant, and Grant's pack would be on his
territory that night. Victor had offered his pack as guards,
but Elijah hadn't thought it was advisable to have energy
from Victor's pack on Grant's territory during the ritual.

It hadn't snowed yet, but the air was wintry and it
would just get colder as the night progressed. Miles and
Grant would be in this clearing until dawn, and Miles
wouldn't have the magic to spare to keep the area warm as
he worked. That was where Liam came in.

After he'd finished his circle, he sat in the center and channeled his magic. Though his access to Kade's energy was limited without Kade there with him, it was so tempting to let the sweet burn of it fill him. He tamped down that desire and set a warming spell over the clearing, giving it enough magic to last until morning.

When he was done, he let himself sense how perfect the spell was. Even with as little of Kade's energy as he'd used, it was still better than any similar spell he'd cast before.

He opened his eyes and saw Miles outside the circle, watching him.

Liam stood and walked over.

"This is beautiful spellwork," Miles said, his gaze unfocused as he took it in, then he blinked at Liam, too nice to ask the obvious question.

"I've been meaning to talk to you about that. Sort of. If your magic and Grant's energy are compatible, be careful how you sever the connection between you after the ritual. Make it a clean cut so there are no side effects like Elijah had."

"Oh. Yeah. I can do that." Miles's cheeks were tinting pink. "Don't want any lasting effects from the ritual. Because we're definitely doing the same ritual Elijah did."

Liam narrowed his eyes at an increasingly flustered Miles.

"Right. Thanks for setting this up. It'll really help. I mean, I'll be wearing a coat. And clothes, of course. You know. Warm clothes. So it's not like I need it. But it'll be good to have. For the ritual. With the clothes. I mean, the ritual doesn't involve clothes, just that I'll be wearing them. Like one does. For rituals."

Well, that wasn't suspicious at all. Miles appeared to be broken.

"Are you okay? If you don't think you can handle the ritual, we can figure something else out."

"No. I can... handle it." He was brighter red than Liam had seen even Elijah get.

"...Alright. If you're sure."

"I'm sure. This was my idea." He swallowed audibly.

Liam stared at him for a beat longer, and Miles vibrated with nerves.

"If you change your mind, we'll understand."

Miles's resolve solidified. "No. I want to do this."

Liam gave him one final skeptical look, but Miles seemed determined and it was his call to make.

Shrugging, Liam turned toward the pack house. Miles took the lead, already familiar with the territory after weeks of capturing spirits on it. But if he hadn't been there, Liam could have found his way without any problem.

Kade was waiting, his presence a beacon that pulled at Liam, drawing him in, luring him closer.

His agitation eased as Liam stepped out from between the trees, the relief of no longer needing to restrain himself from storming into the forest to find him washing over them both. The drive back to Victor's territory didn't settle him, and neither did running with his pack that night. Liam had thought that might help, but he'd been wrong.

Elijah had suggested Liam stay out with the pack's human members at the bonfire that night, but it didn't feel right to Liam. He didn't belong there for this. Elijah wasn't staying there either; he was as wild as the wolves and had slipped into the trees with them. So Liam headed to Kade's room as twilight fell around the house.

But if anything, Kade seemed to be getting more restless as he ran. Liam sensed his exhilaration at running through the forest for the first time in months. It had him pacing the room like he needed to run as well, like he should be out there with Kade, which was ridiculous—there was no reason for him to run with the pack. Running with them was something he should only do if he wanted to stay, but acknowledging that didn't help.

His clothes rubbed against his skin, too rough and too constricting. He couldn't read, couldn't sit still. He was too on edge, too horny, but there was nothing he could do about that either. Not without making the situation so much worse for them both.

Or so much better.

No. Doing that would be the epitome of a poor choice.

A highly pleasurable, mind-blowingly hot poor choice.

He tried to breathe through it. Another thing that didn't help.

The window was still cracked open, the chill night air gusting in, but it did nothing to cool his heated skin.

He tried to focus on anything other than Kade, on his instincts and urges. That became infinitely more impossible as he sensed Kade approaching, stalking toward the house with single-minded determination, like he was hunting down his prey.

The moment Kade entered the house, Liam knew it. Anticipation crackled between them, through their bond, in Liam's blood, as Kade neared, as he climbed the stairs.

Liam shivered.

The only prey Kade wanted to hunt down that night was him.

TWENTY-SEVEN

Kade's paws devoured the ground as he ran through the trees. It was a joy to be out there again, with his pack, running as they were meant to run. But he failed to shake his debilitating need to return to the pack house, to his room, to Liam. To where he was supposed to be.

Victor hadn't lasted long. He'd given them permission to be in the forest provided they weren't alone, but he'd seemed distracted, and soon he was circling back, no doubt heading straight for Elijah. He'd be thoroughly occupied until morning.

Kade wished he could do the same—spend the rest of the night as lost in Liam as Victor would be in Elijah—though even if he returned to his room, that wouldn't happen.

So he stayed out with the pack until that urge was so great there was no denying it. Liam was a restless presence in his mind, one he couldn't ignore. Some of that was the echo of his own emotions; some of it was entirely Liam. It was difficult to separate what came from whom, and he wasn't sure it mattered when the end result was both of them agitated and horny. He ached to reaffirm their bond, to give himself up in any way Liam would have him.

As the night wore on, the little self-restraint he had evaporated, and without making a conscious decision, he was prowling toward the pack house. The knowledge that Liam was there consumed his thoughts.

He drew closer, every inch of his body alive with need as the house came into view. He slunk past the bonfire, incapable of dealing with his pack members. They saw him as he shifted and slipped on his clothes, but didn't comment. He didn't want to dress, not when his skin felt tight and raw from the excess energy inside him. But he was human enough to realize the worst thing he could do would be to leave his clothes where they lay, stalk through the house naked, and enter his room. To see Liam's reaction and let him decide what happened next. Neither of them had the self-control to withstand that.

Over the last few days, something had shifted between them. Liam felt more open to him somehow, his emotions clearer through the bond, and Kade had no intention of pushing that further than Liam was comfortable with. Gently nudging, maybe, but he'd waited this long; he could give Liam as much time as necessary.

Or at least, that was what he told himself. It was easier to remember that when the moon wasn't singing to him, when his wolf wasn't demanding they prove to Liam how good they'd make this for him. When climbing the stairs didn't feel like he was closing in on his prey. When he couldn't smell how turned-on Liam was as he opened the door to find him pacing their room, his eyes wild as he took Kade in.

"How do you deal with this?" The breathiness in his

voice was asking Kade for things he wasn't certain Liam truly wanted.

"It's usually not this bad." Kade heard the rumble in his own words, the panting desire to be near Liam. This was so much worse than the last full moon. He could smell their scents mixed now. They'd be so perfect together, if only Liam wanted it.

Kade didn't dare get closer. He had his limits, and being too close to Liam was far past them. But he couldn't leave either.

Liam sat on the floor, his back against the bed, and looked at Kade. "Okay, let's do this again. East or west?"

"East." Kade leaned against the dresser, but itched to pace.

"Come here. Sit by me."

Kade followed the request, though his instincts urged him to move, to shift, to run, to pin Liam down and fuck him. Reclaim him. Do it right this time.

But that wasn't allowed. Not tonight.

"Where first?" Liam asked.

God, he smelled like everything Kade had ever wanted. Kade inhaled, filling his lungs with Liam's scent, with *their* scent. How would he smell as they moved together, as sweat slicked their skin, as he clung to Kade, Kade's knot stretching him open? How would he taste on Kade's tongue, in Kade's mouth?

Liam shifted his weight, tilting his head from side to side. "Kade. Can you concentrate? Where first?"

"Boston," he managed to get out. "You can show me the library."

He'd never been there, but he knew it was huge. It probably had all kinds of hidden corners they could sneak off to. Liam could clutch the edge of a shelf, biting his lip, trying desperately not to make a sound as Kade thrust into him. Could he knot Liam in the library without someone discovering them? It'd be fun to find out. Or, Liam had an office, right? He could bend Kade over his desk and fuck him. Or Kade could suck him off as he sat in his chair.

"*Kade.*" His name was transformed into a whine by the need burning in Liam.

"Your turn," Kade said in a low growl. "What do you want?"

Liam shivered but steeled himself. "Newgrange, Ireland. There's a Neolithic passage tomb, and mages in the nearby town practice astronomical magic."

Ireland. He could work with that. They'd find some lush green field somewhere, and he'd fuck Liam senseless in it. Yeah, they should do that.

"Next?" Liam prompted, breathless.

"The Sierra Morena in Spain. There are wolf shifter packs there." Maybe Liam would let Kade hunt him down in one of the pine forests, let him stalk him through the trees until the moment was right to catch him.

They continued through another dozen countries, but Kade couldn't focus on the conversation, couldn't focus on anything besides what he might do to Liam in each of those locations.

On this trip, they wouldn't be seeing the sights. It'd be night after night of the dirtiest fucking he'd ever done in his life. They'd take the occasional break for food, but beyond that, it'd be marathon sex. How many countries could they fuck in on one around-the-world trip? Was there a Guinness World Record for most countries fucked in? They'd aim for that.

Liam groaned, his head falling back to rest against the

mattress, his neck exposed, and Kade's canines ached with the desire to bite, to mark, to reclaim.

"God, you're insatiable. I think I've leaked more precome than I knew I could produce." Liam clamped his mouth shut, wincing, then said, "Sorry. That was too much information. In my defense, I've been around you and Aran a lot recently."

It wasn't remotely too much. Kade could smell Liam's lust, could see the bulge in his sweatpants.

"You should take care of that."

Liam's gaze trailed down Kade's body and landed on the tent in his pants. "I'm trying to be responsible here, Kade, but I have a breaking point, and like I said last time, I'm not a saint."

"And I said don't be one."

"Which side of you is in control?"

Kade looked him dead in the eye. "Human." By a thread. "If my wolf side had been in control, that suggestion would have been growled in your ear."

"You'll regret it in the morning."

"Let me decide that."

"Won't it deepen the bond?" Liam's resolve was only marginally stronger than Kade's nonexistent self-control.

Their bond was already deep. It would already hurt to lose, and Kade wanted this. Wanted to do something with Liam, anything with Liam, even if it was just once. The consequences of his actions be damned.

"It's okay. It doesn't count if we don't touch."

Liam didn't look or feel like he believed him, but he said, "I'll take your word for it. I'll do it if you do it."

It was impossible for Kade to deny that.

He palmed himself through his jeans, groaning when he gave himself a squeeze. Liam's eyes stayed fixed on him as he rubbed his palm along his length, his precome darkening a patch of denim.

Kade couldn't breathe as he unbuttoned his jeans. He saw it when the realization hit Liam, sensed the flash of arousal through their bond.

"You're wearing those?" Liam asked, wetting his lips, and Kade pushed his jeans lower to expose the crimson silk.

"Yeah. Can't say I'm a fan of the lacy pairs, but the silk feels amazing." His regular underwear had been returned the day after they'd disappeared, but Kade mostly wore the ones Liam had bought for him. Prank or not, he liked wearing something Liam had given him.

He pushed the silk aside, the fabric gliding over sensitive skin as he pulled himself out. Liam's attention didn't stray from his hand.

"You too." Kade's voice jolted Liam out of the stupor he was in. He shoved his sweatpants down and his underwear with them.

Fuck, his dick was gorgeous. When they'd been together in the clearing, Kade hadn't had the time to properly appreciate the sight. There were so many things Kade longed to do to him. To touch and taste and feel him. To have the weight of that cock in his hand as he moved inside Liam. To have it pressing into him as Liam's body draped over his.

But he couldn't. Not yet. Not until Liam was ready.

"Channel my energy," Kade said, and Liam's eyes snapped to his. "You like how it makes you feel, don't you? Use it."

For a moment, he thought Liam would turn him down, but then Liam was opening to him, to the energy that rushed to fill him. Liam's eyelids fluttered shut, his dick leaking more precome. The tattoos on Kade's chest warmed, and he saw a few swirls peeking out from the collar of Liam's shirt and on his exposed wrists, an orange glow against his brown skin.

"Good." Kade was intoxicated by the heady scent of him, the beautiful sight of him. "Now stroke yourself."

Liam didn't open his eyes, just wrapped his long fingers around his cock, his pleasure flooding Kade as he worked himself over, making Kade's hand move as well. Ecstasy ricocheted between them. If he couldn't have Liam's hand on him, this was the next best thing.

"Show me what you like." The command seemed to remind Liam that he wanted to watch Kade. His gaze swept over Kade's body, landing on his hand.

He rolled his foreskin back, and Kade copied the motion, only for Liam to pause.

"Do you want my magic?" The question was rough and needy.

"Fuck, yes." Kade had scarcely gotten the words out before the connection between them equalized, Liam feeding his magic to Kade as he channeled Kade's energy. Liam's magic filled him, stretching him full, and Kade groaned. "Keep going."

Liam didn't require any more encouragement. Kade matched his movements, the slow drag and pull he was using.

When Liam noticed what he was doing, he slowed further, squeezing the base of his dick. Kade moaned as he did the same to himself, his knot hot and throbbing under his skin, begging to get back into Liam. It had been too long. He should never have to go over a month without touching Liam, without being inside him.

Liam continued to jerk himself off, but more and more, he focused on the lower part of his shaft, feeling the thrill that brought Kade. He sensed how Kade needed to be touched there, needed Liam clenching around him. Liam gripped himself tighter, and Kade did the same, his knot expanding.

Liam's eyes latched on to the now-visible swell. "You're knotting? That's... Is that possible? When you're not in someone?"

Kade wrapped his fist around his knot, making Liam's hips stutter forward from the shared sensation.

"It's rare," he confessed. "You have to be extremely aroused, but it happens."

With Liam, it'd be a frequent occurrence. If they ever got to the point where they could tease each other, edge each other for hours until Kade's knot was so swollen, he'd barely be able to get it in Liam.

He'd always hoped for a mate he was so attracted to, so connected to, that they'd make him start to knot before he was inside them. He'd assumed it would happen whenever he found his mage; he just hadn't expected it would be like this.

"Can I..." Liam cut himself off and wet his lips again, but Kade knew what he'd been going to ask.

He leaned in and inhaled, his nose buried in Liam's neck. "*Yes.*"

Liam shivered and released his own cock, reaching over hesitantly like he was giving Kade a chance to pull away, to change his mind. There was no way in hell Kade would do that.

He moved his hand up his length as Liam's tentatively skated over the swell of his knot. His fingers were gentle as they brushed against Kade and encircled him. Kade didn't bother stifling his moan.

"Tighter," he said, more a plea than a command.

Liam obliged, and Kade's knot swelled, throbbing in Liam's hand as Kade jerked himself off, his fist bumping against Liam's with every stroke, Liam's magic tingling against his skin.

Fuck, this was good, with Liam right there, his scent surrounding Kade. Liam's grip was snug, and he grabbed himself with his left hand, the motion awkward, but he kept rhythm with Kade. His breath hitched, his eyes locked on Kade.

It didn't take much for them to come. Liam's hand stayed wrapped around him as they did. Kade's orgasm hit in pulse after pulse, making a mess of his jeans and their hands. It wasn't the hot, tight clench Kade wanted, but it was enough. It was still better than every single one of his hookups combined.

They slumped against the bed, half leaning against each other, panting, but Liam didn't remove his hand, and Kade was infinitely relieved. He couldn't imagine having a full knot without some kind of pressure on it.

It'd be so easy to lean over, to kiss Liam, but that seemed like asking for something more intimate than Liam's touch.

Slowly, he deflated, and Liam appeared almost regretful as he removed his hand and released Kade's energy.

He cleared his throat. "I shouldn't have done that."

"No, it's fine. It was good." *Really* good.

Awkwardness fell between them, and they sat in silence until Liam spoke.

"I'm going to shower and rinse some of this out." He gestured to the spatters of come that now decorated his shirt.

He stood and walked to the bathroom. Kade followed. Liam turned to him in question, and Kade blinked, realizing what he was doing. He couldn't stand to be separated by even a door. It was pathetic, but he couldn't deny the instinct.

Liam shrugged. "It's fine. It's not like you haven't seen me naked."

He pulled off his sweatshirt, and Kade's breath was stolen by his tattoos. They were glowing softly—shimmering swoops and fiery spirals that graced his skin.

"Your tattoos." Kade had caught glimpses of them, but he hadn't seen their full extent, how they'd spread over so much of his chest.

"Actually." Liam looked sheepish. "Can I see yours?"

Kade snorted. "Didn't we just do that?"

"You know what I mean." Liam rolled his eyes.

Kade shucked his shirt and checked himself out in the mirror. The swirling patterns of Liam's tattoos started at his heart and curled over his chest and left shoulder, an ember orange visible from the strength of the moon.

Liam reached out like he couldn't stop himself. His fingers traced along the tattoos, making them light up brighter. Warmth ran through the lines. Kade had felt them before. Any time Liam used his energy, they heated. It didn't compare to Liam's fingers tracing them—another thing he might never get more of.

Liam shook himself and pulled away. "Sorry. It's so weird to see my tattoos on someone else."

He washed his hands in the sink before rinsing out his shirt, then stepped back so Kade could do the same. He slipped into the shower, leaving the curtain slightly open in a clear invitation for Kade to follow.

There was enough room that they could shower without touching, but Kade wanted nothing more than to pull Liam against him under the warm spray, to soap Liam up and get him clean for the sole purpose of dirtying him again, scenting him all over, marking him until everyone would know who Liam belonged to. Who Kade belonged to.

But he kept his hands to himself as they showered and toweled themselves dry.

They climbed into bed. Kade's wolf was more settled, happy they'd gotten their mate off, but something was missing. It wasn't the lack of sex; it was deeper than that.

Unable to suppress the urge, he gathered Liam into his arms. Liam froze for a second, then melted into him as Kade tucked him against his chest.

His wolf rumbled a deep, contented sound, and Kade inhaled Liam's scent, his nose pressed to the nape of his neck.

This. This was what he needed. Liam boneless against him, smelling of pleasure—a little slice of perfection.

In his mind, Liam felt sleepy and satisfied. He was still unsure about the idea of them together, but he was getting closer. Kade was certain if he gave him time, he'd realize how right they were for each other, how he didn't want to sever their bond any more than Kade did.

TWENTY-EIGHT

Liam woke to late morning light spilling in through the windows and the warm weight of Kade draped along his back, an arm wrapped around him. All he wanted to do was melt into him further, to stay like that for hours.

Kade was awake, and Liam was certain Kade could tell he'd woken as well. But for a few tranquil moments, they lay there, pretending otherwise, neither willing to break the illusion.

The night before had been intense. Their connection had let Liam feel Kade and the sensations echoing between them... It had been the hottest thing he'd ever done, so different from anything else he'd ever felt. What would sex with Kade be like? Unaffected by the spirit, just the two of them and their bond. Liam tethered to him, filled with Kade's energy. It was more appealing than he would have dreamed possible before this trip.

Kade shifted his weight on the bed, and Liam realized it wasn't the smartest idea to think about that while Kade was pressed against him, so he forced his mind to safer thoughts.

He'd figured Kade would regret it, but nothing about Kade's presence indicated that, and Liam couldn't bring himself to regret it either. If anything, he could get used to waking up in Kade's arms and not having a reason to pull away.

When he blinked his eyes open, his gaze landed on the books on the bedside table—three of them from the attic. He'd reinforced the protection spells on them before bringing them down to read.

He'd never cared about his lack of ability to do practical magic. The theoretical was so much more interesting. But looking at them now, there was no denying that this bond was special. It wasn't on the same level as Victor and Elijah's, but would it grow to something closer as they got to know each other better?

If he were being honest with himself, he'd miss this. Miss their bond if they severed it, the magic they did together. Miss *Kade*. But that didn't mean he wanted to stay there. He wanted to set up his archive and create a proper history of mages that filled in the holes left in the official histories. He wouldn't be able to do that in the middle of nowhere.

"Are you still going to tell me you're fine?" Kade asked, his voice a whisper that brushed against Liam's neck, making him jump.

Of course Kade felt how conflicted he was, just as Liam sensed Kade's concern nudging at him. He'd assumed that would be intrusive when Elijah had talked about it, but it wasn't. Not with Kade.

He opened his mouth, then closed it, unsure what to say.

"You don't have to answer. It's fine."

Liam huffed out a laugh. "The irony of you telling me it's fine." He sighed. "This was... unexpected. I'd planned to be here for two or three weeks max, then head back to the library."

Kade waited for him to continue. Something in his emotions said he was bracing himself for the worst. It was too hesitant to be anticipation, though it held a glimmer of hope.

Liam's phone buzzed, and he considered ignoring it, but it vibrated again. He felt like a coward reaching for it, using it for the diversion it offered.

He sat up, and Kade did the same, though he leaned close, his arm pressed against Liam's, and Liam had no desire to put distance between them as he opened the notifications on his phone.

MILES

The wards are reset. Everything went well.

I slept most of the morning, and I'm starving and more depleted than I've let myself get in a long while, but overall, I'm good.

Liam exhaled. One more hurdle cleared. He showed the messages to Kade, and the cooling rush of his relief swept over Liam, but Aran replied before he had a chance to.

ARAN

So... how was that night-long pounding from Alpha Silver Wolf Daddy's metaphorical shifter dick? Are you nice and stretched this lovely morning?

MILES

There was no shifter dick! Metaphorical or otherwise!

ARAN

Who said anything about otherwise? You did get to see him naked though, right? If he isn't an absolute beast in that department, I'll swear a vow of celibacy for a year.

ELIJAH

You'd crack after a week.

ARAN

Speaking of people who got their fill of shifter dick last night... though much less metaphorically.

Elijah sent an eye-roll emoji.

LIAM

Miles, are you up to driving to the shop, or do you need someone to pick you up?

There was a slight delay before Miles answered.

MILES

Actually, Grant invited me to their pack breakfast and said I could rest here until I've recovered.

So I'm going to eat as much food as they'll give me and then sleep until tomorrow.

Liam hummed thoughtfully. Elijah had offered Miles and Aran spare bedrooms multiple times, and they'd insisted it wouldn't feel right to stay on pack land. He was surprised Miles felt comfortable enough to do it now, but with the wards containing so much of his magic, it might feel different to him.

LIAM

Okay, but let us know if you change your mind and are too tired to drive.

We'll come get you.

MILES

Thanks, but I'm good. And STARVING.

I'll see you guys tomorrow.

ARAN

At which point I will expect a lengthy dick report! Both metaphorical and otherwise!

Miles didn't reply. Definitely the wise choice, in Liam's opinion.

He set his phone aside and got out of bed. They got ready in an easy silence, though Liam sensed Kade waiting for him to say more.

He remained close to Liam, like he couldn't bear to be farther than an arm's length away, and Liam understood. There was a pull between them that demanded they get closer. He wanted to be consumed by Kade.

It had to have been what they'd done. They'd deepened the bond, and it was demanding more. That should have made him worry, but it didn't.

As they descended the stairs, the house was quieter than he'd grown accustomed to over the last month. With Grant's pack gone, there was room to breathe. Sure, there were more people than Liam was used to, but it wasn't bad. It seemed like the perfect amount.

He didn't mind all the people there. The sly looks they

gave them, on the other hand... It didn't take a genius to realize they could smell what he and Kade had done.

Victor took a breath, cocking an eyebrow at Kade, and Elijah whipped his head toward Victor, picking up enough to understand Victor's reaction. Elijah's eyes locked on Liam as he sat, delighted mischief in their depths. Liam's cheeks heated.

Like Elijah was one to talk. He appeared thoroughly mauled again, his pale neck marked up with half-healed hickeys. Not that Liam was jealous about that or wondering what it would have been like if he and Kade had exercised a little less self-control.

Before Liam could pick up his plate, Kade was already filling it with everything Liam was craving. Liam stared down at it, and when he glanced up, Elijah was smirking at him from across the table. Some tiny corner of Liam's mind was telling him he should be annoyed, but given how delicious the food was, he couldn't be bothered.

As soon as Liam had cleaned his plate, Elijah was out of his chair, circling the table and grabbing him by the arm.

"I'm borrowing him for a few minutes," Elijah said as he dragged Liam away from the dining room and out of the house.

It was brisk outside, and Liam shivered at the cold. There'd be snow by the end of the week.

"Soooo..." Elijah looked at him expectantly.

Liam refrained from rolling his eyes. "A few days ago, I examined a spell I did with Kade's energy."

"There are very few times I get to say this to you, so you'll have to forgive me for enjoying this, but... I told you so. Now what are you going to do about it? I mean, aside from whatever you did last night."

"I don't know."

"You like him though. You're just overthinking it like always."

Liam couldn't refute any of that. "What does it matter if I like him? Kade's pack is here, and I'd rather not live here forever."

"You should talk to Kade before you make any assumptions. But for the record, I'm all for it. Even if you don't stay here."

"How would that work? He's Victor's second."

"Talk to Kade, Liam."

Would Kade want to leave his pack? He'd mentioned it, but that must have been more of an 'I'm okay with leaving briefly to do some traveling' than an 'I'm willing to leave my pack forever for you.' The latter wasn't something Liam would ever ask Kade to do.

And if he did leave, didn't wolf shifters have an innate desire to belong to a pack? Wouldn't that mean he'd need to be part of a pack somewhere else? How did that fix their situation?

"Talk to Kade, Liam," Elijah repeated. "You aren't an idiot, though sometimes you try to be. Don't be one now."

Liam gave him a flat look. "Fine. I will."

Eventually. After he figured out what he was hoping for.

Kade was waiting by the door and wasted no time getting close to Liam once he was inside. Liam had to wonder how much of his emotions Kade was able to read. He sensed some of it, if the apprehension coloring their bond was anything to go by.

Elijah glanced at Liam one last time before heading back to the dining room.

Liam inhaled, about to speak, but he still didn't know what to say. So instead, he said, "Let's go to the workroom."

He was being a chicken about this; he could admit

that much, but it was upending his entire life. It wasn't something he could research and find the answers he needed.

When they got to the workroom, Kade sat beside him, their shoulders bumping together.

Liam called a ball of fire into his hand and stared into it like it held the answers to his questions.

Kade reached over, and Liam passed him the flame, his fingers brushing Kade's as he did. Kade held the ball before transferring it to his other hand, then back. He offered it to Liam, who took it, copying his actions before passing it to Kade again. Each time their fingers touched, Kade's energy sparked against Liam's skin, accompanied by the occasional flash of memory from the night before.

There was a deliberateness to Kade's fingers stroking along his as they passed the fireball back and forth, neither talking, and Liam couldn't deny that his touch lingered as well. Flames licked over their skin.

They were sitting too close for Liam to make smart life choices. Kade smelled so tempting. Each brush of their fingers lit up Liam's senses. He tried to distract himself, but didn't stop passing the flame to Kade.

"I'm out of ideas. I've tried every way imaginable to destroy these damn spirits, and now I've got no clue what to do or where to look next."

Kade stayed quiet as Liam gathered his thoughts.

"How do you destroy something that's basically an emotion? Anger or hatred or sadness?" Liam was starting to believe the spirits couldn't be destroyed.

"You don't. Or at least, not with real emotions. You can't blow up hatred and expect it to go away. Sadness doesn't disappear if you try to force it. There's always a root cause you need to address first."

Liam paused, his hand on Kade's, not taking the flame Kade had been passing him.

The spirits were formed from corrupt magic. That was their underlying issue. Corrupt magic couldn't be used for anything good, anything pure. Anything like healing.

Maybe he'd been coming at this wrong. Maybe they couldn't destroy the spirits; maybe they needed to *heal* them.

Elijah had tried to heal the forest when the decay spirit was affecting it, but that had been healing its effects, not the cause. Healing the spirits themselves might work.

Liam's first instinct was to call Miles, but he was on Grant's territory, presumably asleep, recovering from the ritual. Liam didn't want to bother him while he was depleted.

He wasn't great at healing, but he could try it. A basic circle below the box, a few standard herbs and stones. It might not require more than that.

He glanced up and found Kade staring at him, a soft smile on his lips.

"You're lighting up in my head again," he said.

"I don't know if it will work, but I want to attempt to heal a spirit."

"Then let's do it. What's the worst that can happen? It blows up in our faces?"

Liam snorted. "Hopefully not. I've had more than enough of that for a lifetime."

They scrubbed the floor clean so Liam could draw a new circle. It was simple and elegant compared to the increasingly complex and convoluted things he'd been trying. He added lavender, rose quartz, and willow for emotional healing, turquoise for balance, and cedar for support, then he placed the box that held the spirit of annoyance in the center of the circle and flipped open the lid. They'd tried to destroy it countless times, but it remained—a yellow ball that pulsed orange.

Liam reached for Kade, their hands meeting over the circle. He exhaled and let Kade's energy fill him. Their magic and energy twined, and the circle began to glow. That combined power washed over the spirit, over the tainted magic it had been born from. And slowly, so gently and slowly, the spirit dissolved, bits and pieces of it fading into nothingness. It took more energy than everything they'd tried before, but when the final wisps of the spirit disappeared, Liam knew without a doubt that it was gone.

Still, he waited, his hands clasped with Kade's, not breathing, expecting it to return.

It didn't.

He tore his gaze from the now-empty box, a wide smile spreading across his face. Wonder and amazement echoed through their bond. Liam's relief was so powerful, his elation so effervescent, that he might have floated away if it weren't for Kade's hands on him. His joy was too immense for words.

They could do this—get rid of these spirits, *heal* the spirits. It took a lot of energy, but if he could do it, so could Elijah. And Miles too, if he used Grant's energy.

They could absolutely do this.

Liam didn't know who moved first, but he found himself pulled across the circle, the box knocked aside, the chalk lines smudging under his knees, the stones and herbs scattering as Kade gathered him in his arms.

Kade's breath ghosted over his skin, and he leaned in, his body warm against Liam's.

"You did it," he whispered.

"Team effort." Liam was breathless from the emotions caused by achieving this breakthrough.

Kade let out a laugh full of delight and happiness. "Sure. If that's what you need to tell yourself."

Liam wanted to argue, but Kade was tightening his hold, pulling him closer, one hand cupping Liam's cheek, his eyes dropping to Liam's mouth.

Magic and energy danced in the air, saturating the room with everything that was them. Liam wouldn't have been able to look away from Kade even if the spirit had chosen that moment to reappear.

God, he'd wanted to kiss Kade for so long, but it was more than that now. Before, it had been a physical desire, but this need felt soul-deep, mirrored back at him.

"Can I?" Kade's voice was a velvet-soft whisper, his expression one of unadulterated longing, matching the emotions thrumming through their bond.

"Your human side is in control?" Liam asked as he pressed closer to Kade.

"Completely."

Was this wrong? It didn't feel like it, but they were caught up in their success, caught up in their bond.

"Your brain never shuts off, does it?" There was fond amusement in Kade's tone, the question a gust of air against Liam's lips.

"No." How could he stop overthinking things? Especially something like this, something heavy with meaning he hadn't fully grasped.

"Can I try?"

"Try? To shut my brain off?"

"Yeah, that. Let me try to do that." There was a promise behind those words that had Liam shivering.

This might be a horrible idea, but that didn't make him want it any less. "Okay."

With slow determination, Kade closed that last sliver of distance between them, their breath mingling as they met in an aching kiss. Kade's lips were warm and soft, sending a jolt of awareness through Liam's body. Kade's energy surged between them, the power of their bond singing at the touch, magnifying every sensation, every emotion.

Liam gasped into Kade's mouth as his magic whirled around them. He gripped Kade's shoulders like he needed an anchor in that blissful storm. The raw connection between them had him trembling, anticipation a wildfire in his veins, the air charged with the intensity of the moment.

A low rumble built in Kade's chest as he deepened the kiss for one far-too-short minute that had Liam losing track of reality, the edges of the world around them blurring, before Kade eased back to a lingering tenderness, then pulled away.

Liam opened his eyes. Kade was staring at him with a hooded gaze. The roaring inferno of his touch subsided to a banked warmth that wouldn't take much to rekindle into a consuming blaze.

"Why'd you stop?" Liam asked, his voice rough.

"Because I want you certain, and you aren't yet."

Liam wasn't so sure. If Kade had kept kissing him like that, he would have been certain real soon. "You said you've thought about leaving your pack."

"I did, and I have."

"For how long?"

Kade's hands tightened around his waist. "Forever, if I needed to."

Liam blew out a breath. "But don't you need to be with a pack?"

Kade looked him straight in the eye. "My mate could be my pack. That's all I'd need."

That sent another shiver through Liam. "You'd want to travel the world?"

"Yes."

"But you're Victor's second."

"I don't have to be."

"You'd honestly leave your pack forever?"

"Ideally? They'd still be my pack. I'd be gone for a few months, return for a few weeks, then head somewhere new. But if that wasn't possible, I'm flexible."

Liam swallowed. Could that work? Could they use Lost Creek as a base? Travel the world together, then come back home.

Kade's expression grew wicked. "And just so you know, when I say I'm flexible, I mean that in more ways than one."

Liam laughed despite himself.

"Alright," Kade said, disentangling himself from Liam. "You need to think about this, and when you're this close to me, it's hard for me to remember I want to give you time to do that." He stood and offered a hand to Liam, pulling him to his feet.

Liam would be thinking about this. It'd be impossible for him not to. But they had other things they needed to do.

He glanced down at the ruined circle and brushed as much of the chalk off his knees as he could before he sent a message to Elijah.

LIAM

Can you meet us in the workroom?

Bring the spirit of your choice.

I think we found something that works.

He'd barely grabbed a rag before Elijah was rushing into the room, three boxes tucked under his arm, Victor a step behind him.

"You figured out how—" Elijah cut himself off. "Did you try to clean that circle up with your knees? No, wait. Don't answer that. I'm not Aran. I don't want to know." He set the boxes on the workbench. "You destroyed a spirit?"

"No. I *healed* it."

"You... healed it?" Elijah turned that thought over in his head, his mouth hanging open. "Well, fuck. How did we not think of that before?"

"We were too fixated on destroying the things."

"True. That doesn't make me feel less like an idiot though."

Liam was in total agreement. He'd been spinning his wheels on this for far too long. He reset the circle, then walked Elijah through what he'd done.

While Elijah wasn't the most proficient at healing either, he had more experience with it than Liam did, and he had access to a larger source of energy through his bond with Victor. Liam had confidence in Elijah's skills, but he was still holding his breath as Elijah and Victor took their places around the circle.

They linked hands, and Elijah channeled his magic and Victor's energy. Their power filled the room, the formidable strength of their connection.

The first spirit Elijah had brought oozed in its box, a squirming, sickly green. The mere sight of it made Liam seasick and nauseous. But Elijah's magic gradually disintegrated it until the box sat empty.

Elijah stayed frozen, staring at the box suspiciously, his breathing accelerated, a sheen of sweat on his brow, his hands in Victor's.

"Everything in me is telling me the spirit is gone," he said. "But I've been through this before. Many times. I'm not sure I trust it."

"Same," Liam said. "But I think they truly are gone."

Elijah looked up, cautious optimism in his eyes. "Did it work? Can we defeat these evil bastards for good?"

"We can." Liam felt almost giddy.

Elijah sat back on his heels. "I knew you'd figure it out."

Liam shook his head. "Team effort."

Kade snorted. "Some members of the team contributed significantly more to the effort."

"They did," Elijah agreed. "This takes a lot of magic, but it's doable. I could do a few a day without draining myself too much, as long as I didn't have to do anything else. I bet Miles would be even more efficient at it. He might have less access to Grant's energy, but if he was able to reset the territory wards properly, he'll be able to do this. We'll have to have him try it after he's recovered from the ward ritual."

That was what Liam had been thinking.

They had another piece of the puzzle solved. There were a few small spirits left on Grant and Victor's lands that they were having difficulty tracking down, but their packs were mostly safe, and now they could handle the spirits. They just needed to take out the paranoia spirit and get Niall's territory cleaned up, and hopefully that would happen soon, which gave them four or five days to heal spirits before they had to conserve their magic for that.

For the first time in weeks, Liam saw an end to this. He was worried about what was happening to Niall's pack, and there was the issue of who was behind this and where they were, but if they could heal the spirits, they'd figure everything else out.

Realistically, at the rate they'd be able to heal the spirits, and given how many they'd captured, it'd take them a while, but they'd get it done. It would be time-consuming to do them individually, but if he altered the spell to do several at once, it would speed things up. It was something he'd have to brainstorm. Though it would take a ridiculous amount of magic and energy to do that, there was a chance they could manage it. A ritual with the four of them to amplify each other, fed by the energy of three packs. Yeah, that might be doable.

Things were looking up, and that was confirmed when Elijah and Victor healed another spirit. It worked exactly like it had previously, though Elijah appeared more strained by the end.

Liam let out a relieved sigh. Something was finally going right for them.

Victor side-eyed Kade, then looked at Liam. "I owe you. Anything you want, name it and it's yours."

The first request that jumped into Liam's head was downright inappropriate. Kade was his own to give.

He was about to say Victor didn't owe him, but stopped as another thought hit him. "Actually. Would it be okay if I were to archive the books in your attic? Not any you consider too personal to be shared widely, and you'd have final approval over everything, but those books are a priceless resource. I'd like to make them available for anyone who needs them."

Victor glanced at Elijah and got a nod before answering Liam. "Have at it."

Liam beamed at him.

If they each healed one or two spirits a day, archiving the attic would give him plenty to do in the downtime while they waited to meet Pierce. Plus, it offered him an excuse to go through every single book up there. The next week was going to fly by.

With everything that had gone wrong lately, today was turning out to be an amazing day.

The following day, Liam healed a spirit with Kade, then spent the morning in the attic, organizing the books and preparing them to be archived.

The scanner in Elijah's office had been damaged during the break-in, so Liam had to order a new one, but that was alright. He had plenty to do before it arrived, and he was excited to get started on this project.

His mind was brimming with visions of how many other family libraries might exist and how much knowledge he'd find in them.

The books that were most fascinating to him were the ones about pack history, the ones he would not be archiving publicly. He had an unedited source of information reaching back to before the abductions, and it was filling in so many blanks for him.

Reluctantly, he emerged from the attic for lunch and found Aran was already there. Shortly after that, Miles and Grant arrived, and as much as Liam longed to return to the attic, they had more important things to do.

"Are you up for doing this?" Liam didn't want Miles straining himself if he was depleted. He should rest another day or two. It wasn't that urgent. But Miles waved him off.

"I'm surprisingly good. Not nearly as drained as I expected to be."

"It was all that metaphorical alpha dick, wasn't it?" Aran asked.

Kade chuckled, and Liam glanced at him, only to get feigned innocence and a feeling of evasiveness in return.

Whatever. Liam couldn't focus on Kade's perverted thoughts.

Miles's cheeks were pink, but he ignored Aran.

"So, you healed the spirits?" Miles was attempting to change the subject, and Liam was happy to assist.

"Yes. Both Elijah and I were able to do it, so you'll definitely be able to."

Miles sat on one side of the circle, with Grant opposite him. Grant held out his hands, and Miles placed his on top of Grant's. His eyelids slid shut, the light blue tattoos on his arms glittering to life. And then he did what Liam and Elijah had already done, but faster and needing less energy.

Liam had known Miles was a world-class healer—his affinities were suited to it, and he was more precise with his use of magic than the rest of them were—but it was always impressive to see him work.

Letting his hands fall from Grant's, Miles blinked away the blue glow in his brown eyes.

Aran whistled softly. "Not bad. You really are getting used to that alpha energy, aren't you?"

Miles cleared his throat and stood. "I can do a couple of these a day. Provided Grant is willing to let me use his energy."

Grant's voice was gravelly as he said, "Anything you need."

Miles's gaze darted toward him, then back to Elijah. "We can do this."

They exited the room, Miles and Grant walking past

Liam and Kade on their way out. Kade inhaled, the corner of his lips twitching.

"Well," he said, "that was not entirely surprising."

Liam nodded. "Yeah. I knew Miles could do it."

Kade smirked at him. "He certainly did."

He turned to leave, his amusement shimmering in their bond. Liam narrowed his eyes at his back before following. He probably didn't want to know whatever dirty thing Kade was thinking. Probably.

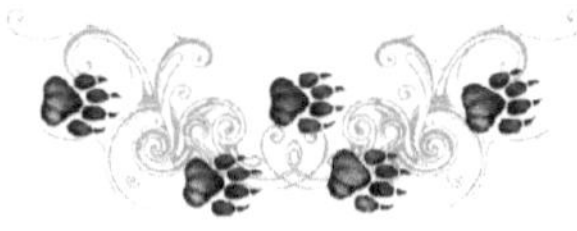

Liam set a stack of cardboard boxes on the floor and rolled his shoulders. The boxes were full of books from the attic. He'd packed them up the evening before, and that morning, Kade and a few other shifters from the pack had hauled the furniture downstairs. The bookshelves, drawers, and chests now lined the walls of the workroom, waiting to be filled with books again. Books that Liam would put in the proper order so Elijah could find whatever he needed.

He, Elijah, and Miles had already healed two spirits each, and with nothing else to do for the day, they were setting up a workroom for Elijah. The trove of books and magical artifacts was too valuable to be gathering dust up in the attic.

"I still say we can't trust this Pierce guy," Aran said as he arranged vials of dried herbs in an apothecary cabinet. "We shouldn't be going into their territory."

They'd been discussing the situation as they worked.

Miles looked up from the chest he was organizing. "We can't abandon them. They're so affected by the spirit, it could do anything it wants to them. There's no way they can survive that on their own. Why haven't we seen or heard from them?"

Liam didn't trust Pierce either, but he agreed with Miles. They had to help the pack. If there was a pack left to help. "Any luck with breaking through the wards, Elijah?"

Elijah grimaced. "I can do it, but not fast enough."

They fell into silence, Liam considering the few options they had. He unpacked the books and began to place them on the shelves.

If they ensured Niall's pack was safe before they tracked down the people behind this, it would give him some peace of mind. It'd be one less thing to worry about. Deal with Niall's pack, then handle the mages.

But if they were going to do that, they needed to find them, and the stone hadn't locked onto their hideout yet. They needed a backup plan if that didn't work.

"Is there something we can do to locate the previous shop owner?" he asked. "What was his name again? Darius?"

"Yeah. Darius Caldwell." Elijah grimaced. "Victor and the pack never say it, for understandable reasons, but the council wouldn't even tell me his name. I found it on invoices in the shop."

"We could ask them. They might know where he is," Miles suggested, and Liam winced.

"Do we want to get them involved?"

"Hell no," Aran said.

Elijah shook his head. "I doubt they'd get involved anyway. I think the only reason they bothered in the first place was because he was running one of their shops. They can't allow corruption there. It'd ruin business if word got out. But he's no longer an official representative of the council and they've punished him for what he did to Victor's pack, so they've washed their hands of it. We could try, but—"

Aran cut him off. "I'd rather not deal with those ancient bastards while everything else is going on. No good can come from their involvement."

"But we don't know what he's doing," Miles said. "Surely they'd help."

Liam doubted that. The council never did anything unless there was profit in it for them. They were... Well, they were the council. They had control over far too many things, and they didn't like change.

"Speaking of," Elijah said. "I've received notice that there have been complaints about my shop being closed so much recently. I told them I was remodeling, and it'd be up and running in the next few weeks. They seemed skeptical, so who knows how long they'll buy that. I didn't tell them about the break-in or anything else."

Liam didn't blame him. If they were lucky, they'd avoid dealing with them until this was finished. But even if they couldn't go to the council for help, they should still track Darius down.

"I guess that leaves Victor contacting his father?"

Elijah looked less than thrilled. "He'll do it if he has to, but there's an open wound there. If we've got nothing after we've cleared the largest spirits off Niall's land, we'll contact him and see if he knows anything. Or, more likely, if he's willing to share what he knows."

Liam grabbed another box of books as he considered that. "The fact that those two mages we saw ran away makes me think they don't want an all-out confrontation, but I'm worried they might cause more problems. They must have realized the spirits are no longer affecting our pa —Victor's and Grant's packs."

Elijah grinned, but didn't call him on the slip. His amusement gave way to a sober tone. "They might be planning something as we speak, but if they could attack us, wouldn't they have done that by now? There must be something holding them back. But that doesn't change the situation. While we have a credible suspicion of who's behind it, we can't search a two-hundred-mile radius in the hopes that we stumble upon them and that whatever protection spells they're hiding behind magically reveal them to us. We need more to go on than that."

Liam didn't love it, but Elijah was right.

"As much fun as it is to discuss things we don't have answers to," Aran said, "I'm still waiting for that detailed dick report. So, Miles, how'd the ritual go? Give me specifics. Exactly how big are we talking?"

Miles's face was burning a bright red.

"Ignore him," Elijah said. "But I do want to know how the ritual went. Should I check over the wards and make sure everything is okay? You've never done anything on that scale before."

"No, I checked them. You don't need to." Miles suddenly seemed fascinated by the contents of the chest. "Oh, that reminds me. Any luck with that flower, Aran?"

Aran groaned. "No. I swear I've tested it against every herb and flower in Elijah's shop, and it didn't react to any of them other than moonflower, and it's not registering as having any magical properties either. It's annoying the hell out of me, but I will figure the fucker out."

Liam had complete faith in his ability to do that. If anyone could identify what it was, it'd be Aran.

The lack of information about Niall's pack and who

they were up against ate away at Liam, but there was nothing he could do about it for now. They had a week to wait, and until then, they had enough to keep them busy. They had spirits to heal, and he had books to archive. And he was more than capable of doing both as he worried.

Pack dinners were kind of fun. Chaotic, yes, but fun.

Liam let the chaos flow over him. The good-natured ribbing, the easygoing camaraderie, and the pack children constantly asking to see more magic tricks, *bigger* magic tricks, like Elijah was going to split open the dining room floor so he could do whatever Oliver wanted him to do with his earth affinity.

He even got in on it. After Oliver had discovered his main affinity was fire, he'd run to the living room to get candles for Liam to light and extinguish as he pointed to them, conducting them like a symphony was playing in his little head.

Kade's happiness and contentment settled over Liam, sinking deep into his bones. He sort of loved this. He wouldn't want it every night, but he understood the appeal of coming home to this.

The warmth of the meal was offset by the howling wind outside. It started snowing shortly after dinner. Liam had never been fond of snow, having lived most of his life in places without it or with very little. It hadn't been until he'd moved out to the library that he'd experienced months of snow. It was pretty, but he hated being out in it. Maybe if he and Kade did travel the world, they could hit up the southern hemisphere from December to February.

They headed up to their room after calling it a night. Once inside, Liam shivered. The window was open a crack, and the air in the room was frigid. A tiny drift of snow lay on the sill.

He walked over and shut the window. A sharp pang flashed through his mind, and he spun to look at Kade.

"Oh. Do we still need to keep it open?"

Kade shifted on his feet.

"Are you going to say you're fine?"

Kade forced out a breath. "Yeah, I kind of was, but I honestly think it'll be okay."

Liam studied him, sensing him through their bond, but Kade didn't feel unsettled. None of the panic Liam had grown accustomed to during their first days bonded was coming through their connection. Aside from that spike of anxiety, Kade genuinely seemed alright.

Kade was capable of making his own decisions, so Liam took him at his word. They couldn't have the window open while it was snowing.

They changed and brushed their teeth, Kade sticking close to him, occasionally leaning in and inhaling his scent. Liam smiled, enjoying the almost inaudible rumbles Kade let out every time he did it.

When they climbed into bed, Kade didn't hesitate. He wrapped an arm around Liam and drew him in, fitting his body along Liam's back. Liam bit his lip and grinned to himself. This was better than he ever would have imagined it could be.

There were so many things they had to do, but together, they'd overcome any obstacle in their way.

As he drifted off, he had to admit—to himself, at least—that he didn't want to lose this.

TWENTY-NINE

Water closed in over Kade's head. His body itched as decay skittered along his skin. He shuddered and gasped, trying to take in air, but there was none, only filthy water burning his throat, choking him. Bands of iron clamped around his chest. No matter how hard he struggled, the blackness, the oil-slick rot, coated him, clogged his lungs, and stole his ability to breathe.

The vice grip tightened as the spirit dug into his brain and buried itself there until nothing was left of him, stripping him of control over his own body. He thrashed, attempting to throw it off, but it was too strong.

A warm hand pierced through the filth and closed around his wrist. His skin buzzed at the contact.

"Breathe," a soothing voice said.

Waves of calm tried to wash over him, but breathing was impossible in the torrent of decay and rot that had invaded him.

"Kade, I need you to breathe for me. You can do it." The

words were gentle, but they withstood the onslaught of corruption.

The tingling in his wrist increased, sweeping up his arm. A cool, clear presence in his mind pulsed with calming energy that whispered over his skin, and he caught the faintest hint of a scent—bonfire and old paper and pack. His own scent, but more. Better.

He tried to force his lungs to work, taking in a ragged breath, shaking with the effort. His eyes were pressed shut against the filth he was drowning in.

"Breathe, Kade," the voice said again.

Kade took in another painful gasp, then another, until the polluted water began to subside, inch by inch, freeing him from its embrace. It receded until his head was above water, though his chest was still tight.

"That's good." Another calming pulse rolled through him, growing stronger, warmer, driving away the water, the spirit.

He peeled his eyes open and found Liam staring down at him, his expression concerned, moonlight highlighting his features.

Kade sat up, shaky from the nightmare.

"Are you okay?" Liam asked.

Clearly he was not.

"Why am I not over this shit?" Frustration roughened his voice. He dragged a hand through sweat-damp hair.

"You dreamed about drowning? In the spirit?"

For a moment, the water was back, but then Liam's hand was on his arm again. Kade swallowed the bile in his throat.

"When it possessed me, it came out of nowhere and surrounded me, and I couldn't breathe. It filled my lungs like polluted water. Like I was drowning in it."

"We can leave the window open. I'll wear another layer to bed and put a ward on the screen. At the very least, I should be able to manage a ward that blocks snow."

Kade snorted. "No. I have to get over this. It's too cold in here for you with it open, and if I'm being honest, I want it closed so the room smells more like you."

Liam's gaze softened, but then a determined expression crossed his face. "In that case, there's something we need to do. We have to heal the decay spirit."

Kade's brow furrowed. "Why?"

"If we heal it, if you can overcome it, I think it'll give you closure."

Knowing that spirit was gone would be a relief. Kade couldn't imagine the weight of that off his chest.

"To be clear," Liam said, "healing isn't linear. If we get rid of the spirit, it doesn't mean I expect you to never have another panic attack. If you still have nightmares, I won't judge you for that. But let's do this. Let's heal the spirit so it's no longer in this house."

Kade wanted that, but the idea of facing the spirit made his heart race. "We've only done small spirits."

He'd never seen Liam look quite as resolved as he did when he answered. "We can do it. Together, we can do it."

Liam rolled out of bed, and Kade blinked at him. "Now?" It was the middle of the night.

"No time like the present." He held out a hand to Kade and hauled him to his feet.

They didn't change, just slipped through the quiet house in their nightclothes.

Kade followed Liam to the room where the spirits were stored, and they grabbed the cedar chest Elijah had used to capture the decay spirit. His skin crawled as he picked it up.

It had been in the house since his childhood, but now the sight of it made him feel unclean.

In the workroom, Liam drew a larger circle than the ones they'd been using and placed the chest in the center of it.

"Ready?" he asked as Kade sat next to him.

Kade was, but that didn't keep his lungs from threatening to close as Liam flipped the latch and opened the lid. The spirit churned, and Kade could swear there was no air left in the room.

Liam's hand found his, their fingers intertwining. "This is going to take a lot of energy."

Given how much the smaller spirits took, that wasn't surprising. Kade nodded. He'd give anything to lessen the helpless feeling that overtook him whenever he thought about his encounter with this spirit.

Liam channeled his energy and fed it into the circle. At first, it seemed like nothing was changing, like the spirit wasn't being healed. But Liam didn't give up; he simply pulled deeper on Kade's energy and continued to pour his magic into the spell.

He kept working until sweat glistened on his forehead. Until, little by little, the spirit began to fade.

It was a long process, far longer than it had taken them to heal any of the handful of spirits they'd done before. But this one had been so much bigger, and it hadn't completely lost its size while locked up in the box.

The spirit shrank, giving way to the healing spell, and then it was gone.

Kade sucked in a breath and clean air filled his lungs.

The spirit was gone.

He stared at the empty chest, feeling almost numb with shock.

It was gone.

It was over.

Liam's hand squeezed his. "Is that better?"

"I think so."

"Good. But like I said, this doesn't mean you have to be okay."

"I thought I was okay after my sense of smell returned. I... I've been using your scent as an anchor, as something to remind me that I'm in the present moment whenever I start to panic."

"*Oh.*" Liam seemed unsure how to respond to that.

He needed all the information laid out before him in order to make a decision, and Kade could give him that. "I can't describe how perfect your scent is, how well it mixes with mine. None of this is remotely how I'd pictured this happening, but it has, and now I don't want to sever our bond. I want to keep this. I want us to be together."

Liam hesitated, and Kade could only wait for his reply.

Finally, he grimaced. "I don't know if starting a relationship with a mistake is the best idea."

Kade shook his head. "No. The situation wasn't ideal. It was probably the worst way for us to bond. I messed this up, but it wasn't a mistake."

"How can you say that?"

"Would you have given me a chance without this happening?"

Liam inhaled, about to speak, but then he paused, and Kade sensed him wavering.

His shoulders slumped. "I don't think I would have. Sorry, but I wouldn't have been around you enough to get to know you. I mean, I would have thought you were hot, but I doubt I'd have realized how much more there is to you than the terrible pickup lines."

Kade huffed. "Hey. I have amazing pickup lines."

"That has yet to be seen."

"Alright. Challenge accepted."

Liam grinned at him.

Sobering, Kade stared him in the eye. He needed Liam to understand. "This was not a mistake. It wasn't some adorable, fictional meet-cute, sure, but I don't regret it. You're everything I've ever wanted. You're not a mistake. Not even close."

He sensed those words hit Liam, saw the hitch in his breath, heard the skip in his heartbeat.

"I wouldn't want to stay here forever," Liam said. "I do enjoy it here, just not all the time."

"Same. After this is over, I want to explore the world with you. I want to be by your side as you find all the knowledge your heart desires, and I want to help you save it, preserve it."

"So we travel for a few months, then come back home? And maybe we could avoid the worst of winter here?"

Kade grinned. "That sounds perfect."

"How did you picture this happening?" Liam asked.

"This?" Kade's cheeks hurt with the extent of his smile. "Us?"

"With all those books you read, you must have had an ideal scenario. No spirits, no bonding when neither of us was ready for it. What was it?"

Kade drank in Liam's scent, savoring it. There were so many ways this could have played out, but most started in the same place. "You'd come to visit Elijah, and from the moment you met me, you'd think I was insanely charming and handsome."

Liam chuckled. "Okay, we can pretend you're the smoothest wolf shifter to ever exist."

"I'd flirt with you, and obviously you wouldn't be able to resist my charms. We'd edge closer. You'd shoot me looks across the table at dinner, glancing at me out of the corner of your eye. As we got closer, I'd notice your scent and crave more of it. You'd be here for the full moon. You and Elijah would be sitting by the bonfire, and I'd strip to shift, knowing you were watching me. Maybe you'd follow me into the forest, or just think about it the entire night. Elijah would try everything in his power to keep us apart, but you'd be far too attracted to me to stay away."

Liam shook his head fondly. "Sure. You're irresistible. I'm magnetically pulled to you."

"As you should be. Then I'd woo you."

"*Woo* me?"

"Yeah. I'd woo the absolute hell out of you. I'd take you out for a romantic dinner. Candlelight, fine dining, me looking dashing in a suit."

"I am partial to a good candle."

"And then after dinner, we'd end up in my bedroom. I'd go slow, drive you out of your mind with pleasure, until you begged for me to bite you, to give you my knot."

Liam shivered. "I'm not sure I'm the type to beg for someone's knot after one dinner."

"It'd be a very romantic dinner. But I'd be willing to make it into a whole series of romantic dinners. We'd go to a hotel, or find a cabin with a fireplace and one of those overly expensive rugs in front of it. And if none of that works for you, I'd buy you a dozen books."

"Not roses?"

Kade scoffed. "You wouldn't want roses. Books all the way. I'd get ones with red covers, if you wanted. Or I suppose I could give you a bouquet of dick-shaped candles or suckers. Or anything dick-shaped, really."

"I'll take the books, thanks," Liam said dryly.

"Whether it's books or candles or MateHub merch—"

"Definitely not that." Liam's laughter settled in Kade's chest, warming him.

"I'd sweep you off your feet and into my bed. It'd be exactly what we both wanted."

"We should do that." Liam had the softest smile on his face, his eyes shimmering with amusement, their bond full of happiness and delight. "Our order of operations is backward, but after we take care of everything, let's do those dates. I won't be a mistake, and you won't mess up. But maybe tonight..." He slid his fingers along Kade's. "We could do that last part?"

Kade let out a low rumble. "Are you sure?"

"I want to explore the world with you too. I want you to see all the places you've longed to see. In person, not just in the books on your shelf. I want you to go everywhere you've dreamed of going, experience everything you've dreamed of doing. And I want to be there with you when you do. For us to do that together. Travel the world together. Find that future together."

Kade leaned closer and reveled in their scent, in the promise that Liam could be his forever. He rested his forehead against Liam's. "East or west?"

Liam was light and giddy in his mind. "Whichever way you want to go."

Kade didn't care as long as it was with Liam. He ran his hand along Liam's sharp jawline, tilted his head up, and brought their lips together. It was a soft brush that had them both gasping, but he didn't deepen the kiss.

He pulled away, and Liam chased after him, silently asking for more. He blinked his eyes half-open.

"Give me ten minutes?" Kade said. "Then come upstairs."

Liam looked bemused, but he nodded. "Okay. I'll see you in ten."

Kade swooped in for a quick kiss, then hurried out of the room. He had things to prepare.

THIRTY

Liam stared after Kade, wondering what he'd walk into when he got to their room. But it didn't matter; whatever Kade set up would be perfect.

Kade was a jittery ball of anticipation in his head, his excitement zinging in Liam's blood, and it just made the ten minutes crawl by even slower.

He stood and closed the chest, placing it off to the side, then cleaned up the circle. That only killed a few minutes. He spent the rest rearranging things on the workbench, telling himself he was tidying up, though the space was already as neat as could be.

After the time had passed, he left the workroom and climbed the stairs. A hint of nerves mixed with the stirring of arousal, making his heart beat a little faster with each step he took until he was standing outside the bedroom. He inhaled, attempting to steady himself, then put his hand on the doorknob and cracked the door open, revealing the room. Moonlight spilled in from the windows, the only light inside.

Kade spun around from where he'd been lining up candles on his dresser. He winced. "I'm not quite ready yet."

Liam eyed him. "Should I wait another ten minutes?"

"No, I just... I couldn't find a lighter."

Kade appeared flustered, and Liam had to chuckle as he stepped inside the room, shutting the door behind him. He snapped his fingers, and a dozen candles kindled to life.

"I think you found one." He grinned at Kade.

Candlelight played over Kade's features as he closed the distance between them, a hand coming up to cradle Liam's jaw. "I think I did."

He brought their lips together, but there was nothing light or gentle about this kiss. It was deep and slow, Kade's mouth claiming Liam's, his passion and longing poured into it, leaving Liam dazed by its intensity.

"Can I undress you?" Kade asked, pulling back slightly.

"Yes." Liam's entire body buzzed with desire.

Kade stripped Liam's sweatshirt off and ran his hands over Liam's chest, the motion causing his tattoos to light up. He traced the curling lines across Liam's pecs. An orange glow danced under his touch, and he used the swirls as a map to learn Liam's body, following one over the curve of his shoulder and down his arm.

Every caress made Liam's breath hitch and sent a pleasant warmth licking over his skin. His tattoos had never responded to anyone else touching him, not how they did with Kade. It was almost like they were an erogenous zone that only reacted to him, to his energy.

Kade dragged a kiss along a whirl, his tongue darting out to follow the twisting pattern, and Liam shivered. He tugged at Kade's shirt until Kade shrugged it off.

Liam placed a hand over Kade's heart, watching the

tattoos he'd left there flicker as Kade's strong heartbeat drummed a rhythm under his fingertips.

"If we do this tonight," he said, his voice hushed, "can I reset the tether between us?"

"You can fix it? Elijah mentioned it might be messed up because of how it was created."

"This isn't how it's supposed to work. I don't have full access to your energy the way I would if it was a proper tether. Everything I've read stressed that tethers must be consensual or they have consequences. I'm not experiencing any of the problems that would have come up if I had forced it on you, but it's not connecting us completely."

If they had a true bond, that had to be the reason the tether wasn't acting how it should.

"Then you should reset it. I want to have that connection with you. Even if I can't reset the bond, this, at least, can be right."

"I'll have control over your energy if I do."

"I trust you. You can take whatever you want. You'd never use it unless you needed to. So it's yours, if you'll have it. Everything I have is yours."

Liam would take the best care of that gift.

Kade leaned in again, inhaling deeply. "I want to taste you. Last time, I couldn't."

"Yes." Liam had barely gotten the word out before Kade was sinking to his knees, gazing up at Liam as he eased his sweatpants down, exposing his half-hard cock.

"God, you're beautiful," Kade said, taking Liam in hand and rolling his foreskin back to lap at his tip. The possessive rumble that ran through him had Liam threading his fingers into Kade's hair, tangling in the long strands.

Anticipation stole Liam's breath as Kade's lips wrapped

around him, as he let out a low, pleased growl that vibrated through Liam's dick and made him gasp.

Kade worked him over like he'd never tasted anything better. In Liam's mind, Kade was alight with the need to please, to make this good for Liam.

If Kade kept this up, Liam wasn't certain how much longer he'd be able to stay standing. The heat of his mouth, the suction, those rumbles... Liam's legs turned to jelly as Kade swallowed him to the root, his lips gliding over sensitive skin, only breaking away to pepper kisses down to Liam's balls and take them into his mouth, one at a time. He laved and sucked on them until Liam was cursing under his breath, then teased his way up Liam's shaft with his tongue, savoring every inch before taking him in again.

Everything else faded away under the swirling onslaught of pleasure. Liam's climax built, coiling tight. He tugged on Kade's hair.

"If you keep that up..." Liam warned, and Kade pulled off, looking smugly satisfied.

"I said I want to taste you."

"You don't want to—" Liam began, but Kade's grin grew wider and sharper, taking on an untamed, rapacious edge.

"Oh no, I want to, and we will. But I can wait until you're ready for round two."

A shiver raced down Liam's spine. "Okay." The word came out winded, but he didn't care how he sounded when Kade's eyes were locked with his, heady promises smoldering in their depths.

Liam's world narrowed to Kade's lips parting, his mouth taking him back in, his cheeks hollowing as he drew him deeper. He groaned at Kade's redoubled efforts, arching into the pace he set. Waves of hazy bliss threatened to sweep him away. His hands, tangled in those silky strands of hair, served as his only anchor.

Muscles taut, breathing ragged, Liam rode every sensation Kade wrung out of him. His eyelids fluttered shut. A torrent of need pooled in his gut. He gripped Kade's hair so firmly that it had to be painful, but it only seemed to spur Kade on—each tug of Liam's fists, each thrust of his hips made Kade hum and moan around him.

The world spun. Heat scorched through him, consuming him whole. And when his climax hit, it reverberated between them—through him, through Kade, and back—better than anything he'd experienced before.

His knees buckled, and he sank to the ground, mind a blur, body trembling, hands still in Kade's hair. He used them to reel Kade in for a kiss, tasting himself on Kade's tongue.

Liam laughed breathlessly. "With orgasms like that, I might have actually begged for your knot after one dinner. What's round two?"

"I want to make love to you."

No one had ever said that to Liam. There was something so cheesy about it, so stupidly romantic, but for Kade, it worked.

"Okay. Let's do that. Make love to me."

Kade hauled him to his unsteady feet. "Shower first? You seem like a shower-first kind of guy."

Liam nodded, and Kade wrapped him in his arms, kissing him as he walked them into the bathroom where they stripped off their remaining clothes. Kade's dick was hard and leaking, and Liam swallowed, so tempted, but Kade shook his head like he knew what Liam was thinking.

"Not now. But definitely some other time. Hopefully many other times."

Liam could guarantee that would be the case.

He basked in the aftermath of his orgasm as Kade's soapy hands roamed over his body, then gently turned him around to brace against the shower wall.

"Do you usually top or bottom?" His fingers stroked over Liam's hole as his other hand came up to toy with his nipples.

Liam gave a languid shrug. "Neither. I've done both and found them pleasurable, but, well, I've never had a real relationship." He glanced over his shoulder at Kade. "It seemed too intimate to do with someone I had no feelings for, so experimenting aside, I haven't done it often. But with you, I want to. I want that closeness."

"Either way?" Kade looked thrilled at the possibilities that presented.

"Either way. If you want that."

"Absolutely. But tonight, I need to be in you."

Liam's stomach clenched at those words, at the pure desire that shimmered through their bond. He needed that too. "Yes."

Kade pressed closer, kissing along Liam's neck and shoulder, then slipped out of the shower to grab lube from a cabinet. When he returned, he slicked his fingers and skated them down Liam's crack to his hole, circling it before pressing one in. Liam relaxed into it.

He let Kade stretch him open under the hot water, his body loose from his orgasm. Kade took his time, in no rush, even though Liam sensed the fiery pulse of arousal that burned inside him. But Liam also understood his intentions. He wanted to fuck Liam senseless, but he also needed this to be different, for them to do it right. For neither of them to have doubts. To explore each other's bodies, to savor the moment. For it to be good, not just because the spirit was making them crave it, making them think it was good. He wanted Liam so achingly ready for him, so sure about choosing him, choosing their future together.

Liam's body hummed with satisfaction, with the comfort that blanketed him whenever he was with Kade.

He teased and touched until Liam was hardening again. His hands scrabbled to find purchase on the slick tile, and he squirmed, breathless with the slow build, needing more than Kade's fingers.

Reaching down, he stroked himself, and Kade shuddered against him, letting out a shaky exhale. "God, that's good. But if you want me in you anytime soon, I'm going to need you to not do that. It's too much with everything else."

Liam gave himself one last stroke, and Kade's hips flexed, his dick bumping against Liam.

"It's so strange," Kade said. "Not exactly like you're stroking me, but I still get stimulation from it."

Liam knew what he meant. He wrapped a hand around the base of his cock and squeezed where the demanding throb of Kade's knot was in his mind. Kade's hand on his hip gripped tighter as he choked back a moan.

"*Fuck.* One of these days, I want you to do that. Tie me up and jerk yourself off, keeping a hand right there until I'm knotting. Until you make me come untouched."

A vivid image of that flashed behind Liam's eyes. Kade stretched out on their bed, Liam straddling him, getting himself off as Kade watched, as Kade writhed, coming from Liam's pleasure alone. He never would have imagined that would appeal to him, but with Kade, god, he wanted it. He wanted so many things he never had with another person.

Kade hadn't been wrong when he'd wondered if Liam's

brain ever shut off. It rarely did, even when he was with someone like this. But he could fall into Kade until there wasn't a thought in his head except how perfectly they fit together. How their connection resonated on a near primal level.

Kade reached over and turned off the water, then toweled him dry. He led him into the bedroom, where the soft flicker of candlelight illuminated the space.

"Where did you get these?" Liam asked, gesturing to the mishmash of candles scattered throughout the room—decorative votive holders, tea lights, pillars, and more.

"I... may have run around the house, frantically searching for every candle I could find."

"No dick-shaped ones?"

"I know it's not as romantic without them, but I promise, after this, you'll always have the most realistic dick candles I can buy you. Only the best for you. Dozens of girthy, veiny—"

Liam cut him off with a kiss.

He marveled at this ridiculous, sweet, beautiful man. He had a feeling everybody's first impression of Kade was incorrect. That all they saw was the carefree fuckboy. But there was so much more to him. He was so much deeper than that.

They settled onto the bed, Liam pulling Kade on top of him, the hard length of him pressing into his hip.

"I'd bet every single book I own that you have lube in your drawer."

"Would you expect anything else?"

No, Liam would not.

Kade reached across the bed and retrieved another bottle of lube. Liam took it, snapping open the lid, slicking his fingers, and stroking them over Kade's dick. He rolled his foreskin over the head, teasing the edge with his thumb, then eased it back.

Kade grabbed his wrist and tugged his hand away. "I'm not going to last if you do that."

"Then we should get to this whole lovemaking thing."

Kade's hand glided over Liam's, stripping off some of the extra lube, then he held it out for Liam to coat his fingers with more.

Liam spread his legs wider, giving Kade all the access he could want, and Kade slipped two fingers inside him, stroking over his prostate and making them both shudder, before he lined himself up.

"You good?" he asked.

"More than good."

Slowly, he pushed inside, and Liam gasped, partially at Kade's thick length filling him, but also at the sensations he was getting from Kade, at the hot clench engulfing his cock a fraction of an inch at a time as Kade slid into him, finding a home in him.

The way Kade had described it was right. While it wasn't quite like being inside someone himself, it wasn't entirely different either. It was an echo of that—the euphoria of that sweet embrace. It had him moaning and arching from that one thrust alone, until Kade was fully inside him, leaning over and bringing their mouths together in a heated kiss, both of them panting before Kade had truly started to move.

"God, you feel amazing," Kade whispered against his lips. "I've never felt anything half as good as this."

Pleasure danced through their bond. Liam sensed Kade's wolf; its raw, wild contentment at finally being inside their mate, finally being where they were supposed to be. Kade's knot throbbed beneath the surface, and Liam groaned at how much he wanted that, how much he needed that. It had been too long since they'd done this, and they'd never done it properly—with clear minds and the knowledge that they were in control of their own actions and choices, without hesitation or doubt.

Kade withdrew as deliberately as he'd pushed in, carefully, like Liam was the most precious thing in the world and he didn't want to hurt him. Then he thrust forward again, the slow drag of their bodies maddeningly divine. Neither of them would last; it was too new, too intense, too overwhelming in all the best ways.

Nothing would ever compare to this, to them moving together, entwined.

Kade gradually picked up his pace, setting a rhythm that thrummed with the demands of their bond, with the desire to be connected in every way imaginable.

"Can I knot you?" His voice was rough, and he studied Liam's face, his eyes yearning and hopeful. But he didn't just want that. He wanted more. He needed to do this right. His *wolf* needed it. To bite Liam, to reclaim him. To have that reassurance that Liam was theirs, wanted to be theirs, wanted them in return.

The force of those instincts inundated their bond, leaving Liam trembling.

"*Yes.*" That one word was a tender whisper laced with unwavering conviction. He brought his hand up to press against Kade's chest, anchoring it over his heart, and he tilted his head, offering his neck.

Kade's mouth found the mark he'd left over a month ago, his teeth sharper than any human's as he scraped them over it, making Liam buck against him.

The moment Kade bit down, breaking skin, magic streamed out of Liam, through his hand, and into Kade, realigning the tether, opening it up further, as it always should have been. It twisted around the bond, washing away the influence of the spirit, fixing their connection, no longer tainted by the lack of choice. Somehow it unfurled even more. Kade wasn't a mere presence in his head now, but a part of him, *seamlessly* a part of him, breathing with him, his heart beating with him, their sensations and emotions flooding through them.

Liam let out a laugh filled with stunned, airy delight at the difference, at how perfect this was, at how everything he'd felt before seemed a pale imitation.

Kade looked at him in wonder. "How did you…?"

Liam shook his head. "Team effort."

The relief on Kade's face was blinding. He surged forward, capturing Liam's lips in another kiss, and Liam clung to him, gathering him as close as possible. So close, Kade could only grind into him—anything more than that was too much distance.

Liam's breath caught as Kade's knot expanded inside him, stretching him full, tying them together, pressing against his prostate. The ecstasy was so intense it had him arching up into Kade, his cock trapped between their bodies. It built to the point where Liam couldn't breathe, couldn't think, couldn't do anything but cling to Kade.

"You're everything I've ever waited for, everything I've ever wanted," Kade said. "Everything I've hoped for, dreamed of, dared to believe in."

Liam held him tighter. "This wasn't how I imagined my life going, but I'm glad I ended up here. With you."

Kade trailed kisses over the bite mark, and Liam moaned. When Kade bit down again, Liam's orgasm hit. He spilled between them, clenching on Kade's knot.

His climax dragged Kade along with him, growling

against his shoulder as he released inside him, that euphoric crescendo whiting out Liam's vision.

They stayed like that, panting and shaking, floating in rapture, until Kade had the presence of mind to flip them over, settling Liam on his chest, his knot pulling at Liam's rim as he did.

Liam relaxed against him.

"You still good?" Kade asked, running a hand down his back.

Liam sighed in contentment, not sure he had words for how good he was.

"I think you should know," Kade said solemnly, "if you say you're fine after that, I'll never recover from the emotional damage."

Laughter shook through Liam's body. "I'm so much better than fine. Better than I've ever been."

"Did I manage to shut your brain off?"

"It may never work again."

"Mission accomplished. But if it ever gets too noisy in there and you need it turned off, you know where to find me."

Liam would certainly be doing that. He nuzzled Kade's shoulder, and Kade angled his head to the side. The urge to sink his teeth into Kade swept through Liam, so strong and undeniable that it left him quivering with the instinct to claim. He had no idea how much of that was him and how much was coming from Kade, but it didn't matter—they both wanted it.

"*Please*. God, yes," Kade said.

Liam kissed along the juncture of his neck, sucking at it for a few seconds, but Kade's need was too profound, too bright. He couldn't deny it. He latched on to Kade's shoulder with his teeth until he broke skin. The iron tang of blood hit his tongue as Kade arched up, crying out, his cock pulsing inside him, releasing another couple of spurts that had Liam's dick twitching in sympathy.

This. This was perfection. He smiled against Kade's skin, his mind warm and fuzzy with ecstasy as they lay there, wrapped up in each other, until Kade's knot deflated enough to slip out of him, his come leaking out of Liam's ass.

Liam rolled onto his side, his fingers tracing the glittering tattoos that spiraled out from Kade's heart, glowing in the dim room. His gaze roved down Kade's body to where his come decorated his abs, then to his spent cock, messy with his release. Kade preened under the attention.

A thought struck Liam.

"Uh." He couldn't tear his eyes away. "Can I request something?"

"Anything."

"Could you maybe…" Liam winced. "Change your MateHub profile picture?"

"Ooh." Kade grabbed his phone off the bedside table. "Can I use your dick instead?"

"No." Liam attempted to sound stern, but knew his amusement was bleeding through.

"Both of our dicks together?"

"How would that not be twice as bad?"

Kade pouted at him. "Alright, but I need you to do me a favor. Channel my energy?"

Liam narrowed his eyes, but did as Kade asked. The tattoos on his chest lit up even brighter. Kade sucked in a breath, his body writhing, his toes curling against the mattress, but he steadied himself and ran his fingers through the mess on his stomach. He smeared it over his heart, then snapped a picture.

He angled his phone to show Liam. The tattoos illuminated Kade's skin, now adorned with streaks of Liam's come. A possessive heat shot through Liam, and he suddenly understood the growls Kade gave off.

Kade grinned. "I believe that was a yes."

Liam nodded and swallowed hard, and Kade cleaned his hand before uploading the photo to his MateHub profile, setting it as his user picture—no longer his cock, but instead Liam's tattoos, Liam's come, clearly marking him as owned for anyone on the forums to see.

Kade's phone buzzed a minute later, and he snorted, then showed Liam a message.

MagicalHWood:
Just got a notification that you uploaded a picture.
Nice. Tell him well done.

Two seconds after that, Liam's phone vibrated with a notification from the group chat.

ARAN

Is there something you'd like to share with the group, Liam?

Liam's cheeks burned.

LIAM

Why are you even awake?

It's like…

He glanced at the clock.

LIAM

6AM.

Okay, that wasn't particularly early for Aran.

MILES

Why is Aran cackling like a madman? He woke me up.

What's this about Liam having something to tell us?

LIAM

Um, about that…

Kade and I had a talk.

ARAN

Some talk that must have been.

LIAM

It started out as a talk!

ARAN

Didn't end that way.

MILES

What's going on?

LIAM

So…

The thing is…

Kade and I decided we're staying together.

ELIJAH

Let me take a moment to say… I TOLD YOU SO.

Also, congrats!

MILES

That's amazing! I'm so happy for you!

ARAN

Same, but I'm going to miss Kade's
previous user pic.

MILES

What does that have to do with anything?

Aran, stop typing. We're in the same room.
Just tell me.

ARAN

Kade uploaded a new picture to the
MateHub forums, and it left little to the
imagination. Never would have believed our
dear Li-mom would be involved in that kind
of debauchery.

MILES

Oh. I didn't need to know that.

LIAM

It's not what he's implying!

ARAN

Shall I show the group?

Miles and Elijah replied with quick "No's," though
Liam's beat them both.

Kade was reading the messages over his shoulder and
chuckled. "I don't know. It's pretty hot. How about we
make it our holiday card this year?"

Liam groaned. "We are *not* doing that."

His phone buzzed again.

ELIJAH

So I take it I won't be seeing you today?

Kade took the phone from Liam and typed out a
message.

LIAM

This is Kade. You're not going to be seeing him for multiple days. If anything urgent comes up, we'll be in our room.

ARAN

Have fun! I can't wait to see Liam after the stick has been thoroughly removed from his ass. And replaced by something else.

Repeatedly.

Liam snatched the phone back.

ELIJAH

Not to sound like Aran here, but seriously, enjoy yourselves.

We don't need you over the next couple days.

MILES

Yeah, we've got this covered.

But please don't tell me the details.

Liam didn't know how to respond, but Kade plucked the phone out of his hand again.

LIAM

Thanks, guys. We will.

He hit send, shut off the screen, then set it aside before rolling Liam over.

"So. Any suggestions on where to start 'having fun?'"

Liam had more than could be considered decent, but then, decency and a bond with Kade would never align, and he was surprised to find he didn't mind that one bit.

When hunger compelled them to go downstairs for breakfast—or, honestly, a very late lunch—they found Victor and Elijah sitting in the living room.

Elijah smirked at him, and Victor gave Kade a once-over, his expression flat. "Kade, you're a terrible second-in-command. When this is over, I'm demoting your ass."

"Understandable, Alpha," Kade said, tucking Liam against his side. Their bond sparkled with happiness.

A smile cracked through Victor's unimpressed glower. "Congrats. I'm glad you guys figured it out."

When they returned to the room, Liam checked out his tattoos in the bathroom mirror. The amount of skin they covered was closer to Elijah's. Not quite as much, but not that far off either.

Without touching Kade, he had full access to his energy, and when he grabbed one of Kade's travel books off the shelf and set a protection spell on it, it was even more exquisite. This stunningly balanced magic rivaled everything that had ever been created, an elegantly entwined beauty that spoke of the elemental nature of their connection.

He didn't have long to marvel at it though; Kade was already pulling him back to bed, the low rumble of his wolf informing Liam that the hour they'd been downstairs had been too much time apart.

It took them days to untangle themselves, and Liam got enough teasing from his friends to last him a lifetime, both in the group chat and in person when they eventually emerged from Kade's room.

But as the moon waned and the day they'd planned to meet Pierce neared, their little cocoon of pleasure burst. They couldn't ignore the outside world anymore.

As much as Liam enjoyed getting lost in Kade, there were things they still had to do. They just had to hope that Pierce showed up, that he wasn't too affected by the spirit to help them, that they weren't walking into a trap. And no matter how good it felt to lie in Kade's arms, it was impossible for Liam not to worry about what was about to happen.

THIRTY-ONE

The hike to Niall's territory was as long and dark as last time, but now they had to wade through drifts of snow while a frigid wind whipped at their clothes. Kade and the other shifters were largely unbothered by it—especially those in their wolf forms—but the mages shivered at the arctic blasts. The lights in their hands cast eerie illumination that twisted the trees into hulking monsters looming over them.

Kade crowded close to Liam, as close as he could on the winding paths, finding comfort in being able to touch him as much as he wanted, pulling him even closer to warm him with his body heat and feeling Liam melt against him when he did. It was too soon for them to be out of their room, out of their bed. Risking Liam by crossing through those wards into who knew what was making his wolf half-feral. The idea of losing Liam to one of the spirits, of something happening to him, had an uneasy, anxious sickness squirming in his gut as they neared the border of their territory.

Ahead of them, Victor was also sticking close to Elijah,

and Kade noticed Grant hovering beside Miles as well. Although he didn't lean in to warm Miles up, the way Grant held himself made Kade think he wanted to do exactly that.

Behind them, Aran grumbled to himself. "Excuse me, but where's my large, muscly wolf shifter to keep me warm?"

"Please don't let that happen," Liam said under his breath.

When they reached the meeting place, they didn't have to wait for Pierce. He was there, standing inside Niall's wards, casting furtive glances behind him, twitching when they emerged from the trees and passed into the neutral area between their territories.

The icy brush of the wards swept over Kade as he crossed that line.

Pierce's eyes darted around their group, then back to Kade. "Why did you bring so many people?" His words were quiet and agitated.

"They're here to guard us from the spirits." Elijah's voice was low and soothing, as if he were trying to calm a frightened animal.

Pierce's head jerked toward him. "You shouldn't have all come."

"It's okay," Elijah said. "They aren't going to hurt your pack. The last two times we fought a spirit as large as this, it created golems to attack us, and we assume this one will do the same. We need them to protect us as we trap it."

Pierce glanced over his shoulder. "You shouldn't all be here. The rest of you should go. Just the mages stay."

Kade's hand settled on Liam's back, and he saw Victor do the same to Elijah.

"No," Victor said. "We do this together. I give you my word. We're here to help your pack."

Pierce pressed his eyelids shut like he was fighting against his instincts and trying to gather himself. He shook his head. "No. You don't…"

"You have to trust us," Elijah said.

Kade couldn't breathe as he watched the exchange.

Finally, Pierce opened his eyes. He took a step forward.

"Why didn't you meet us on the new moon?" Aran asked, and Pierce lurched to a stop, his gaze shooting toward the mage.

"*Aran.*" Elijah's warning was clear. He didn't want Aran scaring Pierce off.

"No. We need a reason. Why didn't you meet us?"

Pierce winced. He lowered his voice further, whispering harshly and staring at them with wild eyes. "He ordered us to stay inside. I couldn't leave. He's too strong. When he uses his alpha command, I… I can't… He's…" His breathing accelerated, and he fisted his hands in his hair.

"After we capture the spirit, it'll no longer affect him. He'll return to the alpha he used to be." Elijah's calming tone was back in full force.

Pierce looked up at him, desperation stark on his face. He was so different from the kid Kade had gone to school with—sweet confidence replaced by a hunted, cornered skittishness.

"We can fix this," Elijah said, "but you have to let us."

Pierce darted another glance behind him, then raised his hand to the barrier, giving them permission to enter. It rippled under his touch, becoming a visible, twisting black. Silver energy leeched from his palm and corroded as the swirling darkness devoured it.

Kade sucked in a sharp breath as Victor walked through the wards, followed by Elijah. They both shuddered. Grant and Miles went next, and Miles turned to stare at the barrier, his expression horrified. When Kade stepped across, he understood why.

The wards didn't feel like any he'd touched before. The closest he'd ever felt to them was the decay spirit descending upon him. This wasn't that, but it was still corruption and filth crawling over his skin. He shuddered, and Liam did the same.

"You okay?" Kade asked.

"Yeah. You?"

Kade nodded, but he was far from okay. Eyes were watching him from every direction, following his every move, waiting for him to make a mistake.

He spun around, peering into the trees, and Liam grabbed his wrist, his touch bringing Kade back to reality, allowing him to recognize the paranoia suddenly gnawing at his mind, like he couldn't trust anyone. Anyone but Liam.

He forced out an exhale, taking Liam's hand and using it to remind himself that those thoughts were the spirit's influence, and he had no intention of letting them control him again.

Above them, lightning flashed, though there was no storm that night. But what Kade saw between the skeletal branches of the trees stole his breath and clamped around his chest with oppressive horror.

A bluish fog floated in the sky, blocking out the stars and waning moon. Cracks of jagged yellow shot through the haze, shattered and broken.

"*Holy fuck*," Aran breathed.

Kade couldn't have agreed more. The spirit was *massive*. The pack wards had been hiding it from view. He squeezed Liam's hand, anchoring himself in Liam's presence.

"We've got to move quickly," Elijah said. No one argued.

Kade still felt jittery. The eyes were still on him, but his bond kept him as grounded as possible.

Paranoia was written on the face of every shifter who crossed the barrier.

"It's the spirit." All of Victor's command and authority was in his words. "*Remember*, the spirit is making you paranoid."

They nodded, but that didn't stop them from looking around like they expected something to jump out at them.

"Get into position," Victor said, and they spread out.

Rick brought the chest he'd made to Elijah and set it on the ground. "Good luck," he said, then headed into the forest.

"Let's do this. I don't know how long we can last in here." Elijah knelt and placed his light beside him. Shivering, he stripped off his coat and rolled up his sleeves, exposing his arms.

Liam extinguished the fireball he was holding and reached out, placing his other hand on Elijah's bare arm. Miles did the same with Grant on the opposite side. Victor took his place behind him.

Kade resisted the urge to check to see who was staring at his back.

"Let's hope I can use your energy," Aran said, eyeing Pierce. He pulled out a small knife and sliced it across his palm. "I'm not taking any chances with this. Do the same to yours."

He held the knife out to Pierce, handle first, and Pierce hesitated, debating whether or not he should take it.

Before he could, there was a shout Kade recognized as Rick. "There are shifters in the forest! Their pack is here!"

Kade jolted at the warning. Were there really, or was the spirit making Rick imagine things?

Snarls rose around them, too many to be just their pack and Grant's.

Kade pulled Liam closer, spinning to find the threat, but the sounds were coming from all sides, closing in on them.

"Did you betray us?" Aran demanded, flipping the knife around and glaring at Pierce.

More snarling rang through the night. Pierce took one step backward, like he might try to flee, but then a voice, deep and commanding, said, "*Pierce, do it.*"

Kade's gaze snapped to the forest, but it was too dark for him to see past the first couple of trees. The illumination from Elijah's light didn't penetrate deeper than that.

Pierce flinched and, as if he had no control of his body, knocked the knife out of Aran's fist, sending it flying. Aran raised his hands and the trees shook, but Pierce was too fast. He struck him across the head hard enough that he crumpled to the ground.

The forest stilled.

"Aran!" Liam cried, stepping away from Elijah.

Kade moved with him, but it was no use. Pierce was already grabbing Aran, tossing him over his shoulder like he weighed nothing, and sprinting off.

Liam's shock staggered Kade. He went to run after Pierce, but Niall materialized from the trees, his eyes feral as he stared them down.

"You're on my territory uninvited."

"We're helping your pack," Victor said.

Niall scoffed. "You're here for my land."

"We aren't," Kade said, but Niall wasn't paying him any mind.

Half of Niall's pack sprang out behind him in their wolf forms, and the forest exploded into chaos.

A ball of fire appeared in Liam's hand, and he lobbed it

so it landed in front of a wolf stalking toward them. The wolf flung itself back, but it was unharmed, and Liam repeated the motion, throwing a second fireball at another wolf, though he wasn't aiming to hit or hurt them.

The growls and snarls of wolves boxed them in.

"Stay back." A cool threat lingered in Elijah's tone, but Niall strode forward and pointed at Victor.

"You. You and I will fight."

"We're not here for that," Victor said.

"Have it your way. If you won't fight, I have no other choice." Niall tilted his chin up.

Snow crunched, and Kade turned in time to see one of Niall's betas slipping out from between the trees, a knife in his hand. It glinted as he sprinted toward Victor.

Kade lunged between them, catching the beta's arm, but it was too late.

The knife plunged between his ribs, burning as it sliced him open, cutting off his breath. Scorching heat spread through his body, starting at the wound and searing through him. Warm blood gushed down his side.

Fire whizzed past Kade, hitting the beta square in the chest.

"Miles!" Liam yelled. "It's wolfsbane!"

Kade gasped for air as he sank to his knees, but his lungs weren't working. He thought Victor's hands were on him, catching him as he fell, but he couldn't feel them.

Wolfsbane. Yeah. That was what that was. Made sense. It explained the agony lancing through him, eating away at him, destroying him from the inside out. Blood no longer ran through his veins; it had been replaced by blistering pain.

Liam's magic poured into him through the tether,

cooling and welcome, but the wolfsbane clawed at it, ripped at it, tore it apart the moment Liam fed it to him.

The edges of Kade's vision began to darken, and his eyes locked on Liam.

Liam.

The only light in the world.

His rage and panic flooded through their bond. He threw fireballs at the wolves surrounding them, not pulling his punches, his aim deadly accurate. The scent of singed fur and yelps of pain filled the clearing.

"Fall back!" Victor shouted, the sound muffled like Kade's ears weren't working right.

Kade struggled to focus on the blurry shape of Liam. He opened his mouth to call Liam's name, but only a rattling breath came out.

"*Shit,*" a voice said. Miles? Kade wasn't sure. It had come from so far away.

Tingling magic spilled into him, but it did nothing to quell the fiery pain.

Kade tried to blink, tried to move, tried to go to Liam. His body refused to obey.

Liam was still throwing balls of fire, beautiful and vengeful in the night that just kept getting dimmer and dimmer until all that was left was Liam.

Then even he faded into darkness.

THIRTY-TWO

Pain seared through Liam. He felt the twisting agony of the poison in Kade's veins, and rage filled him. Fire formed in his hand before he processed what he was doing, and he threw it at the bastard who had stabbed Kade, at anyone he didn't recognize as one of his own, driving them back, wanting nothing more than vengeance for what they'd done.

He reversed the tether as much as possible while still throwing fire, feeding Kade his magic with the meager skill he had. He couldn't heal him, not from wolfsbane, but he might be able to slow its effects enough to sustain Kade until Miles saved him.

"Fall back!" he heard Victor yell, and wolves howled in response.

Above them, the spirit churned, hanging low in the sky.

Niall watched the chaos, and Liam threw a fireball at him, though Niall moved too fast, dodging it, only to stand there again, staring them down.

Elijah hooked an arm around Liam's waist and pulled him backward.

"We have to go," he said, but Liam kept throwing fire at anyone who approached, stumbling over the uneven ground as Elijah guided him toward the wards.

For the first time in his life, he was grateful for his affinities and their offensive capabilities, for them enabling him to protect his friends.

He sensed Miles's magic pulsing through Kade, slowing the spread of wolfsbane, attempting to counteract its effects, but it wasn't healing him. He glanced to the side and saw Grant carrying Kade, Miles's hands on Kade's neck as they backed across the border. The corrupted wards swept over them again.

Liam held Niall's pack off, pausing at the edge of the wards, giving cover to the shifters from Victor's and Grant's packs. He waited one final beat before letting Elijah pull him across. When he tried to throw another fireball through the wards, it fizzled out against twisting blackness.

He ran to Kade, crossing into Victor's territory behind Miles and Grant. Panic clamped around his lungs, making him unable to breathe.

When he reached Kade, he grabbed his hand and found it cold and limp. Kade was faint in his mind, no longer vibrant with life. Liam poured his magic through their bond, through his hands, knowing it wasn't enough.

There was activity around them, and some part of Liam knew Victor was checking on his pack and Grant's, ensuring they were safe, but he couldn't tear his gaze away from Kade.

Grant went to lay Kade down, but Miles shook his head, his eyes bright blue, channeling more healing magic into Kade, sweat beading on his brow even in the frigid night. "I can't heal him here. Not properly. Elijah, is there—"

"Yes. There's wolfsbane in the house," Elijah said, his tone grim, already leading the way.

Victor rushed over, taking Kade from Grant. As soon as Grant's hands were free, they were on Miles's neck.

"My pack?" he asked Victor, his voice tight.

Victor confirmed what he'd likely sensed through his pack's bonds. "They're accounted for. Some injuries, nothing life-threatening."

"Then let's go."

The journey back was longer and darker than the one there. Liam stumbled over the ground and through the snow, trying desperately not to slow Victor down. His numb hand clung to Kade's, needing that connection with him as their bond dimmed and Kade faded.

Miles kept his hands on Kade too, counteracting the constant damage the wolfsbane was causing. Grant was there to steady him as he ran.

Wolfsbane harmed shifters regardless of how they were exposed to it, but it was deadliest when it was in their blood. It wasn't about healing then. It had to be pulled from their veins using more wolfsbane, like calling to like, the strength of the plant—

"*Aran.*" Liam faltered, half turning as he clutched Kade's hand, but Victor continued moving, forcing Liam to follow. "They took Aran." Horror welled in his chest.

Elijah spun around, his eyes flashing purple, anger and pain on his face. "We *will* get him back. We'll rescue him. But we can't do it now. Not like this. We have until the full moon."

Liam's stomach lurched at the thought of what Niall would do to Aran if they held him captive then. They wouldn't kill him; mages were too valuable for that. What they'd do would be so much worse. Bond him against his will, take control of his magic. Bile rose in Liam's throat.

The full moon. They had three weeks.

Kade had only hours, if that.

Liam's lungs ached, the icy air whipping at his face as they ran. Kade's presence grew fainter and fainter, even as Miles did everything he could to keep him alive.

After far too long, they reached the pack house.

Once they were inside, Victor laid Kade carefully on the kitchen floor. His expression was pinched with worry as he stepped away to give them space, and Elijah sprinted toward the workroom.

Liam knelt on one side of Kade, Miles and Grant on the other.

No matter how much magic Liam gave him, no matter what he did, Kade kept slipping further and further away. Liam inhaled shakily. When he exhaled, it came out as a sob. His eyes burned.

Elijah dashed back into the kitchen, landing beside Miles with an audible thud as his knees hit the floor. His hands trembled as he uncorked the vial he was carrying.

Miles held out his hand, and Elijah dumped a purplish-blue petal onto his palm. Miles's other hand pressed against Kade's side. He began to work, pulling the poison from Kade. It oozed out of his wound, between Miles's fingers, a sickly black tainting the red of his blood.

Liam did his best to sustain the healing as Miles worked, giving all of his magic, all of his power to Kade, focusing as much on his vital organs as his limited skill allowed. He kept his heart pumping, his lungs working, while Miles extracted the wolfsbane.

It was slow, painfully slow. Each moment an eternity,

each second agony. A fine purple dust settled on Miles's palm around the petal as he called it from Kade's body.

The scorching pain retreated one capillary, one vein, one artery at a time. Until finally, *finally*, the last traces of it left his system.

Miles slumped forward, caught by Grant's hand on his shoulder, though Grant shied away from his open palm.

"I think I got it," Miles said, his voice weak.

Liam nodded numbly, too drained for anything else. "You did."

Kade's presence had stabilized; still faint, but not fading further. Liam could only sit there and stare at his face, at the sallow tone of his skin.

Elijah helped Miles to his feet, taking him to the sink to wash away the wolfsbane on his palm.

"How is he?" Victor asked.

"He'll recover." Miles's exhaustion was evident in every line of his body. "He just needs time to heal."

"Oh, thank god." Victor pressed his eyes shut.

Grant looked at Liam. "He wouldn't have survived without your bond."

Liam gave another nod. He'd felt that much, felt how quickly the wolfsbane had taken over Kade's body, how quickly he'd been fading away. But to hear Grant say it, to think what would have happened if they hadn't been bonded... He could scarcely breathe around the lump in his throat.

Miles slid onto the floor next to Kade again, his hand resting on his neck, checking him over once more, then roughly stitching together the wound on his side with his magic.

"Thank you," Liam said in a cracked whisper.

"Sorry I couldn't do more. I should—"

"No," Liam cut him off. Miles would burn himself out healing others if they let him. "You've done enough. More than anyone else could have. We've got it from here."

He already sensed Kade's enhanced healing kicking in. It was sluggish, but working.

"How are you?" Miles asked, his expression concerned.

"I'll be fine," Liam reassured him. No one called him on the blatant lie.

"Let's get him upstairs," Victor said, and they stood. Miles swayed until Elijah wrapped an arm around him, supporting his weight.

Grant shifted on his feet, like he wanted to go to Miles, but he restrained himself.

Liam followed as Victor carried Kade up the stairs and set him on the bed. He squeezed Kade's shoulder before stepping away. "Do you need help cleaning him up?"

"No, I've got this." Liam was tired, they all were, but he could do this much. He could take care of Kade.

Victor slipped out of the room, leaving Liam and Kade alone.

Liam undressed and rinsed off the sweat from the fight, then stripped Kade out of his clothes and wiped him clean of blood. He crawled into bed with him, wrapping himself around Kade, careful of his wound. It looked fresh and raw, but it was closed, at least.

But even though he was exhausted, sleep didn't come. He stared up at the ceiling as the darkness outside the window gave way to dawn, but he couldn't stop dwelling on everything that had happened, everything that could have happened. Everything that might still occur.

He'd nearly lost Kade. Their bond was still so new, but it had almost been taken away from him. He'd realized he couldn't picture his life without Kade, and then he'd been faced with that exact scenario. He breathed through the panic that thought caused. That reality had been too close for comfort.

How had things gone so wrong? They'd been suspicious of Pierce, of Niall and his pack, but Liam never would have imagined it would end up like this. Kade almost dying, and Aran...

Aran. Fuck.

That sick feeling bubbled up into his throat again. They had to get him back. Before the full moon. Liam gripped Kade's hand. No one was going to take away any of the people he cared about again. He vowed that to himself and Kade.

But Elijah was right. They needed to recover and regroup. They were no good to Aran like this.

"I could use that magical ability of yours to shut off my brain," he whispered to Kade.

It didn't have to be sex, just something to distract him from the sickening worry that was spiraling through his thoughts.

There were books on his bedside table that he'd already finished. He'd been meaning to get more, but now he didn't want to leave Kade alone, even for the few minutes it would take.

His gaze landed on Kade's nightstand. Maybe Kade could distract him after all. He reached over Kade and pulled open the drawer, grabbing the Kindle that was tucked inside.

"I hope you're okay with this. Relationships are about sharing, right?"

He turned the Kindle on.

"Let's see what you've got in here."

Not wanting to lose Kade's place in the book he was

currently reading, Liam backed out to the home page. He was greeted by an extensive series of collections, starting with All-Time Faves and ending with Utterly Trashy Fun.

Knowing he'd regret every life choice that had brought him to this moment, he clicked on that last folder, his curiosity getting the better of him.

The first book in the collection was titled *Love's Hot, Throbbing Arrow*.

Well, he was making questionable life choices today. Why not continue to do so?

He opened it and began to read chapter one aloud.

"'Matteo shuttled his thick lovestick through his fist.' *Oh*. We're getting right into it, aren't we?" Liam asked, glancing at Kade.

The collection's name seemed thoroughly justified, and he hadn't even gotten ten words in.

He swore Kade felt like he was listening. He'd read that coma patients supposedly heard what people said to them. This might do them both good.

"'His turgid, fiery man-meat wept like a one-eyed widow as he stroked it with purpose.' If his man-meat is fiery, he should see someone about that. You know, get that thing checked out?"

Liam exhaled. Alright, so maybe he wasn't an utterly trashy kind of guy. At least not tonight. But there were other folders to explore, and he was impressed with Kade's organizational system, even if he didn't fully grasp the difference between fluffy spice and spicy fluff. Was this a bluish-green versus greenish-blue situation? And if so, where was the line between the two?

He scrolled to the top of the collections, noticing the folder labeled "Author: Y. Jesus."

Could he deal with sweater shifters? He didn't think he

was mentally prepared for that. He'd have to work his way up to it. Instead, he opened the All-Time Faves folder and hoped for the... well, the best might not be accurate. He doubted Kade was miraculously hiding a bunch of academic texts in the collection, but he'd settle for anything that didn't include the word lovestick.

He wasn't surprised to find *Howling Hearts and Hidden Heats* in there.

"I'm reading this, but we are absolutely not telling Aran about it, okay? Okay."

He forced his mind away from the fact that Kade couldn't tell Aran, none of them could, and braced himself for what he was pretty sure would be the worst read of his life. But as he read the first chapter to Kade, he couldn't say he disliked it. It had this whole sweeping, epic fantasy vibe. If sweeping, epic fantasies were allowed to have more sex than plot.

He could see why someone might enjoy it. There were two hot alpha princes who definitely hated each other. Loathed each other's very being. Except they had to meet to negotiate an alliance between their kingdoms, and the moment they shook hands, they realized something neither would have predicted. They were fated mates. It was a twist that threatened to expose that one of them was not an alpha at all, but secretly an omega, hiding his designation because only alphas could inherit the kingdom.

It wasn't Liam's thing, but when there wasn't any weeping man-meat by chapter eight, he counted it as a win.

Kade grew stronger with every word Liam spoke, until he wasn't just a ghost of himself, but slowly healing, slowly returning to Liam, and that alone eased a fraction of Liam's worry.

He tapped the screen and blinked at the highlighted

text on the next page. "'A true bond is a fate one such as myself can only dare to aspire to. For as the moon casts its silvery glow upon tranquil waters, so does a true bond cast its luminous radiance upon the lives of those blessed enough to bathe in its glorious effulgence.'"

Where had he heard—

Wait. Wasn't this what Kade had said to his mother on that video call? Kade had been quoting from this book? And his mother had recognized it? Well, no wonder she loved Kade so much. They had the same taste in books.

Oh god. His *sister*. She'd recognized it too. Did that mean she'd read this? He winced when he remembered chapter seven, which had made it exceedingly clear the two princes didn't despise each other as vehemently as they claimed.

"Kade, I really need you to tell me my sister hasn't read this."

Instead of being reassured, another thought hit Liam.

Wasn't this the book MateHub had adapted into its first original drama series? He just had to pray his sister hadn't seen *that*.

"You wanted me to watch this?"

Kade didn't deny it.

Shaking his head, Liam started reading out loud again. It didn't erase the world outside their room entirely, but it distracted him enough that, eventually, he was able to doze off and get a little sleep.

THIRTY-THREE

The darkness slowly receded as Kade regained consciousness. Every fiber of his being ached. It was the main reason he believed he was alive. Surely being dead couldn't be this painful. Just the thought of moving hurt; his limbs felt steamrolled into the mattress. But he didn't care. He sensed Liam in his mind, smelled his scent, and as he surfaced closer to waking, he heard him too. He let Liam's voice wash over him, that faint accent of his adding a little extra warmth to words Kade had read half a dozen times before.

"'She stared in horrified fascination as her big, fluffy sweater began to glow, a radiant light spilling forth as it lifted up from her bed and into the air, hanging there like a shining angel from heaven. And then it transformed. Its soft, luxurious fabric magically changing, *shifting*, into smooth, hard muscle until it was no longer a sweater, but a man. Every inch of his body was chiseled like it came from stone, not cotton. A Greek god hewn from marble, so unlike her favorite sweater, the one she had worn so many times.'"

Liam sounded as if he'd been talking nonstop for days,

but he continued. "'She shrieked, and in her surprise, her hands flew up, dropping the towel she'd wrapped around herself as she'd gotten out of the shower, leaving her bare in front of this naked man, this naked *sweater*.'" Liam started laughing. "Oh my god, Kade. I don't think I can do this. Next, is she going to run away and he chases her and somehow they both fall on top of each other?"

"No," Kade said, his voice jagged from disuse. "That's book five, *Slipped on by the Robe Shifter*. And book eleven, *Stretched by the Pantyhose Shifter*."

Relief and shock rushed through their bond. "You're awake!" Liam's hand found his arm, and he squeezed. Kade hissed, and Liam jerked his hand away. "Sorry."

Kade cracked his eyes open. Fuck, how was it possible for eyelids to hurt? The room was dim, only lit by the lamp on Liam's side of the bed, but that alone was searingly bright.

Kade's mouth was dry, his throat raw, but he took in Liam's appearance—the dark circles and pinched, exhausted expression.

"You okay?" he croaked out.

"Am *I* okay? Jesus fucking Christ, Kade. I'm fine. You're the one who almost died. Are *you* okay?"

"I'm alive. I'll take it. How's everyone else?"

Liam's face twisted with worry. "It's been two days. We're alright, but we haven't heard anything about Aran."

"What's the plan?"

"We think Elijah will have to break through the wards."

Kade knew how that would play out. Niall's pack would be there by the time Elijah got through. There'd be no avoiding a fight.

"We'll get him back," Kade vowed. "Before the full moon. Whatever it takes. When are we doing it?"

"You're doing nothing until you're fully healed."

"Another couple days and I'll be good as new. He's my friend. I'm not leaving him behind. I'm not going to let Niall bond him against his will."

That had to be why Niall had abducted him. He'd said as much to Victor.

Liam gave him a concerned look.

"Are you okay?" Kade asked again. Liam opened his mouth to speak, but Kade cut him off. "You know you don't have to be fine, right? Your friend was abducted, and it feels like you haven't slept properly in days. It's okay if you aren't fine. You don't need to put on a brave face for me."

Liam deflated. He pressed his eyes shut. "I'm not fine."

Kade forced his arm to move until his hand was brushing Liam's. His skin still hurt, but his need for a physical connection with Liam was greater than the pain. "That's okay. This situation is fucked up, but we'll fix it. Together."

Liam nodded. "Yeah. We will."

"So," Kade said, trying to distract him. "Why are you reading trashy books on my Kindle?"

Liam's cheeks took on the faintest of pink glows. "Because there's nothing else on your Kindle?"

"But the sweater shifters? Really? That's not entry-level PNR right there."

"You said they were good. *Good* did not mentally prepare me for a page-long description of how turned-on she gets whenever she's wearing only the sweater. I mean, an entire paragraph dedicated to the delicious friction of the chunky weave against her nipples?"

"I said they were addictive, not good. Those are two separate things. But seriously, there are well-written books on there."

"Like *Howling Hearts*?"

"Yeah."

"I, uh, already read the trilogy. It was... not bad."

"The whole trilogy? Did you read them out loud? To me? When I couldn't hear them?"

Liam made a noncommittal noise.

"What did you think of chapter seventeen in *Shattered Souls and Secret Scents*?"

The pink tint to Liam's cheeks grew darker.

"Read it to me?"

Liam swallowed. "Maybe not while you can't do anything about it."

Kade groaned, then whined, "Fucking wolfsbane. But when this is over, we are doing that. What else did you read?"

"A few things in your All-Time Faves collection. Though, I have to say, I wanted to punch the wolf shifter in *The Wrong Wolf* for what he did to the human character. Pretending to be his twin brother to bond him? That asshole."

"You and everyone who reads it." Kade's words were starting to slur, his eyelids too heavy to keep open. "Read me to sleep? You haven't gotten to the second part of the tagline yet. 'Usually, she wears him. Tonight, he wears her.'"

"Okay, if that's what you want." Warm, fond amusement threaded through their bond, and Liam began to read again. "'His gaze slid down her body, a caress as gentle as the cycle she used whenever she washed him.' *Kade*. No. I can't do this."

Grinning to himself, Kade drifted off as Liam continued to read.

Kade managed to stay awake for longer periods over the next day. He felt tired, but more like himself, and Liam got some food into him, though Kade couldn't handle much more than broth. Even chewing seemed to exhaust him.

That evening, Victor and Elijah came to the room. Their relief when they saw him sitting up in bed was clear.

"You've been unconscious too much lately," Victor said. "Could you stop that?"

"Is that an order?"

"Yes," Liam snapped.

Victor snorted. "Exactly. Don't do stupid shit like that again. But thank you."

Elijah leveled a look at Kade. "For the record, I kind of love you for what you did. You can tell me as many dick jokes as you want for the rest of your life, and I won't complain about them. I'll even try to phrase things in ways that absolutely call for 'that's what he said' jokes and thinly veiled innuendos."

Kade grinned, but the mood in the room sobered quickly.

"Miles sent a message," Elijah said. "The stone has locked onto the shifter we're searching for."

Liam sucked in a breath. "Where are they?"

"It seems they're hiding in a nearby ghost town."

"Do we go check it out?" Liam asked, but Elijah shook his head.

"Let's get Aran back first."

Victor grimaced. "I contacted my father yesterday.

We're meeting tomorrow. I'll try to get some information out of him."

That had to have cost Victor. It wouldn't be a pleasant reunion.

After confirming their plans, Victor and Elijah left the room.

Kade sensed Liam's brain churning with worry and doubt, and as much as he'd have liked to turn it off in more pleasurable ways, propping himself up against the head-board was about the extent of his physical abilities at the moment. So instead, he asked a question.

"East or west?"

Liam didn't hesitate before answering. "East."

Kade laced their hands together. "First, I want you to meet my parents."

Liam smiled softly. "I'd love that. The final stop can be you meeting mine."

And then they were off on another trip around the world, just as perfect as the others they'd planned.

They couldn't leave yet. They still had to save Aran and help Niall's pack, then defeat the people behind the spirits. But Kade knew without a doubt that they'd go on these trips. Their future held hundreds of destinations for them to explore, and he couldn't wait to see where they went.

EPILOGUE

Victor opened the door to the diner where he and his father had agreed to meet. He wrinkled his nose, catching the reek of corrupt magic that blotted out his father's scent.

His father was sitting in a booth toward the back, away from the other customers, and Victor took a seat across from him. Two glasses of water sat on the table between them.

"It's about time you contacted me," his father said, his voice laced with disdain. "You're too weak to handle this without me."

Victor repressed a growl, but before he could reply, Elijah slid into the booth next to him. He inhaled sharply, glancing at the table, then said, "We're doing fine on our own, thanks."

Victor's father snarled. "I told you to come alone."

"Like fuck that's happening." Elijah gestured for the waitress to bring a third glass of water.

"Does he have you on that short of a leash?" Victor's

father stared at him with a cool gaze, and they fell silent as the waitress brought over Elijah's glass.

When she set it down, Elijah switched it out with the one in front of Victor.

Victor shot him a confused look, and Elijah shrugged. "What? You know I don't like ice. Yours has less in it." He didn't take a drink though, just kept his hands loosely around the glass.

What was he doing? Elijah didn't mind ice in his drinks. But he must have had a reason, and Victor wasn't going to question him about it, not right now. He turned to his father.

"You called me and said there was something you could help me with. If we did want your assistance, what are you offering?"

"I thought you were fine on your own."

"We are. That bastard of a mage has to have realized his plan isn't working, but we still need to know what he wants from our packs."

His father scoffed. "What makes you think he wants anything?"

"The fact that he let spirits loose on our pack territories in an attempt to weaken us."

"Spirits that showed up after Darius left town and your new little fuck toy moved in? Are you sure he isn't behind it? You ran to him when you couldn't protect my pack, and he got access to all their energy out of the deal. Nice and convenient for him, isn't it? Probably even worth letting you screw him a time or two."

"They aren't your pack anymore." Victor found he wasn't bothered by his father's comments about Elijah. None of it was true. The bond they had was worlds apart from whatever twisted arrangement his father had with that asshole mage.

"Why are you working with him?" Elijah asked.

Victor's father stood abruptly. "We aren't going to accomplish anything with him here. Contact me again when you're ready to talk alone."

He grabbed Elijah's glass and downed its contents, then glared at Elijah for a beat before walking away.

"What the hell was that about?" Victor asked.

Elijah frowned at him. "You can't smell that?"

"Smell what?"

Elijah held the empty glass up to his nose. "This. It's so strong."

Victor sniffed the air, but it was only filled with the usual scents of the diner—the fried food and sugary drinks. There was nothing special about that glass that he could tell. "It just smells like water."

"No, it smells like the white flowers they broke into my shop to steal."

Victor's stomach dropped. His father had tried to poison him?

Elijah looked grim. "And now we have another reason we need Aran back. We have to figure out what that flower can do. Whatever it is, it isn't good."

"We'll get him back," Victor vowed with unwavering determination.

They already had the raid planned. Four more days, and they'd save Aran, no matter the cost.

End of Impulsive Connections (Elemental Bonds Book Two)

Thank you for reading!

Sign up for my newsletter to receive the itinerary of one of Kade and Liam's trips and a bonus scene of Liam reading Kade's Kindle. You'll also get regular updates on my upcoming releases and an occasional free short story.

UNEXPECTED ALLIANCES

The story continues in *Unexpected Alliances, Elemental Bonds Book Three.*

Aran's Story. Coming soon.

Join my mailing list for exclusive updates and sneak peeks!

MATEHUB: LEGEND

Aran nodded solemnly. "Richard Knotz. The love of my life. Making people come together around the world."

Meet Kade's and Aran's favorite MateHub star, Richard Knotz, in *MateHub: Legend.*

The contract was simple: three months, seven scenes, zero feelings. Following it was not.

In the world of supernatural adult entertainment, Richard Knotz is a legend, and knotting scenes are his brand. No human could ever threaten to tear his empire to the ground, no matter how tempting that human smells.

Available now on Amazon and in Kindle Unlimited.

FIVE STAR REVIEW

"I have Richard's merch, but have never used its... most famous feature."
"Most famous feature?"
Kade leaned in. "It has a fully functioning knot."

Kade might not have used it, but Zayn has. Meet him and his mate, Aiden, in *Five Star Review*.

Gravity, love, and other inevitable falls.

Aiden Lucas is used to a steady stream of discreet packages arriving on his doorstep. It's part and parcel of living with an adult toy reviewer, but nothing could have prepared him for the next toy his roommate receives—something that hits a little too close to a secret Aiden has longed to confess for years.

Available now on Amazon and in Kindle Unlimited.

Acknowledgments

This book and I had our own little enemies-to-lovers arc. When I started writing it over a year ago, it was supposed to be the same length as book one—115k or shorter. Close to 170k words later, I was threatening to throw it off my balcony. It seemed bound and determined to make me miss every single deadline I set for it. But I ended up absolutely adoring Kade and Liam, and I even managed to trim nearly 20k off the word count.

I must also tragically inform you that a *MateHub*-related plotline involving the sweater shifter books has taken root in my head. So that might eventually happen. I'm going to be in serious trouble if every novel I write spawns a ridiculous spinoff. I may or may not have the entire *Howling Hearts* trilogy outlined too. ^_^;;

I'd like to thank my amazing beta readers, Amy Pittel and Megan Dischinger, for their work on this novel. It would not exist without their encouragement and support. I'm equally grateful to my wonderful editor, Kate Wood, for hunting down more typos than I care to admit. All three of them were infinitely patient with me constantly running late on my deadlines, and words cannot express how much I appreciate them.

Additionally, I owe a big thank you to Kate Munro for always letting me bounce ideas off her and for giving me additional feedback on this.

And finally, thank you, dear reader! Many of you waited

quite a while for this book, and I sincerely hope you enjoyed it! I will do my best to get *Unexpected Alliances* out as soon as possible. I'm so excited to write Aran's book, and I look forward to sharing more stories with you in the future.

If you could spare a moment to leave a review of *Impulsive Connections* on Amazon or a site such as Goodreads, StoryGraph, or BookBub, it would mean the world to me. Reviews help indie authors gain visibility, and I appreciate each one, no matter how long or short.

Please feel free to reach out to me on any of the social media platforms listed on my About the Author page. I'd love to hear from you.

Thank you again, and happy reading!

About the Author

Marie Reynard is an American in Japan, teaching English by day and writing M/M paranormal romance by night. Her steamy, snarky stories will take you from first kiss to forever with a few Fs in between—including found family, flirty banter, fake dating, and a fair amount of fu...n. Check out her website for more information on her books, and join her mailing list to get a free story or two and be the first to know about upcoming releases!

Website - https://www.mariereynard.com/
Newsletter - http://subscribepage.io/qVn7di
Facebook Group - https://facebook.com/groups/
mariereynardsden/

facebook	facebook.com/authormariereynard
tiktok	tiktok.com/@marie_reynard
x	x.com/marie__reynard
instagram	instagram.com/marie__reynard
amazon	amazon.com/author/mariereynard
goodreads	goodreads.com/mariereynard
bookbub	bookbub.com/profile/marie-reynard